MW00527926

FOR ALL THE WATER

FOR ALL
the
WATER

STEWART FLINK

FOR ALL THE WATER
By Stewart Flink

First Edition
Copyright © 2023 by Stewart Flink

Published by Forces of Rationality, LLC

All rights reserved. No part of this publication may be reproduced, distributed, or transmitted in any form or by any means, including photocopying, recording, or other electronic or mechanical methods, without the prior written permission of the publisher, except as permitted by U.S. copyright law.

The story, all names, characters, and incidents portrayed in this production are fictitious. No identification with actual persons (living or deceased), places, buildings, and products is intended or should be inferred.

ISBN# 978-1-960299-09-3
Printed in the United States of America

DEDICATION

To Jennifer, my four children, and four grandchildren, who inspire me daily. I pray (not hope) that you never face freshwater scarcity in your lifetimes, for hope is not a strategy.

To my editor, Thalia Mostow Bruehl, for being in the trenches with me for months on end and being a guiding light for my writing style.

To Charlie and Lily for facilitating my ambitions and fueling my passion. You know who you are.

To all the hydrologists, researchers, and scientists who work tirelessly to find global solutions for the freshwater shortages that are both upon us now, and in the foreseeable future.

PROLOGUE

January 2045

I*can smell their fear. Don't need to see the look in their eyes. Ain't gonna go away on its own, they need to jump through it.*

High above the Mojave, the only light was a slivery moon illuminating the sky. Jon Oliver Buckingham, the alpha and driving force behind the Forces of Rationality, was pensive as he tossed his half-smoked Cuban on the ground and stomped it out with his boot before boarding the bare-bones cargo plane that would carry six F.O.R. team members deep into the desert night.

"Y'all, welcome aboard for Round Two. The first practice jump we did a week ago didn't go so well. And that was in broad daylight. Let's nail it this time," Jon stated with soul-crushing persistence.

Too bad Diaz has a fear of heights, the poor bastard, Jon thought to himself. *Each time I look at his face, I see a death mask of fear. He's runnin' with the big dogs and needs to keep up. Hope he took his medication.*

Jon looked down at his illuminated satellite watch, the date read August 1st, 2044. "Perfect. Right on schedule. 10 p.m. on the dot." It was the team's last practice jump before heading to Asia for F.O.R.'s mission; Jon had committed the circuitous route—avoiding both the Chinese and Russian borders—to memory.

In 2044, the planet shuddered as if Atlas himself had lost his balance and was about to drop the world from his weary shoulders. Environmental epilepsy and subsequent hemorrhaging were present on every continent. Greenland was now hotter than at any point in the past one-thousand years, sending the third planet from the sun into disequilibrium. Like a pendulum swinging back and forth, the earth had been held hostage between floods and droughts.

Jon phoned Wolf, his partner in F.O.R. and best friend of twenty years, who was eight hundred miles away in Frisco, Colorado. "I'm sensing some primal emotions over here," Jon whispered into his headset, so as not to be heard by the other members of his team.

"Buck, just speak in plain English, please." As patient as Wolf was, he could be short with Jon, who was known to talk around a subject rather than being direct. Wolf remembered his father's sage advice. *It takes few words to speak the truth.*

"I can practically see the terror rising off their bodies like steam, except for Sol and Sapphire. For the others, it's a constant rumble like the plane's engines readying for takeoff. A clear sign that we're all human. Not sure if it's the fear of failure or dying, but aren't they connected anyway?" he asked Wolf rhetorically.

Jon thought he heard Diaz let out a gasp as the plane began rolling down the runway.

"You do realize that there are only three constants in life. Fear, change, and ignorance," Wolf stated. Jon's headset clicked off as Wolf hung up his phone.

The team huddled in the back of the cargo plane near the exit door, firmly closed until the jump. There were three women and three men originating from five continents and collectively fluent in eleven different languages. All of them PhDs in hydrology and water research with naval combat experience.

Freshwater shortages had been a constant due to the inability of most populated cities around the globe to develop large-volume desalination technology able to convert seawater into drinking water, leading certain Armageddon evangelists to conclude that the end of civilization might occur before the turn of the twenty-second century. The only question for them was where Armageddon would take place, as it had morphed from the Middle East to somewhere else.

Many contributors to the Armageddon theories were borne in the geo-political winds of change, causing an ever-shifting global landscape. The initial catalyst was the fatal heart attack of Kim Jong-un and China's subsequent annexation of North Korea. It was a calculated risk by the PRC given Kim failed to groom a successor, the result of an arrogant leadership style, and a deep-seated, flawed view of his own mortality. With China's reflexive land grab, the PRC had instantly leapfrogged the U.S. and Russia, an action that created the largest submarine fleet and standing army in the world.

"Hope you're ready," Jon shouted over the thunderous roar of the plane's strained engines as they took off, the plane lifting higher and higher in a steep ascent. He felt his stomach tighten. "Let's not fuck this up."

The ancient Russian Antonov AN-74 cargo plane careened over southwestern Nevada at five-thousand feet, climbing steadily towards its predetermined altitude. The team sat on hard steel benches, nervously fidgeting, tapping their feet rapid fire on the vibrating floor, or obsessively adjusting their night vision goggles. They were waiting for a signal from Jon, who was deep in thought, leaning against the cockpit doors, eyes closed. He was a leader whose moment-to-moment decision-making style was a trajectory led not by emotion, but meticulous planning and intent. Slowing down was never an option. Jon, consistent with his personality, hit the accelerator hard. He had two gears, sleep and fifth.

Jon stood up straight and faced his carefully handpicked team.

"OK everybody, y'all listen up! Our good friend Wolf has a saying. 'Energy follows intent.' We go real-time three weeks from today and will be jumping out over the Gobi around 4 a.m. In the spirit two thousand years ago of the great stoic philosopher Epictetus, *Expect Nothing. Be Prepared for Everything.* Keep in mind that the weather ain't gonna be tropical over there. The place is like all hell breakin' loose. Mongolia has the most volatile weather of any country in the world, with temps ranging from one hundred and ten degrees to minus forty in the winter months. Summers are hotter than a firecracker on the 4th of July. Three weeks from today, it could be twenty degrees, or eighteen below zero in the same twenty-four hours! Remember, the colder it is, the more it plays to our advantage."

"Speak for yourself," said Yael, who looked calmer than many of her teammates. "Coming from Israel, I like it steamy. If I had my druthers, I'd take firecracker weather any day." Everyone laughed, enjoying the break in the tension.

Jon tried to ignore Yael and gather his thoughts. "I know y'all fully appreciate the significance of the mission before us. Tonight's jump is designed to simulate similar conditions as much as possible. There's no pressure, but if y'all can't find your way to our meeting point within three minutes of the target ETA, you won't be going on the mission." Jon had zero tolerance for mediocrity, especially something that could put F.O.R. lives in danger. "Check your NGVs, courtesy of Sol. If they don't fit right or aren't functioning properly, we have spares upfront. Other questions?" Jon asked.

An raised her hand like a confident student. "Jon, I have one, and it's..."

Jon cut her off mid-sentence. "Jon! Who the hell is Jon? From this point forward I'll be addressed and respond only to my code name— Buck. Y'all got that? What's your question?" he shouted in a thick Southern drawl.

"Are we going to land anywhere near Joshua Tree National Park?" An asked. "I hear it's beautiful this time of year." Her giggle was audible.

"Cut the crap, Angie. If you're tryin' to be a comedian, you'd better keep your day job," he said with a sarcastic bite. Jon was, in fact, a secret admirer of people who could inject levity and ease the tension in high-stress situations, but they were getting close to their jump point and Jon needed to rein his team in.

"Tell you what, if our mission is successful and we all come back in one piece, I promise I'll take you there," he added with a reassuring smile.

"I'm gonna hold you to it," said An, who moved toward the exit door. "You're not going to get out of this one."

"Anyone else? Speak now or forever hold your..."

Diaz, loudly clearing his throat, spoke up. "How in God's name did you manage to get your hands on a Russian transport plane in the U.S.? It's a good trick. You must be a magician." Jon ignored his question.

The winds of change had blown fiercely across Russia as Vladimir Putin suffered a debilitating stroke in December of 2029. His self-appointed successor and twenty years his junior, Sergei Cherkov, more than eclipsed Putin's thirst for conquest and had been ruling with an iron fist.

Both the political and environmental sectors had reached the apex of instability. The U.S. was a laggard in the establishment of federal water policies, but one Hail Mary did occur with a joint venture between NASA and the Jet Propulsion Laboratory in Pasadena. Through their collective efforts, the two entities were able to tap into the geothermal power underneath Yellowstone at a time when the hydroelectric power sourced from certain lakes, rivers, and dams in the western U.S. was dwindling.

"Can I get your attention?" Jon asked. "We're going to mix it up. First up, Angie and Fran. Sol and Court, y'all let ten seconds pass and then hit the exit door. Sapphire, you're going last with me. Got it?" Jon liked to change things at the last-minute, choreographing practice jumps to make them slightly more challenging than the actual mission.

"Anything else we should be aware of?" Phillippe yelled out from the back of the plane in his dark blue ski pants, a white turtleneck, and a jacket that could withstand temps of ten below. Everyone had on long underwear under their outer gear, a mishmash of bright colors and clothing.

"Oh yeah! Y'all watch out for those Mojave Rattlers, I hear their venom's a bitch!" Jon howled in laughter. "Remember, three minutes or less, so don't be late. See y'all on the ground!"

No one said a word. Everyone was tuned into their own breathing. The anonymous pilot broke the silence and spoke to the team directly into their headsets. "OK, everybody. Grab your helmets and NVGs."

Jon noticed that Diaz, who was set to jump first, was engaged in last-minute dilly-dallying with his helmet strap. It looked like he was fidgeting with dread.

"C'mon, Fran. Hurry the fuck up!" Jon insisted. "Need to stay on schedule."

Morale was high, and everyone was in sync. "Look. I'm not great at giving pep talks, and you are all motivated ball players, so you don't really need it. You know damn well how high the stakes are. Most of y'all have been in tough situations before, at least until we get to Mongolia. You guys have come up a steep learning curve in the past ten days, so keep striving towards excellence."

The team was busy adjusting their parachutes and jet packs; the two pieces of equipment added almost eighty pounds to their physically fit frames. "Listen up everybody. Ninety seconds to jump. Let's synchronize our NGV timers to zero in three-two-one."

The pilot engaged a button that opened the wide rear door of the cargo plane, an invisible veil separating its passengers from the cold desert air. Jon went through the details one last time, like a daily mantra.

"Remember, ten seconds of free falling and then pull your ripcords. The red handle glows in the dark, so don't be concerned about finding them out there. At two-thousand feet, engage your jetpacks and release chutes."

The temperature at 6,000 feet altitude was a brisk eighteen degrees. Except for a silver crescent moon, the night sky was pitch black. The sun had yet to show the slightest glimpse of its rays. Diaz and An jumped first. Jon practically had to shove him out the door as he watched his team plunge into darkness.

"Ready, Sapphire? This is our first jump together," Jon said. "Let's do it right." He put his arm around the Russian's stalwart shoulder. She smiled at him through her helmet, and after a few seconds, they were freefalling. At a ten count, they each pulled their ripcords and the sandy-colored chutes opened, just enough to buffer their fall as they fired up their jetpacks exactly as planned. Camouflaged parachutes jettisoned into the night air, floating toward the desert floor like a sheet wisping in the wind.

Stabilization took a mere three seconds; they were heading toward their pre-arranged coordinates of 112.13 east latitude and 46.83 north longitude. They were gliding through the air, exhilarated because there was no enemy to worry about. Everyone was on the ground at the precise rendezvous exactly two minutes and twenty seconds after jumping, except Diaz, who arrived twenty-eight seconds behind everyone else.

"Nice of you to join us, Fran," Jon said in a deadpanned voice, staring at his state-of-the-art watch. "It took you twenty-eight seconds longer than the rest of the team to find the meeting point." He looked at An who had jumped in tandem with Diaz. "Hey Angie, I'd like to have a word with you when we get back."

Yael shot poison darts at Diaz with her eyes. She knew all too well from her IDF experience that a half-minute delay from F.O.R.'s predetermined timetable in the Gobi might be the difference between evading Russian and Chinese drones, or missile-toting helicopters, and not. A margin defined not only by success and failure but life and death.

"Fran, don't tell me you got lost at night in the desert?" Jon said, looking at Diaz with total frustration. "You do realize that if you were late by another four seconds you weren't going on the mission with the rest of us. *Comprendez?*"

Diaz froze, looking like someone put a live wire down his pants, dangling millimeters from his testicles. "I'll do better next time. You have my word," he said with a noticeable crack in his voice.

"You'd better because our next jump is real-time." Jon looked around, removed his helmet to scratch his head, and asked, "Any hitches y'all? Feedback? Mine worked like a charm. Those last-minute adjustments to the tanks and parachutes did the trick." The team gave Jon a unanimous thumbs up. He looked at them with pride, and Diaz with disdain.

"Ready to head back to the van?" They switched on their jetpacks one more time as Jon turned and took off. The team followed closely behind him like Canadian geese in a V-formation to the pickup point two miles southwest of where they landed. Everyone noticed how much easier it was to navigate their jetpacks while a few feet off the ground.

Jon activated the high-powered flashlight on his helmet, and noticed the damage done by the wildfires of the twenties and thirties blowing west. The landscape was open, a combination of half-burnt, twisted Joshua trees and rocky landscape. There was scant green, the ground covered with gravel and dark brown clay. So much of the earth was still trying to recover from the mutilation caused by sun-scorching temperatures, fires, and floods of the last half-century.

Note to myself. This sure ain't what it used to be, Jon observed. *Fuckin' one hundred fifteen degrees in summer and that's in the damn shade. Assuming you could find shade to block the blistering sun beating you down. Hard to fathom the Fenner, a massive underground aquifer stretching over 700-square miles sitting in the middle of the goddamn Mojave. It's enough to flood 32 million acres under a foot of freshwater.*

Suddenly, a large unmarked black van appeared on the side of the road, engine running. The team gently placed their gear in the back, stacking their jet packs two high in rows of three. Jon closed the rear door and hopped in the front seat as the driver maneuvered through the desert mountains toward their original take-off point, a private airstrip in the middle of nowhere.

If not for Diaz, it would've been a near-perfect jump. Hope he falls into line, and sooner rather than later.

CHAPTER 1

SPARKS FLY

August 2044

It was a crisp early fall afternoon, and Jon Oliver Buckingham was in his element wearing a classic yellow and black flannel shirt, sitting on a rocking chair made by the hands of his late maternal grandfather Al. He was Jon's main mentor in business and life. From the cedar deck and porch that Jon had built with his own hands, Jon had an idyllic view of Lake Dillon. Solar panels, facing south, covered his rooftop. He felt safe. With a combination of solar, geothermal, and green hydrogen providing his power needs, he could live off the grid indefinitely at the flip of a switch.

Wolf had arrived four days earlier from his home in Copper Harbor, a stone's throw from the shores of Lake Superior in upper Michigan. His home was adjacent to Porcupine National Forest, 65,000 acres of pristine nature, where he could easily bond with the abundance of moose, deer, eagles, and beavers busy at work while simultaneously disappearing off the grid for days.

He built his log cabin out of beech, a conscious decision because beech trees were far more fire resistant than most trees found in North America. It was a quaint two-bedroom, complete with a fireplace, a full bath, a modest kitchen, and a storage room for all his hiking and hunting gear, 100% off the grid, just the way he preferred.

Wolf was visiting his best friend because after almost perfecting the extraction of microplastics from fresh and saltwater on an industrial scale, his lab partially funded by Jon was raided ten days earlier. Jon was concerned about Wolf's safety and protecting a discovery that was worth billions. *In the wrong hands, Wolf's stuff could shift the global balance of power.*

Something else was gnawing at Jon, like a tick had just burrowed through his skull, penetrating his brain. Aimless mutterings began spilling from his mouth as if fear itself were interrogating him. 'What if' scenarios clouded John's mind. "Did you ever have one of those days when you're walkin' outside on a windy day, and no matter which way you turned, the wind was constantly in your face?"

"Can't say that I have," Wolf responded, girding himself for more questions.

Jon glanced at Wolf and then back at the multi-colored sailboats moored on the Frisco side of Lake Dillon. They both endured a minute of silence before Jon responded. "You know what? I realize that I'm fucked up, but sometimes you're really fucked up!" Laughter emerged from deep inside Jon's belly.

Wolf, unfazed by his friend's response, was still basking in the afterglow of his meditation. "Whatever you say, but not as fucked up as getting an extra million for the sale of your drone company QB23 so the sale price of $793 million would equal a prime number. You have a terminal case of the quirks and you quants are all the same. Still debating whether one plus one equals two, three, or five."

"You're just jealous that I have the financial chops," Jon said kiddingly.

"You wish," Wolf returned a smile.

Jon cast a glance at the evergreens, the ones that survived more forest fires than one could count. Dotting the landscape was an unobstructed, intoxicating view of the 270-degree fourteen-thousand-foot mountain chains with jagged edges punching holes in a neon sky. An adjacent icy stream flowing down the mountain provided nature's perfect percussion music.

He exhaled a sigh of beauty. "Just shy of perfection. Hey, Wolf. Wasn't it Voltaire who said, *Perfect is the enemy of good?*" His head tilted back slightly, squinting at the glare of the remaining one-quarter sun sinking rapidly below the horizon. He lowered the sunglasses on top of his head to shield his eyes. His face exuded a shallow smile, a smile that reflected contentment without deep meaning. A faint, percolating thought occupied a remote corner of his mind.

"I've got a question for you. How do you make big decisions in your life, especially ones where no amount of advice can help you?"

"Simple. I just tap the universe."

"Wait. What?"

"I ask the universe for advice and the right answer for me, and eventually it flows back through me." Jon had a stunned look on his face, staring into space where silhouettes of stars and planets were starting to appear.

Well, I'll be a rooster that sleeps through sunrise. Something's still missing. With all that I've accomplished, why am I having this over-whelming feeling of incompleteness, a life void of authenticity? Unlike Wolf, Jon was constantly asking himself eschatological, soul-searching questions. Wolf warned him about the incessant monkey chatter rattling his brain, thoughts that could grind him down. *Why am I here, and what am I supposed to do with the rest of my life?* were enigmatic queries haunting him since the day he sold his drone business.

Jon was conveniently distracted, watching two of his homemade drones disguised as hawks gliding overhead above the perimeter of his property. In the background, cirrus clouds were scattered among a dark blue dusk, painted with streaks of orange and violet. Jon watched the night skies shift colors as he gazed at the celestial sunset in the southeastern sky. Jupiter and Mars shone brightly, visible to the naked eye. Jon was in his own world, so deep in thought that he couldn't hear the birds giving their nightly concert or the rushing water from the stream a hundred paces away.

He placed the Cuban cigar in a ceramic ashtray dotted with flecks of steel grey, black, and cardinal, the school colors of his alma mater. Jon picked up a high-powered hand-held telescope he'd recently purchased. It had small print on the side that read 'Made in the U.S.A.'

He could see Jupiter with the naked eye, but needed amplification to see Europa, Jupiter's largest moon. "I can't believe that the top astronomers still maintain that the water underneath Europa's surface is the same as the subglacial lakes of Antarctica."

Wolf took an audible inhale from deep within his diaphragm. "We're merely one tiny piece of a massive universe that's at play right now." The crisp Colorado air was devoid of any traces of smoke from the incessant forest fires drifting eastward from California, Nevada, Arizona, and New Mexico. The pristine body of water in front of them had become the largest freshwater source in Colorado. A lake with a perimeter equivalent to the distance of a marathon.

"And access to freshwater right on my front doorstep, even though Lake Dillon has dropped seven feet in the past decade. Up here, water is scarce ever since the Colorado River dried up. It's that goddamn alfalfa," Jon spewed.

"What are you talking about?" Wolf urged.

"I'll tell you exactly what I'm referring to. For the last forty years, 80% of the Colorado River was used for agriculture, and that almost one-third was used to grow alfalfa." Jon ranted. "And for what? To turn it into hay that fatten up the cattle and the cows. Another 20% went to grow frickin' cotton. All this accomplished was to just drain the shit out of our water supply. It was plain reckless. And highlights the lack of foresight by not having a national or even an interstate water conservation policy!"

"You know what I have to say to that? In a word, *stupility*." Wolf said emphatically, as Jon gave him the look of disbelief. "It's a word I made up recently and is a combination of stupidity and futility. Think I'm gonna trademark it so no one steals my original thought," Wolf stammered in between bursts of laughter.

Jon looked bewildered but managed to continue his train of thought. "Like I said five minutes ago, you're really fucked up! Remember when we were kids and drank from our faucets or hoses, had water fights, and took for granted that clean water would flow indefinitely? There are some places in California and Arizona where you're only allowed to take two showers per person per week. They have fuckin' drones monitoring it! If that ain't Big Brother at work, then my shit don't stink and..."

Jon gently closed his eyes in mid-sentence and listened to the breeze rustling multi-colored leaves. The smell of a sentimental fall invaded his senses, reminding him of his younger days growing up in the foothills of Tennessee. He reflected. *Things are so messed up compared to my childhood. A perfect storm of environmental chaos. Mead and Powell and the Great Salt Lakes dried up. The Colorado? Practically gone. The ice at Glacier National. Melted. What's next?*

Wolf stood up and went inside. Jon loved Wolf unconditionally and trusted him implicitly. He was the ultimate net-giver, and Jon was honored to have him as a co-founder of F.O.R. He felt that Sally, his mom, was the only one that could possibly hold a candle to Wolf. Thoughts were swirling around his head like a Midwest twister and Jon felt compelled to write them down, but not before playing a song that was his grandfather's personal favorite called *Hands on the Wheel*, a Willie Nelson classic. He turned up the volume of the speakers imbedded into his sunglasses.

At a time when the world seems to be spinning hopelessly out of control, There's deceivers, and believers, and old in-betweeners that seemed to have no place to go. Well, it's the same old song, it's right and it's wrong, and living is just something that I do. And with no place to hide...

Jon picked up his laptop, the one he made from scratch with used parts that created a mini quantum computer. Furiously, he began typing in a free-flowing, stream-of-consciousness style that could have made Faulkner envious, with his run-on sentences that turned into paragraphs.

This certainly ain't gonna win me any Nobel Prize for Literature, that's for darn sure. Here goes nothin'.

There are myriad classes and archetypes representing the nine and a half billion people on this planet. For my own simplicity, I will subdivide them into two distinct groups: Net Takers and Net Givers. Both come in all shapes, sizes, sexes, races, and guises. Most net takers are bad actors who slyly engage others with cunning finesse, making them difficult to spot, even after working or living side by side with them for years.

Eventually true nature reveals itself, particularly when they find them-

selves faced with moral dilemmas that collide with fear, greed, and an ego longing to win at all costs. Do the means always justify the end? Hell, if I know, but I think not.

Net takers constantly keep score, buy material things to impress others, are users and may choose to be involved in charitable causes, albeit for none of the right reasons. They are human chameleons. Why do these takers bother with their ruse? They are obsessed with what they believe material wealth yields and how people view them, boost their fragile self-esteem, image, and mixed reputations. Driven by well-disguised, unrelenting need to prove their superiority to others, they're convinced that they deserve all the accolades and privileges they inherently crave.

And to a great extent, the control over others they seek is captured with an ever-widening net with every word or lie that spews forth from their mouths. Or worse, they feel compelled to prove they're the smartest to keep their feeble self-esteem afloat. The harder they work at preserving this false persona the less personal growth they can achieve with their shallow existence.

Lost in their mirrors of vanity and whether their physical appearance looks younger than their chronological age, they fumble about searching for their own fountains of youth. They toil during their workdays uselessly spent, stroking their misguided egos. They couldn't find the South Pole if they were leaning on the flag.

Human nature hasn't changed much from the days of Shakespeare all the way back to Plato and Aristotle, and biblical times. The ultimate question I ask myself is not how much money I'm making but what kind of lasting value am I creating. I need to surround myself with net-givers, people that are eager to hand off what they've received and pay it forward.

Net givers have great expectations as to how their good deeds or helping to make the world a better place will benefit, and possess an innate sense of purpose. This is their main concern, and it's about who they are and what they stand for, not what they've accumulated. Like an instinct, they do the next right thing, and if they are unsure of what to do, they ask trusted friends, family members, or advisors for help.

They humbly roam the earth with the ideology that they can learn from everyone and realize that each is their teacher. Full of wisdom and grace, *they are fiercely self-reliant and independent thinkers, unafraid to go against the grain of the majority's words, deeds, and actions.*

Jon stopped typing. He felt exhilarated yet questioned if he was just spinning his wheels. As a self-described atheist who studied the Old Testament religiously, he listened to the silence as a wellspring of inspiration burst forth. *He leadeth me beside still waters; He restoreth the soul.*

Jon closed his eyes. *That's it!* he thought, hands trembling ever so slightly, as he tapped the keyboard again. Three billion people suffer from lack of freshwater or from water insecurity. *Almost three-quarters of the planet's land mass is arid, and the depletion of soil suitable for growing crops due to microplastics ingested by the animal kingdom and humans had become wholly inadequate to nurture the planet.*

"It's settin' right in front of my own damn face," he shouted to the mountaintops that surrounded his view. Snow-capped, 14,000-foot mountainous peaks that reached up to the sky like outstretched arms. He forged ahead.

We use it to bathe, clean, travel, fish, swim, manufacture and create power with it. I will use every ounce of energy to preserve, defend, and promote the equality of access to freshwater.

Jon recalled a conversation with Wolf back when they were seniors in college. Wolf told him that in the Shamanistic practice energy flows like water, but Jon struggled to recall Wolf's message. *Something like energy is force that follows thought. Intent precedes thought. Wolf could feel the presence of ancient infinite wisdom present on Isle Royale, an island over a billion years old.*

Wolf's Native Ojibwe ancestry had been ingrained in him since he was a child, in that although the ether is the final resting place of the soul, you will never find a clearer, more life-enhancing medium than water. It mirrors life and is among the greatest of all teachers. It sends us all multiple messages a day. Wolf was not afraid of dying because he knew what he was living for.

He remembered his insides twitching when Wolf told him that he was not afraid of dying, an acknowledgment that Jon couldn't admit to. He was still afraid of dying and still not sure what he was living for.

Jon viewed himself as having a foot in two worlds, surrounded by friends and colleagues on the one hand, but less frequently with true kindred spirits on the other. He possessed profound abilities that when in combination enabled him to succeed at any challenge that lay in front of him. Total recall of conversations he had at any point in his life from childhood to the present was one of those gifts. A close second was his enormous physical and mental energy, and the ability to concentrate for often up to eight hours without needing a break, all while navigating on four hours of sleep. Jon was a natural albeit adaptive leader. There were occasional drops of arrogance in his everyday presentation of self, but he had begun his journey of personal growth. Like a drum beating louder and louder, he was keenly aware that time was finite and of the essence.

Jon would need some assistance from past, present, and future friends he had yet to meet. He was keenly aware that the world was designed to be forever imperfect, and he was part of a species with a dichotomy of emotions about work, money, sex, relationships, creativity, power, passion, love, and truth.

I'm gonna preserve the freshwater on the planet if it's the last thing I ever do. I don't care what happens to me, but I do have an issue with risking the lives of others.

CHAPTER 2

A UNICORN OF THE NEGEV

September 2044

Jon was ready to start building his team and identified Dr. Yael Solomon as his first recruit. His innate curiosity about her was a big part of the motivation behind an excursion halfway around the world to a continent he'd never before set foot in. It was the main catalyst for his impending visit to Be'er Sheva and Sde Boker, where most of the water breakthroughs, including cutting-edge desalination technology, had been developed.

Jon had a secondary motivation in that he needed to see what the fiercest drone competitors were up to on the other side of the globe. Everyone he spoke to told him that the Chinese were on the cutting edge of drone production, but Jon knew the Israelis were best in class and were licensing some of their technology to the PRC.

From his most recent PhD in hydrology at Cal Berkeley, he had a burning desire to learn about desalination from the experts. He arranged a meeting with the thirty-six-year-old phenom, Dr. Yael Solomon, one of Israel's most well-respected water and desalination gurus.

Upon arrival and stepping outside of Ben Gurion airport, the blazing heat and humidity of Tel Aviv caught him off guard. Once on the high-speed, air-conditioned train to Be'er Sheva, Jon pulled out a spare shirt neatly folded in his backpack and changed in the train's bathroom.

It's a good thing I pre-booked the car service that Yael recommended from Be'er Sheva to Sde Boker. In this oppressive heat, the less time I spend outdoors the better.

After finding his seat, Jon quickly noticed that Israelis and foreigners alike were immersed in discussions about Israeli politics, breathing the thick air of opinions that were omnipresent. Fifty minutes passed, and he arrived in Be'er Sheva, exiting the train. The five-minute walk outside in the scorching dry heat was almost more than he could bear. It felt like someone was walking in front of him holding a giant hair dryer in his face set at maximum heat.

Jon was beyond excited to meet Yael but had an hour to kill before meeting his driver. On a whim he decided to call a professor at Ben Gurion University Yael had referred to him. Dr. Sharon Weiss was an expert in technology that was able to detect malicious drone operators. Weiss also oversaw the leading anti-missile laser technology research team in the world.

He glanced at his watch. The brief hour had passed and he excused himself, thanking Weiss profusely for her time. His driver, a former Israel Defense Forces soldier in cyber, spotted Jon outside the building he had just exited. For a trained IDF military man, Jon was an easy mark as an American in the middle of Be'er Sheva, a thriving city filled with Israelis, Arabs, and Bedouins.

Jon was scheduled to meet Yael at the main entrance of the Sde Boker at fifteen hundred hours. He dozed on and off most of the drive and was dropped off with five minutes to spare. Jon peered out his darkened window, and spotted Yael standing casually inside the entrance, arms crossed.

Jon climbed out of the back seat with only a dark blue backpack on his shoulder, dressed in faded blue jeans that were stuck to his legs, and a multi-colored dashiki, scattered with brown, beige, blue and maroon patterns. On his feet were blue and white Nike running shoes that were made from his 3D printer. He had no idea of what to expect as Yael began sauntering casually toward him.

She's stunning, at least on the outside. Jon's wire-rim, mirrored sunglasses reflected her perfectly. His eyes swept her face, and then her body. A few seconds passed before his brain caught up with his eyes. Yael stood before him with her angelic face and toned body. Jon sensed harmonic vitality along with an energetically grounded spirit.

"Shalom, Jon. I'm Dr. Yael Solomon. Welcome to Sde Boker," as she extended her hand with a warm welcome. Slowly, Jon removed his sunglasses as the hot, unrelenting desert sun ablaze in the western sky caused sweat to drip down his neck and his back. He barely noticed, as Yael's majestic beauty literally stopped him in his tracks. She was the kind of person who would turn the heads of either men or women as she walked down the street, and sat outside her favorite café sipping pomegranate tea.

Whether it was her aqua-lacquered nails that matched her beautiful teal-colored eyes, her strong but gentle voice, her golden-brown wind-blown hair, or her modesty, Jon summoned all his willpower to focus on the business at hand and not be taken in by the dazzling scientist standing before him. Yael was blessed with many gifts, including brains, athletic ability, warmth, grace, a sense of humor, and stunning good looks.

Both her parents were PhDs, and Yael's older brother Tal was the commanding officer of an undisclosed IDF air base. Besides earning a doctorate from Sde Boker in hydrology and desalination, Yael received her undergraduate degree from Technion in mechanical engineering. In six short years after completing her post-graduate work, Yael had established herself as a world-renowned expert in two critical areas of the global water crises.

One was large scale desalination using a combination of solar and green hydrogen. The other was working in conjunction with researchers at Technion in Haifa to find ways to remove dangerous PFAS, or forever chemicals from the water. She saw the world and its diminishing water supply literally coming apart at the seams, and desperately wanted to do something to soften the inevitable blow of a deteriorating planet.

They strolled lazily through the hydroponic labs and greenhouses toward the desalination technology housed in a locked-down facility. Jon asked the first question. "I take it you served in the IDF? What division were you in?"

"The Navy and I was trained in underwater demolition," Yael answered in her Israeli English accent.

"That must have been interesting. Were you ever on a submarine? I saw that Israel bought some new subs from Germany a while back."

Yael glared at Jon like he was a scorpion about to sting her.

"Excuse me, but that's as far as we go with my military background, OK? We are not allowed to talk about the specifics of what we saw and did in the IDF."

"My bad. I'm so sorry. I didn't realize that my questions were crossing lines. Promise it won't happen again."

"What about you? Do you have any formal military training?" Without hesitation, Jon answered. "Training, yes. Actual combat experience, no."

Yael had a quizzical look on her face. "What does that mean?"

"I was in my second to last day of Seal training in San Diego," he responded. "Assume you know what hell week is?" Yael nodded.

"I got a call from my older brother that my mom was extremely ill and was days away from passing. She was admitted to Vanderbilt Hospital and was in the ICU. I was young and naïve, so I asked my commanding officer what he thought I should do."

Curiosity invaded her senses, and as she leaned in a few feet away from Jon's face, she asked "What did he say?"

"I recall it verbatim. 'Buckingham, that's totally your call and I'm not going to make it for you. Leave now and you will have to start all over with another class when you return.' It was short and directly to the point."

"And what did you decide?" Yael asked, wanting to know the outcome.

"That was the easiest, no-brainer call I've ever made. I bolted from the West Coast and caught the first plane back to Nashville," Jon smiled.

They were walking toward the desalination plant powered by solar. Jon watched the door open after placing both thumb prints, followed by an iris scan of both eyes, and finally a twelve-digit code.

"Did you get there in time to see your mother?" Yael asked, her brown hair dancing from the powerful fans above. Jon appreciated Yael's family orientation.

"Sure did. She recovered fully and is still going gangbusters to this day!" he said grinning with delight. They were in front of steel door that led to highly secretive technology. "Wow, that's some security. What are you hiding?"

"You know Israelis. They are into tech and cyber. Did you return to San Diego and start over again?" Yael asked, locking eyes.

"Hell, no. And if I had to do it all over again, I'd make the same decision. 100%. The Seals are possessed, and they want your heart and soul. My motto is 'family first, country second.' On a certain level, they remind me of organized religion. And the way I see it is that most organized religions are nothing more than a form of mind and crowd control," Jon stated emphatically.

Yael's eyes narrowed. "I'm sorry you feel that way."

"Am I wrong?" Jon asked.

"Actually, I'm sorrier that you may be right," she laughed. "I understand and it's a deeper conversation for another time. Let's continue with the tour, shall we?" They walked along inside on a stone path in comfortable silence. Jon's Seal training had only provided a glimpse of underwater drone technology, something the Chinese were at the forefront of for naval use in the South Pacific.

Jon was wowed by the desalination technology he was shown. He reflexively went to take a picture with his eyeglasses. "I guess I'm not allowed to take pictures either," he uttered. Yael's eyebrows furrowed beneath her forehead while her eyes smiled through her sunglasses.

"What do you think?" she asked sarcastically. Jon hid his Seal training like a concealed weapon. *Probably shouldn't mention that I passed the initial training to become a navy helicopter pilot and that the Seals were preparing me to be a sniper sharpshooter. Too much info for a first dance. Hell, I just met her an hour ago. How do I know she's not a spy?*

He equated sharpshooting to the practice of Zen. It wasn't so much skill or a contest but self-mastery, something that Wolf had taught him as well. Jon was convinced that Yael's IDF Navy demolition expertise would come in handy and make her an invaluable asset to the team.

As if she was reading his mind, she smiled flirtatiously and continued the tour. Jon found himself doubly captivated. First, by the cutting-edge water technology he was witnessing, and then by Yael's allure. Her pheromones were working overtime on his senses, and Jon hung on to her every word.

Jon noticed Yael's visible tattoos in Hebrew, one on each of her inner forearms. "What do they mean?" he asked. She held out the underside of her right arm. "This one says, *Genesis*. And on this arm is the word, *Exodus*. It symbolizes birth and freedom." Jon nodded his approval.

Yael was slightly underwhelmed that *shalom* was the only Hebrew word that Jon had spoken in an hour. He'd learned the bulk of his Hebrew and Yiddish from Bill Engel back at M.I.T., but he'd forgotten more than Bill taught him. She continued to explain how Israel's prowess in desalination allowed them to export excess water to its neighboring countries. Alongside it military superiority export drinking water was a sign of innovation and power in the Middle East.

"Countries like Egypt and Saudi Arabia have been importing water from Israel since 2029, and Jordan as far back as 2016. It brings in mid-nine figures of annual revenue straight to the bottom line," Yael added. "Dubai got its desalination technology from us, and the UAE is running short of groundwater. I believe they are down to seven billion cubic feet."

Jon yawned, trying in vain to cover his mouth. "I hope this is not boring you," Yael said, flashing her glistening, slightly imperfect teeth. "Would you like to take a break?"

"Boring? Are you kidding? My apologies. It's gotta be a combination of jet lag and the heat. I just need some green tea on ice and a liter of water, and I'll be fine. Please continue." Yael punched in a few commands on her phone that were sent wirelessly to the kitchen. Minutes later, a robotic server arrived, and she handed him a liter of ice-cold *Eden* water, Israel's leading bottled water.

"I've read about your involvement in finding solutions to eliminate PFAS from groundwater, fish, and soil. Anything you can share with me?"

"Certainly. My team has been working in conjunction with a

research team at Technion. This joint research endeavor started two decades ago before I entered university. The inherent issue is that environmental scientists have identified over 13,000 different types of PFAS."

"And how many types of PFAS have you been able to eliminate so far?"

"That's the problem. As of last year, we've been able to identify and eliminate about 425 different PFAS we can remove from the water. So, less than ten percent."

"I see," Jon replied, disappointed at the lack of progress. "By the way, I had a productive meeting with Dr. Weiss at Ben Gurion earlier today."

"Great. I'm glad that worked out. How is Sharon?"

"She's awesome. I was dazzled by her brilliance and her candor. I guess she trusted me because I was an acquaintance of yours," Jon shrugged his shoulders. "She was extraordinary in her knowledge of laser defense systems."

Jon felt the coldness of the bottled water on his hand and relished in it. The bottle was sixty degrees cooler than the desert air outside and provided immediate relief as he pressed it against his forehead and held it to the back of his neck. Yael looked at him playfully. She noticed the inner child in Jon and liked that he didn't take himself too seriously.

"The bottom line is until other countries develop or mimic our desalination expertise, our technology gives Israel more leverage than Iron Beam."

After an hour of stimulating discourse, Jon sensed that he had his first F.O.R. recruit, although he couldn't explain why. Yael told him that her mother originally came from Ukraine to Israel, and that she was fluent in Russian. *Yael is the perfect fit with her fluency in Hebrew, Arabic, English, and Russian.*

The tour concluded in just under two and a half hours. At the end, they chit-chatted about their respective families and bantered about educational backgrounds until Yael went directly and rather forcefully for the jugular, like a jungle cat lunging for the neck of its prey.

"Look. I'm flattered that someone of your caliber, background, and experience came all the way from Colorado to Sde Boker to get a tour of our desalination facilities, but what am I missing here? There's got to be more, something else you had in mind?" as if she were looking right through him.

Jon peered over his shoulders to see if anyone was in earshot before he answered. "Well, if you must know, the reason I came to Israel was to meet you." She raised her eyebrows.

"I'm forming a special international task force, whose mission is nothing short of saving the scarce freshwater resources remaining. And in the process, I hope to prevent a possible WWIII scenario. My colleague and I happen to be privy to Russia's intentions regarding China. These are premeditated decisions made by Russia toward the PRC due to its continuing military and economic dominance, and as a response to the PRC's annexation of North Korea."

Jon was convincing in his role as a recruiter. Yael's piercing eyes were wide open. She hadn't blinked once since he started his pitch.

"A contributing factor is Russia's rather careless, almost flippant attitude about their own habitat. Actions that are destined to have repercussions for all humanity. Hundreds of millions, if not billions of lives are at stake. And that is only a piece of the overarching plan, the part that pertains to F.O.R.'s mission."

"Please get to the point. You know, about the mission. And what the hell is F.O.R.?" she asked in an incredulous tone.

Jon hesitated and for a millisecond cringed that he may have divulged too much information. *Giving her more detail might prove fatal if she decides not to join F.O.R. I've already crossed more than a few lines. Shit!* Yael was locked into Jon, as if they were the only two in all Sde Boker.

"To answer your other question, F.O.R stands for Forces of Rationality."

"I see," said Yael without flinching.

"My best guess is it will involve a handpicked team of seven that will undertake secret missions to save the world's freshwater supply in two particular regions and prevent it from falling into the 'wrong' hands. I know that sounds crazy and all, but that's it in a nutshell."

"What do you mean by nutshell?" Yael asked, gathering herself, trying to stay composed. "Never mind. How'd you get to seven as the optimal number?"

"It was the original plan, assuming I can recruit them all."

"Am I your first recruit?"

"Kind of. You're the first *outside* recruit," Jon answered, responding with bravado. He rose from his seat, and started pacing back and forth, as he explained the plan to Yael. "The others I've identified will be hand-picked from China, Russia, Chile, Canada, and possibly India or Denmark. If all goes according to plan, there will be only one person from each of those countries joining F.O.R."

"Interesting, but why Denmark?" Yael asked.

"Because Denmark still controls Greenland and the Faroe Islands."

She continued to drill Jon with questions, almost as if she were interrogating a prisoner. He held his ground and chose to answer only a select few. He deferred the others telling Yael that he would get back to her when he was able.

Abruptly, Jon looked at his watch, stood up, and then gazed into Yael's aqua pools one last time. "Yael, thanks for the green tea and the *mayim*," he winked, proud that he threw in a second Hebrew word. "It was a pleasure meeting you. I really appreciate the tour and you spending time with me."

Yael didn't react as Jon uttered the Hebrew word for water. "The pleasure was mine. Listen, I'm going to digest all this and give you a call in a couple of weeks. I will have many more questions. How do I get in touch with you?" she asked, looking directly into the sun behind Jon's broad shoulders.

Jon clicked his sunglasses twice, sending Yael his vCard electronically. He also pulled out a physical card from his shirt pocket with a private number that only his mother and Wolf had. "Not to worry. I'll find you."

Jon couldn't help but notice for a second time that Yael's aura practically placed him under a hypnotic trance. Yael never looked away. "Man! Israeli women are something else!" Jon mumbled under his breath as he turned away, hoping Yael wouldn't hear him.

"What did you say, and what's with the grin on your face?" she asked him, pulling a card out of the front pocket of her slim-fitting, blue-jean skirt, and handing it to Jon.

"Nothing. Nothing at all."

"Here's my card." Yael had scribbled her private number on the back before giving it to Jon. To Yael, a physical card was more secure than an email over the internet, especially one with her private number written on it. He held it gingerly with two hands and memorized the number before placing it in his shirt pocket.

"My ride's here. Gotta go. Shalom, Yael," he said as he extended his hand to meet hers.

"Shalom, Jon." Their eyes locked one final time. Jon felt a tingling on the top of his head as he walked to the car. "Where are you headed next?"

Jon stopped and turned to face her. "Moscow," was Jon's one-word reply.

Her face turned an angry shade of red. "Oh, you mean that terrorist-supporting country that has been fucking with the balance of power in the Middle East since the 1967 war! And whose complete failure of a government run by mindless, oppressive, overbearing lemmings who manage to perpetrate their evil-minded, ambient violence at every turn. Be careful."

"Hey, Yael. Why don't you tell me how you really feel about the Kremlin?" He laughed, enjoying the banter with her. He entered the back seat of the car and lowered the window.

"I thought I just did." She shrugged her shoulders, waved, turned, and walked back to her office, smiling like a child who just had her first piece of chocolate cake. She walked through the double doors but couldn't shake the feeling that her life was about to change.

———

Jon settled into the air conditioned car, and immediately noticed it was a different driver who had dropped him off. Initially, he thought nothing of it.

"Hey, what happened to my other driver?"

"Sir, he became ill. I was called in to replace him," he answered in a thick Russian accent. Jon tried to relax until he noticed what looked like a trace of blood smeared onto the back of the driver's beige-colored leather seat.

The driver hit the gas and took a left turn on the highway toward the Be'er Sheva train depot. Jon didn't hesitate to trust his instincts. He pulled out his Glock, leaned forward, and pressed it firmly against the new driver's temple. Jon's heart raced, as beads of sweat rolled down his forehead.

"OK, my friend. Pull over at that abandoned gas station up the road on the left and keep your hands on the wheel where I can see them."

Jon kept his pistol pointed at the driver's head as he exited the car. "Give me your cell phone. And your gun," he motioned. "Slowly exit the car and kneel with your hands behind your head and do exactly as I say." Jon was standing directly behind the bogus driver.

"Please don't shoot, mister. I'm a..." Jon pistol-whipped him hard on the back of the head and knocked him out cold.

That should keep you for a while. He dragged his victim behind a dumpster in the parking lot, the black sedan's engine still running. As Jon got back in and sped away, he tossed the Russian's cell out the window onto the highway where it splattered into a dozen pieces. Jon's phone lit up. It was an unrecognizable number. He answered, putting it on speaker.

"Jon, are you OK? I just got word from the car service that your driver was found on the side of the road bloodied but still alive. What's going on?" she said in a concerned voice.

"The guy who picked me up was a phony driver. I took care of things. Left the bastard unconscious behind an old, abandoned gas station about five kilometers from Sde Boker. Just tryin' to cool down," Jon replied with the AC blasting in his overheated face.

"Baruch Hashem," Yael uttered. "I'm sorry."

"It's not your fault, so don't sweat it. I'm driving directly to the airport, and then leaving the car in short-term parking. Tell the car service about my plans. Appreciate your concern. Gotta go." He hung up.

Twenty kilometers away, two Russian men were waiting indiscriminately at the Be'er Sheva train depot, wondering why their accomplice had failed to show up with the package.

Jon felt relief as he turned on a random Israeli radio station, heading northeast on a six-lane highway toward Ben Gurion Airport. Even though he was far from fluent in Hebrew, the music soothed him. He was preoccupied, mentally preparing for his next call with Yael. It was mission critical that as little time pass as possible. He couldn't afford to lose the momentum that he'd gained in Sde Boker. But he didn't want to seem too eager either. He compartmentalized his thoughts for the time being and set his sights on tomorrow night's dinner meeting with Dr. Elena Safina in downtown Moscow.

He boarded the plane, got situated, tilted his Boston Red Sox cap forward over his eyes, and folded his arms over his chest. He hung on to a bad habit from his childhood of taking off his shoes on a plane without regard to his fellow flyers, hoping they wouldn't notice. Jon finally began to unwind when he was startled by the loud rattling of the self-automated beverage cart rolling down the aisle.

Fifteen minutes after take-off, Jon had talked his way into a first-class upgrade. He put on his wireless, noise-canceling earbuds and leaned his head back against his cushioned seat. Approaching Turkish air space, his phone began vibrating inside his coat pocket. It was a restricted number, but curiosity overshadowed initial reluctance.

"Shalom, Jon. This is Yael. How are you feeling? Are you in the air yet?" Jon was fumbling for the right words to say, but all he could manage was, "Yes, I'm in the air and thirty minutes from landing in Ankara to change planes. It's two o'clock in the morning there. To what do I owe the pleasure of this call?" Jon asked, trying to sound engaged.

"Well, I never hesitate once I've made up my mind. After unpacking your proposal, I'm in. But I do want to know more details about the first mission. As you might have guessed, I've still got a lot of questions. Sorry to have disturbed you at this hour but thought you'd want to know."

"You're not disturbing me at all, especially with that kind of news. I'm honored and humbled that we will be working together on such a critically important mission. And I've got a few things to share with you, but all I'll say is that besides me, you're the third member of the team."

"Third?" she exclaimed, her voice trailing off.

"Remind me to tell you about Wolf the next time we speak. Once I'm on my way from Moscow to Toronto, I'll be in touch, and we can talk at length more freely. Sound good?"

"Yes. That will be fine. Shalom, Jon."

"Shalom. And thank you!"

Before he hung up, Jon asked Yael why she had decided to sign up for such a dangerous mission. Her answer caught Jon a bit flat-footed.

"Tikkun Olum," was her cryptic answer.

Jon shook his head. "Huh? Please tell me exactly what that means."

"I believe you already know what it means, and you're in alignment with its inherent philosophy. You just don't understand the Hebrew part, and that's your first assignment from me," she said laughing.

Jon could feel Yael smiling affectionately through the phone. As he hung up, he felt the adrenaline from his first outside F.O.R. member chugging through his veins. *Looks like I'm not going to get much shuteye after all. Too wound up at the moment. I'd best figure out what the heck Tikkun Olum means.*

CHAPTER 3

MOSCOW: A PASSION PLAY

September 2044

Jon was still groggy as he exited the plane. A rough zigzagging driverless car arrived forty minutes later at the hotel he booked. A bit nauseous, he checked into his room, took a shower, and crashed on his semi-hard mattress. His incessant travel schedule had finally got the best of him.

He awoke sluggishly at 11 a.m. the next morning and had no desire to check his emails that were piling up by the hour. He strolled around Moscow staying within three kilometers of his hotel to make sure no KGB were tailing him. Dreary, drizzling gray weather persuaded him to cut his walk short and head back to his room. *I can't possibly fathom that Russia borders fourteen countries and they're able to police Moscow with such complete efficiency. And China's worse. They border fourteen countries and share maritime borders with six others.*

"Mr. Walker?" the woman behind the front desk asked Jon.

"Yes, that's me." Jack Walker was the alias Jon used, the name derived from Jack Daniels and Johnnie Walker, the most popular blended Scotch in the world.

"You have a message."

"Thank you. I'll check it in my room."

Thoughts echoed in his paranoid brain. *How'd she know who I was? She wasn't the one who checked me in last night.* Ever since Jon set foot in Moscow, he fretted about being harangued by Chirkov's pesty government foot soldiers. The message was from Wolf asking Jon to call him. *Why didn't he try me on my glasses phone?* Jon had forgotten that he had switched to a burner phone when he arrived in Russia. He assumed the worst case, but it turned out that Wolf was calling about how to activate a certain drone that wasn't responding to his command at Jon's fortress in Frisco. *Problem solved,* he said silently.

In preparation for his meeting with Dr. Safina, Jon had done extensive research on water in this controversial country loaded with natural resources. Moscow was home to Russia's largest water company, Moscowkanal, a conglomerate that provided water and sewage to more than fifteen million people in the city and surrounding areas, yet only covered twelve percent of Russia's total population. Jon realized that the Kremlin had two festering issues.

The Moscow water supply system was old, causing drinking from the tap unsuitable. Many citizens were forced to boil their tap water which did little to ameliorate the problem, and the privileged few who could afford it bought bottled water for consumption. The other problem involved the outskirts and rural areas, where the water was scarce, and much like in the U.S., water quality was waning due to chemicals causing industrial pollution as well as contamination from pesticides used in agriculture.

The sign in Jon's hotel room warned visitors to brush their teeth with only bottled water and to avoid foods or salads washed with tap water. *No wonder Russians drink so much damn vodka. It's cleaner than the water, and safer too. Even the ice made from un-bottled water is risky for chrissakes. Now I get why Russians don't use ice when drinking hard.*

Russia was currently down to four brands of domestic bottled water that had gained the right of usage from 2034-2038. *Aquaniqua, Volzhaniqua, Novoter*stoya, and *Prosto Dobronaya.* Rumor had it that Chirkov had personal ownership stakes in Aquaniqua and Volzhaniqua, a catalyst for ugly bribes to bureaucrats that had become commonplace. *Who knows what Chirkov's got his greedy paws into?* There was also a clear distinction between bottled drinking water and bottled mineral water. Bottled drinking water was just slightly better than tap.

Dr. Elena Safina did her homework on Jon and was duly impressed with his accomplishments. She assumed correctly that Jon didn't speak a lick of Russian yet managed to find out that he loved sushi. She had gone the extra mile and arranged for a car to pick him up at the hotel so he could avoid navigating the shuffling madness of downtown Moscow on a Friday evening.

Jon was still unnerved by what happened with his Russian driver in Sde Boker. His gruff-looking driver was housed tightly inside a white shirt with the two top buttons open, and a thin black tie hanging from his size twenty-one neck. He drove Jon to Foster Cinema restaurant, and Elena chuckled at the thought of Jon telling the driver, "Take me to *Frunzenskaja Naberezhnaya* 30 Street 19." Fortunately for Jon, Elena's second language was English. She spoke French and Mongol as well.

On the way from the hotel to the restaurant, Jon couldn't help but notice the post-Communism architecture that still lingered outside the big city. As the driver weaved his way toward the center of Moscow and began driving down the busy two-lane street, Jon saw a stark change. The thick-necked driver tapped the horn of his black Mercedes sedan with his pudgy hands to clear the way through a stable of tourists crossing the jam-packed streets. Everything resembled euro in style, from the shops to the restaurants.

The buses used natural gas and had not yet graduated to hydrogen. Russia was still behind the times and had been making half-hearted attempts to clean up its own environment and the air pollution from decades of operating chemical and oil processing plants that converted thick heavy crude oil to gasoline and diesel. Considering the modernization of Moscow, Russia in 2044 was still a country in the grips of a mercurial and highly corrupt leadership, subjecting its people to an oppressive lifestyle. A society that was thin in numbers at the top, and prioritized profits and power over its people.

The car eventually arrived in front of a neoclassical building, a heavy steel structure with glass windows. An oblique-shaped facade housed the restaurant on street level. Jon thanked the driver and walked into the restaurant as he was looking at a picture of Elena on his OLED-embedded glasses.

Like Jon, Elena had a stellar academic career and received her PhD when she was twenty-four. She had an undergraduate degree from Moscow University in Biology and obtained a PhD in water conservation and hydrology from the Russian Academy of Science. A giant piece of Jon's puzzle was that by focusing on water conservation, he had accurately surmised that Elena had extensive experience working at Lake Baikal, the deepest and oldest freshwater lake in the world. Sitting smack in the southern region of Siberia, Baikal was still the single largest freshwater lake by volume with the equivalent amount of freshwater as the five Great Lakes combined.

Jon stared at her picture. *Fascinating*. Elena showed jet black hair that draped across her shoulders, a slender physique and looked to be about 5'9" tall. He knew in advance that she would be wearing a solid black shirt and a red skirt. *She'd be hard to miss, even in a crowded stadium*, he thought. Sensing Elena's presence, he looked up from his phone. She was standing three feet directly in front of him by the maître de. Her perfectly curved lips reflected in a smile that lit up the room, and for an instant had the same effect on Jon as if he'd injected ground coffee beans into his veins.

The restaurant had all the charm of Tokyo or San Francisco, despite being dead center in a city where Western and Southeast Asian cultures still coexisted as a minority influence with a dreary, dull Communism and a little socialism mixed in for good measure. Jon had yet to see a menu but was already excited about Elena's choice of dining establishments.

"Hello, Jon. I'm Elena. Pleased to meet you. I've got a table in the back where it's relatively quiet. Shall we?" She motioned him with a hand to follow her. Jon noticed with intense curiosity the black and white Italian marble floor that was part of the décor of the Japanese restaurant. *Kind of eclectic,* he shrugged.

As they strolled past the bar, Jon viewed a wide variety of well-stocked local and imported beers, as well as more types of vodka and whiskey than he could count. Most of the labels were in Russian, but he did recognize a few classics, especially in the scotch department. He knew that Balvenie 25 or Glenlivet 40 in a Moscow restaurant would cost him the equivalent of a dilapidated used car.

They were seated toward the back of the restaurant. Jon was stunned to find someone with equal beauty, intelligence, and radiance as Yael. The only things lacking were the subtle presentation of herself in public. *She reminds me of a neon sign hanging in Vegas. You can't help but notice her.*

"Good to finally meet you, Jon."

"Likewise," Jon responded as the waiter pushed in his chair and placed the red linen napkin in his lap. He could barely detect a Russian accent and realized that Elena's command of the English language was formidable. After being seated and ordering four distinct kinds of sushi from the menu, Elena jumped right in. Jon asked if he could see a list of scotches and bourbons.

"What brings you to Moscow?"

"For starters, I'm trying to live life with no regrets."

Elena laughed. "How on earth are you going to do that? Regrets pile up in my flat on a weekly basis like unread books next to my bed."

The waiter returned with the cocktail menu. "Would either of you like to start out with a vodka, tequila, scotch, or something else?" he asked. Jon ordered one of his favorite bourbons native to Tennessee. *I can't believe they have this stuff on the menu of a restaurant in Moscow,* he thought.

Jon was riding a wave of confidence about Yael joining F.O.R. and decided to go for back-to-back wins. "Good question. This is going to be a long answer, so please bear with me. I'm on a personal mission and Lake Baikal plays an integral part of the story. Like Brazil's Amazon twenty-five years ago, I couldn't help but notice that for the last three decades, your country is well on its way to wasting away one of the world's most valuable resources."

"I assume you're referring to the water pollution, illegal poaching, increased tourism, and to top it off, radiation. Correction. This has been going on for the better part of four decades. And yes, someone needs to stop it before it's too late."

Elena cast him a reassuring glance. "Elena, didn't the Israelis created an innovative technology a decade ago that could remove the algae in freshwater lakes like Baikal?"

"That's true, but the problem is that the algae blooms were less than twenty percent of the cleanup task." Jon had poured over Elena's unparalleled data analytics, and coupled with her breakthrough scientific discoveries, placed her on a pedestal for saving the behemoth body of water from further destruction. There was another reason why Jon needed Elena, but he was reluctant to tell her until they got further along. Jon drummed the fingers of his right hand on the white tablecloth. *Too risky*, he thought.

The waiter returned with their dinners. "That was fast!" Jon commented.

Out of nowhere, the hair standing up on the back of his neck was sending him subliminal messages that there were eyes in the restaurant on them. Jon had noticed two guys near the front of the restaurant that stuck out like sore thumbs when he first walked in. Dressed like undertakers in black suits, white shirts, and black ties, they were easy marks. *Not much of a disguise*, he smirked.

A busboy crashed into a waiter carrying several drinks, and suddenly the noise from breaking glass enveloped the entire restaurant. There was silence as everyone stared, and just as quickly, they resumed their conversations. Jon swallowed hard. "I need to ask a question that might offend you."

"Nothing you're going to ask me will ever offend me."

"OK. Here goes. Are you wearing a wire?" Jon asked timidly.

Elena threw her head back and started to laugh insanely.

"What's so funny?" Jon inquired.

"What century are you living in? I think you've been watching a few too many old crime shows on AppleNetflix? Did you ask me that so you could see the color of my bra? Here. See for yourself." Elena quickly unbuttoned her shirt and opened it down to just above her waist, revealing a laced, black bra filled with supple breasts.

Before Jon had a chance to look away, he noticed that Elena was ripped.

"Go ahead, check me out. I want you to be able to trust me implicitly," she said with a comical certitude that belied her Soviet upbringing.

Jon shielded his eyes. "Geez, Elena. In a public restaurant for chrissakes."

His face exuded embarrassment and bright shades of red. He was still trying to read Elena. Still holding his hand up in front of his eyes, he turned to face her.

"OK. I believe you." She quickly buttoned her shirt, still chuckling. "You're incorrigible," Jon said under his breath.

"Two FYI's. The bugs today look like soft, clear contact lenses. I could literally stick one under our table to capture and record our entire conversation. Wires are kind of passé, at least in Russia. And one other thing. I have a nanodevice in my purse that can detect bugs within a twenty-meter radius, and there are none around us."

Jon nodded humbly. "Moscow's become like your Beverly Hills, except without the weather." Her head tilted back, she continued to laugh, entertained by her sense of humor.

"Thanks for the tutorial. I've been tracking the pipeline via satellite that Russia and China have been building from the base of Lake Baikal in Siberia through Mongolia with its destination Lanzhou, and ultimately Beijing. As the pipeline goes through Dundgovi, it swerves southeast and then crosses the Chinese border with Lanzhou as its first stop."

"Yes. I'm well-versed in the project. One of my colleagues helped design it in collaboration with Chinese engineers. What about it?" Elena inquired partaking in her fifth sushi roll. Her appetite resembled that of a large squid.

Jon leaned over the table. "What else do you know?"

She gave him a quizzical glance. "After extensive testing, the water will start flowing by the beginning of April. Why?" she responded, feeling as if she had missed something obvious yet significant and shot him an irritated look.

"That's all you've got. Nothing else? What about water quality, the filtration?" he drilled down with penetrating eyes.

"Am I missing something? The Chinese will handle the filtration on their side. End of story. Why do you ask? And what's with the look of panic on your face?" Elena was starting to worry that something awful was brewing with the pipeline and Lake Baikal. Her curiosity to know the truth was starting to overwhelm what little patience she had left.

It was like déjà vu with Yael, except that Elena was more forceful and to the point. "Let me explain," Jon acknowledged with a feral grin.

Elena powered right through Jon's attempt to explain why they were meeting, and in Moscow no less. He struggled mightily to get a word in edgewise.

"I mean, don't get me wrong, Jon. I appreciate your brilliance and what you've done with your research eliminating microplastics from water, but I don't get it."

Suddenly, Elena cut loose as if she was escaping earth's gravitational pull, heading into orbit. "I have these recurring nightmares that I'm driving down a one-way street the wrong way and I'm about to drive off a cliff. If I stay in this country one more year, something in me may rust forever. Who wouldn't cave, given the kind of leader that Putin was and Chirkov is?" Jon was stymied as Elena continued like a freight train rumbling through a small town, brakes worn thin. "You have to help me get out of this place!" she whispered forcefully.

Elena eventually paused to catch her breath after she told too much to a man sitting in front of her, someone she had met for the first time forty-five minutes earlier. Jon's mouth went agape as he shook his head to make certain he'd just heard what he thought Elena said. It was the D word. *Defection*. The line about 'staying in the country one more year would rust her out' was still ringing in his ears as he nursed a rare Kentucky bourbon. There were two non-stop conversations happening at the same time. One with his own palate and the other with Elena.

Elena subtly opened her black leather purse sitting firmly in her lap, flashing the contents. Jon couldn't help but notice a handgun resembling the new Glock.

"I heard something last month that stopped me like death. The Kremlin has their agenda," Jon said looking directly into Elena's eyes.

"Like what?" she shot back, fear dancing in her eyes.

How about injecting a deadly, undetectable chemical into the water, starting about five kilometers south of where the pipeline crosses over into Mongolia? It has no cure and is going to make the Coronavirus outbreak of 2020 look like child's play," Jon said with bitterness.

"Who are your sources?" Elena asked, starting to squirm uncomfortably in her chair.

"Remember that fiasco around the turn of the century when DuPont was dumping chemicals in the water and half the city in Parkersburg, West Virginia got cancer from it? And then when these same forever chemicals started showing up in the fish in Lake Erie, Huron, and even Michigan?"

"Vaguely. Why?" Elena asked, leaning forward on the edge of her chair, hands clasped with both elbows firmly planted on the white-laced tablecloth.

Jon had Elena's undivided attention. "You know as well as I do about the forever chemicals, PFOA or PFAS. These substances can never be broken down in the environment, and more importantly in our bodies. And I'm sure you've heard that most fine dining establishments now test their fish as they come in. So much for the cities surrounding our Great Lakes being a reliable supply of fresh water."

"I'm aware of it," Elena shot back. "Alex Temkin, the Russian-born PhD toxicologist in conjunction with the Environmental Working Group, published studies and white papers about the dangers posed by PFAS. They've been detected in the blood levels of nearly everyone in countries that use 4MDupont products.

"What's your point? Is this a quiz?" Elena said half-jokingly.

"My point is this. Dupont operates in over seventy countries, two of which are the Czech Republic and Russia. I got wind through my network that instead of disposing of it safely in those two countries, they've been storing it and selling it indiscreetly for a profit to a division of the Russian government that no one outside of the Kremlin walls is aware of."

There was nothing except uncomfortable silence from Elena's side of the table. "What? How did you find out?" Elena muttered, shaking her head in disgust. "This is like the future of chemical warfare but it's water contamination instead of an aerosol delivery." Elena's mind ran wild like a ravenous hyena.

"Exactly! You can't see it, smell it, or taste it, and it has a delayed and deadly cumulative effect. And the only country that can test accurately for these chemicals is the U.S. because we had to deal with the problem thirty years ago. And you know what those motherfuckers did? They spun out their business that released PFAS into the water into a new company in 2015. Heard from partner that their plants emit HFC-23 into the air, too."

"Wait. Slow down? What partner?"

"My partner who's a long-term colleague and happens to be my best friend. I'm not going to give up his name yet. We met at M.I.T. twenty years ago." Jon said, then quickly changed the direction of the conversation. "I noticed you served in the Russian Navy for three years. Did you see action or was it more along the lines of basic training?"

Jon was feeling gassed from the three shots of vintage 2025 Pappy Van Winkle bourbon he had with dinner. It cost him as much as his one-way ticket to Tel Aviv. He was fading fast and desperately needed to get to the punchline.

"I served my despicable country for three years and continued working on my PhD in the process. I spent four months on a submarine. It was the highlight of my brief military career."

Jon gently encouraged Elena for more. "What type of sub?"

"It was the B-274 Petropavlovsk-Kamchatsky, conventionally powered sub." Jon suddenly got a second wind. "You mean no nuclear reactor on board?" he asked with an astonished look.

"That's correct," Elena stated. "It still uses lead-acid batteries to power the propeller and can be occasionally charged using a diesel generator. The last time your navy commissioned a conventionally powered sub was eighty years ago!"

"I don't get it. Why would the Kremlin do that?" he inquired.

"Look, I'm no expert, but from what I understand nuclear submarines are faster and with surplus energy that can be used to power massive sonar arrays. In open water this makes them much more strategic because they can hear the enemy further away, and then move faster to get into an attack position or get out of trouble," Elena said fervidly, her forehead crinkled.

"Yes, but in the end it's all about two issues. One, are these subs capable of firing hypersonic missiles with nuclear warheads that travel at speeds of Mach 20? I believe the answer's yes. And the second is about money. What you're missing is that conventional submarines are smaller, cheaper to build, and less expensive to crew. Compounded by the depressed prices of oil and gas given that hydrogen and electric-powered vehicles have taken over," Jon stated, hoping Elena would hit her pause button, but no such luck.

"Yes, but the critical advantage is that conventionals can turn off almost all systems and sit silently on the ocean floor, making them more stealth and extremely difficult to detect."

"That makes more sense. Let's get back to the matter at hand. All this will come into focus after we complete our first mission," Jon uttered with a tone that lacked humility.

"The first mission? What are you talking about?" Elena exclaimed with a surprised voice, shaking her head in disbelief. "As hard as it is for me, I'll try to shut up and listen. Go on."

"I need you to join a team of six others, including me. The first mission will involve blowing up a water pipeline that originates at Lake Baikal and runs the length of Mongolia. Russia's plan is to contaminate the water just over the northern Mongolia border. The worst part is that C8 is a slow-working poison, and it will take years to source and link all the disease-wracked citizens in China to this liquid cancer flowing through the pipelines originating an alleged viable water source." A voice inside her head started to scream as she leaned in to hear more.

Jon paused, waiting in vain for the noise level to die down just enough so he wouldn't have to shout. Jon's voice was now audible to the people sitting closest to their table. "And China is paying Russia for the privilege of exporting water, for chrissakes!"

"Please keep your voice down," Elena motioned, noticing the guys in the front of the restaurant were still seated. One of them was looking back their way. "Is that it or is there more?" Elena asked in a more moderate voice.

"That's the gist of it," Jon said in a more relaxed voice.

"The plan is pathetic, sad, and soulless all at the same time," Elena said with her index finger in front of her mouth. "I don't fully understand. There are plenty of capable Russian hydrologists who are working on the Lake Baikal project," Elena spurted.

"Why me and not someone else?"

"Because of your military experience, you're the ideal candidate. Plus, it's a catalyst to get you out of Russia once and for all." Jon glanced forward at the two men in front of the restaurant as the bigger one pushed back his chair and walked toward them on his way to the bathroom.

"And why would Chirkov commit such a horrendous act?

"Simple. So that the Russians can finally get the upper hand over China once and for all. This contaminated water, if consumed over a sustained period, will eventually cripple China's infrastructure, along with its military and healthcare resources. The only businesses that will thrive will be funeral homes. And in the case of cremation, the chemicals would outlive their own bodies. Chirkov, along with his semi-permanent sycophant Sergei Prikhodko, will have defeated the Chinese super-dragon without firing a shot or sacrificing a single soldier."

"Sounds familiar. Maybe in Sun Tzu's Art of War?" she pondered.

"Exactly," Jon replied. "And at the same time, they will be squeezing India, a country that desperately needs water as much or more than China. In effect, almost one-third of the world's population will be at the mercy of Russia."

Elena slumped back into her chair. For a moment, she could not hear the loud laughter and shrill voices bouncing off the tile floors and the ceiling. She was so deep in self-talk she felt like she was drowning in the back of the restaurant and completely missed the next four sentences that came out of Jon's mouth.

"Elena? Are you in? Elena? Say something," he asked repeatedly.

She snapped back to the present. "In for what?" Elena responded with a perplexed look on her face. The man exited the bathroom, staring at them. Jon waited until he was out of earshot.

"Are you down for the mission?" he asked. "I'm all in! Your timing is impeccable. Just let me know when we can begin, and what you need me to do."

Jon was brimming with satisfaction, ecstatic that he had secured his second team member within forty-eight hours. He looked around the room and noticed the two goons in front of the restaurant had a half-empty bottle of vodka and no food.

Elena stared intensely at Jon. "I noticed them when we walked in. What do you take me for anyway? I have an idea. Get up and head for the men's room. I'll get the bill and order a couple of Ochakovo's for our friends in front of the restaurant and pay the bill from my phone. Open the bathroom window and slip out the back. There is enough room for you to escape. Close the window from the outside, and then head east for three blocks until you are facing the GUM department store. I'll do the same. My driver will meet us there in eight minutes."

Jon froze and did nothing.

Elena rolled her eyes. "Don't just sit there. Move!" Jon pushed his chair from the table and wiped any remaining food from his mouth with his red cloth napkin. He reflexively placed his hand on his backpack where his Glock was safely secured inside.

Elena waived over the server and instructed him to bring a couple of beers to the two Russian stiffs sitting and laughing at the table by the front door, who were served by the unsuspecting waiter. The two conspicuous-looking men turned around to see that the table that Jon and Elena dined at was empty. They quickly got up, tossed some rubles on the table, as one bolted out the front door and the other darted to the back toward the men's restroom.

By the time they reunited at the front of the restaurant, Elena and Jon were long gone, sitting comfortably in the back of the Mercedes, the same vehicle that brought Jon to the restaurant. Jon leaned over, and whispered something Elena's right ear, and then pulled back as he uttered the words, "Enlighten me." She shook her head, her silky black hair moving in all directions, and told the driver in Russian to head to Jon's hotel. Upon arriving, Elena asked the driver to wait for them around the corner.

They ducked inside and strolled to the bar in the back room, out of sight from people hanging around the lobby. Her answer was direct and to the point. "I'd prefer Canada, but the U.S. would be a close second. There's no third choice, but I'll give it consideration over the coming weeks."

Jon nodded as he sipped his Balvenie 25. The hard part was over, and they could both unwind, as he talked about what it was like growing up in Tennessee. Certain people talk incessantly under duress, and Elena was one of them. There were tears forming in Elena's eyes.

Jon looked her way. "What is it?" he asked. The word *synchronicity* went off like a light bulb in his head. Elena pulled a cigarette and went to light it.

"Please don't," as Jon adeptly swiped the cigarette from between her index and middle fingers.

"Hey. Gimme that back?"

"You're not smoking in front of me. Those goddamn tobacco companies. Over fifty trillion cigarette butts have been discarded globally in the last decade. The executives are so fucking callous. They cannibalize their own customer base and don't give a shit. Wolf told me that 98% of vape as well as the filters in cigarettes poison global water supplies. Cellulose acetate degrades slowly, but not before it emits lead and arsenic. The same arsenic that's used to poison rats!"

Elena got a text from her driver Boris that the two chumps at the restaurant who were following them just pulled up in front of his hotel. She motioned to Jon and went to an unmarked exit door at the back of the hotel. Once outside, he handed her a wad of rubles. "It's for dinner. Don't argue with me. I flew here to ask you to join me. It's the least I can do. Just take it. Please."

"But it's more than the dinner cost, including tip."

"The lady doth protest too much, methinks..."

"Ooh. A cultured American scientist who quotes Shakespeare's Hamlet."

Jon shrugged his shoulders. Boris took Jon's luggage and tossed it in the trunk. Jon hugged Elena goodbye, and then he slipped into the back seat and mouthed the words, "Be safe," through the open window, knowing he would see her again in six weeks. Standing outside on a clear night under the moon's gaze, the stars and Venus shone brightly. Elena had the feeling she made the right decision and had found new meaning in her life.

Jon admired her, along with her spectacular feistiness. He inhaled and let out an audible sigh, loud enough for Boris to glance at Jon through his rearview mirror. Jon was oblivious, observing Moscow's nightlife one last time through his darkened window.

"She's full package, yes?" Boris exclaimed as he revved the engine.

Jon remained silent, nodding. *She's flawed and beautiful, crazy and passionate, angry and brilliant with an intellect to match her street sense. She doesn't want safety anymore. She wants justice and truth. Next stop, Warsaw.*

CHAPTER 4

WHITE HOT

October 2044

Dr. Phillippe Courtier, the consummate Canadian hydrologist, and diplomat, seemed to be a no-brainer since he already knew both Yael and Elena from their research and work in hydrology. He was also primed because of all the mischief the Russian Navy had caused for the past two decades near the Canadian side atop the Arctic Circle. Whatever he could do to slow down the Russians was his highest priority, especially since the Canadian Navy ranked dead last among first tier countries around the world.

They discussed everything, from politics to food to what gave life meaning. After an hour-long dialogue that covered the gamete, Jon posed the question.

"Will you join F.O.R.?"

"I was wondering what's in it for me, but think I know the answer. You've made me an offer I can't refuse, so consider me part of the team. Give me a sense of timing and next steps so I can plan my life accordingly." They stood up.

"Court, with your service in the Navy and your experience with the

Canadian Security Intelligence Service, I believe we have the beginning of a meaningful relationship.

The last time I checked, Canada had one-fifth of the world's fresh water with over two million lakes in your backyard. There's a lot to protect, eh?"

"Yes indeed. Thanks for making the trek to Toronto," Phillipe said to Jon as he left and proceeded to the airport.

———

Jon sat in the airport lounge waiting to catch his Miami flight to meet with Dr. Francisco Diaz, someone who Jon had checked out with Phillipe and Yael. Diaz was born in Brazil and currently was working as a hydrologist out of Santiago, Chile. He had a master's degree from the University of Tromso, the Arctic University of Norway. In two years, he earned an M.Sc. in marine biology and freshwater ecology. Being the only student from South America that year, his was the beneficiary of free tuition.

It was serendipitous that Diaz was giving a lecture at the International Water Symposium in Miami the week after Jon was in Tel Aviv and Moscow. They had agreed to meet in Miami. Jon was excited about the prospect of closing in on what hopefully would be his second to last recruit, as he wanted to avoid the long flight to Santiago at all costs.

In terms of hands-on experience, Diaz came from the best of both worlds. While living in Brazil, he was part of a research team whose task was to oversee the highest volume of renewable freshwater in the world, a rate that hovered at eighteen percent consistently. Strategically, the value that Diaz brought to the table living in Chile for the past decade increased the odds of success both in Mongolia and a second mission that Jon and Wolf had been planning.

As Jon walked to the rental cars, a shit-eating grin formed on his face. He spotted an electric, metallic blue electric Mustang convertible at the car rental agency that appealed to his id. After charging the car on his glasses, he was heading south from FLL to meet Diaz in Miami.

Jon put the car on auto drive temporarily and began to daydream.

Lauderdale has changed, 'specially since the last time I was in south-eastern Florida over five years ago. Shocked to see the intercoastal half-submerged by the Atlantic. Doubt Miami looks any better, and the Keys are only accessible by boat and seaplane. I remember reading in high school about Florida, and how its freshwater supply days were numbered. Something like 900 million gallons a day being used to water lawns and golf courses. What a waste! And including industrial and agricultural use, it was another seven or eight billion gallons. Most of that came from the Floridan aquifer. They were screwed from the get-go.

He almost missed the exit as he jerked the steering wheel at the last second, veering off I-95. He arrived early, uncharacteristically valeted his car, and walked around the back toward the outdoor café of Ocean Gabbiano's. With a bird's eye view of the ocean creeping up the sandbanks, he grabbed a chair facing the Atlantic, the smell of saltwater wafting through the air. The large red umbrella conveniently blocked the sun.

Diaz arrived from Chile at Miami International about the same time as Jon's flight, but Jon was unburdened by avoiding the customs process. With a moment of quiet, Jon reviewed notes that he'd scribbled in his green-bound recycled notebook with a sketch of the new underground bunker that he was contemplating.

Hypnotized by the rhythm of the waves, he didn't notice a tall, deeply tanned gentleman in a white suit and chapeau that approached the table. Diaz cleared his throat.

"Jon? I'm Dr. Francisco Diaz, but please call me Fran." Diaz tipped his hat and extended his right hand. He looked like he was straight out of an old movie, wearing a tailored white suit, a black cotton shirt and a black silk tie.

Jon rose from his chair and shook Diaz's hand. "Pleased to meet you, Fran. You got here sooner than I expected."

"It was fortuitous that my plane arrived early, and customs were a breeze. I travel light." Diaz held up a tan backpack, his only piece of luggage. They sat down at the table. The waiter with a bulging stomach and a black mustache came to take their orders.

"I'm hungry. What would you like?" asked Jon.

"My good man, I'll have an iced tea with lemon and a shrimp cocktail."

"I'll have an iced tea and bring me the house salad as well." Jon handed the menu back to the server.

As the wind changed directions, Jon caught a whiff of the cologne that Diaz had slapped on his permanently tanned face after arriving on his overnight flight. *Geez, that stuff is strong. Gives me a frickin' headache.*

While Diaz chatted about his past achievements, Jon kept getting distracted because he observed Diaz undressing a blond waitress serving the table next to them. *And the fuckin' guy is married with three kids?*

"I am curious why you moved to Santiago from Rio in 2031."

"It was a straightforward decision. Before the United Nations and America took over the wildlife administration and protection of the Amazon region in late 2028, I could see the writing on the wall. They weren't wrong, mind you. When you factor in fires, deforestation, weather coupled with cattle ranches and rubber plant expansion, it doesn't take a rocket scientist to figure out that my country had squandered one of earth's most precious resources."

"The methane and nitrous oxide being emitted from the Amazon basin had already offset and likely exceeded the region's ability to absorb carbon dioxide in the atmosphere. That line was crossed in early 2024."

"The UN and the World Bank acted just in time. While there was serious damage done, Chile had begun to see reversing trends in our region and even in certain parts of South America."

"Can't argue with you," Jon acknowledged.

"I was invited by the Chilean government to do research at Puerto Williams in southern Chile's Magallanes region," Diaz continued "It has some of the purest water in the world and still does. And they enticed me with a great offer," he said with a wry grin.

"Quite the opportunity. Let me guess. That makes you fluent in Portuguese, Spanish, and English, and maybe a little bit of Norwegian?"

"Never mastered Norwegian, and even if I did, there aren't many places outside of Norway where I could've used it." Diaz chuckled.

"Impressive. Have you spent any time in Antarctica as part of the Chilean research team?"

"Yes, indeed. Mind if I smoke?" as he pulled out a pack of hand-rolled cigarettes and a lighter from his coat pocket. He didn't wait for Jon's answer.

"No problem," Jon said effusively. He couldn't stand the smell of cigarette or pipe smoke. It was the only thing on the planet that made him nauseous. Ironically, he loved the luxurious odor of cigars, an acquired taste passed on from his grandfather.

"I've made three trips to Antarctica over the past five years. Given the geographic proximity and my background, I was a natural. Why do you ask?"

"Not important. Say, how far is Trondheim from Oslo?" Jon asked, assessing the authenticity of Diaz's story.

Diaz exhaled after a long draw on his cigarette, tilted his head upward, and blew out a cloud of smoke whisked away by the prevailing winds and the fan swirling overhead. "It's about 390 kilometers north of Oslo, about seven and half hours by train. I took it to visit friends or relatives who came to visit. It was quite relaxing with many beautiful panoramic views."

"Did you ever spend any time in Longyearbyen?" Jon posed the trick question to Diaz to see if he really knew about Norway's northern-most city in the world, typically reserved for the rugged and tough-minded individual.

"As a matter of fact, I spent a month there researching the permafrost melt. It's a sad situation as global warming has really done a number on the town and its inhabitants. I'm afraid its destiny has been determined."

"Anything else I should know about you or your family?"

"There is. In the spirit of full disclosure, I've been known to have bouts of anxiety and dizziness from a fear of heights." The arrogance on Diaz's face faded like air just let out of a balloon. "I do take medication daily and believe I've got it under control, but just wanted to be upfront, to give you the entire picture. I need to own it."

At that point, Jon was eager to have Diaz join F.O.R. His hydrology experience, his military background, and his transparency made this decision easy yet he still felt slightly uneasy somewhere in the vicinity of his gut.

"It's kind of 'the good, the bad, and the ugly' right?" Jon said as they both had a good laugh. "Thank you for your candor. It doesn't bother me, although in the spirit of full disclosure, there will be one parachute jump that is required to complete the mission, and a few practice ones as well. I really appreciate your transparency and willingness to talk about it. Welcome aboard! If I can speak for the other members of F.O.R., it is an honor to have you on our team."

"No worries. I'll handle the jumps," he said confidently, his dazzling arrogance came back with a vengeance. *No Hay Mal Que Dure 100 Anos Ni Cuerpo Que Lo Resista.*

"Sorry, my Spanish is a bit rusty."

"My apologies. Loosely translated it means 'nothing bad lasts forever.' And what about the others? Can you tell me a little bit about them?"

Jon deliberately ducked the question. He was cautious about revealing the identities of F.O.R. "Yeah, we'll talk about that later, but suffice it to say I think you'll be impressed with the caliber of the team."

Diaz looked at the gold antique Rolex watch hanging from his left wrist. The conversation felt as if five minutes had passed, but it had been over an hour.

"Pardon me. The conference begins in an hour, so I'm going to head to downtown Miami. Would you care to ride with me?"

"I'm going to sit this one out. I've been traveling almost non-stop during the past month and have some close friends in Orlando. I'm going to head up there for the day. Good luck with the conference. What's your topic?"

"A comparative analysis of Greenland versus Antarctica's glacier melt. I genuinely enjoyed our meeting and appreciate the offer to join F.O.R. I gladly accept. Here's my personal contact info." Diaz handed him a card with white print on a solid, black background.

"Thanks. I'll be in touch in a few weeks about what happens next. I'm zeroing in on my final recruit."

"Anyone I might know?" Diaz asked in his nonchalant manner, continuously probing for additional information.

"I doubt it, but you will find out in due time. Promise."

Jon shielded his eyes from the Florida sun as he watched Diaz stroll toward his black UberLyft with darkened windows waiting at the entrance. The sound of waves in the background created an idyllic scene, almost a distraction. Jon couldn't figure out what was lurking underneath Diaz's snarky personality, as if a tepid, lukewarm soul was encased by an exterior composed of good looks and a charming personality. Something lingered in the air. *Hmmm. Diaz laid all his cards on the table, but it still seems like he was holding something back. Principals before personalities,* Jon thought, shrugging his shoulders.

He walked around to the front, got into his blue Mustang rental that was charging at an electric station and headed north to Orlando on I-95. It was an unusually humid day. He gunned the car to eighty, top down, as the wind blew back his hair.

Jon was going to see friends. But not the kind of friends he'd led Diaz to believe. He had an appointment with his 'friends' at NASA, people who he was introduced to by Bill Engel after they had sold their drone company to DARPA.

His agenda was about discussing the satellites that NASA had launched in the spring of 2040, designed to defend against and take out supersonic missiles.

Jon met with the lead engineer for NASA in the design and production of next-generation anti-drone lasers, who had just flown in last night from the Jet Propulsion Lab in Pasadena and headed up the division in US Space forces.

His specific task was laser development design for military satellites to aim lasers and track foreign missiles.

They were as much interested in Jon's former drone company's next generation AI chips as Jon was learning about their anti-drone laser technology, a joint venture between the two agencies and DARPA. Jon was concerned about how little progress had been made on hypersonic missile defense systems. Both Russian and Chinese hypersonics had advanced to the point when the U.S. was playing catch-up with its development of missile defense lasers.

The view from the window at sunset highlighted neon-blue sparkling water with reddish orange from a citrus sky overhead. The two men revealed little, as they were reluctant to discuss any recent breakthroughs. Jon did glean certain intel about anti-drone laser tech. He yearned to find an edge for his team.

Jon shook hands and headed to Orlando International to drop off his new car crush and catch a flight back to Denver. He had just recruited members from three different continents in eight days, and it was starting to wear thin. He needed a shot of Colorado to recharge, and embark on a side journey, one that would involve some cutting-edge construction.

Once on the green hydrogen-fueled jet that would take him from Miami to Denver in one hour and thirty minutes, he pulled out the green notebook made of 100% recyclable materials and began to draw. Jon decided to use the plane ride to sketch out an architectural design of an impenetrable underground bunker he had informally dubbed Darwin's Cave.

He sketched out the geothermal design. *Electric ground source heat pumps are connected to an underground loop to collect heat trapped in the earth and use it to both heat and cool the bunker with the ability to store excess electricity. In winter, the heat pumps pull heat from the ground directly into the bunker. In summer the heat pumps take heat from the building to cool it down. May install vertically or in a nearby lake. Requires backup system.*

Infra-red heated floors will eliminate germs, microbes, and mold. Solar powered cameras set on trees, pointed in all directions, four attack drones. Exit 90 meters to Cyber Stealth camouflaged with interchangeable outer wraps. LED and OLED grow lighting for vegetables and micro-greens using latest indoor farming tech and chemistry developed by Wolf. Eight gas marks, attachable to NVG's commercial-size refrigerators and one freezer. A washer-dryer that blows air into an underground vent. Parallel vents eliminate smoke from cooking. Secure air intake system, complete with HVAC underground.

A library/office, three bedrooms, kitchen with dishwasher, three full bathrooms with steam showers, vertically stacked washer-dryer, tool kits for repairs, and a surgical room with robotics using cold plasma.

Two camouflaged secret entrances on either side with automatic spring-loaded features. Same tech used for naval sub hatches. Full lab with quantum computers (redundancy). Note: Bunker able to withstand 25-kiloton nuclear blast.

Jon arrived back in Denver, walked to his car, typed in the autopilot coordinates for self-driving mode to his home in Frisco, and then started it using a voice-controlled system. He felt stymied for the first time he could remember. He was in desperate need of a credible ally within the walls of China that he could use as a proxy to forewarn the sprawling nation about Chirkov's grotesque plan.

After arriving back home with three hours of sunlight remaining, Jon found himself talking to Wolf on his deck outside, surrounded by an idyllic backdrop of some of the best that nature had to offer.

"I trust you understand that the vulnerabilities and flaws of a plan are about people, not systems. As far as I'm concerned, we humans are a failed experiment, and it's been a baffling decline in the last two millennia. Look no further than the story of Noah to understand that humans were going to be wiped off the planet, save one family. The supreme being was using water and floods to accomplish it."

"Pretty dismal, or should I say, fatalistic outlook for a perennial optimist," Jon mentioned.

"People are the weak link, but I do agree that getting An involved is mission critical, especially since this has to do with the PRC. Your patience and persistence will prevail. Just step out of your own shadow, and let it go. Then things will come your way." Wolf was steadfast in his advice borne of Shaman wisdom.

"Remember, energy follows intent — all ways and always." One of Wolf's assigned tasks was to call Jon out on his flaws and weaknesses, and reel him in when he was going astray or acting impulsively.

The next day, Jon got the break he'd been impatiently waiting for and was ready to pounce. He received an email invitation to participate on a panel at an International Water and Ice Symposium held annually in Reykjavik. He was selected by the committee to speak on the topic of microplastics. Naturally, he asked for a list of the other speakers before agreeing.

If I'm brutally honest with myself, Wolf should go in my place, but I can't take the risk, Jon thought. *Especially given how close we are to the mission. If he got kidnapped, we'd not only lose our leverage, but I'd never forgive myself.*

"Hey, Wolf, check this out!" Jon said with such excitement that Wolf thought he won something outsized.

"What is it? Did you win a ten-figure lottery?"

"A billion doesn't buy what it used to. What I just found is better anyway. This conference in Iceland. I looked at the speaker list and An Shui is on it. This is our big opportunity. Can you believe it?"

Wolf was trying to keep Jon's emotions in check. "This is not a done deal. What if she is unable to attend because she gets sick, what if you talk to her and she says 'no?' There are a lot of 'what ifs' here that you can't control. You need to keep your expectations balanced."

"C'mon. I'll figure out something. Maybe I'll just kidnap her and hold her hostage until she agrees to join F.O.R. How about we send out some positive vibrations into the universe and eliminate the negativity for the time being? I need all the help I can get."

The conference was scheduled for October 15th. Jon decided to use the time to learn a little Mandarin. Wolf thought he was certifiable.

"At least I'll know the basics. Hopefully, Dr. Shui is fluent in English, and she'll bail me out, so I won't embarrass my ass too much." Wolf almost fell off his chair laughing, imagining his friend speaking Mandarin with a Southern drawl.

The day before his arrival to Reykjavik, Jon flew to NYC and had a debriefing with Phillippe, who was also participating in the Reykjavik conference. Jon wanted to pick Phillippe's brain about bringing An into the fold. Jon figured tag-teaming An would increase the odds of a successful outcome since Canada was not part of the Cold War with China. However, they were barely on speaking terms with Russia, due to its decades of threatening actions near the Arctic Circle.

CHAPTER 5

F.O.R. ALL THE MARBLES

October 2044

Jon was finally back in familiar surroundings. A month passed, and he was glowing about the opportunity to recruit his seventh and final member of F.O.R. He had a huge grin on his face borne of anticipation that he would successfully convince Dr. An Shui to join him, and that he would be able to operate in a place underground with no interference from anyone above ground. He practiced his pitch to An in front of a mirror.

In his Frisco home overlooking a bountiful Lake Dillon, rested a framed quote prominently displayed on a large wall overlooking his fireplace. 'It is not the most intellectual of species that survives; it is not the strongest that survives, but the species that survives is the one that is able best to adapt and adjust to the changing environment in which it finds itself.' *Charles Darwin*

Jon knew exactly what came next and hatched his plan. He and Wolf had to be protected 24/7 when he wasn't globetrotting across different continents. Wolf needed absolute impenetrable security from the unwelcomed predators that might come knocking, especially when he was out of town and Wolf was alone.

"It's imperative that we defend ourselves from all the power-hungry, greedy sons of bitches, the same ones who broke into your lab twice in the last year. That was a warning shot across the bow. It strikes me that they were hoping to steal whatever they could, and then reverse engineer your microplastics research. I doubt that they'd ever be successful, but it doesn't mean they wouldn't use you as leverage to hold other governments hostage to extract a large premium."

"I am curious about what you have in mind about 'protecting ourselves.' Please enlighten me." He folded his arms and stood firmly in place. Wolf was eager to find out exactly what Jon was plotting upstairs in his mind.

A smile formed on Jon's face. "Trust me, Wolf. Let's discuss the details later. We've got much bigger catfish to fry."

Jon made sure that he and Phillippe were on the same flight with seats across the aisle from one another. The plane took off on time. "An is without question the number one choice among 1.2 billion Chinese to round out our team. She's perfect," Jon's face beamed with optimism.

"Any ideas of how I should approach her? Do you know the names of any of her colleagues, or have you had any interaction with Chinese labs in the last couple of years?" Jon was probing like a dentist scouring a patient's mouth for cavities.

"It is curious that while I don't have any direct contacts with anyone who might know An, my sister's husband has been doing quite a bit of work with a lab in China focused on freshwater solutions. Let me call Pierre and see what I can find out."

Phillippe stared at his watch. *Half hour before boarding. Plenty of time.*

"Great. I'm gonna get some green tea. Want anything while I'm up?"

"No, thanks. I'm good." Jon turned and strutted towards the cafe as Phillippe speed-dialed his brother-in-law.

Jon and Phillippe deboarded the plane and noticed how clean and orderly things were in Iceland, starting with the airport. They had been unable to get seats together and had some catching up to do. Jon was acutely aware that most of Iceland had been powered for decades by geothermal and hydroelectricity from the glacier runoffs. The latter had been waning due to climate change, and while the melting of the glaciers yielded short-term results, the long-term renewable energy sources from hydro were drying up.

They proceeded to the exit and caught a driverless, hydrogen powered UberLyft to the hotel where the conference was being held. Electric vehicle transportation was available and although there was a premium charge for hydrogen, Jon was happy to pay extra.

"Jon, I've got a little surprise. Turns out that Pierre knows one of An's cohorts, and he arranged a dinner for us with her tomorrow night. It's at a low-key restaurant off the beaten path, and far enough away from the conference that we won't run into anyone." Phillippe said, giddy with excitement.

"That's great, Phillippe. What's the name of the restaurant?"

"It's called Bryggjan Bruggerhús."

"I just want to make sure they have Arctic Char on the menu. I've been dying to have some fresh fish. I only get the frozen variety at home, except for Colorado trout, but most of that is farm-raised." Jon's adventurous palate was always excited to try new restaurants. "I'll meet you in the lobby in the morning. Get some rest."

"You as well. 8 am sharp, eh!" Jon went straight to his room and started reviewing his notes about An he had gathered from Chip, his childhood friend and CIA contact. Jon realized what he'd been able to dig up was full of holes.

Dr. An Shui was part of a lab consortium with offices in Beijing and Shanghai. She had been toiling with her own discoveries and patents for over two decades, struggling to protect them from the PRC stealing them outright. Her mother was still alive. Her father was murdered when she was two years old.

That night he called Wolf for his usual update. "An's father was murdered on June 4, 1989. Any guesses as to what happened on that day?" Jon asked as if he was challenging Wolf's knowledge of world history.

"Chinese history for $10,000. What was Tiananmen Square?" Wolf responded as if he was playing Jeopardy 2044.

"You never cease to amaze me."

An Shui witnessed a constant stream of air and water pollution that was slowly poisoning the vast majority of her people. The Chinese government had been talking out of both sides of its mouth for the last thirty years and continued going to great lengths to cover it up from not only its citizens but from the rest of southeast Asia. They were preaching zero carbon emissions while opening a record number of coal-fired plants until 2029 and then closing them down, only after severe, irreparable damage had been done.

Jon was pleasantly surprised to get a call from Yael within minutes of hanging up with Wolf. He was sitting in his room eating dinner consisting of salad with hard-boiled eggs, roasted vegetables, and a non-dairy dessert covered with a variety of nuts. He never drank his tea during a meal; always afterwards.

"When are you meeting with Dr. An?"

"Tomorrow night for dinner, and Court's going to join us. He arranged the whole thing with one phone call."

"Do you have a plan? You do realize that An and I have met and bonded at several previous water conferences."

"Not really. I'm just going in there and winging it," he said half-kidding.

"Really? Would you like some old-fashioned friendly advice? Don't wing a first meeting with a Chinese hydrologist."

"I was kidding, of course. I'm going to find out what she's most concerned about and what her fears are." Jon started to wonder if somehow Yael, An, and he were somehow connected from a past life, a concept Wolf had championed since they first met at M.I.T.

He and Phillippe arrived at the restaurant five minutes early. An was already there standing by the maître de. Jon didn't know whether to bow or shake hands, so he put out his right hand, which was met by An's soft, uncalloused touch. Jon was immediately taken in by her energy. Much like Wolf, her spirit emanated a calm, unrelenting force. Not fire, wind, or stone, but water. Her face was radiant with not a wrinkle to be found anywhere, including her neck. She was all of five foot, four inches tall, but Jon suspected she was an absolute powerhouse.

They sat down at a table in the corner and began to do a verbal dance. "Nothing surprises me anymore, and my government loves to rewrite history by hiding both the past and the present and then kicking the can down the road to a future where they would ultimately over-promise and under deliver," An said.

"If given the choice, would you rather live in Beijing or Shanghai?"

"Well, it's not much of a choice, and that's why I live in Shenzhen," she laughed. "Shanghai peaked decades ago and is literally consuming itself. They are living off the fat of a previous and more prosperous era. Beijing is pathetic. They have dwindled and squandered away all their natural resources. I can't find a city block that is devoid of air and water pollution, and the corruption and power mongering have resulted in them ignoring the basic needs of their own citizens."

Jon was staring at An. When he discovered that An was fifty-six years old, he was stunned. She didn't look a day over forty. Her stride was spritely, as if there was a hoverboard under her feet as she seemed to glide effortlessly across the floor. "The hands of time have been kind to you," Jon reflected aloud.

Phillippe was content to be a spectator watching two brilliant minds go at it. Jon and An proceeded to speak about their respective government faux pas before they got on to the topic of why they were dining together. Jon's intention was to be low key, and not seem too eager. He could barely contain his excitement about An rounding out his stellar F.O.R. team. *She would raise the bar from good to great.*

"Tell me about your childhood," An asked with intense curiosity.

"I grew up in a small town in the foothills of Tennessee. Once you get outside of Nashville, you're pretty much in the deep south. Let's just say that there weren't too many bright lights in my community, if you know what I mean. I skipped the seventh grade and graduated high school right after I turned eighteen. I always looked older than my age. It helped in the drinking department, but that was a double-edged sword. The only thing that I didn't like about growing up in the South is that people *grin-fucked* you to death!"

"Pardon me? Or pardon you?" An exclaimed, startled by what she heard.

"Oh. You mean *grin-fuck*? It's an expression about fake Southern charm. You know, when people smile in your face while they are secretly trying to take your job, steal your girlfriend, or just plain stab you in the back."

An looked at Jon as she started to laugh uncontrollably.

"What's so funny? You never heard that expression before?" Jon asked.

She finally calmed down enough to utter a few concrete sentences. "Can't say that I have," she said, dabbing tears of laughter from her eyes with a napkin. "In China it's just the opposite. People don't smile when they are sticking a knife into your chest, but they do look you right in the eyes."

"Ouch. Guess you'd know." An continued to be amused by Jon's self-effacing humor, and was listening intently to every word above the loud chatter and clanking of dishes in the restaurant.

Phillippe interjected briefly and asked what everyone was ordering so that he could tell their server without interrupting the flow of conversation. Jon ordered the char. Broiled, with roasted potatoes and a salad. An duplicated Jon's meal.

"Tell me about your parents." An asked politely.

"My parent's divorce became official on my twenty-second birthday, and was the main catalyst in my pursuit of a second PhD," he told An. My mother Sally looked a good fifteen years younger than her age and was the consummate net giver." He pulled out a picture in a hidden compartment of his wallet.

"Oh, she's radiant!" she exclaimed in her best Mandarin-English accent.

"My father Chuck was off the charts brilliant but was cursed with multiple demons. He never finished high school and went off the rails when I turned five. In hindsight, he seemed to be living behind the veil of denial in terms of who he was and the damage he was doing to Mom and our family."

It wasn't lost on Jon that he wanted An to do most of the talking, and needed to exert maximum self-control. Jon strained to hear her soft-spoken voice above the roaring background noise in the restaurant, steadily rising as the restaurant became stuffed to capacity.

"What about you, An?"

"My father was killed when I was two when the Tiananmen Square massacre happened, so I never really knew him." Jon noticed that An had tears rolling down one cheek.

"That's awful and I'm sorry."

"He died doing something he believed in, protesting against the corruption of the Communist Party. He was a PhD student at the time and considered an intellectual. I was an only child, so my mother raised me by herself. In that era, the government was 'strongly encouraging' one child per family."

"How about you, Jon? Any siblings?"

"Yeah, I have one older brother who resembles my father. I haven't really spoken to him much in the past six or seven years. Let's just say I'm extremely grateful that I turned out like my mother. I was fortunate to get a full scholarship to college because, at the time, Mom couldn't afford the tuition. They were still supporting my older brother."

"How was your university experience?" An inquired, as she instinctively looked around the room to see who was listening.

"Except for one close friend and a few interesting professors, I was slightly bored most of the time, and graduated in the middle of my final year. I took about eight months off and was fortunate to be accepted into Cal Berkeley's doctorate program in hydrology. They covered all the tuition, and I received $65,000 a year stipend to cover living expenses. I was blessed to earn my PhD at twenty-three."

"What did you do with your eight-month hiatus? Travel?" An inquired.

Jon was sweating on the inside and was struggling to keep his story brief. He brushed her question aside and kept firing back at her.

"What about you, An? What was it like being raised as an only child by a single parent?"

An cleared her throat. "After my father died, we moved to Shenzhen. I was brought up by my maternal grandmother because Ma Ma was working fourteen hours a day in a factory to support us. She struggled mightily, but I'd like to think that her hard work paid off. After earning a PhD, I was in the workforce for five years, and had saved enough to buy her a small house. She was able to retire from full-time work by the age of seventy, but still works part-time two days a week and takes care of Lao Lao. My mom is my hero, but my Lao Lao is my rock. And remember the positives. At least you had two parents and a brother growing up."

"That isn't exactly how I remember things. It was a classic toxic father-son relationship. My father could violate his own standards faster than he could lower them. He was a drunken sailor without a sail and with a broken rudder, and really didn't give a shit about anyone else but himself and his female companions. All of whom proved to be short-lived."

"What was it that turned you against your father? How do you say, the piece of straw that broke a camel's back?"

"That's an easy one. When he asked Mom to pay him alimony as part of the divorce settlement and got it, I couldn't stand the sight of him anymore. Truth is I haven't seen him since. Talked to him a couple of times by phone in the last fifteen years. On top of it all, my brother turned out to be a clone of my father."

"Was it really that bad?" An asked innocently.

"Let me put it this way. The only thing my father ever did that was remotely positive was contribute to my conception, and that was it. He served as my motivation to be successful, and it manifested into a twenty-year dance with the devil as a chronic overachiever so I could offset his failures in life."

"You never answered my question about what you did during your eight months off between undergrad and your PhD program," An persisted.

"In the interest of time, I'd like to defer my long-winded explanation for now. Let's just say I did Seal training in San Diego for those eight months. We live halfway around the world from each other, but it's pretty much the same."

"What do you mean?"

"We both have governments who have made mockeries of environmental privilege and providence, at least up until this point. It's all about the money, big business, and abuse of power at the expense of citizens. Do you have any idea that the U.S. military is one of the largest polluters in history?"

"You need to check your facts," An said politely. China's military surpassed the U.S. military seven years ago as having the largest carbon footprint of any military or organization that ever existed. And what's more, our wasteful country has consumed over fourteen trillion gallons of water annually for the past decade."

Jon's jaw dropped slightly. "What the fuck? What are they using it for?"

"You know, the usual. Agriculture, industry, auto manufacturing, running coal plants and utilities, with a little left over for personal consumption."

Jon took a deep breath. "In our defense, our military has been developing alternative energy sources like biofuels, but these are only a tiny fraction of its spending. Nevertheless, it remains that our military, mostly the Army and Navy, is the single largest consumer of hydrocarbons in the world. Trying to shed their old ways is like climbing uphill with the wind in their face."

An nodded. "You are correct." "At least you have some basic rights as citizens and the freedom of expression. So, what is so pressing that you had to meet me for dinner on our second night in Iceland?" An asked with a feeling of trepidation.

Jon had his opening. He seized the opportunity and started talking about the plan and the team, and how the person sitting across the table from him was the last piece to give his mission the greatest chance of success. "Well, I've been cooking up a plan, and have already built a world-class team to execute it."

"I can already tell I'm not going to like this," a mischievous smile formed around her lips. "And what does this grand plan have to do with me?"

"You're the last piece of the puzzle. Like the queen on a chessboard. It's not a matter of want. It's a matter of need."

An was mesmerized given that she had no inkling that they were going to discuss such a sensitive topic. She showed no signs of fear. Jon admired her courage. He spoke to her about each member of the team and what the mission was, and how An could play an integral role in F.O.R.

"May I ask who else is on the team? It appears you only named three people, excluding you and me. I thought you said there were seven?" Phillipe sensed this might be her final question before Jon would ask her to join the team and jumped into the fray.

"I like that you're paying attention. I'm the sixth member and Wolf is the seventh," Phillippe asserted.

"You've got to trust us on this," said Jon raising his voice.

She did a double take. "Trust? That's rich. You're asking me to trust two people I met for the first time in my lived-in life an hour ago? Wow, you've got some set of cojones, Mr. Buckingham!"

"I didn't know you spoke Spanish," Jon responded, slightly embarrassed. "And you don't even know the half of it." They both had a hearty laugh. It turned out that An knew everyone on the team by reputation and had even met Elena briefly at a Eurasian water conference several years back.

"You have one-third of the team sitting right in front of you! Whaddya think? Can we make this work without putting you and your family at risk?"

She hesitated a long time before speaking. Jon had hit her right in the vagus nerve, the very nerve that connects the brain to all the major organs. An knew that she would never be able to share any of this with her mother or grandmother. The anxiety began to stir inside her, and her stomach tightened, followed by shallow breathing. This was part and parcel of An Shui's daily reality.

Phillippe stayed the course. "We can only begin to understand your risk, and it's not lost on us that your own government threw you in prison for three months after you organized a protest. You even wore masks to throw off the AI security cameras and drones being used to identify citizens."

Finally, An spoke in a whisper, glaring from the corner of her eye around the restaurant, a reflexive action she acquired while living in China all her life.

"The only way this could work is for me to arrange an extended joint research project abroad. Israel would be my first choice since my government is still on good terms with them and there is still active trade and technology transfer going on between our two countries. It would be ideal if I could work with Yael to do hydrology research with her in Sde Boker. Yael's reputation is legendary for water conservation in arid climates, using desalinated water as the main supply for agriculture and raising farm animals."

Phillippe jumped into the fray. "That's a tremendous idea, and a brilliant solution to our dilemma. I'm willing to bet that the guy sitting in front of you can help make it happen."

Phillippe glanced to his left. "Jon, can you phone Yael early tomorrow morning and run this idea by her? Too late to call now. It's 3 a.m. in Israel."

"One more thing," An asked for her own edification.

"What's that, An?"

"From my limited perspective, there are only two reasons to be involved with your F.O.R. group. One is out of desperation. What I mean by that is there is no other alternative to resolve the issue at hand."

"Understood. What's the second?"

"For revenge. And I'm in for both reasons."

"Makes sense to me. I'll take it from here." The timing was nearly perfect. Jon paid for the meal, and they walked back to the conference hotel. An was constantly looking over her shoulder at three Asian males who seemed to be following them ever since they left the restaurant.

"Don't look back. Keep walking as if nothing's happening and look straight ahead. I got you covered," Jon assured her.

The conference ended at six p.m. the following evening, and Jon was the second to last speaker. Everyone would be going their separate ways. The plan had taken on an inertia all its own. After a twenty-minute conversation with Yael, Jon was assured that with some help from one of Yael's colleagues, she could pave the way to make An a welcomed, albeit temporary colleague. Yael was genuinely excited about the prospect of working with An in her lab and with F.O.R.

The next morning, Jon and Phillippe met An in the lobby, and she did a quick turn to make sure no one was within earshot. "Well, how did it go last night, Jon?" An said with a wide smile of anticipation.

"Couldn't have gone better. It's down to the small details, and if I know Yael, she is already working on things from her end. Here's her private number." Jon discretely handed his Jack Walker business card to An with Yael's nine-digit cell number scribbled on the back.

She paused. There was a mutual silence borne of gratitude and admiration. Gazing up at Jon, her eyes were a misty red, as tears welled up in the corners of his eyes. He could only imagine how much she had to overcome living in China as well as losing a father as a young child, someone who stood up for his beliefs. *The antithesis of my father.*

Phillippe held his emotions in check until after An left the hotel. "Well done, good form, indeed." They were both ready to leave. The bell captain arranged for a taxi to Keflavik Airport. Both were admiring what remained of the glaciers on the horizon. As they exited the cab, Phillippe gave Jon a hug goodbye before they went to separate terminals to catch their respective flights. Jon reflected upon the irony that he was able to slip through the cracks and recruit An in a single night.

Once he was seated on the plane, Jon began to dissect his face-to-face encounter with An. He was already missing her energy, and was keenly aware of the risks An faced when she chose to join the mission. This final and perhaps most invaluable recruit would round out Jon's world-class team. He had pursued her covertly, like a junkyard dog lurking silently at dusk. With drones that recorded comprehensive facial recognition, An could never be seen in public with an American in mainland China. If found out, the Chinese authorities would be content to lock her up with her family in Qincheng maximum security prison, branding her and her family as traitors.

Jon had less fear that Elena could suffer a similar fate to An's. Elena did not have an extended family. The damning irony of it all was that the former Soviet Union helped build QinCheng in 1958, the only remaining prison belonging to China's Ministry of Public Security.

Jon returned to his house in Frisco later that night and phoned An. "My sources tell me that the pipeline was completed less than a month ago. The good news is that they're still in the testing phase for another ninety days, and it appears that this is the ideal time to strike. And once they find out we have technology that can take plastic and other deadly particles out of the water, we have the ultimate leverage against both countries and can put a wedge between them. Our pipeline demolition buys us three months, enough time for the entire world to know."

"Plus, China is going to be quite unhappy that they spent $17 billion on a pipeline, lining Chirkov's pocket with a smattering of rubles, dollars, gold, and cryptocurrencies, only to discover the water had been contaminated by its corrupt, alleged ally. According to my sources, that plan has been in the works since 2030 and was supposed to be completed four years ago. The destination? Langzou in northwest China, then Beijing and Shanghai. What are four years in the scheme of decades?" An quipped sarcastically.

"An, I respectfully disagree. There were some big Chinese businessmen involved early on with the plan designed to reap big profits importing water from Lake Baikal."

"How?"

"By controlling the distribution, that's how. Either as bottled water or through an intricate array of pipelines to Beijing and Shanghai. Jian Songdeng, who owned dozens of mines in Mongolia, was the first to propose a pipeline to move water across Mongolia thirty years ago. Jian's initial idea was to divert water from several rivers in northern Mongolia, including the Selenga River that flows into Lake Baikal, and then into southern Mongolia and ultimately Langzhou.

Jon heard a knock on An's door through the phone. An got up and approached the door. As she approached the door, Jon sensed that something bad was about to happen. A split second later, he shouted, "Angie, don't answer it."

An reflexively grabbed her nun-chuks. She cracked the door open slowly, leaning against it. She held the nunchucks firmly in her right hand behind her back, hidden from view. A Chinese man wearing sunglasses lunged at her with a knife. She nimbly side-stepped him while the nunchucks came crashing down on the back of his head. He hit the floor with a thud and was out cold. As if nothing happened, she calmly continued the call and said she'd dispose of the garbage laying on the floor of her hotel room after her call with Jon ended.

"Nice move, Angie. You still got it. Look, all we need is to get you safely to Israel, and then you're skiing downhill. Any other questions?"

"Only one. Will you at least consider the possibility of helping me leave China permanently after the mission is over, and Mama and Lao

Lao out of that cesspool too? I'm letting you know up front that it's a package deal. I couldn't live with myself if I left them behind."

Jon noticed An starting to cry. "Understood. You have my word on this."

That was all she needed to hear to commit wholeheartedly.

CHAPTER 6

DARWIN'S BUNKER

Late August 2044

W olf's breakthrough research in removing microplastics on a large scale made him a likely target from a plethora of sides. Jon insisted that Wolf spend most of his time in Frisco, given he had Seal training and Wolf's expertise was his crossbow. Together, they could defend themselves against any predators.

"Look. It's not just about me. This is for your well-being and safety, too," Jon said, staring into his confidante's eyes. "I considered all our options."

"We've got to locate our bunker far away from the rest of the world. Remote is the operative word. It will be so rock solid that if the enemy stumbled upon our exact whereabouts, they could never penetrate the fortress I'm planning to build. Think of the Bat Cave on steroids."

Wolf didn't have a cynical bone in his body and his moral compass pointed true north, but he was a tad suspicious. "Let me see if I've got this straight. You want to build an underground bunker and want my help because I am running my uncle's construction business until he gets out of the hospital," Wolf sighed. "Is that the sole reason why you're including me in this conversation? And where did you suppose this impenetrable fortress is going to be located, Yosemite?"

"Just humor me, will ya? My number one choice was somewhere in New Zealand. I was there in that part of the world back when I tested the jetpacks outside of Sydney. No one knew I was scoping out the country for underground bunker locations."

"Why not New Zealand? I like the sound of that. New Zealand has no natural enemies and is isolated, too. It's twenty-five hundred miles away from the nearest civilization. It's also closest in proximity to northeast Antarctica. The least you could've done is ask my opinion," Wolf said, leaning back in his chair with his hands laced around his neck.

"Listen, back in 2022 one of my colleagues at MIT got wind of a 150-ton survival bunker that was being shipped from some God-forsaken warehouse in Texas to New Zealand. According to the press release I read, it was ultimately buried fourteen feet underground."

Wolf was leaning in with his elbows resting on his knees, his hands clasped in front of him. "Just think. If there was some Asian land or naval war, an incurable virus, or a nuclear apocalypse, New Zealand might be the last country standing. A nuclear safe haven, if you will. Possibly Greenland. And they have an abundance of freshwater, sheep, agriculture, and natural resources, especially when you measure it on a per capita basis. In a word, they are self-sufficient."

"What about China taking over New Zealand? And where in particular were you thinking of building this so-called bunker?" Wolf asked quizzically. "And I suppose it was attached to a house above ground?"

"There was some vacant land overlooking Lake Wakatipu in Queenstown. There was also property in two other locations I loved. One was near Lake Pounui, and the other was Wanaka. Both had spectacular views but were too damn hard to get back and forth from the States or Europe. And yes, they were attached to magnificent homes above ground."

"It never stopped you before. You know, the distance thing. Supersonic jets can get you from New Zealand to LA in eight hours. What's the issue?"

"There were other factors. For starters, it is extremely difficult to be anonymous in NZ as there are strict citizenship requirements. On top of that, I would need a private jet at my disposal at a moment's notice. Just owning or leasing a jet would make us visible. I need a place much more inconspicuous."

"I get it. The location must be practical," Wolf surmised. "And I suppose you, or should I say 'we' have a definitive location?" Wolf asked.

"C'mon, where do you think it is? You know me well enough by now."

Wolf had no logical response and threw his hands up in the air.

"Brace yourself. I've decided on Porcupine State Park, right in your own backyard." Wolf practically jumped out of his chair, sitting outside on the deck at Jon's Frisco dwelling.

"Before you give me your infamous naysayer look, consider the positives. It would be easy access for your construction crew, and we could build it right in the middle of the forest preserve where there are no access roads. If we're going to pull off the master plan, protect what we already have in the way of breakthrough science and chemistry, then it better be a goddamn secret to the outside world. And the locals, too. It's perfect."

Wolf sat in stunned silence and didn't move a muscle, except his vocal cords. "It's not only illegal trespassing, but on state and federal land. It simply won't work," Wolf responded with a barrel of doubt in his voice.

"That's what I thought at first. And guess who's gonna build it for us? Your uncle's construction company! At least part of his crew."

"Do you know how outside of your mind you are right now? You're my best friend, but there's no way that I'm going to put my uncle's company in double jeopardy by committing a Class A felony. If we get caught, we have no recourse. All the lawyers in Michigan couldn't defend us." Wolf was projecting a feeling of doubt into the air, but Jon was three steps ahead of him.

"I've already thought this through. I'll form a new, single-member LLC with Jack Walker as the sole member and manager. Then, we'll 'borrow' eight or nine of your best crew for four months while we build our underground dream house complete with a world-class lab. Your uncle will see revenue flowing in, so he won't be suspicious. That way, there is no liability on your end. I'll take care of the LLC this afternoon. Wolf, say something."

Wolf was pacing deliberately back and forth on the deck in total silence, as if he was a Buddhist monk on a meditation walk trying not to step on any bugs.

Wolf was not close to being sold on the concept, but Jon continued his sales pitch just as Wolf was about to respond.

"C'mon, you've got to trust me on this one. I built, ran, and sold a drone company with fifteen electrical engineers, five material science engineers, two salespeople, and four support staff collaborating with me. This is a piece of cake."

The words 'trust me' echoed through the chambers of Wolf's mind. Jon was lobbying hard for his idea, and clearly wasn't going to take 'no' for an answer, especially from his best friend who he was altruistically trying to protect.

Wolf shrugged his shoulders. "I'm going to take the rest of today to think about it, but if I decide to take one for the team, here are my conditions. One, I assume you're footing the bill. If that's the case, you'll have to pay the crew members in crypto and need to figure out a way to do this without my uncle knowing about it. If he ever found out that we were doing something illegal, there's no tomorrow for me, and I'm exiled from the family."

"Done. Next."

"I also need to be able to handpick my men."

"I've got no problem with that and leave the decision in your capable hands. Keep in mind that I would have to start ordering materials in a couple of days, given that we need to finish before winter freezes the ground. I've targeted around Labor Day as our start date. I'm willing to pay double the normal hourly rate that they would be making working at your uncle's company, even though we are coming into a slow season." In his methodical way, Jon was slowly persuading Wolf over to his point of view.

"I need it done before winter sets in. Do you think you and your uncle's men can hit the deadline? And how much will it cost for labor and materials?" Jon asked, wanting to make sure his timeline was realistic.

Wolf started to laugh. "What's so funny?" Jon asked with a puzzled look on his face.

"It's just like you to ask more than one question at a time. And I haven't agreed to your cockamamie plan yet. I imagine we can dig the hole and clear the trees in about ten days tops, assuming no inclement weather. Cement, wood, steel, and infrastructure will take a good two weeks for delivery, and I would do that in short order to minimize our downtime. Figure two weeks for the foundation to dry and another two months to complete the internal construction, like wiring and plumbing. It's optimistic, but we should probably be in before Thanksgiving."

"What about the hardware and materials we're going to need? Is that factored into the cost?"

"Not at all. The cost of the underground bunker doesn't include any of the lab materials, supercomputers, AI, and ventilation for cooling the servers as well as the heat you will need in the winter. I imagine we could power and heat it with geothermal. And keep us off the grid so there are no utility bills, although most of Michigan's power is provided by wind energy. It's imperative that the utility companies don't have an address for us, and geothermal will do the trick."

"C'mon! What's the bottom-line cost already?" Jon's impatience was growing like a weed in the rainy season.

"We will have to do some of the work at night. Can't draw too much attention that we are building in a national park, even if it is 65,000 acres. We'll need electric backhoes and hauling trucks to minimize the noise and exhaust so no one will be able to hear the construction. My uncle has some portable solar cells to charge them during the day."

Wolf was trying to cover as many details as possible in his mind. "We're talking three and a half months all in, and maybe a bit quicker."

"Yeah, that sounds about right. I also ran some preliminary calculations. Tell me what you're thinking."

Wolf was in deep thought trying to estimate the costs in his own head. "OK. Got it. I'd say approximately $995,000 for labor and materials. I'd like to price in a new 1,000-qubit quantum computer for my research to protect and encrypt all our data systems and intranet. My best guess is a million eight."

"Are you sure we need something this extensive and impenetrable?"

"I'll let you answer your own question. You've had two serious break-ins to your office in the last six months, and it feels like if you were there at the time, you may not be standing right here."

"Under $2 million? Where do I sign? 'Specially since the quantum computer computers have come down 90% in price in the last ten years. Remember back when 100-qubit quantum computers were more powerful than all the supercomputers on the planet combined? Times have changed."

Wolf was still tentative, although he found himself moving closer toward Jon's way of thinking. "I need a day to contemplate this but considering we don't have to 'buy' or 'zone' the land, the path is clear. I would order the materials in a couple of days. We'll have to play the weather by ear, but since climate change has started to bring more temperate weather, it's very doable."

"OK. When you decide, let me know how much crypto you need to order all the materials. I'll have it for you by tomorrow, whatever you need."

"Here's a design sketch of how I want the interior laid out. I'm a novice when it comes to architectural renderings."

Jon was giddy about one thing. The idea that the bunker could withstand a 25-kiloton nuclear blast. A huge grin appeared on his face, borne of anticipation that he and Wolf would be able to operate in a place underground with no interference from anyone above the surface. He was also excited about Wolf's knowledge of the territory, and his ability to work at night to minimize the possibility of attracting unwanted attention.

Jon was about to be hung by the impatience wrapped around his own neck. "Whaddya think?"

Wolf finally relinquished. "It's paramount that the buildout be kept airtight with no leaks. The only wild card left is choosing the eight or nine workers who would be aware of its whereabouts."

"I trust your judgment and your relationships with your hand-picked team implicitly, so no problem from my perspective."

"I can assure you these guys are like family and would never betray the location, not even to their wife and children. They know what's at stake here. Besides, they're all like brothers. When they find out they'll be making double wages, no worries." Wolf smiled and then spoke with a calm authority. "Look. I trust these guys with my life, so don't give it another thought."

Jon nodded. There was one final reason he was set on the location. It was surrounded by freshwater on all sides. Not only was Lake Cloud right around the corner, but to the north and northeast was Lake Superior, and to the south and southwest Lake Michigan. Jon could also land a floatplane on any of one of the three lakes nearby, something he'd learned to do in his spare time. A floatplane docked nearby could take them out of harm's way at a moment's notice.

———

A week passed, as Wolf and two of his most able-bodied crew surveyed the 65,000-acre wilderness for a suitable location. Jon worked up the final designs and architectural drawings from the drafts he'd made earlier. He scrutinized what was available in the way of underground bunker construction and spoke with a manufacturer of prefab underground bunkers, asking dozens of questions under the guise that he might be a prospective buyer. While Jon abhorred lying, he gave them a fake name and address to stay far away from the anonymity that Wolf and he maintained.

Wolf left the next day, headed back to the UP. Two days passed, and he phoned Jon to give him the good news.

"We found the ideal location, and I'm happy to take you there as soon as tomorrow. It's mission-critical that no one has a clue, including the state of Michigan, Keweenaw County, and surrounding towns like Copper Harbor and Ironwood. Best if you get your ass on a plane to Detroit Metro, and then take a charter to Houghton County Municipal. I'll pick you up."

"Don't worry. I won't tell a soul," Jon teased in between huffs at nine-thousand feet altitude. In the second week of September, Wolf and his construction team began building the 8,000-square-foot fortress right on schedule. The location was pristine, an area located due west of Lake of the Clouds and White Pine. It had easy access to Lake Superior as well, a location of paramount importance for emergency escape routes and water testing.

Wolf and his crew of nine worked ten hours a day in two shifts. They started in the early morning, took an afternoon break for lunch, and then went back at it again from 5 pm until the moon was high in the clear UP sky. Jon installed cameras all around the perimeter that could be used to spot intruders or wandering hikers. Wolf alternated crew members one at a time to watch the perimeter for hikers or an occasional forest ranger.

The ceiling of the bunker was fifteen feet underground, slightly under two feet thick, and built with a combination of cement and steel. The sheer volume of dirt and trees that required clearing and hauling was a full-time job the entire first week. Although it was paramount to leave as many trees, shrubs, and grass intact, the crew ended up hauling a dozen trees to the owner of a lumber yard that Wolf knew. He and his crew had figured out a way to dig underground while leaving part of the natural habitat on the surface.

It was the end of September, and when he wasn't traveling, Jon was on-site six days a week, helping where he could. He and Wolf slept in a log cabin about three miles up the way, a place that they would walk to and from daily. It was the property of Wolf's father handed down from his grandfather. Originally constructed in the late 1960's, the cabin was so remote and naturally camouflaged that only Wolf and his immediate family knew the whereabouts. No one used it much after mid-September.

"I suppose your grandpa got a permit to build this?" Jon teased Wolf when he put the key into the lock of the front door and then set foot into a well-insulated shack in the middle of nowhere. The only thing close by was a small lake that Wolf and his father used to catch fish when he was a boy.

"And if you mind your manners, I'll take you to a hidden lake and show you how to fish for the best perch and whitefish in the Midwest, including Lake Superior."

"C'mon, Wolf. I grew up in the hills of Tennessee. There were lakes in every direction. You don't think I know how to fish? You're just killin' me."

Shaking his head, he bedded down in a cabin that only Wolf, his father, his uncle, his grandfather and grandmother knew the whereabouts of. His grandfather had built it from the ground up some eighty years ago and had never told a soul, with the exception of his immediate family. Before Jon could finish writing in his journal, Wolf was fast asleep but never snored.

Jon sat up in his bed at 3 am, rubbing his groggy eyes. "What's the matter? Do we have uninvited guests outside?" Jon reflexively reached for his Glock.

"Put that thing away. You might hurt someone. Go back to sleep. I heard a sound out there. When I went to check it out, I saw a moose having a midnight snack." Jon was not at all surprised that Wolf had left the cabin and was already back by the time he woke up. He felt safer sleeping in a cabin in the woods with Wolf in the next room than any hotel at which he could ever stay. *How else could someone explain how this man of Ojibwe descent could be woken at 3 a.m. under a full moon from the sound of a twig snapping fifty paces in the distance?*

With Wolf in charge, the two intrepid explorers were in Darwin three days before Thanksgiving, an idyllic fall day smattered with yellows, greens, reds, and browns. Jon took care of the food, and Darwin was fully stocked with grains, nuts, tens of pounds of fresh fish that they put in a large freezer, eggs, energy bar meals, and frozen fruits and vegetables stacked three by four feet in a second, smaller freezer. Water was not an issue. Wolf had engineered an underground pipe directly from a nearby lake with filters that he had constructed in his lab.

Wolf and his crew had delivered, coming in slightly ahead of schedule and under budget. The first night in, Jon and Wolf tested and retested all the electronics, appliances, and technology to make sure they have backup systems in case the power crashed. At 1 a.m., they fell asleep in their respective rooms, and rested easy. For the first time that Wolf could remember, he slept soundly.

The next day, refreshed from the prior night's sleep, they climbed out of the bunker to a sunrise on a crisp late fall cloudless day. "You know what type of Tomahawks? The kind that travels at 550 mph and carries a 1,000-lb payload."

"With a little help from my Navy friends, I designed the entrances into Darwin to act like a spring-loaded submarine hatch, but smaller in terms of both weight and density. At the push of a button, each entrance can open or close within two and half seconds, despite that it weighs close to four hundred pounds and is ten inches thick. Without the button, it's impossible to lift it on your own."

Jon was uniquely qualified to build the technology, both inside and outside of Darwin. His ability to merge a telecommunications and engineering background with his knowledge of quantum physics was unique. While earning his PhD at MIT, Jon had implemented the creation of a new, hack-proof intranet for the Navy, rendering its prior system obsolete.

He channeled that experience as he worked on making Darwin's perimeter secure. Three cell towers about five hundred meters apart were disguised as trees that stood thirty to forty feet high. An unsuspecting hiker or camper could be walking right past one and would be unable to differentiate between the towers and authentic two-hundred-year-old White Pines.

Jon had also installed an underground electric charging station to fuel his self-driving 2039 Tesla CyberStealth, as well as air filtration systems that from the outside were camouflaged as small, shrub-like moss and lichen. At night, a dim green light would flash at the entrance to Darwin, and at the click of a button from their watches, Jon and Wolf were assured a quick getaway underground.

"I've seen that look before. How can I help to alleviate the pain coming from that face of yours?" Wolf asked in a calm yet firm voice.

"There's one thing that I left to chance. It could be our Achilles Heel. I keep weighing the pros and cons but can't come up with a resolution. Not sure how to say this, but the only way to find out if Darwin's missile proof is to test it out."

Wolf was stunned. "How on earth...? Please tell me you're not considering doing something like that?"

No one would be looking for Darwin here, and even if they knew we were in Porcupine, the odds of them finding us were equivalent to being struck by lightning and bitten by a shark on the same day, Jon thought.

CHAPTER 7

A PRIME PARTY

Late October 2044

J on eagerly awaited the arrival of his five dinner guests. An eclectic, handpicked group of PhDs with high level naval training, in transit from four far-flung continents to be with Jon on his birthday. His left hand fidgeted with the butt of a Cuban Montecristo No. 2, while his right coddled a glass of Balvenie 40-year-old single malt, ice rattling around the glass as he swirled it unconsciously.

Wolf sat cross-legged on Jon's deck in Frisco. He turned and faced Jon. "My friend. If you were firmly in the present, then you would shed your worrying like a snake molts its skin."

Jon deliberated before responding. "Look. It may be challenging for you to accept with your spiritual upbringing and all, but the *real* world is a stream of perpetual trade-offs, 'specially when it comes to saving civilization from itself while trying to preserve the dwindling supply of freshwater. It's so damn complex when lives are at stake, 'specially those I'm holding in my own palms." Jon gestured with his two hands cupped together. "The good thing is it seems like the older we get, the more power we possess to create real and sustainable change."

Jon's glasses showed a call coming in, and he answered reflexively without looking at the caller's number. "Hey, Ma! How're you feeling?"

"Fit as a fiddle. I wanted to tell you how proud I am of you, but more important is that you be proud of yourself and all that you've accomplished in your young life. Happy Birthday, son! How's Wolf?"

"Thanks, Ma. Wolf is Wolf. He's settin' right here. You wanna say hi?"

"Hi, Mrs. Buckingham. How are you?"

"Great, now that I'm talking to both of you." Her voice turned into a whisper. *It wasn't so much that Ma considered Wolf her other son who fucked up his life and became more like my old man as much as she knew deep down that we had each other's backs and were playin' for keeps.*

Wolf was so grounded in the Ojibwe and Shaman traditions that he could disentangle his best friend's fears and anxieties at a moment's notice. And reel him in when he was drifting too far out from the sea of his own consciousness. Jon admired Wolf's tenacity toward living an altruistically centered existence and his propensity to help others. "Gotta go, Ma. Catch you later."

He turned toward Wolf. "These folks shine in all the categories that are necessary to pull off the missions we have planned to protect freshwater supplies and shield them from falling into the wrong hands. Their native intelligence, integrity, experience, and athletic prowess make them unique among all the candidates. I just cringe at the thought of putting this cohesive, like-minded group in danger on the upcoming mission to Mongolia." Consistent with the values instilled in him by his mother, Jon was first and foremost concerned with the team's safety, his own well-being a distant second.

Jon was squinting at the glare of the remaining one-quarter sun moving rapidly below the horizon. He lowered the sunglasses on top of his head to shield his eyes. The smell and sight of fall invaded his senses. The multi-covered panorama and the aroma of burning leaves reminded him of his younger days growing up in Wartrace. Jon shut his eyes and listened to the sentimental breeze rustling leaves. His face exuded a shallow smile, a smile that reflected contentment without joy. A faint, percolating thought occupied a remote corner of his mind.

"And what about the replacement of hydroelectric power for the twenty-five-million customers that Mead provided up until eight years ago?" Jon asked rhetorically. "Gone. Hell, it's not like we didn't see it comin' for decades. Yup, we really fucked ourselves good, didn't we?"

"Yeah, and it's a damn good thing that NASA and the Jet Propulsion Lab decided to tap Yellowstone for geothermal. That source is producing enough energy to power twenty million homes for at least fifty years at about ten cents a kilowatt-hour. Considering that it's a carbon-free source and that the Yellowstone caldera was ready to blow anyway, it was like a two fer one. Saved the planet from a volcanic winter that would have led to mass starvation," Wolf pontificated, always concerned about protecting the masses beyond himself.

"Amen to that, brother," Jon explained to Wolf. "I'm still pissed about the lack of any cohesive US national water policy. And consider yourself one lucky sonofabitch that the Great Lakes Nation was formed weeks before our unconscious, half-assed government tried diverting water from the Great Lakes out west using old natural gas pipelines. Phillipe has heard rumblings that the next shoe to drop will be the southern province of Ontario, including Toronto, when they will join the Great Lakes Nation."

Canada's beacon city, Toronto, had been eyeing the Great Lakes Nation as a potential solution to its own water pressures, trying to spread the wealth of freshwater in and around Lake Ontario to the western and central provinces of Canada.

"Seems like time accelerated nature's revisionist tendencies," Wolf reflected. The clock struck midnight in broad daylight, and the Great Lakes Nation was the only response that made any sense."

"You know what really chaps my ass?" Jon added. Russia and China's plundering of the Arctic Circle's natural resources. Do you realize that the Russians have built eight new naval bases in the Arctic since 2026? And that these areas are constantly patrolled by a small fleet of nuclear submarines? Russia has a terminal disease. It's called military expansion to secure Arctic resources no matter what the cost."

Just then a phone number flashed onto Jon's organic light emitting display glasses including the date and time, that only he could see. Jon reveled in cutting edge tech. His first guest had arrived from Moscow via Charles De Gaulle Airport.

As usual, she's right on time, even from almost nine-thousand kilometers away. Elena arrived promptly at 6 p.m. Jon opened the door to greet her. She stepped into the foyer and stood under a sparkling chandelier with glass reflections dancing on the walls. Elena, in red high heels with a red satin top and matching black leather jacket and pants, stood out like a white river birch tree in the middle of Sequoia National Park.

"You'd be easier to spot in a crowd than a great white in the Great Barrier Reef hunting a pack of sea lions. Welcome to the party. Jon hugged Elena and gave her a light kiss on the cheek. "It's good to see your smiling face again."

Elena, with a complete disregard for Jon's Southern charm, was all business. "Cut the crap! I already agreed to join F.O.R., so as far as you're concerned, flattery is the law of diminishing returns." They both laughed. "I'm hoping that we can discuss the upcoming February mission this weekend. And what's with the airport bottled water costing $20 a liter? It's cheaper in Moscow!"

"That's because your bottled water is shit and worse than our tap," Jon fired back. "And in case you haven't noticed, the price of water per gallon worldwide has more than tripled in the past five years. I think the state governments outside of the Great Lakes Nation have finally woken up. And yes, I'll be happy to discuss the mission. What can I get you to drink?"

"Russian utilities discourage us from taking baths or long showers by charging its citizens an exorbitant rate. I need something smooth to wash down the shots of cheap vodka I had during my layover in Paris. You don't, by chance, have any Jewel of Russia or Beluga Gold with a twist lying around?" she smiled devilishly, knowing full well that Jon's bar wouldn't be stocked with either.

"You underestimate moi. I bought some Ultra Black Label Jewel of Russia just for you. And I do have fresh lemons. Not easy to come by these days. Nothing but the best for my guest who traveled 5,000 miles for my birthday."

"How thoughtful of you. That would be wonderful." She paused, looking Jon up and down. "Great shirt, by the way. You didn't disappoint." Jon handed her what he assumed would be the first of many drinks that evening.

"Thanks. I designed and made it myself with a 3-D printer from a friend at MIT who built it. The printer lets me design and make clothes from almost any material with a perfect fit every time." Jon pointed to the hummingbird on his multi-colored shirt. "It's also made of a material that can be dry cleaned with UV lighting. And the dyes used in it are sustainable. Not like the bullshit petroleum-based dyes and all the chemicals that are still used in certain parts of the world. You know, formaldehyde, benzene, and hydrogen cyanide, the hat trick of common carcinogens."

"Impressive. Where do I place my order? And I want the Buck discount," she teased. Jon gently grabbed Elena's hand. "C'mon, I'll introduce you to Wolf."

They strolled leisurely toward the back deck through his house with vaulted ceilings anchored with natural cedar. *Getting Elena to focus on F.O.R. in Moscow was like playing craps and Texas hold 'em at the same time at two different tables.*

"Isn't she perfect, Wolf? Highly Intelligent, experienced, quick on her feet, served in an elite division of the Russian navy with a major academic career."

Elena interrupted Jon's sugarcoating. "A pleasure to meet you, Wolf."

"The pleasure is all mine," Wolf responded.

"By the way, I recently learned of your service in the Naval Spetsnaz. I'm sure you're aware that it has been compared to our Team Seal 13. That's no easy feat. And you spent over half your time onboard a K-571 Krasnoyarsk M class series nuclear sub." *That may come in handy on our second mission, assuming we make it out alive from the first one.*

"When can we speak about the upcoming February mission? Are you holding out on me?" Elena asked, slightly annoyed.

Jon deflected Elena's question. He continued to shower her with praise. "And that you were appointed right after your military service as the top hydrologist to do research and cleanup on Lake Baikal in Siberia. That's serious! Isn't Lake Baikal the deepest and oldest freshwater lake in the world with the same water volume as our five Great Lakes combined?" Elena nodded affirmatively.

"We have a star-studded line-up tonight. An arrived earlier this afternoon on a supersonic flight from Shanghai and is taking a fast nap. She is under the guise of attending a hydrology conference in Denver. Sol just landed in Denver directly from Tel Aviv, and Court's en route from Toronto. He's delayed a half hour going through customs. Due to a scheduling conflict, Fran won't be arriving until tomorrow morning."

Elena took a sip of her drink. "That's the real stuff. Damn that's tasty."

"How're things going at Lake Baikal?"

"Come on. You know the drill," Elena said sarcastically. "It's more of the same. Pollution, radiation, poaching, tourism, and development. All courtesy of Chirkov's regime. You know that American expression, 'You can't fight City Hall.' In the past eighteen months, three highly trained members of my research team have resigned out of frustration. It's an untenable situation, and despite my best efforts, it continues to worsen."

Jon knew of Nikolai Chirkov and coined a nickname for the despised leader. "*Jerkov* is rapacious and a depraved SOB. Uncivilized as they come," he stated vehemently to Elena.

Jon noticed another number flash on his glasses. "Looks like Sol has arrived. Excuse me for a moment. Make yourself at home. I've been told the view back here is spectacular. I'll return before you can say *Vladivostok* twice."

Jon felt a visceral excitement, causing him to perspire while his heart raced. The emotional aftermath from his initial visit with Yael back at Sde Boker still lingered like smoldering embers. *Deja vu,* Jon thought as he steadied himself.

He reached for the copper handle attached to the six-inch, steel-reinforced door at the front entrance of his home as he watched her approach from the feed of fifty some odd cameras scattered in the trees around the property. His security was top drawer, courtesy of his lifelong friend Chip Johnson at Langley.

Jon forcefully yanked open the door. "Hello, Sol. Welcome to my humble abode." He pulled her in and gave her a huge bear hug that lasted a couple of breaths. Can't tell you how much I appreciate you making the trek from the Sinai to the Rockies."

"How could I not?" she said, wondering if she was the first to arrive.

Jon was mesmerized, oftentimes vexed, by her combination of beauty and boldness. She had a gravitational pull on his soul, and a glow inside that continued to manifest itself into something greater. Her intellectual capacity, athletic prowess, passion for doing good, and sense of humor were a rare combination. Originally born in Russia, Yael's parents had emigrated to Israel in 2011 when she was four years old. She received her PhD in water sciences with a focus on desalination from Sde Boker situated deep in the Negev, a satellite of Ben Gurion University situated thirty miles south of Be'er Sheva.

"So why am I here other than to celebrate your birthday?"

"I'm not even gonna answer that. All your breakthroughs in desalination and being fluent in four foreign languages doesn't hurt you any. Neither did your stint in the IDF Navy learning underwater demolition and your time on one of the nuclear submarines that Israel purchased from Germany in 2029." He snapped himself back to the present.

"Sapphire's in the back with Wolf. Still waiting on Court. Fran will be in tomorrow morning. What can I get you to drink?"

"You know I'm a simple girl. I'm going to assume that you don't have any Arak or TUBI 60 in this part of the world. Guess I'll settle for an Ice Café."

"Hey, there's no compromise in Frisco. Of course, I have Arak. TUBI 60 was a different story. To use a baseball analogy, I'm batting .500."

"Why did you name your drone company QB37?"

"Actually named it after the first modern drone in England called the Queen Bee. The thirty-seven represents the age I wanted to sell. Today's my 37th birthday. And besides, thirty-seven is a prime number and you know how much I like primes," he replied, pouring her drink. Jon heard a faint rustling in the woods but ignored it, figuring it was the wind or a deer roaming about.

"Tell me about Wolf?" Yael asked with a look of intrigue on her face.

"He can make the invisible, visible? It's hard to explain," he said earnestly.

"Oh, I know a lot of people like that," she said with a straight face, until she burst out laughing. Jon adored her sense of humor.

"Let's go meet Wolf and you can find out yourself what he's like." He put his arm around her and escorted her to the back.

"How's the desalination business these days?"

"We are close to hydrogen as an end solution," she said, beaming with pride.

A third phone number appeared on Jon's glasses. "Hey, Sapphire," he yelled. "Looks like your defection mentor just arrived." Jon walked away toward the front entrance to greet Phillippe.

Yael looked at Jon and then at Elena. "What's that all about?" she asked. Jon turned his head around, shouting in a whiskey sour drawl, "I'll explain later. Trust me. And we need to speak about the drone bees developed by that Israeli firm. What's it called again?"

"Do you mean B-Pol Drone?"

"Yeah, that's the one." Wolf desperately wanted to find a way to piece together a deal with the Israeli company, as he helplessly watched 85% of the bees that pollinated the planet's produce disappear over the last twenty years.

"Hey, Wolf? How much is it worth in dollars of lost annual food production with the decimation of bees?" Jon shouted from a distance.

"Best guess is a $400 billion, except that the drone bee technologies have already cut that number in half," he yelled back.

As Jon approached the front of his house, he noticed the hawk drones scanning his home from above using the high-resolution night vision minicams. This time, Jon buzzed open his front door and welcomed his third guest.

"Court, you made it. Welcome. Heard customs in Toronto is a real bitch, especially since you are an antelope hair away from joining the Great Lakes Nation. Come on in. Excited for you to be here."

"Yes, and I've been asked by the governing body to revise the Great Lakes Nation's declaration of independence to include southern Ontario. The authorities in Toronto are putting up a big stink, so it's going to be a dogfight, but I'm hoping we prevail. I'll show you the documents later and would welcome your input."

"That's a big honor they bestowed on you. Happy to help in any way I can. How are relations between Canada and the PRC these days?"

"Same as always. The strain began twenty-five years ago in 2020

when the PRC, or should I
China, tried to buy a
mining operations ar
ment was a bit taken
were eyeing the mining cc

"Remind us again what

"No surprise to anyone,
teeth. Behind the scenes, the PR
access to minerals as they tried an
ulterior motive was the establishmen
Turned out that the mining operation ha
to the Northwest Passage, and then multiple
and Atlantic due to the acceleration of the Arcti

"Makes sense. I remember reading a white pa
PRC nautical engineers, showing their hand to the W
called it the Polar Silk Road. Bottom line is it will dran
transportation and shipping time between Asia and Europe

Jon escorted Phillippe around back. They entered the back
lit up with a variety of solar colored lighting.

Before Phillipe could greet anyone, Elena leaped into his arms.
had been planning Elena's defection with her, and she considere
Phillippe like a surrogate father. "Sapphire! Good to see you," holding
both her shoulders with his outstretched hands.

Jon, Elena, and Phillippe had discussed the idea last month. "Too
risky to do it before," Jon said. "You've got to trust me on this. I will
take personal responsibility for getting you safely into Canada, and then
into Toronto, with the help of Phillippe, of course," he said
emphatically.

"I'm eager to live in *le ville d'eau douce*. My reservoir of good will for
Mother Russia ran dry years ago."

"What does *le ville d'eau douce mean*?" Jon asked. "Seems like
you've forgotten that some of us aren't fluent in French yet."

"It means 'city of freshwater.' Moscow's water quality is somewhere
between awful and putrid. It's not suitable for hand washing. I
wouldn't even wash my dirty socks in that water!"

Out of the corner of his eye, Philippe noticed several triangular-

shaped, aqua-tin
approached and
Vilcabamba! I
you manage t
list." Phillip
"Ah, V
certain res
It's been
"W
that sh
aver
Ph

ed glass bottles on the table set for five. As he
picked up a bottle, he exclaimed, "Buck. Water from
am duly impressed. You've outdone yourself! How did
pull that off? I've never been there but it's on my bucket
e proceeded to translate the label in Spanish out loud.
lca Bamba. The English translation is Sacred Valley, and
archers believe it represents a modern-day fountain of youth.
a well-hidden secret indeed."
ere the heck is Vilcabamba?" Elena asked, a bit embarrassed
e didn't know the answer.
nd what's the big deal anyway?" Yael added. "They look like your
ge bottles of mineral water, except for their color and shape."
lipe was about to open one and pour its contents into a glass.

"So, the deal is that drinking this water will keep you young? It's too
ate for me anyway," Elena chuckled.

"Besides Greenland, Iceland, and Chile, Vilcabamba is known to
have some of the purest drinking water in the world, blessed with an
optimal balance of calcium and magnesium. Virtually untainted by
modernization, it's situated in a mountainous region at the southern tip
of Ecuador near the border of Peru. No pesticides or industrial pollution of any kind. A pristine place in every sense of the word. It's a shame
they limited tourism starting way back in 2030, but I don't blame them
one bit."

"Can I indulge?" Phillipe asked, holding up a bottle in his right
hand.

"It's yours for the taking. Y'all ready for a spectacular meal prepared
by Wolf and yours truly?" Jon stared at the time on his glasses. *I need to
go wake up* An or she'll miss half the party.

Jon looked at his bulletproof sliding glass doors, the entrance to the
deck. "There's Angie, everyone. We can officially start the party."

He walked briskly to the open sliding doors and escorted her to the
others. *Angie clearly doesn't look any worse for the wear from her flight
out of Shanghai to Denver. She always shines.*

"Hey Angie, glad you could join us," Wolf yelled from across the
deck.

"I couldn't agree more."

"More importantly, what's on tonight's menu?" Elena inquired, as her stomach growled from too much alcohol and too little food.

"For the main course, we have bug burgers and fresh trout almondine. I have a stocked pond back in the woods protected by an electric fence and cameras mounted in trees," Jon grinned. "The sides are sauteed green beans with macadamia nuts, freshly cooked spinach smothered in garlic, and last, but not least sweet potatoes. All home-grown on raised beds over there." Jon pointed to a fenced area that faced south. "Including the garlic." Jon's guests appreciated how rare the dinner food was in the culinary world of 2044.

"Buck. That sounds fabulous. I'm practically drooling. Let's eat," An said with a ravenous look in her eye.

"Patience, please. Your meal will be served shortly. Another drink anyone?" Jon asked just before Wolf strolled toward the house. Minutes later, he emerged onto the deck, with both hands full of delectable food. Jon took the cue that Wolf needed some help and walked back to the kitchen to get the rest of the meal.

As Wolf humbly served their dinner guests, they could not help but notice the dichotomy between Wolf and Jon. Wolf was a constant even flow of energy like a thundering waterfall in the distance emptying into turgid waters below. Then there was their leader, who at times could be full of frenetic energy. It was not lost on this intimate gathering that Jon was an enigma of sorts, a known atheist with a passion as a self-taught student of the Old Testament.

"Would you like to introduce yourself by your real name?"

"If you insist," Wolf said reluctantly. "My birth name is Mikom Venne. Mikom means *ice* in Ojibwe. My paternal great-grandfather was a warrior and the last great chief of the Ojibwe nation. The Apostle Islands in Lake Superior remain to this day the spiritual center of the Ojibwe."

"I'd like to share that An means 'peace' and Shui means 'water' in Mandarin," An interjected. Everyone sat stunned, including Jon.

"How ironic." He looked at Wolf. "C'mon, give 'em a bit more."

"He was also a close friend of Goyahkla," Wolf said, flashing a grin. "For those of you who don't know, Goyahkla was an Apache warrior, better known by his American name, Geronimo. Legend had it that he managed eight wives and still fought on the battlefield right before he died."

"Allow me to fill in the gaps," Jon said as he stood up. "Not only is Wolf a tremendous athlete and deadly accurate with a bow, but he's also wicked smart and has more humility in his pinky than I do in my whole damn body."

"Well, that's not hard," Elena quipped.

"And he has singlehandedly discovered a breakthrough technology combining advanced chemistry and biology that can effectively dissolve microplastics on a large scale from both fresh and salt water. Isn't that right, Wolf?" Jon gazed at his friend with immense pride.

"Yeah, something like that," Wolf shrugged modestly. Jon raised his glass to propose a toast. "To my friend Wolf and to all of you, the backbone of the Forces of Rationality. Here's to a safe and triumphant mission in Mongolia! Remember what Churchill proclaimed a century ago. 'Fortune Favors the Bold.' Let's eat. Bon Appetit everyone!"

"Mongolia?" Elena stammered looking up from her plate. "You never said anything about Mongolia. My father used to take me fishing in the northern parts. You told me the target was somewhere in Southeast Asia, remember? How in hell are we going to get in and out of there without being noticed, let alone unscathed? With Russia's grip on the northern half, and China in the south, we might as well put our heads in a vice and start tightening it."

Jon paused. "Y'all, can we just enjoy our dinner and talk about it later?"

"Alright," Elena nodded as she dove headlong into the food in front of her. Jon finished eating the delectable meal and started one of his ideological rants. "It is with great humility and irony that Wolf and I will lead you on an incredible journey, one that could endanger y'all on the way there and back, and at any point in between."

"I hear Wolf's humility but where's yours?" Yael chided him.

"Nice, Sol. I'll remember that. How strange that we are living at historical levels of freshwater scarcity, and a biblical God that unmistakably destroyed mankind with a flood. And that the Ark containing Noah and his family landed atop Mt. Ararat intact after one-hundred and fifty days at sea."

Wolf knew that Jon was as frightened as everyone else yet managed to hide his fear behind a wall of bravado. "If we are to succeed, we will need to question everything we hear, and believe only half of what we see. To paraphrase a past president, we must 'Verify and never trust.' We are about to embark on a journey to fix a world that began to break in earnest over seventy-five years ago."

"Wolf? Would you like to add anything?"

"Why not? The planet we now inhabit is unable to co-exist with its harmonic and biological intentions because of the tendency for two powerful countries that govern their nations by fear, greed, force, and cowardly oppression. They coerce citizens with a mindset of scarcity. That perception has now become reality and is being imposed on much of the free world. We are all bound by the same objective. To save humanity by protecting the freshwater that remains." He raised his glass. "F.O.R. the water!"

Wolf could sense that Jon's mind seemed to be anywhere but in the present. He was looking out into his expansive backyard as if he was on guard against an anonymous enemy that could strike anytime. Wolf understood Jon's tension.

"I want to share something with you that I was taught as a child and still live by today," Wolf said humbly. "Let's not get confused with the notion that Spirit created humans to love and things to use, not the other way around. Spirit does not put obstacles in one's way that one cannot overcome. Gratitude and faith are the antidotes for fear and anxiety. It's our destiny to be part of the solution."

Everyone was trying to absorb the wisdom emanating from deep within Wolf's soul. The celebration continued until midnight. After escorting everyone to their rooms, Jon decided to linger outside in the brisk mountain air. Without warning, the solitude was broken. A bullet fired from a silencer hummed by his right ear and slammed into the fire-proof, log-constructed structure behind him, a house reinforced with an inch of steel. The bullet was absorbed and came to a grinding halt as it hit metal. *Shit. That was close. And Wolf thinks I'm paranoid?*

Jon quickly crawled inside military style, grabbed his AR-20 with night scope, and a handheld shotgun for good measure, exited out of a side door, and was now lying prone on his stomach adjacent to the deck.

Wolf overheard the bullet ricochet off the house. With an AI-driven locator connected to Jon's phone, and with his crossbow in his left hand, quickly joined Jon outside. As Jon lay flat on the ground Wolf calmly scanned the woods with his keen night vision, searching for any movement or sound. They braced for an onslaught or a possible second and third shots. Jon launched a flare in the direction of the shot to see if he could spot his unknown enemy, but the uninvited guests had already slipped away silently into the dark night, the sound of rushing water acting as their cover.

Jon and Wolf reviewed the video footage minutes after they went inside and noticed there were two intruders. Jon decided to let it lie for the time being, and not tell the others. Wolf slept with one eye open. Jon was struggling to keep his adrenaline in check, as his mind shuffled between the mundane details of life, and the thought that the intruder could have seriously wounded, or worse, killed him. *Maybe it was just a warning. Got to stay focused on the mission. F.O.R.'s going to rewrite history... before it's too late.*

CHAPTER 8

BARROOM BRAWL BY THE SEA

January of 2045

Apart from Wolf, who needed to stay back to continue his research and manage Darwin, the team was scheduled to meet in Tel Aviv five days before launch to review the plan and make sure everyone had made their arrangements to exit Mongolia once the mission was complete. Yael would be staying at her flat while Jon, Phillipe, Francisco, An, and Elena would check into the Tel Aviv Virgin Hotel by the sea.

Everyone arrived at Ben Gurion Airport on schedule from their respective countries. They would be meeting in a conference room on the top floor of the Virgin. The room was chilled to a comfortable of 68 F as opposed to the outdoor steamy, sticky, and oppressive 33 centigrade with no breeze.

It was four days before the mission began, and Jon was up to his eyeballs, drowning in anxiety. It was the first and only time Jon hadn't been totally forthright with F.O.R. He had chalked up his failed mission in Mongolia to knowledge management and his own learning curve. *My preparation was downright sloppy, and I'll never make that mistake again.*

Hiding the truth was part of a gambler's mindset. A game they played with others as well as themselves. *Never heard a gambler brag about all the big losses they had. Besides, why would I ever want to give the team a reason to doubt, to balk about the trust that we've built up together.* The entire team met in Jon's suite for a couple of hours to run through the final details of M-Squared, the code word for the Mongolian mission. The meeting had just ended, and Yael was the last to leave the room. The yellow sun hung lazily on the other side of the window. As soon as they were alone, Yael pulled Jon aside to speak with him privately.

"I want you to understand one thing. You don't need to shoulder all the responsibility of keeping everyone safe during the mission. We all know the risks, and there are always certain things beyond your control."

"You're right. Thank you." She kissed him on the cheek and turned toward the door. Jon sighed from the lingering feeling of her lips on his face and the pleasant smell of a lilac fragrance that went with it. He watched Yael's bright turquoise summer dress sway as she reached for the doorknob.

It was essential that Yael go on conducting her life as usual and cause no suspicion about what she was going to do next. And that Israel or respective countries of the team were able to trace their whereabouts prior to the launch.

Jon had arranged to meet Yael earlier that afternoon on the beach of the Dan Hotel, located about half a mile north of the Virgin. He needed to review with Yael the anti-drone technology that he had created with the help of DARPA, MIT, and his friends in the Navy. Yael chose that specific beach for reasons of convenience and privacy. It was fortunate that the strong prevailing winds had whipped up, whistling across the surface of the Mediterranean because no one would be able to hear their conversation.

At 2:55 p.m., Jon was laying on the beach six feet from the tepid water, resting comfortably under his mirrored sunglasses on a white towel he had borrowed from the hotel. He was admiring the wind-surfers with their bright, multi-colored sails, going randomly in all directions. Suddenly, a strong breeze swept past and rattled a few large beach umbrellas when a shadow appeared over him, blocking the sun. As Jon looked up, there was Yael staring down at him, a mountain of beauty that surpassed any view of nature he'd ever seen.

"Ma nishma Buck! I like the way that sounds," she laughed playfully, hovering over Jon with a smile that highlighted her exquisite face.

"B'Seder. Have a seat." He patted the sand next to him, motioning Yael to lay her multi-colored beach towel down next to his.

"Once again, you've shocked me with your mastery of Hebrew," Yael teased, as she bent down to lie next to him. Jon was aroused all the way from the soles of his feet up to his lips.

"You're right, Yael. Damn perceptive on your part."

"You know, I did serve three years in the naval anti-terrorism unit of the IDF, so it shouldn't come as any surprise that I can read people." Her glistening skin formed tiny beads of sweat on her neck and shoulders. "I suppose you are interested in the anti-drone technology developed by my country?" Yael said, gazing into Jon's blue eyes. He was having a tough time concentrating and had to look away towards the clear bluish-aqua-colored water to gather his thoughts.

Jon nodded. "You did say you interacted with Raphael at one point about the Israeli drone technology that is in development?"

"Yes, but that was eighteen months ago before we ever met." Yael was now leaning into Jon's bare shoulder, wearing nothing but a revealing, peach-colored bikini that was attracting looks from beach strollers like honey to a hungry bear.

Without warning, Yael ran toward the water and dove into the blue sea, took a few strokes, and was soon walking back toward Jon. The view was stirring up every hormone in his body. With her hair slicked back, she sat back down next to him. She shook her head back and forth, saltwater drops flying in every direction.

"Just what the doctor ordered," Yael said toweling off. "I told you everything I remembered from my conversation with Air Terminator, the top drone joint venture partner with our defense contractor. What do you have that will protect us from incoming Russian or Chinese drones?"

"I've developed a lightweight, hand-held anti-drone device," said Jon. "It's embedded with an onboard AI computer and connected to a smart scope. It can identify a drone and analyze enemy movements real-time to ensure disablement. It uses infrared, subversive electrical blocking to take out UAVs, GPS, and ISM signals up to two kilometers away, rendering the drone useless and to drop like iron from the sky." Yael spoke in a tone that Jon interpreted as condescending, especially to someone who had built a drone company from the ground up.

Jon stood up, visibly upset. "Spare me the technobabble, Sol. Besides GLONASS serving the same purpose as GPS, it is owned and operated solely by Russia with its own limitations. What if it was a Chinese-made drone that wasn't using GLONASS?" Yael stared at him, searching for the right response.

"Hey, I'm sorry for the sarcasm. Guess my ego got the best of me. It's just that I'm feeling a bit anxious about the mission."

"I understand completely. That's exactly how I used to get before naval missions where the potential to see live action was high. Israeli women who've served in the IDF can manage almost anything," Yael replied empathetically. "So, tell me, is there any good news?"

Out of nowhere came shots fired from the direction of the hotel. Without thought, she reflexively grabbed the Glock from her purse, got up, and took the safety off, scanning the busy boulevard. Jon went for his gun but realized that he left it back at the hotel. With no way to defend himself, he lay in a prone position on the sandy towel, head down.

"What is it?" Jon asked in a muffled voice.

"Nothing. Looks like the police resolved the situation. You can come out now," she said laughing.

Jon rose from his prone position and dusted the sand off his face. "Shall we continue?" Jon asked. "The good news is that my former company built and shipped several thousand drones, and I know how to program them. I'm aware that the Russians launched GLONASS KM 2.0 in 2032. Unlike earlier versions of GLONASS, this advanced version can't be purchased commercially. Even the IDF, with all its cutting-edge technology defense systems, is unable to access and use drone shields in the middle of the Gobi. Ordinarily, we would be flying blind, but I managed to build in a detection system that would lock on to any drone using GLONASS 2.0."

"What about the new laser that DARPA developed in 2038? Were you able to make any contacts there?" Yael asked, eyes wide open, her Glock still resting next to her, safety on.

"I consulted with them five months ago and managed to incorporate parts of their laser technology into a handheld, lightweight anti-drone device that we'll use on the mission. They're embedded with firing codes that need to be activated. It's a special seventeen letter-number-symbol sequence that is not hackable with AI."

"I trust you. All I need is for you to show me how it works within the next day or two and I'm good," Yael said, staring at windsurfers directly in front of her with lime green and orange-colored sails. They got up, walked along the beach, ripples of water caressing their feet. Nostalgic memories from teen years flooded her mind. Yael felt happy, remembering the times when she windsurfed.

"I took the liberty of arranging for us to test anti-lasers tomorrow morning at a private base outside of Tel Aviv. Hope you don't mind. Practice makes perfect."

They were about two hundred meters from Jon's hotel. She wanted to ask him a question, something that would reveal more about where Jon came from and who he was. She hesitated.

"I have a question for you. What is the sagest advice you've ever gotten?"

"Oh, that's an easy one. It was my grandfather, and he told me to always trust my gut, but this surpassed them all. 'Johnny, my boy, the only time I was ever wrong in my life is when I thought I was wrong, and I was right!' Then he winked at me. It took me a while to figure out what he meant, and when I finally did, I couldn't stop laughing." Yael had a confused look about her.

"Think about it, and then you'll understand," Jon said. She gave him a deadpanned look before nudging him in his ribs with her elbow.

"Touché," she said right before giving him a long hug. Jon told Yael that he would take her, An, and Elena out to dinner that night, leaving Phillippe and Diaz to do some bonding on their own. He texted the three femmes fatales to meet him in the lobby of the hotel at 7:30 p.m., where they would walk to the restaurant together. *See you later.*

Yael was half-hoping Jon would ask her to spend the rest of the afternoon in his room. She almost got her wish. As Jon opened the door to his room, he pulled out his phone and as if he were on autopilot, dialed Yael's number, but stopped short of pressing send. He gingerly placed the phone down on the nightstand, kicked off his shoes, and laid down, still contemplating what it would be like to have a romantic interlude with someone as sensitive and intuitive as Yael.

He set his alarm for 6:30. *Whenever I stand near her, she draws me in. It's like she owns me and hasn't a clue*, he thought to himself as he nodded off.

The alarm went off, and Jon quickly dressed in his favorite Hawaiian shirt and navy-blue jeans. Yael recommended a popular hole in the wall along the strip in Tel Aviv, and they arrived promptly at 7:30 p.m. It was buzzing with conversations in Hebrew, American, French, and Russian.

During the meal, Elena engaged in some intermittent eavesdropping on Russian patrons within earshot. She made it part of her entertainment. The TelAviv air was a hot, dense invisible fog with only a slight breeze to ease the intolerable heat. Jon and Elena were enjoying the evening, though acclimating was a struggle for them.

Jammed with locals drinking, vaping, and chatting the night away, the noise level from clinking glasses and dishes made it almost impossible to hear, only compounded by the horns on the street from late rush hour traffic. Jon and the more capable half of his team huddled at a small table overlooking the bluish-black methodical waves across the street. Jon leaned in toward the three of them, his hands folded on the tablecloth. Inconveniently, they had attracted unwanted attention from the Israeli machismo males hanging around the bar area.

Jon raised his glass. "A toast to the success of M-Squared," as they raised theirs in unison. Jon then opened Pandora's box. "You know the water tables underneath Long Island, Miami, and Tampa have been drawing saltwater into its aquifers for ten years. Rumor has it that they triggered sinkholes. All the garbage about them not knowing what caused them was utter nonsense. Just another example of the frickin' politicians hiding things from their constituencies while lying through their rotten teeth."

"That's nothing compared to the Kremlin and what they've been getting away with forever and a day," Elena said bitterly.

An threw her hands up in the air. "And you think the PRC is Snow White?"

Jon smiled and continued the rant. "And to think during the state of Georgia's prime growing season, thousands of farmers in the lower Flint River basin pull hundreds of millions of gallons of water– not a month, not a week, but every goddamn day. It's not sustainable. Never was."

People at tables close to them were trying their hardest to eavesdrop. "Then Florida and Georgia got into it. A well-publicized lawsuit over the Apalachicola-Chattahoochie-Flint River basin landed in front of the U.S. Supreme Court, the sole arbiter of water conflicts between states. So and so Senator is from Florida, and who is he going to side with? He should've recused himself from the hearing and decision-making process, for chrissakes."

An responded with sarcasm that could take a bite out of a Doberman. "That's a no-brainer, except that never happens in our country. Corruption rules the day. There are no Supreme Courts, no judges, or juries in the PRC. It's nothing but a charade."

Yael gazed at Jon. "It's a tragedy that the US government never got around to establishing a national water policy. Israel did it out of necessity borne from scarcity. And trust me, it takes a whole lot of screwing up and political dysfunction to end up where your country is today."

A mid-twenties-something waiter with slick-backed hair approached the table with their drinks. He seemed a tad infatuated and distracted by the women sitting with Jon. He set the drinks down one by one, his hand shaking slightly. True to his taste buds, Jon was the recipient of a special Tennessee bourbon that he worshiped growing up.

"Let's skip the politics for now, OK? I don't know how y'all feel, but all this talk, well it's starting to grate on my nerves." Jon took a sip of his bourbon.

"Sorry, but I've got one more question before we cast aside this topic," said An. Not waiting for Jon's response, she asked, "What caused the drain of the major aquifers in the U.S.?"

"After all the water used for agriculture and the subsequent polluting of the water from pesticides and fertilizer, fracking came along. Texas, Oklahoma, and Pennsylvania jumped into the fray.

Fracking used up obscene amounts of precious freshwater and left the water tainted, resulting in real scarcity."

A server in the corner dropped a dish that shattered into a hundred pieces, something that interrupted his train of thought. "Consider that Texas is still one of the largest growers of cattle, and Georgia the largest of the peanut growers. Both industries consume enormous amounts of freshwater."

"Peanuts?" An asked incredulously.

"Yes, peanuts. Take JIF-Smuckers. Its Lexington, Kentucky plant is the largest producing facility of peanut butter in the world. There's something like twelve hundred peanuts in a twenty-eight-ounce jar of JIF peanut butter, and Americans consume more than 270 million pounds of just JIF every year." Jon gazed up at the stars that resembled rubies in the night sky.

"They should have a water tax on peanut butter, kind of like the tobacco tax," Yael suggested.

"It'll never happen because of the political gamesmanship going on under the table between big business and local politicians."

Just then Elena turned her head to the right and overheard two Russian men, sitting at a table in full view across the restaurant. Out of the corner of her eye she noticed one of them was packing what appeared to be a 9mm. She downed her second vodka. *How did Israeli security miss that one?*

Jon sensed that something was off. "Everything OK, Sapphire?" Yael flagged down the waiter to take their dinner orders.

"Let's order. I'm starving," Jon said, perusing a Hebrew-English menu.

"The states that get the most rain already have the most water, one of mother nature's jagged laws of inequality."

The waiter appeared. "Yael, you order for us," An chirped.

"I just noticed the name of the restaurant. *The Old Man and the Sea*. Read that book in high school. Love Hemingway, but he was a crazy motherfucker. Think it was from all the concussions he got when his small planes crashed in Africa when he was big game huntin'."

Yael ordered in Hebrew. "Bring us four sea bass with a side order of potatoes and the dinner salad to start. Todah." She handed the menus to the waiter.

"What'd you order, Sol? I'm famished," Jon asked.

"It's a surprise, but let's just say you'll like it."

"Keep me in suspense, why don't you? Wanna know what's really dysfunctional? The sources of electricity today for utilities in certain countries. Hydrogen came along just in time to *buck* the trend, but it's still providing only thirty percent of U.S. energy needs."

"Ha! Nice pun," Yael blurted out. People stared at Yael from all directions, particularly the testosterone-laden crowd hovering around the bar. The place was loud, a merry-go-round of conversations that overlapped, and then trailed off.

"Here's the deal, guys," Jon pontificated. "Eating behaviors have begun to change the game of water conservation."

Yael took the floor. "I studied this at university. Beef requires 1875 gallons of water per pound, with pork and chicken far behind, at 728 gallons and 293 gallons per pound, respectively. Chicken, at least in the states, has a similar requirement of water per pound as wheat does. All 241 gallons of it. If that were true in Israel, we would only be able to consume meat, chicken, or wheat on rare occasions. The good news is that fish, on a per capita basis, is all over Israel."

Jon was pensive, eating bites of fish and potatoes between sentences. "If you want to get sick about water consumption, consider this. To produce one new car, tires included, takes about thirty-nine thousand gallons of freshwater in the states."

"The reality is that the United States has high-class problems when it comes to water usage," Elena said with forte. "I came here to have some fucking fun."

"Sapphire, I hope that you never grow old or up," he said with a wide smile.

A half hour passed, and Yael noticed that An was fading, so she motioned for the bill. Elena went to take a bite off An's half-eaten plate, and An reacted by pricking her hand with a fork. "Let's call it a night. Angie's about to pass out."

"Is everyone else ready to go?' An asked. Elena rose, pulled Jon aside, and whispered something in his ear. The group thought nothing of their close encounter. They were going to take an UberLyft back to the hotel. After speaking with Elena, Jon insisted they take Yael's private car service.

Jon and Yael found themselves alone. She was still verbally stiff-arming unwanted advances of Israeli men trying to pick her up. Jon laughed it off, but there was a slight twinge of jealousy that manifested itself somewhere in the region between his stomach and his groin. He wasn't accustomed to the boldness that Israeli males displayed with women, single or married.

Just as An and Elena disappeared out of sight, Jon leaned over to Yael and quietly whispered some instructions. Out of the corner of his eye, he noticed the two Russians in the corner getting up, as if to follow An and Elena, who were now waiting downstairs for their driver.

Yael abruptly stood up as heads turned to gawk. Half of the restaurant watched her hips sway as she approached the two Russians in the corner. For the moment, Yael had thoroughly distracted them from their pre-planned agenda. Jon rose from the table and headed to the bathroom. Jon noticed one of the Russians tried to push Yael out of the way and snuck up behind him. Unnoticed, he drew his gun and armed the chamber.

The Russians escalated and became verbally aggressive with Yael asking where her Russian friend Elena was. That infuriated Yael as fear for Elena's life bubbled up inside her. When one of them drew a weapon from his coat pocket, Jon put his adversary in a chokehold as Yael, with the element of surprise to her advantage, mercilessly struck down the other with the full force of her right fist. It was the last thing the thugs with vodka-soaked brains were expecting. One of the two men tried to rise from the ground. Yael, loaded with white-hot fury, had her foot on the unsuspecting mercenary's throat with her gun dawn, aimed between his eyes. A suspicious scowl appeared on her new victim's face.

"If you so much as flinch, I'm going to bitch-slap that smirk off your face for the last time." His lantern-shaped jaw tensed. "You're just a small dick attached to a brainless body!" Yael barked in Russian.

Just as the other Russian was about to break Jon's chokehold, Elena appeared out of nowhere, Glock drawn, and in Russian said, "Freeze shitbag."

Everyone in the restaurant turned to stare at the sudden, unexpected turn of events. Yael continued shouting in Russian, directing her energy to the man lying on the ground, her pistol about six inches from his head, finger on the trigger. As Yael took her boot off the dazed man's throat and lifted him off the ground and onto his knees, the restaurant broke out in thunderous applaud.

She turned her fierce gaze at the other Russian, whom Jon had locked in a chokehold, a lit cigarette still dangling from his lips. She motioned to Elena, who took the stunned Russian's gun before releasing him. Yael put a knife to his throat. He winced. Jon grabbed her shoulder. "Sol, please, not here. It's not worth it. Too many witnesses," as she slowly withdrew the blade from the fear-filled eyes of her new nemesis.

Abruptly, Yael yelled for the security guards, who were now at the back of the restaurant watching Yael loosen her vise-like grip of the Ivan. Security was composed of ex-IDF soldiers, and she quickly explained in Hebrew what had happened and who her brother was. The seasoned security officer cuffed the Russians to a heavy metal table and called the police, as part of the restaurant staff proceeded to clean up the mess that Yael created.

———

An was in the lobby cheering wildly, as Jon, Elena, and Yael calmly walked down the stairs of the restaurant. Jon put An and Elena in the car that Yael had called. As the car service pulled away, Jon and Yael walked along the promenade. Both were on high alert, looking for any 'friends' of the Russian thugs.

Jon noticed Yael's knuckles on her right hand were bleeding, as it tremored from the unanticipated brawl. When they were finally alone, he decided that they needed an hour to air things out.

"Good show back there," Jon complimented Yael. It's the first time I've seen you in action. Maybe I should consider you as my personal bodyguard while I'm in Israel?"

"That'll be the day. Nothing I'm not used to. It's second nature for me."

"Buck, what's your middle name?"

"What? You've just been through a shitshow and that's what you want to know? Why?" Jon responded defensively.

"Just curious. That's all," Yael smiled into his eyes.

"It's Oliver." Jon grimaced slightly as if he released a secret part of himself. He knew exactly what was coming next.

"Hmmm. Jon Oliver Buckingham," she said quietly. "So, your initials spell JOB? That's ironic, don't you think, especially given the mission we're all on."

"What about the name Yael? Isn't the direct translation from Hebrew to English 'Child of God'? And if I'm not mistaken, isn't Yael, or Jael, the woman in the Book of Judges mentioned in the Hebrew Bible who was the heroine after she killed Sisera by driving a stake through his temple and into the ground to deliver Israel from the army of King Jabin? Is there something I should be concerned about here?" Jon said, erupting in laughter.

"Nothing I can think of at the moment," she responded right on cue. "I see you've been doing your homework, studying the Old Testament."

And then, as if in a mystical trance, Yael began quoting: *"Behold, he withholdeth the waters, and they dry up: he sendeth them out, and they overturn the earth."*

"Sol, where did that come from?" Jon asked with a stunned look on his face.

"JOB 12:15, King James version," she respectfully replied.

"You know what? I'm taking the fifth on this entire conversation and tabling it for a later date. I don't want to spoil the mood." They ducked around a corner and made sure they weren't being followed. Jon gazed at Yael's moonlit face, as the waves in the background clawed the rocky beach. Jon pulled a Cuban cigar out of his inside jacket pocket, one that he'd bought in Tel Aviv the day before.

"What type of cigar is that? My Abba loved smoking cigars and I grew up liking the smell. It reminds me of him."

"It's a Cuban Monte Cristo Churchill No. 1. My personal favorite." He pulled out a lighter that was more like a small blow torch. As Jon pushed down, it produced a reddish-blue flame. He took a couple of puffs and spun the cigar to make sure it was evenly lit. Jon was looking through the flame into Yael's eyes, as if time stood still. He closed the lighter with his thumb.

"One day we are going to have a conversation about this whole JOB business. For some reason, I don't believe it's a coincidence," Yael said as she leaned in and kissed Jon on the lips before he could take the first draw of his Cuban. Jon's entire body tightened and then indulged. It was the welcomed advance he'd been waiting for since the indelible day they had first met at Sde Boker. Jon had only one word to describe her sensuality. *Intoxicating.*

For the time being, Jon let Yael call the shots. *I feel like I'm flying blind here, and I don't like it one bit,* Jon thought. They ducked into a low-key, local café in northern Tel Aviv. As they settled into the back of the restaurant, Yael faced the entrance, keeping one eye out for her new Russian friends. Yael ordered coffee. Jon had green tea.

Jon looked at Yael. "So, what's your deal?"

"That's a fairly open-ended question. Can you be more specific?"

"I mean, what makes you tick?" he searched Yael's eyes for a clue.

"It's simple. Most people spend their lives between love and fear. The harder I work on fear, the more capacity I possess to give and receive love. Does that answer your question?"

"I admire your boldness, your passion. That's all."

"When can I see Darwin?" was her not-so-subtle way of inviting herself to Darwin and he knew it.

"In due time. Do you know what I love about Wolf? He's so talented as a chemist that he can turn goat piss into gasoline!"

Yael smiled, and they clicked glasses, toasting to their mission. She found herself knocking on love's door each time her eyes gazed into his and heard his wry sense of humor with a thick Southern drawl. Yael was the antithesis of Jon, and she relished in the irony.

Without warning a voice welled up inside Jon's head, as if his brain had been overtaken by alien forces. *When this mission is over, only then I can give my full attention to the incredible woman across the table from me, but not a moment before. Otherwise, it's going to cloud and affect my judgment.*

Then he spoke his truth aloud, staring at Yael's flawless face. "Yael, I loved being with you tonight. I sincerely hope you can understand that as much I'd like to spend the night with you rolling around on the moonlit beach over yonder, but we can't take a chance now that the Russians have entered the picture. I am just askin' that we hold off until after the mission is over. I'm just not good at mixin' business and pleasure."

"What makes you think that was my agenda?" she said with a dead-panned look. Until she couldn't maintain a straight face anymore and burst into hysterics. Jon stood there exposed, caught completely off guard.

"As you wish," Jon responded. Yael subconsciously batted her eyelashes in Jon's direction, putting up her golden-brown hair in a bun. They had one last passionate kiss, hugged each other goodnight, and went their separate ways. He put his key against the lock, turned the bronze handle, and placed the key in the slot by the door, causing all the lights to turn on. *Israel's way of conserving energy. Smart.*

He quickly threw off his clothes, washed his face and the cigar smell off his hands and mouth, reached for his King James Bible and turned to section 12:15.

CHAPTER 9

AND THE CLOCK STRUCK FOUR

February 2025

Jon gave F.O.R. strict instructions to travel by train from Tel Aviv to Beer Sheva, with no two members allowed to sit in the same train car. Jon was unwilling to assume the risk of discovery. The next morning everyone arrived at the Hilton Be'er Sheva lobby ten minutes early.

The van was scheduled to pick them up 8:20 a.m. sharp, and F.O.R. had a half hour to kill. Everyone grabbed coffee at the hotel bar except Diaz, who was in a corner hammering away vigorously with both thumbs on his cell phone. Each member of F.O.R. had one small sack attached to their back. There was just enough room to pack a change of street clothes so they could blend in as tourists once they fulfilled their mission and were heading out of Mongolia.

Elena was nervous. Less than twelve hours after their previous encounter at the restaurant, she overheard several Russian-speaking men in the hotel who put her on edge. *What if they are on to us and have bugged my phone? That might explain what happened at the restaurant last night. Not going to mention it to Jon. He has enough to think about.*

The inconspicuous white travel van pulled up in front of the hotel, and F.O.R. climbed into the back of the vehicle, except Jon. The driver played the role of a tour guide picking up his group to go on a day tour in the Negev. He greeted his passengers with *Ani Uri* as Jon hopped into the front seat. Shutting the bullet-proof door behind him, he noticed a v3 Uzi sub-machine gun laying at his feet.

"Is this thing loaded?" he asked the driver, who rolled his eyes in response.

"Don't touch."

After thirty minutes of driving on a road to seemingly nowhere, Yael was growing impatient. She was the only one in the group with desert combat field experience and who had been trained as a paratrooper. She was tightly wound and getting tighter by the minute.

"Uri, I don't see any signs of the base. How much longer?" she snarled in Hebrew. The driver ignored her and said nothing, but Yael was her persistent, intense self and was not to be denied.

"Did you not hear me, or do I have to ask the same question twice?" she demanded in English.

The driver finally yielded. "We are 3 1/2 kilometers from base entrance."

Uri was a gruff, unshaven ex IDF Air Force mechanic and cargo pilot who served directly under Yael's brother. The van swerved and was now traveling up an unmarked road at a six percent incline. The driver's jerky movements rolling over the rubble of the unpaved road startled Phillippe and Diaz awake. Bleary-eyed and groggy, they could have used more shuteye. An rarely slept in moving vehicles.

Minutes later, a smile formed around Yael's mouth as she heard the familiar sound of an F-16 engine rumbling on a hidden runway. She knew that sound by heart just as Uri had committed it to memory. The road's incline got steeper, and dim lights became visible eastward on the horizon. They arrived at the base entrance, and Jon's eyes strayed into the distance.

"Is that a Cobra?" Jon asked Yael. "Those things cost $40 million each."

She pointed to her left. "You mean the Bell AH-1Z Viper over there? No, I believe it's an AH-64 Apache," Yael gloated as Uri nodded affirmatively. With his fourteen years of service in the IDF Air Force, Uri was able to recognize by sight or sound any flying machine in the IDF, including any of the unmanned drones.

"That thing is beast and flying wrecking ball in air," Uri added in broken English. "It has nose-mounted sensor suite for target acquisition and night vision system, and thirty-millimeter M230 chain gun underneath between landing gear. 114 Hellfire missiles mounted under engines with Hydra 70 rocket pods destroy anything in its path. U.S. use them in Afghanistan, and we got some leftovers from war. We retrofit and modernize them with our own technology. I know because I work on personally," Uri said with an air of pride and defiance.

Elena yelled out something in Russian from the back of the van, and Uri nodded his head up and down. Yael was busy checking in with security. Yael's brother was the highest-ranked commanding officer of the base, and he had pulled more than a few strings for his sister. The base would be used as a launching off point to Mongolia in a Russian cargo plane that F.O.R. assumed would be flown by the Russian-speaking Israeli pilot.

"Sapphire, what did you say to our driver?" Jon inquired.

"I asked him if he was going to be our pilot on the mission, and he grunted with a yes." The pilot, Uri Abramovitz, was trilingual and uniquely trained in both the Russian and Israeli air forces, and had defected from Russia to Israel almost two decades prior. He asked that everybody refer to him by his nickname, Abe.

Everyone turned their heads toward the direction of a deafening roar. "That is sound of F16i taking off," Uri smirked.

"What do you mean an F16i? What does the *i* mean?" An chirped loudly from the back of the jeep.

"They are U.S. F16s retrofitted with special Israeli technology that would make a MIG blush and scramble the other way with its tail between her legs," Yael answered. Elena laughed audibly, nodding because she knew it was true. The most sophisticated Russian fighter jet pilots were no match for their Israeli counterparts. The same was true in drone warfare.

As they arrived inside the base, Uri dropped them off at a remote, barebones barracks. Yael had arranged in advance with her brother to have camouflage gear for desert warfare, including boots, night vision goggles, and helmet. And last, but not least, six Glock 25s. *I'm not taking any chances in Mongolia,* Jon thought.

Diaz was familiar with the 25s and while walking towards the cargo plane, he started spewing all kinds of random data about them. "Sol, where did you get your hands on these Glocks? These babies are illegal in the U.S., but still quite available in South America," Diaz boasted. "For self-defense only in my country."

Jon quickly corrected the South American's doublespeak. "If I'm not mistaken, these are semi-automatic handguns loaded with 380 caliber-bullets and a 15-round magazine capacity," Jon recited. He knew a lot more about Glocks, but the cocky Diaz countered anyway, sounding like a kid giving a book report who had only read the first few chapters.

"That's correct. Law enforcement agencies can order them by letter. You can't import them to the U.S. Not my preferred weapon of choice. I'd rather have a 9mm. The .380s have more recoil and don't perform." Jon rolled his eyes.

Jon heard the engines of the cargo plane roaring. "Let's go everybody. We've got a flight to catch."

The plane piloted by Abramowitz rumbled down the runway at precisely 11 a.m., heading southeast over the Gulf of Aqaba toward Ethiopia. The most direct route to Mongolia was due east. *We need to avoid Iraqi, Iranian, and Saudi airspace at all costs.* Everyone had settled into a resting position, some using their packs as makeshift pillows. The endless humming of the craft's engines had lulled asleep most of the team. Six jetpacks and three electric ATVs for ground use were placed neatly in the back of the plane.

Several hours passed. Jon could feel the air growing drier with each breath. He quickly chugged a couple of water bottles and then went to take a leak. Jon was a strange being, who relished, and practically thrived in high humidity. In dusty, arid climates, he was like a Tennessee frog out of water. Wound tight as a drum, he tried closing his eyes, but a deep sleep eluded him for hours. Hands behind his head, he stared pensively out the small window. His face reflected a thoughtful pose. In less than seven hours, they would hit the rugged, borderless edges of the Gobi Desert. Except for the looming white moon, the Gobi was a sea of darkness, save the occasional fire down below, glowing from a nomad family cooking dinner or trying to stay warm.

Without warning, the nose of the ancient Russian flying machine pointed in a downward trajectory and began its descent for refueling. The plane glided over northwest India, landing at Sri Guru Ram Dass Jee International. The Amritsar airport was a hub of cargo exchanges, and the unidentified plane easily blended in, especially a Russian one. F.O.R. was one step closer to its destiny.

Yael, An, Elena and Jon got out of the plane to stretch their legs. They were still concerned about getting into Mongolia without encroaching on Chinese and Russian airspace. The dryness prompted Jon to clear his throat before speaking.

"It makes me sick to think about what my country's done."

"What do you mean?" An asked in an empathetic voice.

"The Ogallala aquifer has become the black hole of aquifers, under eight states in the southwest and western U.S."

"And your point is?" An inquired.

"It's a boatload of territory used freely by those states that has drained one of our most precious water resources. It's criminal that the U.S. Department of Agriculture never developed a policy that allocated the water instead of the free-for-all we've witnessed. Since the 20th century, farmers have drained ninety-three trillion frickin' gallons from the Ogallala aquifer and irrigation has caused ninety percent of the drawdown."

"It's like a modern-day Shakespearean tragedy. But that's not the crux of the issue," Yael interjected. "It's because your government subsidizes farmers and pays them not to grow certain crops to the tune of $45-50 billion a year."

"Yeah. Subsidies cause overproduction that leads to an increase in water usage. The bastardized results were a precipitous drop in crop prices. It's criminal because the net result was less income to farmers. As Wolf says, Stupility."

"What does that mean?" asked Elena.

"*Stupility* is a word that Wolf made up to describe what most people in life struggle with, finding equilibrium between surrender and control. It's part stupidity because most people believe the stories they tell themselves are the absolute truth. The illusion they have control over people and events in their lives when in fact they have little."

"Interesting," Yael responded.

"The flipside is the futility of thinking that surrender is a sign of weakness, like waving a white flag. It's not only acceptable to surrender in life but knowing when to surrender is a sign of unmitigated inner strength."

"Yep. And then your country ended up exporting the water for three decades it took to grow the crops overseas, mainly to China," An commented.

"It's called water arbitrage," Jon replied. "China imports crops grown using our precious water, something they don't have much of anymore, and the fuckin' PRC gets the water for free. All they pay for is crop exports. It's a political clusterfuck supported by the large lobby representing our farming community and trying to capture the farmer votes. You never had that issue in China or Russia. No free election, everything centrally controlled."

Elena spoke freely. "Angie, let's face it. Economics, communism, and capitalism don't mix, and government subsidies can't solve issues because they create imbalances. The model has been broken for over a hundred and twenty-five years."

Just as Abramovich got back in the plane, readying for take-off, Jon jumped up to answer his wristwatch phone, as a live picture of Wolf popped up. Without thought, Jon's mind leaped to a worst-case scenario. "Excuse me, ladies. This is business." He walked toward the front, earbuds blazing with panic.

"We have a situation here!" Jon, a concerned look on his face, was eager to diffuse the situation as quickly as possible.

"Tell me this is not happening when I'm thousands of miles away."

"We've got a problem. I've detected some unidentified mercenaries in tight formation working their way toward the direction of the bunker. I can tell by their movement they aren't hunting for elk or hikers out for a stroll. And it's raining rhinos and elephants out there, not cats and dogs. It's like a monsoon. Thank God our warning system worked without a hitch," Wolf spewed.

Jon tried to remain calm. "You know what to do. We trained for this situation dozens of times. Keep me posted." *It's uncanny. It's as if someone knew I was halfway around the world.*

"Are you sure these guys aren't hunting for wolves?" Jon chided, standing in a corner of the vibrating cargo plane. Wolf didn't appreciate the unwelcomed humor being hurled at him by his friend. Jon was a good 7,000 miles away from Darwin as the plane took off from India, climbing above the cloud cover.

"C'mon, give me a little credit here. I detected a dialect from the interlopers that sounded either eastern European or Russian. I can see the formation of their bodies. It looks like they're wearing sophisticated night vision goggles. I'm not sure they know exactly where they're going, but they're getting too close for comfort. These guys are about five clicks out and moving methodically. Walking like they are trying to avoid tripping a land mine. The only good news is that they aren't wearing gas masks."

"Jesus H. Christ! No one knows the location of the bunker except you and your men. Alright, you know the drill. Just make sure you move the assholes after they're resting peacefully. Over!"

"Will do. Good luck and keep me posted when you can. Remember, no pressure. There's not much at stake. Just the stability of the freshwater supply for over a third of the world's population riding on the outcome. Possibly worse." Jon heard a faint laugh from Wolf right before the click in his earphones.

Jon got up, and took a few nervous paces, as the plane flew at a low altitude somewhere over the northwest corner of India. *Just fuckin' dandy. Why is this happening when I'm in the air facing one of the most critical points of my life? Damn it!* Jon ran his right hand straight back through his thick brown hair, reflecting on what they'd painstakingly installed around Darwin's perimeter.

Fifty-eight miniature wireless cameras that were solar powered, embedded into the bark of the trees at least ten meters off the ground. Courtesy of Chip. The tranquilizing gas emitters were scattered randomly within a mile of the bunker in all directions. Not sure importing them from Bulgaria's black market at the behest of Elena was a good idea. Time will tell.

Jon's train of thought got sidetracked by Elena and Yael in the corner, laughing and transcending the fear that was engulfing the rest of F.O.R. Yael looked at Jon and mouthed, 'Is everything alright?' She knew it wasn't but was curious about the call. Jon nodded and gave her the thumbs up.

The conversation shifted. Court and Diaz engaged with Jon. "Do you think there's any solution to the water shortages in the western and southwest?"

Yael weighed in. "When Lake Mead lost over 9.5 trillion gallons of water since 2000 before it dried up in 2027, it was a damn shame that your government didn't supersede the rights of individual states and come up with a comprehensive national water policy like Israel was forced to do seventy years ago. The formation of the Great Lakes Nation was a nasty result of a lack of vision and failed politics."

"Good Lord. Gimme a break, will you? We are about to do battle with a country with seven time zones that has a history of withholding energy and using military violence for coercion," Elena stated, with a fearful tone in her voice.

"Wait a second. Did I just hear our in-house atheist refer to the Lord?" Yael asked with a sarcastic tone.

———

From inside the bunker on three of the eight screens staring back at him, Wolf counted five moving targets using the sophisticated infrared heat sensors that they had meticulously installed. There were four marked green buttons to his left, each one signifying a different direction. The intruders were now within a kilometer of the bunker and closing fast. Wolf had no choice but to follow the protocol that he and Jon had established when planning Darwin over a year earlier.

He knew that the soldiers approaching had no clue exactly where the bunker was and how difficult it would be to pinpoint their exact location in a 65,000-acre national forest. It didn't matter. Their closeness in proximity guided Wolf's fingers to press the north and east buttons together. *Buck, I sure hope you're right about this. Here we go.* Wolf closed his eyes as his hands trembled. Seconds later, an odorless, undetectable gas was released in a tight circumference around the unsuspecting terrorists. Wolf grinned as he watched them fall silently to the ground. It was a thing of beauty, especially since it had no effect on animals of any kind. It was the kind of gas where the recipients would not be able to remember a thing that happened hours before being hit with a silent, invisible knockout punch.

That ought to do the trick. They'll be out cold for at least five, Wolf thought to himself rubbing his eyes. He promptly called four of his best trackers, part of the crew who built Darwin. Wolf, using a miniature satellite phone, called Jon.

"Do you copy? What should we do with these sleeping beauties?"

"Have your men load them in the back of their pickup truck and take them to Tom's liquor store on Highway 12. Then leave them on the side of the building where the green recycling bins are. Make sure you confiscate all their weapons and replace them with some old deer hunting rifles with ammo and hats. Have your men sprinkle some beer cans and cheap bottles of vodka around them. Pour some in their mouths and on their clothes for good measure. Try to source their gear from its country of origin if you can. Wish I could be there with you, but duty calls. Appreciate you holding down the fort."

"It's not like I had a choice. Are you sure this gas is going to make them forget everything that happened in the last twelve hours? And shouldn't we be holding them for questioning?"

Jon paused for a moment. "I'm damn sure they won't remember a thing. And don't think they are going to talk. Your men might want to search them for suicide pills or whatever they're using these days. Our best-case scenario is that they are locked up and convicted of being spies."

"Whatever your say, partner. I'll call the Copper Harbor police anonymously and tell them that I spotted these drunk excuses for wannabe hunters, and they will take care of the rest."

"Make sure there are no witnesses at Tom's so the police can't trace your men's license plates. Over and out."

"Got it." Jon knew without a doubt that their countermeasures had worked perfectly. He could rest easy Wolf was safe for now. Other than Jon, Yael, and the pilot, no one else knew the whereabouts of their drop-off destination. The route would have them enter Pakistani airspace for a brief fifteen minutes, crossing over northeast Pakistan to avoid China's border.

Even the Pakistanis wouldn't be stupid enough to fire on a Russian-marked cargo plane, although I do recall when the Turkish missile defense systems took out Russian MIGs that entered its air space. Not once but three times. F.O.R. would fly along the border of Tajikistan and then head northeast again over Kyrgyzstan, continuing east of Alma-Ata in Kazakhstan. For the final leg, they would fly northeast near the Chinese border crossing into Mongolian airspace.

Jon was concerned about how to finesse the neutral zone of Mongolia, a seventy-kilometer strip that ran east and west the entire length of the country. Elena's contacts had alerted her that the Russian Army didn't have any ground to air missiles in the territory they controlled in northern Mongolia. This information did little to alleviate Jon's concerns. *Why would they have Mi-24s and Mi-28s traversing northern Mongolia on a routine basis?"* Jon wondered.

"The good news is the same holds true for fighter jets," Elena commented. "The bad news is the Russian military has deployed Ka-52 reconnaissance-strike helicopters in the neutral zone. They are patrolling the area in four shifts, five times a day. There's only a four-hour period where nobody's home. These choppers have heat sensors, capable of striking both armored and non-armored vehicles as well as air targets," Elena said with grave concern. "The only palpable relief is they tend to stay farther north. Hopefully, they won't be roaming around during the midnight to 4 a.m. shift."

An sighed. Jon noticed a concerned look on her face. "What's the matter?" "According to my sources, China has a newer version of the Z-10, the Zhishengji-20, powered by the WZ-16 turboshaft engines. And here's what really gets to me. The Former Z-10 was developed in partnership between the Kamov Design Bureau of Russia and the Chinese 603rd Aircraft Design Institute for anti-tank warfare. It's a bit of overkill, don't you think?" Embers of fear were masked under her smile.

Jon had done significant intel through his own sources but hoped that both Elena's and An's military intelligence were rock solid. Otherwise, there could be unanticipated complications, especially if either country's military choppers wandered into the neutral zone. Jon was prepared for drones, but attack helicopters were something else altogether. Knowing these choppers had heat sensors able to detect humans on the ground left Jon twisting in the wind, preparing for the worst.

In preparation for the mission, Jon managed to have one meaningful conversation with a former U.S. paratrooper about gear and equipment. The team's lightweight, sand-colored packs would blend in perfectly with the desert terrain. They included food, water, street clothes to fit in with other tourists, and a couple of desert-camouflaged hydrogen-powered ATVs. The silent componentry would allow them to move undetected around the desert. Jon was also outfitted with the latest watch technology that allowed real-time communication between Wolf and him in every continent except Antarctica.

Jon and the team were resting peacefully in the back somewhere north of the Indian border. Jon made a conscious decision to avoid refueling in Bhutan, given the difficulty of landing in one of the most dangerous airports in the world. Jon's relaxation was interrupted. With a wave of his hand, the pilot signaled Jon to the dilapidated cockpit, big enough to hold two people maximum.

"Boss, we got slight problem, but I think I handle them OK. Pakistani fighter jets approach from the west, crossing over Indian border few minutes ago. When they saw we were Russian-marked cargo plane, they high-tailed it out of there."

"Good work, Abe. Thanks for the update."

"Buck, come in please. Do you read me?"

"Yeah?" Jon spoke into the microphone of his headset. How can I help?"

"Where are you? Over." Wolf inquired.

"We are somewhere over Kashmir heading toward north Tajikistan and then to the border of Western Mongolia. Why? Over."

"There's a potential problem brewing in your neck of the woods. Seems like there was a skirmish in the Chinese part of Mongolia, and by mistake, some Russian helicopter missiles took out a couple of Chinese drones performing drills. Tensions are high. Repeat. Tensions are high. Do you read me?" Wolf said with the slightest tremor.

"I read you. Appreciate the update. Will keep you posted."

For the first time, Jon seriously contemplated aborting the mission.

After a few minutes, he took a seat in the rear next to An, and he relayed what Wolf had told him, debating whether he should let the team know about the skirmish in southern Mongolia. He decided to share the info with An, seeking her advice on whether the Chinese would retaliate.

"What good would it do to tell them? They might panic," she reflected. "On the other hand, you believe in transparency and not withholding info from them."

An persuaded Jon to share the news with Yael as she was one of two team leaders. "Fascinating, but not surprising," Yael said gazing into Jon's eyes with one hand under her chin, her elbow braced firmly on her helmet.

"You're not concerned?"

"Not in the least. I like a challenge. Look, compared to Israel and fighting Hamas, Hezbollah, Syria, and Iran, this seems like a cakewalk. They don't know we're the enemy. That doesn't mean I'm not concerned. I am, but it's no reason to abort. Besides, it might serve as a distraction that could help our cause."

"How much do you wanna bet that we make it to our drop point without being detected?" Jon teased. "C'mon, let's make it interesting. I'll bet you the fanciest bottle of wine in Israel."

"That's unfair and you know it. I can hardly afford that bet. I haven't sold a company like you, let alone started one," she said with a deadpanned look. "I thought you didn't gamble anymore?"

Jon remained stoic. He loved tough, intellectual women while Yael was attracted to men like him. Men or women willing to risk it all for the mission of making the world a better place. She liked the sound of his voice, admired his self-confidence, and self-deprecating humor, particularly in moments of danger.

"How do you feel about your group of Sapphire and Court versus my group of Angie and Fran?"

"It seems equal to me and makes perfect sense to have one Russian- and one Mongolian-speaking person on each team. My group seems stronger than yours though. Fran looks kind of scattered. And his fear of heights is a major wild card."

"I know. That's why I wanted him in my group. I can keep a closer eye on him and make sure he doesn't freak out too much on the jump."

"Sounds like a good idea. If I were the group leader for Diaz, who knows how he would react to an aggressive Israeli IDF woman? Besides, I'm tougher and smarter than him. And a lot more good-looking. I probably intimidate the living shit out of him." She gave Jon a subtle wink.

"Amen to that. And wait till the ten-degree bitter cold hits his South American tan ass. It's been a lifetime since he left Norway, and he's gonna be mighty uncomfortable with the harsh weather conditions," Jon grinned. "Get some rest." Jon put his hand on Yael's quad for leverage, got up, and moved across the rear of the plane to check in with An, who was wide awake.

"How's it going, Angie?"

"OK. Just reflecting on my country's human rights record. They treat some livestock better than their own citizens."

"I'm sure it has to be tough living in China and not being in a position of great power or wealth," Jon added, biting his lower lip. "Lying and deception are part of the culture, although I'm not sure my government is any better with those concepts."

An motioned with her hands, putting them to her throat. "I am fed up to here helping a country that has flunked Environmental 101 time and time again."

"Yeah, given what I've heard and read, it's been an abysmal situation."

"Ninety-nine percent of my people still live in a state of grinding poverty and helpless desperation. The crux of the problem is that they refuse to be accountable to anyone but themselves. Everyone knows they have been making Uighur women sterile for the past three decades, but no one raised a hand to stop them." her voice rising in tempered anger.

"Here's what really chaps my Tennessee ass," exclaimed Jon. The others who were awake had perplexed looks on their faces and were listening intently. "The damaging issue with C-8 is that it affects certain blood types more than others. It is devastating to people who ingest it if they have either type A+ or 0+."

"Crap!" An shouted. "That represents about seventy-five percent of the Chinese population, including me and my immediate family. If the C-8 gets in to the water system in any material way, and people in China drink it, that could spell disaster and weaken the PRC for decades, perhaps permanently. And the PRC's plan to encourage two children per family hasn't been effective at all in curbing the declining population."

Jon invited Yael to join the conversation. He had one of his vintage worried looks carved into his face. "It gets worse," Yael interjected. "Given the research we've done on PFAS in Israel, we've found that the only blood type totally immune from absorbing the C-8 compound is AB+. Only five percent of the Chinese population is AB+, and now you get why our mission is so critical."

"The insidiousness of Russia's plan is that it will not kill or become debilitating to all of China. Approximately 25% will be spared the agony. The tragedy is it will take the Chinese longer to figure out what is going on unless we tell them first," Jon pointed out.

Yael motioned to Elena to join the discussion. "Do you know what percentage of the Russian population has A+ and O+ blood types?" Yael asked.

Elena was still trying to absorb the evil that her country was about to inflict on innocent victims of a bordering country.

"Sapphire?"

"Sorry. My best guess is that it's a little under seventy percent, but that's not what I'm worried about. India has one of the lowest percentages with respect to A+ and O+ blood types, coming in at just under fifty percent. With a population approaching 1.5 billion, that makes 750 million people vulnerable. Let's assume seventy-five percent of China's declining population of 1.2 billion is susceptible. Between China and India's 23% of the world's population, poisoning the water would give Chirkov the biggest bang for his buck," Elena said, practically in tears.

The thought of the potential destruction of so much human life punctured her soul. "You know what I'm really concerned about?" Elena asked. "Because India has the largest democracy of any country by a factor of four, Chirkov wouldn't hesitate to group them in the same category as the U.S. Except for one minor issue. India was in striking distance geographically whereas Russia and the U.S. are separated by the Pacific Ocean and the Arctic Circle."

"I'm envious of you, Phillippe," said An, "and what Canada has done to preserve its freshwater resources along with its progressive, forward-thinking environmental policies. Several of my friends moved to Vancouver and seem happy there. China is the *amoral* equivalent of Russia, or is it the other way around?" An smirked.

The group went back to their respective resting places, and An stayed with Jon. "One more thing. Have you ever heard of *Shiji*?"

"Can't say that I have," Jon said, scratching his head.

"Never mind. It's a conversation for another day," she replied.

"Tell you what. I'll take a rain check until we get to Joshua Tree." An observed the lines wrinkled on his forehead. She knew that when he squinted with his eyes that something was wrong, like a nervous twitch. especially when the mega-vein on the left side of his neck bulged at the same time.

Jon noticed Yael staring at him. As he looked at her out of the corner of his left eye, he noticed Yael was mouthing some words, and walked toward her.

"Were you just meditating?"

"Not exactly," she responded in a raspy voice. "I was reciting the Hebrew prayer for safe travel. How do you think this is all going down? Be honest with me. Do you think we'll succeed?" she asked in a rare moment of vulnerability.

Jon smiled, looked directly at Yael, and put his hand on her shoulder. He refused to sugarcoat it, especially to people who were putting their lives on the line for a cause bigger than themselves.

"I can't even predict the past, let alone the future," he smiled. "I believe in process, and a good process will eventually lead to optimal results. Our process and our team are beyond reproach, so I just hope for the best. That's all I got."

Yael nodded, accepting her fate as her fears subsided. Jon leaned on the cockpit door, slightly ajar, busily eyeing the four others around him. His mind was rolling obsessively in a continuous loop about the leak of Darwin's whereabouts, and he couldn't shut it off. Like a faucet that dripped no matter how many turns of the wrench.

How on earth did they find Darwin anyway?' Who could it be? Someone savvy enough to have been given the whereabouts of the bunker and possibly the contents located inside. 'Is the enemy within'? OK, Jonny.

Keep your shit together. Focus. He felt trapped between the impossible and the inevitable.

Forty minutes later, Jon was awakened by an air pocket that shook his body violently. From the other side of the cargo plane, Yael as if reading his mind, gave him a thumbs up. Meanwhile, other team members slumbered through it. There was still a good four hours to the drop zone. The plane had just passed over eastern Kyrgyzstan and was now bearing down on the northeast part of Kazakhstan about thirty kilometers west of the Chinese border.

So far, so good, he thought, folding his arms across his chest. Jon, in a feeble attempt, tried to doze off one more time. Alternating thoughts like electrical currents ripped through his brain. He remained tormented about who could have tipped off the uninvited circus clowns to the bunker's location. *Wait a sec. Didn't Wolf hear them speaking Russian? It can't be, or could it?*

CHAPTER 10

THE PURGE

February 2045

There was something else gnawing at Jon, a haunting memory that only Wolf knew. Eleven months earlier and before F.O.R. was a thought, Jon had tried with his half-baked plan to derail the pipeline project in Mongolia by himself and had, in his own words, *failed incomprehensibly.* His cover was a business trip to Seoul selling a few dozen drones to the South Korean military. After the three-day stint there, he flew to Mongolia on a fake passport to meet up with his guide, Bilguun, meaning 'sage' in Mongol.

They met at the airport. "Hello, Jack. My friends call me Billy. If all you have is American dollars, we should convert it to crypto before we leave here. I just don't want to be walking around town with a wad of U.S. bills in my satchel. Make sense?"

Billy took Jon deep into the belly of his country by jeep, an electric vehicle he had purchased for his guide business. Jon was relieved to be away from Ulan Baator, among the worst air-polluted cities in Asia. *I could only see the outlines of buildings through the dense brown haze, though it was a cloudless day.*

Even though it was now scarce in most countries and banned in others, coal remained abundant in Mongolia's frigid capital. It lay beneath the towering smokestacks of power plants in piles as big as football fields. Drivers hauled it through town in open beds of pickup trucks, the road marked with stacked bags of coal. Random pieces spilled from metal buckets in the areas around yurts where the poorest families inconveniently burned the black stones to repel winter's cold and soulless blasts.

"The smoke in Ulan Baatar is too thick for children to breathe," he informed Jon. And the smell is acrid and inescapable. The sooty air stings the throat and wafts into the gleaming modern office buildings in the center of town and into the blocky, Soviet-style apartment towers that sprawl toward the mountains on the city's edges. Even on good days, handheld pollution monitors maxed out, as readings soared dozens of times beyond the city's recommended limit. Levels of the tiniest and most dangerous airborne particles, known as PM-2.5, exceeded the World Health Organization's suggested maximum limits by 175 times."

"I no longer know what a healthy lung feels or sounds like," said Billy on the drive heading southwest from Mongolia's capital. "It's quite sad. This winter authorities closed the capital's schools for two full months, from mid-December to mid-February. Hospitals are stretched to their limits with pneumonia cases that spike every winter. I once heard a mother of three small children say she has no confidence in the future of our country, as I watched her shovel coal into a small burning stove to heat her yurt during cold winter months where it can drop to between -40 to -50F."

Jon looked at him incredulously. "That's awful."

"This place just brings out the worst in people. Except for certain parts of Ulan Baator, the country was ossified over the last four decades, as if hanging in a state of suspended stagnation. Do you know today's biggest imports are?"

"I couldn't even muster a guess," Jon answered.

"Air filter systems in the schools and hospitals to protect our children. The only two cities that have poorer air quality are New Delhi and Dhaka."

"Hmm. Not Beijing? What about the water pollution?"

Billy continued the drive toward inner Mongolia. "That's the second biggest business in Mongolia. Just as bad as the air, if not worse, is the freshwater issue. Boiling the water doesn't help. Once it's in the groundwater, it never really goes away. The Gobi and the rest of my country don't take water for granted anymore. As mining accelerated, it did irreparable damage to the vegetation and grasslands. No remediation was enforced. And it caused another problem. Nomads are moving in droves, and over two-thirds of our population now dwell in or near our capitol."

"What's the educational system like?"

"It's improved, but it's the only real ticket for people to haul themselves out of here and make a better life for themselves. The problem is that all the smart, young industrious people who could make a difference are leaving. The wealthy people are living in apartments with double-layered air filters, the ability to recycle water, and indoor hydroponics. Unfortunately, they are few in numbers."

Jon had trusted Billy implicitly to get him near an unprotected part of the pipeline, attach highly potent plastic explosives in the wee hours of the morning, and then get back to Ulan Baator without being noticed. There was no plan B. As they approached the pipeline, a Russian patrol equipped with night vision goggles ambushed them a quarter mile from the pipeline. When they saw Jon's U.S. passport, they turned him away and followed Billy's jeep back to the capitol.

"We're extremely fortunate that neither of us had weapons and the patrol didn't search our jeep. Either they would have blown my head off or thrown me in the gulag somewhere in Siberia," said Jon somberly. The soldiers took a picture of Billy's license plate number that was permanently stored in some unknown database and hit him with a whopping fine for trespassing.

Unbeknownst to Jon, Billy had purchased the plastic explosives from a middleman who turned out to be a double agent. Jon's first mistake was allowing Billy to purchase the military-grade explosives from what turned out to be an arm's dealer who worked both sides of the fence. Billy told him that he bought them from an Uzbekistani woman who went by the name Wafat.

After returning to the States, Jon checked her out through Chip, his buddy at Langley. Turned out that Wafat was the code name for Ruqqia

Hashid, a Pakistani terrorist working with the Russians. She also turned up on the CIA's top ten list of most wanted terrorists. *Wafat* in Pakistani means death and destruction.

Lessons learned, Jon said to himself as he wrote an email to Billy to let him know that he should be extra careful about who he deals with in the future. His second mistake stemmed from his ingrained gambling persona. He overestimated his ability to get close to the pipeline undetected by the Russians, who pathologically patrolled the area on a strict schedule. He had been careless.

Jon was in a deep sleep with his arms crossed when he felt a tap on his left shoulder. He opened one eye and saw Uri standing in front of him. The pilot signaled with two fingers on his right hand and walked back into the cockpit. That was the sign to Jon that the plane had crossed unnoticed into Mongolian airspace. *It was 1470 miles from one end of the barren, mountainous country to the other. At an average speed of 350 mph, it was slightly under two hours to the drop point.*

Jon had managed to take his obsessive thinking about the Darwin incident down a few notches, but the idea that Wolf was there alone rattled his cage. Two hours later, F.O.R. was in full gear ready to jump. "Listen up, everyone. We've trained for this moment. I have de-risked the situation as much as humanly possible. Stay with your group all the way until the pipeline's lit up. That's what I'm asking of y'all. Any questions?"

An raised her hand. "How fucking cold is it outside right now?"

Jon glanced over at her. "It's -5 degrees, cold enough to freeze a hawk's nipples. That's without the windchill. Is that cold enough for y'all?"

Yael was about to respond. "That's so cold it scares the crap out of me. I just hope my eyeballs don't freeze." As planned, the F.O.R. team jumped in two teams of three each. The jump was meticulously executed right up until the point where Diaz veered off course 180 degrees in the wrong direction.

Jon scanned the mayhem. He struggled to keep his emotions in check as his entire world instantly fell apart at the seams that he had methodically sewn. He felt like he was outside of his own body, looking down from above, and knew instantly that Diaz hadn't made a mistake.

He observed the image of Diaz moving away from his carefully laid plan. *It's your fuckin' funeral, Diaz. Going to Plan B. Just in case you set a trap for us.*

Plan B was four clicks south of the originally intended landing spot. He had pre-programmed the exact coordinates into his and Yael's jet pack systems like a driverless car toward its destination. The embedded AI in Jon's NGVs could tell him the exact distance to any target he would view from the air, like an eagle eyeing its prey from a distance.

How in the hell did that traitor Diaz figure out how to manually override the system? Jon wondered into empty space. *His technological competence was under-whelming. He must've had help. If I ever catch up with that sonofabitch, I'm gonna barbeque his ass in Tennessee molasses. On second thought, I wouldn't waste it on that worthless piece of shit.* Jon knew intuitively that Diaz had a deep cynicism, the kind harbored by an unprincipled and insecure person.

Jon diverted his attention back to business. As he and An ducked out of sight away from the desert lights towards the alternate destination, Jon's adrenaline flowed through his body like water through a firehose. "Angie. Do you copy?"

"I'm here, Buck. Looks like the sandstorm is our lucky charm. What's up?" "The South American asshole took off on us. Definitely on purpose. I'll be damned if I'm going after him. Follow me. We are heading to a safer area. I have a feeling that there's a party waiting for us, and the shitbag choreographed the whole thing. You need to manually override the system. Quickly hit the black button and then punch in the coordinates 45.9283 latitude, 104.6855 longitude. Got it?"

"Yup. 45.9283 and 104.6855," she repeated back. "Read you loud and clear, I'm right behind you." Jon had every right to be demonstrably paranoid about what might happen next. He prayed in the silence of the desert hinterlands that the sandstorm would continue to act as cover from patrolling Russian choppers.

Jon knew his fate if captured, whether by the Russians or Chinese. He would be tortured until he spilled his guts about the mission, and after confessing they would kill him on the spot and bury him in the Gobi. Or worse, leave his dead corpse for the buzzards or some desert animal to devour him at its leisure.

Jon was still trying to push the simmering rage out of his mind and refused to let *that motherfucker live rent-free in my head*. Every cell in his body was obsessed with blowing the pipeline and getting the hell out of Mongolia. He'd meticulously planned it out. They would complete their task in fourteen minutes.

As they touched down on the desert floor about one hundred meters from the pipeline, Jon's brain was now swirling with worst-case scenarios. An stared intensely at Jon through her night vision goggles. "You know what? I don't have a damn clue what happened with Diaz, and I could give a flying fuck about that weasel. Let's just take care of business and high-tail it out of this god-forsaken place. And I got some news for you."

"What's that, Angie?"

"No way I'm going back to fucking China either," she shouted in anger laced with fear. "For all we know, Diaz might have tipped off the Chinese in exchange for something. As I said before, it's either Canada or the States for me."

"Let's blow the pipeline first, get the hell out of here, and then we can have a conversation about it." An removed four plastic explosives from her pack, readying for the purpose of why she was in the middle of the Gobi blowing a pipeline built by China.

"Let's proceed with caution just like we practiced. I'll be on the lookout for drones. Don't forget I have the Boar in my back pocket. Doubt if they have men stationed this far away from the original drop point, but not taking any chances."

Jon was hurled right back to the present like his worst nightmare had come true. The sandstorm was now a combination of sand and snow. As if the free-floating snowflakes were bound together and could turn into a roaring avalanche at a moment's notice. The noiseless desert night revealed a distant sound of something he had hoped to avoid.

"Hear that?" Jon probed.

"Hear what?"

"It's a Russian chopper. Maybe two. I'm sure of it. Get down." He readied the Boar for combat, while the sandstorm continued to work in their favor.

Jon and An lay flat on the desert floor, eyes on the silvery oblong target no more than one hundred meters ahead. They were looking for any movement on the ground. Nothing in sight, not even an ibex. It was still dark, with the sun yet to appear on the horizon. The only semblance of light was a dull crescent moon hiding behind a gray cluster of clouds.

"Let's move." Without hesitation, she lifted her light frame from a crouch to a full standing position, explosives in her right hand that she carried like a football. Jon spoke into the mic on his headset. "Set your timer for..."

Thump! A bullet whizzed by her left ear. She heard it crash into the rocks behind her. As the wind intensified, sand and dirt beat against her NGVs. She froze and closed her eyes sensing energy to her left about 150 meters out rapidly approaching on foot. She quickly turned in that direction and dropped the explosives behind her. They were smothered instantly by the swirling sand.

Her suspicion was confirmed in seconds. Instinctively, she quickly removed her NGVs, and dropped them behind her. Jon lay still and watched as An wrapped a bandana around her mouth and her eyes to look like a lost tourist in the rocky terrain. She grabbed a switchblade from a side pocket in her vest.

Her eyes spotted a lone soldier appearing on the horizon at ten o'clock trotting toward her. He was toting what appeared to be a modern version of the Lobaev sniper rifle, but An couldn't make it out with the wind-borne swirl all around her. The mercenary zig-zagged on the desert floor, shouting something unintelligible in Russian. She dropped her knife by her right foot in the sand. A high-voltage surge kicked in as An transitioned to the realm of hand-to-hand combat. Visibility had maxed out at ten meters.

As the Russian approached, he was completely unaware that Jon was twenty meters behind An, camouflaged and lying in a prone position on the chilled desert floor. She casually walked up to the Russian soldier while frantically waving her raised arms speaking the words, "Don't shoot" in rapid-fire Mandarin.

The lone soldier waved a flashlight in her general direction but couldn't make her out. Only that she appeared to be a female Mongolian or Chinese tourist stranded in the desert storm. As fortune would have it, this disarmed the sniper long enough to bring him into her personal space like a black widow about to eat its mate.

Still approaching, An could hear him breathing audibly through the fierce, howling wind, asking questions in Russian. She shook her head, attempting to communicate that she couldn't understand a word he was saying. His suspicions were slightly heightened, as he asked himself what a single woman would be doing this deep in the desert traveling by herself. Or maybe she had lost contact with her traveling companions. Either way, she appeared unarmed and small in stature. His finger was on the trigger of a high-powered rifle. He took nothing for granted. An had persuaded him to carelessly let his guard down for a split second. That was all that she needed. She sensed her opening. Standing 5'4" as an Asian woman, she had the element of surprise, and would use it to her full advantage. The door was open, and she eagerly stepped into his space.

Jon was riveted, ready to defend her as he drew his Glock, pointing at the chest of the approaching soldier. Seconds later, before Jon could cock his weapon, An went on the attack. Jon had never seen Wing Chung inflicted on another human being, a jaw-dropping experience for him. *It seemed like a way to squeeze more life out of its victim, like squeezing a lemon a second and third time to make sure you got every last drop of juice.*

A blinding two fingers struck his Adam's apple, sending the hapless soldier reeling, and writhing in pain, knocking the rifle out of his hand. Followed by a forceful elbow to the solar plexus, taking the wind out of him. Without hesitation, An effortlessly flipped someone at least two times her weight over her left shoulder onto the rocky ground below. Her final, clinching blow was directed to the Russian's unprotected groin with her knee, a strike to his right eye with her index finger, followed by her steely fist into the helpless soldier's solar plexus.

Jon reflexively grabbed his crotch and then his throat, wincing as An crushed her unsuspecting opponent using nothing but her bare hands. She quickly grabbed a loaded pistol exposed in the holster attached to his waist. She put on her NVGs, picked up the plastic explosives, took his flashlight, rifle, and the Russian-made pistol, carrying his guns back toward Jon, grinning from ear to ear.

Jon never felt compelled to fire a shot. The sound could have alerted any potential Ivans near them. The angels favored what remained of Jon's team because it appeared that the soldier was acting on his own behalf. "Looks like a Norinco-made pistol, a Chinese company that sold everything from choppers, tanks, missile systems, and drones," she shouted to Jon.

An understood that China had usurped Russia as the iconic weapons maker and had been prominent on the world's military stage for over two decades. And Iran was not far behind. Fear of her own country's weaponry blinded her soul.

Jon stared through his NVGs in the direction of where An's victim was lying motionless. He sensed no movement. She handed Jon the telescopic rifle. He tossed it behind an errant rock where the unconscious soldier would never find it.

He looked at An. "Did you hear that?" She gave him a blank stare.

"Listen. I hear the Russian chopper again, and it sounds like it's about six clicks away. We gotta hurry. They're gonna be on top of us in eight minutes."

"How do you know?" she inquired briskly.

"Just a hunch. We have a Class 4 shitstorm in our midst, so let's use it to our advantage. We've got a three-minute window to set the explosives!"

An turned her head and screamed at Jon, but he couldn't understand her muffled voice through the thick desert sand swirling in the air. She signaled military style, pointing in the direction of the pipeline. She grabbed the explosives, and they both sprinted to their respective destinations about twenty meters apart. Much to his surprise, An beat him handily to the pipeline, and set four plastic explosives underneath the pipeline before Jon had two in place. She was both efficient and self-sufficient.

It took thirty seconds for him to attach the explosives and set the timer against the cold, cylinder steel structure. As he sprinted back across the desert, he noticed that An was already slouched behind the rocks. He felt his legs burning from lactic acid building in his bloodstream. His oxygen-deprived body was pulsing, his lungs clawing for air, as he lifted his jet pack over his shoulders. An slid hers on with relative ease and was breathing normally.

"Stay with me," Jon barked. "No more than three meters behind, OK? By the way, nice moves back there. Did they teach you that in grad school?" he laughed into his mic through the howling sandstorm. He could hear the choppers growing louder. Jon continued shouting commands. "Vision will be limited going forward. We'll head due west with our jetpacks and leave the ATVs behind. Maybe it will throw that flying eggbeater off our trail and give us enough time to get in the clear. Our ride is waiting for us three clicks from here. We should be in the truck before the pipeline blows."

Suddenly, An turned her head in the direction of the chopper approaching, and she shouted the words "Enemy 3 o'clock" into her headset. Jon hit the brakes on his jet pack, and turned 180 degrees, almost colliding with An, who dodged him at the last second. He descended to the ground, readying himself for the most crucial battle he'd ever faced, and in unfamiliar territory.

Here goes nothin'. C'mon Boar. Don't let me down. Light 'em up." He raised his right arm, programming the device steadily with his left hand, and then pressed the launch button. An witnessed the laser as it honed in on the chopper. The last thing she saw was a flash of light as the explosion rocked the night sky.

The force of the blast almost knocked them both to the desert floor. The chopper ignited, instantly incinerating the flying gas can and the human contents within it. It crashed into the dark terrain below. Fifty meters south, the explosives sat strapped to the pipeline, ready to obey the timer.

"Good shot," An said with relief. "Glad to know it really works. Nothing worse than a Russian chopper bearing down, especially one that you can't see."

"OK. Let's boogie. I'm pretty sure there's another one a few kilometers behind, and they must have seen the explosion. Hopefully, the diversion will give us enough time to safely reach the train."

Jon was concerned about leaving the Boar behind. For a tidy sum, he had pre-arranged with one of Elena's ex-military Mongolian contacts to secure the missile-guided laser drone and ship it back through Kazakhstan by truck, with Be'er Sheva being its final resting place.

"What about the others?" An shrieked through her headset.

"They're on their own. Can't worry about them. Besides, Sol is a seasoned pro, and could find her way out of Mongolia with her hands tied behind her back and her ankles chained together. I have total faith in her. And if by some chance the Russians should capture them, Sapphire can talk her way out of anything. She'll tell them in Russian that they are a bunch of tourists who got lost in the desert. It's the best we can hope for, and it's out of our hands."

Yael picked up Jon's communication. Her body tensed slightly. She knew exactly what to do and set her jetpack two kilometers south of her original destination. Elena and Phillipe fell in line behind her, heading further away from the troops that were lurking around the initial drop points.

They had placed their explosives under the pipeline just shy of five minutes after when Jon and An had placed theirs. That way both sets of charges would detonate back-to-back.

Yael saw the explosion caused by Boar's laser lighting up a chopper. "Holy Shit!" she shouted loud enough for Phillippe and Elena to hear. "Looks like the Boar came in handy after all." Yael pumped her fist in the air.

"Just enough time to ditch The Boar in a place where no one would find it," Jon said with his finger on the digital controls. Both Jon and Yael's control panels would record and store the exact longitude and latitude of their respective Boars for pickup later. Plan C was in Jon's capable hands. He had the ability to self-destruct his highly efficient defense machine remotely from anywhere on the planet, but only as a last resort to avoid it falling into enemy hands.

"Let's go, guys. Follow me. Set your jetpacks at twenty feet altitude," Yael shouted decisively through her headset. "We are heading southwest to our pickup point. Vision is limited, so for God's sake, stay with me." *Wonder why Jon instructed me to leave the ATVs behind. Guess he had his reasons.*

Elena was hoping that the Russian driver she secured was on schedule to take Yael to a landing strip ten kilometers away from their pickup coordinates. At that point, she would separate from Elena and Phillippe. Each would be following their own escape plan.

Elena's body froze as she spotted a drone, and screamed into her headset, "Sol, drone one o'clock!" Yael deliberately raised her left hand with the anti-drone laser, locked on her target, and pressed the blue button, leaving the defenseless drone inoperable in less than a second. Elena watched as the drone fell helplessly to the ground, crashing onto the rocks below.

"Way to go, Sol! Let's get the hell out of here before they wake up and realize what happened and send reinforcements to track down who fucked with their drone," Phillippe said euphorically.

Jon's premonitions proved so accurate that he could not have written a better script. The second Russian chopper, having spotted the first helicopter's wreckage and the ATVs about one hundred meters from the pipeline, took the bait. They lowered two men on rope ladders to the desert floor within seconds of when Jon and An reached their ride near the western border of the province of Dundgovi.

An spotted the truck parked on the side of an endless winding road. They quickly landed, took off their jetpacks, turned, and marched toward the rear door. An was right beside Jon, proving to be his equal at every turn. They threw their jetpacks in the back of the truck and jumped into the back seat. The driver promptly hit the pedal of his incognito electric van.

That's when they heard the roaring chopper blades in the distance followed by a deafening explosion. Seconds later an angry orange ball of fire was released into the atmosphere from the explosives An and Jon attached to the now decimated pipeline. The dazzling fireworks lit the sky for a moment and then subsided. The troops inside the $45 million chopper were incinerated as the gas tank exploded with a bang that could have been heard all the way to Ulan Bator. They were exterminated like people whose bodies had just run through the crematorium.

With the immediate pressure relieved, they changed clothes in the back seat to blend in like tourists. For an instant, Jon noticed An's taut body gleaming with sweat in the shimmering moonlight. Just as they began putting on their civilian shoes, the vehicle lurched forward and made a hard right onto a local, unpaved road. With the turn, Jon's body was pressed against the passenger door, and his head lightly tapped the window from the force of An's chi that had flown into him. An was laughing uncontrollably as she disentangled herself from Jon.

"It does feel good to be in an SUV heading toward civilization, don't you agree?" An asked rhetorically. Jon nodded wordlessly, simultaneously recalling the distance of twelve kilometers to the train depot. A full minute passed, and then he gathered what was left of his energy to speak.

"We're heading northwest toward the province of Ovorhangay, where we're going to catch the train." An could still 'see' the second chopper, its muffled rotors in the distance, whipping up sand in the desert storm. Two explosions, minutes apart, left no doubt that Russian forces would be mobilizing to find the would-be saboteurs who had the audacity to blowup a water pipeline in the Gobi.

"What about that poor bastard back there in the desert? Did you kill him or just wipe the hair off his ass?" Jon probed, feeling a little light-headed. Things happened in a blur. It was challenging for him to see what An had done.

An flashed a withering glance at Jon's piercing blue eyes. "I left him alive. Just because I could have killed him doesn't mean that I should've. Just knocked the wind out of him, that's all. He was unconscious but still breathing. He will wake up in an hour or two with a few aches and pains, a sore groin and maybe a few broken ribs."

"Rendered him unconscious? No, really. Where'd you learn that killer stuff?" Jon asked, as he looked at his watch to see if they were on schedule. "Learned most of it from watching old Bruce Lee movies," she responded with a sarcastic laugh that was sharp enough to have taken a bite out of a pit bull.

Jon threw his head back, appreciating An's sense of humor, and whispered, "We're in good shape. Slightly ahead of schedule. Let's just relax." Minutes passed. His eyes were shut, trying to bring his adrenals under control.

"Are you sleeping?" An asked without looking in Jon's direction. He opened one eye, and without moving responded, "You do know that the Chinese military brass have nicknamed their modern military buildup as 'wolf' warrior, right? Don't you think that's ironic?"

Just then, the driver spoke his first words since the ride began. "There is train depot right over there," the driver said in broken English, pointing in the general direction of the entrance. "Safe travels, my friends."

Jon got out after An, shut the door, walked around to the driver's side, leaned in, and said, "Bayaralaa," as he shook the driver's hand good-bye. He handed him instructions as to where the two jetpacks would be delivered.

An told the driver in Mongolian that he would be well compensated when they arrived safely at their destination point. Jon, who was translating through An, made clear that his compensation would be significantly more than selling them to the Russians or the Chinese, who would probably just confiscate them anyway.

An looked at Jon with a smile. "We are just full of surprises today, aren't we? When did you have time to learn Mongolian?"

"In my spare time. Let's board the train and get the hell out of here before the Ivans start snooping around as to the whereabouts of those lunatics who had the balls to blow up their newly constructed pipeline, and two choppers."

Along the walk to the train depot, an old Mongolian woman shuffling in front of them inadvertently dropped her shopping bag, causing a few cans to roll downhill in Jon and An's general direction. Without hesitation, she gingerly knelt, gathered the woman's belongings, and placed them gently into her bag. The woman thanked her profusely. He had seen an act of kindness and humility in An that shook him to his core, especially given they were in a hurry to get out of town.

An bought the tickets with 29,800 Mongolian tugriks that Jon handed her, the equivalent of $16 USD apiece. They walked about twenty meters, boarded the train, and found two barren seats away from the rest of the crowd. They were both trying to avoid the hard stare of the disheveled Mongolian conductor, who clearly was not used to seeing a Western white male with an Asian woman. Jon sighed in sheer exhaustion, but was still alert, eyeing the train for any active military.

"What did the woman say to you?" Jon asked as he leaned over. The smell of her sweat was as sweet a smell as sweat could ever be. He felt the heat of her body next to his on the dark green dilapidated train seat. It was a strange intimacy given they weren't entirely out of the woods. The train abruptly pulled out of the station right on time.

"The woman thanked me and said that she hopes her grandchildren grow up to be just like me," she smiled.

Before An could begin to worry about what would happen next with her life in Israel and then back to China, Jon pulled out what was to be the biggest surprise yet. Sitting quietly in a private car, Jon pocketed his phone, forcing his sleep-deprived eyes open as he turned toward An.

"Angie, I hope you appreciate that there was some anticipation on my part of where you would be next, and that returning to Shenzhen was not an option. So, I took the liberty of making certain arrangements for you. I hope that's OK."

Her eyes opened wide in amazement as he pulled out a blue passport and handed it to her. With slight trepidation, An opened it. Her eyes narrowed as she perused the contents. Tears of happiness burst into streams flowing down her cheeks. Jon had just handed her a passport to freedom.

After studying the dark blue document, she hugged Jon, and then stared into his half-mast eyes. "How did you pull this off, and are we really married?"

Jon started to laugh. "For the time being, yes. We are on our honeymoon, Mrs. Angela Walker." An was rendered speechless. She sat there in a daze, and then started rambling, peppering Jon with random questions packed with super-charged emotions.

She felt giddy. "Ugh. Who takes a honeymoon to Mongolia? Where are we headed? What's our ultimate destination? Am I really going to the U.S. with you? I can't believe it, I mean you. Where are we going to live, Mr. Buckingham?"

"Shh. C'mon, Angie. Try not to use my real name, OK? Just take a deep breath and I'll tell you everything you need to know and more. Look, you deserve it, not to mention you did a helluva job back there in the desert."

"I beg to differ with you, but I think we're just getting started. Everything seems bad until you find the inevitable. Something worse. You did say three missions, right?" An said playfully. Jon barely nodded, conserving whatever energy he still had left. She lowered her voice. "And you're putting me in an awkward position, marrying me before asking my permission. And not to seem ungrateful, but where's my wedding band?"

An's spirit was dancing with joy. As if right on cue, Jon pulled two onyx wedding bands out of his pocket, one for each of them.

"That's what friends do for each other," he said, flashing a tired grin. "All you gotta do is trust me, and everything will be alright."

"But I haven't said 'yes' to a question you never bothered to ask, Mr. Walker." An snuggled up to Jon, put her head on his shoulder, closed her tearful eyes, and shut out the world for the next hour.

Meanwhile, Jon continued to process the entire history of his short-lived history with Diaz. He was starting to connect the dots of his fleeting and overconfident interactions, dots that marked Diaz's descent into darkness. The last one to arrive during the Mojave jump. Followed by his constant texting during meetings as well as in the lobby of the hotel in Be'er Sheva. The curiosity about the refueling spots, the final drop point, and so on. Jon continued to beat himself up for not seeing earlier signs. *Where'd this guy come from anyway? Psychos R Us? He lies like he breathes. Fuck it and fuck him. Bottom line is mission accomplished. Everyone is safe and going home. And that's the scorecard I'm using to measure success.*

The train pulled into the station, and they hopped into a taxi to the airport.

"Jack? I am your driver, Chono. Heading to Buyant Ukhaa International Airport," he said in his best English. An asked the driver in Mongolian what the name Chono meant. As he responded, An sat dumbfounded for a few seconds and then turned to face her new husband. "You're not going to believe this, but the driver's name means 'Wolf' in his native tongue."

"He's here, he's there, he's everywhere," Jon responded, shaking his head in disbelief, remembering that Wolf had told him more than once that there are no coincidences, and everything happens for a reason. "What are the odds, Angie?"

CHAPTER 11

LONG NIGHT'S JOURNEY INTO DAY

February 2045

As they arrived at the airport, Jon noticed that except for the airport terminal, everything looked worse than the last time he was there. An was enjoying the reflection of the Khentii Mountains under what appeared to be a full moon. No matter where An was, she loved the mountains. They had a certain healing power, and raised her vibrational energy.

Approaching the entrance, she could not help but notice a life-sized picture of Chirkov and the current president of Mongolia through the sliding glass doors. There were a few soldiers dressed in Mongolian uniforms holding rifles, but no sign of any Chinese or Russian military presence. The airport had been remodeled shortly after the Russian invasion. It had all the charm of the Soviet-style era, with a bit of local architecture mixed in for good measure. Jon spotted a small duty-free shop sign in the corner, and they went up to the third floor to purchase some Swiss chocolate. He perused the store and was pleasantly surprised to see a tiny humidor in the back, and purchased a couple of Cubans. The price was right, and since he was in a celebratory mood, Jon also purchased a liter of Chinggis Khaan vodka.

"Aah, the perfect combination to commemorate our journey. Liquor, chocolate, and cigars," Jon exclaimed. "It's not Scotch, but I'll take it."

An noticed a GOBI sign. Immediately she recognized it as the premier Mongolian cashmere clothing brand and decided to do some shopping. In short order, she walked out with a multi-colored cashmere scarf wrapped around her neck. Jon complimented An on her taste in clothes. She was beaming as they casually strolled through the terminal toward the security checkpoint.

At their gate, they sat eagerly waiting to board their flight as they shared a green tea that Jon had bought from a vendor outside the airport. An couldn't stop staring at her wedding band. She knew her marriage wasn't real, but was still trying to process all that had happened in the last twelve hours, including that they had left their Glocks in the back seat of the SUV as a present for their driver. Hopefully to be used against some abusive Russians.

An was bursting with the anticipation of freedom, praying only that the Russian or Chinese authorities wouldn't be combing the airport and find them before they boarded. She was deathly afraid. *We narrowly escaped one disaster, and being this close to freedom only to be captured by the Chinese would be the equivalent of an annihilating fate.*

Jon was in his own world, staring at the texts lighting up his phone. One from Yael. "All good. Hope to see you soon. Shalom." Another from Elena that had a thumbs up emoji in the message. And a third from Phillippe, who texted, "Can't wait to get back to a milder climate and the freshwater lakes of Toronto. Safe travels, Buck."

Jon sat back, shut his weary eyes, and tried to adopt the more philo-sophical way of life that Wolf had shared with him after Darwin was completed. He no longer subscribed to the saying that knowledge is power. After Wolf told Jon that he believed humankind, both histori-cally and in its current state was a failed experiment, Jon's thinking began to drift toward what Wolf had told him. He shook his head. *Damn that guy. He's always one step beyond my reach, living with 100% integrity and making the world better for others first, and himself a distant second.*

On the tarmac with the plane's engines revving for take-off, Jon happened to look out his window. He had an unobstructed view of the entire terminal lined with tall, vertical glass structures. He noticed a team of Mongolian police accompanied by half a dozen plain-clothed men scurrying through the airport. Immediately, Jon knew that it was the Russians and the Chinese searching frantically for anyone involved in the two explosions that rocked the desert calm a mere two hours ago. He tapped An's shoulder, and as she turned to face him, he pointed out the window. She saw what Jon was watching, as if they were viewing a silent movie. As the plane went rumbling down the runway, she prayed that it was too late for the control tower to halt the plane. As the jet engines lifted the passengers into the empty sky, An let out a sigh of relief that she was truly safe and on her way to a freedom she'd never known. She smiled in gratitude and admiration at Jon's luminous presence and placed her hand on his, praying there were no military planes in the air tailing them. *Not possible,* she thought.

They had a brief layover in Seoul before departing for the states. Long enough to have a meal of Korean cuisine. Since China had annexed North Korea, any existential risk to South Korea had been dramatically reduced. During the eleven-hour flight, An sketched out some of the possibilities in her mind about what her new life in America might look like. Jon was eating his second meal, consisting of eggs, toast, and a salad. He turned his unshaven face toward her with a look of surprise. He was feeling a sense of relief, having led F.O.R. through a dangerous yet undeniably successful mission. He struggled to remain in the present, avoiding the yesterdays and tomorrows.

"Mrs. Walker. I've got another surprise for you, but I'm not telling until we land at LAX." Jon spoke in a soft tone.

An gazed back at Jon in wonderment. How this man had looked after her and guided her through a journey that aligned with her own life's mission, and then taken her future into his strong, capable hands. She was beyond grateful, but anxious to see how Jon was going to rescue her mother and grandmother. "Well, this is a curious way to start a marriage! Does it have to do with the honeymoon you've been planning?" An blushed.

Jon rolled his eyes at An, who was looking more radiant by the minute. "I know what it is. We're going to Joshua Tree, aren't we?" An was giddy with the anticipation of safety and freedom for the first time ever.

Jon, looking into the windows of her soul, faintly nodded, content as a hunting dog with a pheasant in its mouth. In a remote chamber of his mind he was still smarting from being double-crossed by Diaz. His anger festered like an open sore. *Maybe I'm confusing evil intent with raw incompetence.*

Jon, still in an obsessed state of mind, wondered whether Diaz had given up their identities to the Russian or Chinese authorities. *It doesn't much matter any more now that Angie's name has been officially changed and there would be no trace of the former Dr. An Shui. Afraid of heights, my ass.*

Jon had a few additional surprises in store for An. Before they would return to Darwin for safekeeping, they would spend three nights in Joshua Tree and then a quick stay in Frisco to check on the status of his Denver mini-sub. At least until they could figure out a plan to integrate her as a U.S. citizen with a plum research job at a yet-to-be-determined university. Yael told Israeli authorities that An left to go back to China because she had an urgent family matter to attend to.

———

Right after texting Jon, Yael stepped into a private car that would take her to an uncharted runway of a secluded private airport with one landing strip. From there, an eight-seater, twin-engine flown by a former Mongolian Air Force pilot would whisk her away to Ulan Baator, where she would then catch a flight on Turkish Air to Tel Aviv, including a layover in Istanbul. Yael hadn't seen active duty for at least a decade and was relieved to be going home. The thought of sitting on the beach watching a fiery red sun dip below the horizon of the Mediterranean took her anxiety down a few notches, although there was an aura of sadness that it would be without Jon.

It's a good thing that Buck and I figured out a way to stamp our passports with the Mongolian insignia before we left Israel. Otherwise, I'd have a hard time explaining how I got here in the first place, Yael thought.

As the other team leader on the mission, she was harboring a similar resentment that she couldn't shake. *Diaz, that heartless scorpion. There's such a colossal smallness about him. If I didn't know any better, it's almost as if he lusted after betrayal. He will get his, in this life or the next.*

Yael made it through customs with forty-five minutes to spare. As she boarded the plane to Istanbul, she took one last look around to see if any F.O.R. mates were nearby. Yael dreaded the idea that an indefinite amount of time would pass until she and Jon would be together. Yael like to plan her life and was uncomfortable with the unknown. Jon was the one thing she had no control over.

On the flight, she fantasized about Jon traveling to Israel to spend time with her, or how she might fly to Denver and surprise him with a knock on his door in Frisco. Or call from the airport in Houghton County, forty miles from where Darwin lay submerged underneath the forest. *Maybe we could drive to Cal Berkeley together or camp on Isle Royale,* she longed. The thought of her being alone with Jon for a few days excited her, but she understood how the odds were stacked against that either one of her fantasies would happen.

"Sol, without your brother, I'm not sure how we could've possibly completed the mission. Be sure to thank him for me." Those were Jon's parting words to her before the group texts went silent.

Philippe slipped anonymously into the backseat of a private car that was waiting for him, courtesy of one of Elena's many close connections. He was daydreaming about life in Toronto, and how dull life would be compared to the harrowing adventure that he had just gone through. Phillipe was thoughtful and deliberate about ways he could help Elena defect. Phillippe was reluctant to tell a soul, including his significant other of fifteen years. It wasn't in his nature to keep secrets from people he loved. But when it came to jeopardizing the safety of any F.O.R. member, he was stalwart. All of them had become like family to him. His flight would take him through Frankfurt on the way home to Toronto. No one would ever suspect that this mild-mannered, middle-aged Canadian had just participated in a high-risk mission that blew up what he had nicknamed the 'pipeline of death.' He had just committed the biggest international crime of his life, yet barely gave it a second thought.

Phillippe was in a reflective mood. *Do the next right thing, and everything will work out for the best,* his father always told him. *To think that Chirkov almost got away with killing off a quarter of China's stagnating population and was using what remained of one of the poorest, most defenseless countries in Asia to implement his plan. That arrogant, evil no-good sonofabitch,* Phillippe raged.

————

Elena caught a slow train in Bulgar that was heading northwest to Ulaangom, a newer rail route that originated from Ulan Bator and made several stops along the way. She crouched down low in her seat and closed her eyes, clutching her passport tightly in her left hand and making sure she looked like an unsuspecting tourist headed to Moscow through the common northwest border.

The Mongolian conductor had the disheveled appearance of someone who had given up on life. The stench of cigarette smoke hanging in the air from somewhere in the back of her car was overwhelming, as she caught a whiff of a hand-rolled cigarette that had been left smoldering in an ashtray nearby. The air reeked of booze, too. *Probably cheap vodka that someone had picked up at an import/export shop.*

Elena was too exhausted to care, too tired to sleep. The train car was completely dark, except for the sliver of piercing light from the sun beginning to rise on the eastern horizon. The same light that served to keep the passengers with whiskey on their brains from tripping while walking to and from the bathroom. Elena observed a grim silence that gripped the natives aboard, packed shoulder to shoulder in the inexpensive cars. It weighed heavily on her soul. *People suffer here. Then they die for no fucking reason. No escaping it.*

Although she was good under pressure, the last twenty-four hours had stretched Elena to her emotional limits. Her breathing remained slightly labored, and she was desperately trying to rein in her emotions and remain calm. Her eyelids felt like lead weights, shielding eyes that wandered to the scenery rapidly sliding past. Out of the window to her left, she noticed a bus standing in front of the train tracks with lights on, waiting to cross after the train had safely passed. There stood the dark gray vehicle that hauled working-class men and women to their jobs. Dressed in blue garb and work boots, they stared out the bus windows at a collective, hopeless condition. People who had seen misery and death, they sat with destitute eyes, scrambling for a future that was already out of reach.

Elena had a flashback to the stories her parents told her of their early days in the U.S.S.R. *At least education was a way out. These people have been deprived of the one thing that could give them a strand of hope to grab onto.*

Upon arriving near the border at full sunrise, Elena deboarded the train and was met by a Russian driver that would escort her over the border straight north to Abakan, the southernmost airport in Russia. The flight to Moscow departed at 10:50 a.m., arriving at 11:50 a.m. Five hours of non-stop air travel, gaining four hours in a country that had eleven time zones. Once in the air, Elena would breathe deep, exhale long, and doze off for three hours of well-deserved rest.

———

From Ulan Bator, the newly minted Mr. and Mrs. Walker flew Mongolian Air to Seoul, and after a brief two-hour layover, traveled in business class on Korean Air to LAX. On route over the Pacific to California, Jon thought about the western states that had *never built the infrastructure to capture rainwater.*

On the other side of the globe, Wolf had just discovered through one of Admiral Brown's contacts that Diaz had been collaborating with the Russians since 2037 and promptly phoned his friend in mid-flight.

"Buck, you're not going to believe this. The word on the street is Diaz got into serious financial difficulty by losing a small fortune trading the Brazilian stock market and betting on the Brazilian currency right before it crashed. He has a wife and three small children to support. The Russians got to him. Made him an offer he couldn't refuse. He had little choice but to sell his soul and do the devil's work.

Wolf humbly continued. "I have learned from my ancestors and certain Shamans that the ability to put knowledge into action for the benefit of others and not solely for yourself is true power. An altruistic, unselfish kind of power. Buck, are you sitting down? Brace yourself. Turns out Diaz suffered a series of strokes. He was medevacked by helicopter from Ulan Bator to a marginal hospital in southern Russia to be treated for his condition.

"Apparently, those ER docs weren't too swift. It seems as if the strokes had a permanent effect on his speech, his balance, the vision in his right eye and rendered his sex life non-existent. What did Martin Luther King say? *The arc of the moral universe is long, but it bends toward justice.*"

An sat in silence, trying to absorb what Jon had just said. *More like karma than justice. Couldn't have happened to a nicer horse's ass. That mother of all assholes painted himself into a corner with his own paint and his own brush.* "Karma's a bitch," An gloated. "And this is the kind of instant karma that punishes a creature like Diaz living out the remainder of his life incapacitated, unable to enjoy the simple pleasures that money can't buy."

"Yael's brother discovered yesterday that our friendly Russian pilot may have been a double agent. His theory was Diaz and the pilot were in cahoots with each other before the flight took off from Israel. That explains why the Russians were waiting for us at the exact coordinates we planned out. I'm more pissed at myself that I couldn't see something so obvious," Elena said to Jon. "How do you know for sure?"

"I don't, but Yael learned through her brother that after the drop our trusted pilot made a beeline to a Russian air base in northern Mongolia. Both plane and pilot disappeared into the night and never returned to Israel. Turned out to be an easy defection for the pilot. Now that I think about it, Diaz may have planted a micro tracking device in my backpack when I met him for the first time. I left my backpack on the chair when I went to take a leak."

"Bummer."

"Yeah, and Yael feels horrible about the pilot choice. It wasn't her fault when her brother, a commander in IDF Air Force, suggested Abramavitz. She was a victim of no good deed goes unpunished."

"My grandpa had a saying about soul-sucking shitbags like Diaz," said Jon.

"What's that?"

"He's as phony as a three-dollar bill."

"Nothing we can do at this point except to look forward and focus on what's in front of us, not behind us. It's not going to do us any good to dwell in the rearview mirror," said An, trying to turn Jon's attention away from Diaz.

"You got that right. The thought of him makes me burn. He violated the entire group, not just me. I'd like to get a hold of him and throw him in a shredder while he's still breathing, and then send his remains back to Russia. Now I understand why he insisted on making his own arrangements out of Mongolia. It all makes sense," Jon said, his eyes still smoldering with unspeakable rage.

After speaking with Phillippe, Jon phoned Wolf on his way to LAX.

"Forget Diaz. He thought he could ride the tiger without ending up in its mouth," Wolf said.

"Yeah, and the motherfucker thought he'd stolen his way into retirement."

"Do we know who the pilot was reporting to?" Wolf asked.

"I'm not sure yet, but my gut tells me it's Mikhail Mishustin, the guy who's been #2 under Putin and Chirkov ever since the KGB was abolished years ago. I'm gonna get that sonofabitch, too."

Wolf could sense the smoke coming out of Jon's ears. "Breathe, Buck. Just breathe and let it go. You always told me that revenge is for suckers. You need to listen to your own advice. Besides, things went well on the mission, despite the betrayal of Diaz. Count your blessings."

As soon as he landed in the States, Jon located his high school buddy, Chip. He was entrenched with the CIA and Jon told him all about the mission. From there he would contact his counterpart in the Chinese government, alerting them to the potential danger of water sabotage flowing from Lake Baikal to Lanzhou, and the contamination once the water passed into Mongolian territory. Jon breathed easier knowing that the mission had prevented what could have been the most devastating catastrophes in history.

Upon arriving at the rental car area, Jon signed for the pre-reserved electric rental van for his unofficial honeymoon. The drive from LA to Joshua Tree without traffic was a reasonable 2 ½ hours due east, through Anaheim and Riverside to the national park. Given it was the beginning of the weekend, Jon sensed there might be long lines at the main entrance in the town of Joshua Tree and took the west entrance on Hwy 62.

"Hey, Angie. Why don't you share the whole Shiji thing with me now? We have a drive ahead of us to the campgrounds." An noticed the change in scenery driving out of LA toward the national park. She'd read a travel book about Joshua Tree and was feeling a wave of wonderment.

"Shiji is an ancient Chinese text about 526,500 Chinese characters, making it longer than the Old Testament. Historical Chinese scholars say that when planning for battle the focus was on these documents. Are you bored yet?"

"Not at all," Jon replied, trying to manage the traffic jam heading out of LA.

"Shiji are the Records of the Grand Historian. It covered a twenty-five-hundred-year period and began with Sima Tan, also known as Taishi, the Grand Astrologer. Upon his death, this immense, almost overwhelming project was completed by his son, Sima Qian." An paused to lower her window and get a whiff of the fresh air.

"Ironically, the two known surviving fragments that predated the Tang the dynasty has been preserved at a temple in Otsu, Japan. Certain parts are just recordings of history, while others contain the evolution of ritual, music, the Chinese calendar, astronomy, sacrifices, rivers, and records of financial administration." An peered out her window to gather her thoughts.

"Most of Shiji refers to male rulers. One notorious and noteworthy woman who comes to mind is Empress Dowager Lu, her cruelty depicted in vivid detail. Ironically, she was able to bring peace and prosperity during her rule."

"Why Buddhism?" he asked, hitting the brakes as the traffic slowed to a grinding halt.

"Originally, Buddhism appealed to lower castes in China because it emphasized the path to enlightenment in the then-current life and was the great equalizer between the wealthy and the poor."

"Whatever happened to Sima Qian?" Jon inquired.

"He was sentenced to death. I've read in certain sources that a death sentence could be commuted by either a considerable sum of treasure or castration. Pity the person who was poor and couldn't pay." Jon and An both winced.

CHAPTER 12

PREVAILING KARMIC WINDS

March 2045

It was an idyllic experience for An to be in such a beautiful, peaceful place as Joshua Tree National Park, a place that she had been dreaming about for years. The remains of the great fires in 2020 and 2029 that took place in California. Charred trees that had yet to grow back dotted the landscape.

Jon stopped in Riverside to rent camping gear and stock up on food, water, and recycled toilet paper. The two weary travelers arrived at a campsite as the sun was setting and the moon was rising, a yin yang dichotomy of the solar system. Jon set up the two tents side by side.

An was chatting him up. "Did you know that the park encompasses more square miles than the state of Rhode Island? This is my kind of solitude," she cooed. "I love it. No cell service, water, electricity, street-lights, food service or lodging." There were toilets, but not the flushing kind. An didn't seem to care. "As long as I'm away from the far-reaching tentacles of the PRC, and I'm with you, I feel safe. Never felt like this before," she shared wistfully.

Although there was a palpable physical attraction between Jon and An, especially given what they had just been through together, he had no intention of being intimate with her. He refused to leverage that he had gotten her out of China and onto U.S. soil. Besides, his mother taught him how to treat a woman.

As Jon watched the silhouette of An strip down to her black silk panties and white sleeveless, low-necked t-shirt from inside his tent, his resolve weakened. An was so overcome with joy, anticipation, and pent-up energy from the journey that within ten minutes of saying good-night, she tiptoed into Jon's tent, unzipped the flap, and gazed at him. "I can't sleep."

He was lying on his back with his hands clasped behind his head, eyes wide open, locked onto An's toned body. Both were too exhausted to rest. She slipped casually into his sleeping bag. Jon hadn't held a naked woman in his arms for over two years, and immediately sensed her sexual readiness. They made uninhibited love in the shadowed silence of the night, and he couldn't tell if it lasted five minutes or two hours.

Time was irrelevant. It was a welcome release for him, although Jon felt conflicted about his feelings for Yael, who was fifteen years younger than An. He compartmentalized his emotions and decided to live in the moment now that the mission was over. *Who knows what tomorrow brings? And besides, I like what An has to offer,* he thought as An climbed on top of him.

In the middle of the second love-making interlude that night, An was looking down at Jon with wide-eyed innocence. While rocking back and forth, her fingertips lightly touching his chest, she moaned 'four mysterious words in Mandarin.' He grabbed her shoulders, pulled her close, and shuddered violently, climaxing like he'd never done before.

Jon was still inside of her when he smiled and asked, "What was it that you said in Chinese a few minutes ago, Mrs. Walker?"

He could 'feel' her blush from the question, almost too embarrassed to answer. "It means, I love fucking you." Jon was surprised by his reaction, as he broke into gut-wrenching laughter, with tears soon streaming down his face.

"What's so funny? I've never said those words before." She was taken aback as if she had discovered something new about herself. Jon recalled the wisdom uttered by Wolf's grandfather. *'It takes few words to tell the truth.'*

"I'm not sure. Just some raw emotion bubbling up to the surface, I guess. I just hope it doesn't get weird at sunrise tomorrow morning," Jon murmured in between uncontrollable bursts of laughter. "You know something? The longer I live and the more I know, the less I understand."

An assured him it wouldn't, as she hung on to the last words that Jon spoke to her. *The more I know, the less I understand. I wonder what that means?*

The next morning came earlier than sunrise. They had gotten no more than five hours of sleep between them and were still severely jetlagged. Jon was slightly uneasy, concerned if it would damage his relationship with Yael. The last thing he wanted was to follow in his father's footsteps.

Jon was immersed in self-talk. *Wait a second. It's not like I'm married or even engaged to Sol, and these were extenuating circumstances,* he rationalized. Yet he couldn't shake the idea that his body, agitated by the stressful conditions he had just experienced in Mongolia, would do things against his will, things that Jon wouldn't consider under more normal circumstances.

They spent three fabulous days and three sensual nights hiking and exploring the natural surroundings and each other. For Jon, it was like *déjà vu*, as if they'd been together in a past life. After Joshua Tree, Jon and An flew to Denver, and spent three relaxing days in Frisco, but something still nagged at him. He vividly recalled the night a shot was fired from the perimeter woods of his backyard. He felt exposed with An there and knew that she would be safe at Darwin's underground fortress. After expressing his feelings to An, they cut the trip short and headed to DIA, on their way to Houghton Airport.

Wolf met Jon and An at the Houghton airport. As they deplaned, An looked at the car parked on the tarmac and knew without a doubt that it was Jon's truck. Jon was relieved to see his buddy and be back in Porcupine National Forest. Walking toward the car, he gave Wolf a huge bear hug, practically lifting him off the ground.

An was a bit more reserved. "Hello, Wolf. Good to see you again."

"Hi, An. I've missed your energetic vibrations," Wolf responded.

They got into the car and Jon stared at his phone reviewing texts sent by Phillippe and Elena. He was scratching his head, with the realization that he had to be on the move early the next morning. *Won't this ever let up?* he shrugged. A part of him relished in the constant action as if he were becoming addicted to the adrenaline rush that traveling provided him.

Wolf and An were chatting in the front seat, as Jon brought their lively discussion to a grinding halt. "I hate to be a killjoy and end this banter, but I gotta prepare for a trip to Montreal tomorrow. I'm gonna take care of some unfinished business and help Sapphire figure out things with Court at the North American Water Symposium. I'm flying from Houghton to Montreal at 9 a.m, and hoping you can survive without me over the next couple of days," he winked. "Anyone interested in driving me to the airport in the morning? C'mon, don't everybody volunteer at once!" Jon said, shaking his head.

An feigned enthusiasm. "Well, I'd be happy to drive you, but I don't know my way around this area yet."

"Sure, I get it. You need your beauty rest. Not to mention my truck has a self-driving feature and GPS."

"Why don't you just leave your car at the airport," An asked naively.

"No can do." Then Jon glanced at Wolf. "I guess it's tag you're it, Wolf. Besides, you don't require as much sleep."

When it came to Darwin, the basic difference between the two leaders of F.O.R. was that Wolf viewed it more like a spiritual sanctuary, safe from the evil that existed in the world. Jon, on the other hand, put physical safety first and took solace in the notion that Darwin could withstand a direct hit from a Tomahawk missile. Unless Jon was traveling to Frisco from Darwin, each time he left his fortress of solitude he felt a bit unprotected. He couldn't verbalize the feeling. *Exposed?*

———

Phillippe and Elena were sitting at a table in the highly decorated lobby of the Hotel Le Germain in downtown Montreal. The same hotel where the annual North American Water Symposium was to take place over the next two days. For Elena, Phillipe was someone she trusted implicitly, being the conduit for her defection to Toronto. The Montreal conference was a steppingstone and a decoy.

It was 4:45p.m., an hour before the opening dinner would begin. Phillippe had ordered two Angry Canadians- a combination of Canadian Rye whiskey, bitters, club soda, and pure maple syrup instead of sugar, typically used in an Old Fashioned. It was quite popular in Canada and a pleasant surprise to Elana's veteran Vodka tastebuds.

"Court, I grew up on more good vodkas than you can count on both hands, but this is quite tasty. I may have to start getting used to this now that I'm turning the page to a new chapter in my life," she said quite cheerfully. Elena was in good spirits, and in more ways than one.

"Slow down," he whispered leaning over the table. "This conference will be your ticket out of Russia, but we still need to drive to Toronto. You know, get you situated and find you meaningful work."

"I guess you're right. Besides, I need to keep an eye out for Ivans who may be following me." Elena wheeled around instinctively just to make sure there was no one within earshot.

"Let's start with the basics of becoming a citizen and go from there, shall we? Keep in mind that Toronto is advocating for inclusion in the Great Lakes Nation, and we might have to finesse things a bit more."

Elena nodded as she took another sip of what was rapidly becoming her new favorite cocktail. Phillippe was citing chapter and verse about becoming a citizen.

"First, you must become a permanent resident. I own a two flat within three kilometers of my house, and I'm going to rent it to you free of charge until you can get on your feet. This way, you'll have a 'permanent' address when you fill out the forms and apply for citizenship."

"Bless you. One day I hope to repay you, eh?" she winked.

"I'm not doing this with the expectation of getting repaid. You are like family to me. Have you thought about a name change? I would suggest dyeing your hair a different color and changing glasses prior to taking a new driver's license picture. I also have friends who work in the visa department."

"That's great. When I landed in Paris, I changed planes and flew on Air France under an alias with a fake passport that Buck was able to secure for me. I booked a roundtrip flight back to Russia from Paris under my real name to make sure no one was going to check up on me or ask too many questions."

Phillippe was deep in thought. "What do you prefer as your new name? Perhaps we should ask Buck his opinion when he gets here later, eh?"

"Sounds like a plan. But Sapphire is going to stay with me no matter what my name will be." Phillippe smiled as they clinked glasses.

"Given that you are fluent in French and English, there shouldn't be any issue with getting you a work visa and on the path to citizenship. Your hydrology background and extensive research at Lake Baikal will be kept secret for a while. I'm hoping to get you a job in my department."

"Sounds good to me," Elena responded enthusiastically.

"And that's not all. To circumvent any skepticism that you are defecting from Russia, we will need to reinvent your background from either Minsk or Kyiv. This will be a way to leapfrog the process of getting into a Great Lakes Nation city without arousing any suspicions. There is one other way to get in front of the line."

"What's that?" she replied with a bit of skepticism.

"You can always marry a Canadian," Phillippe chuckled.

"Nyet. I refuse to marry for citizenship and plan to keep it that way. I have a numbered Swiss Bank account in Geneva that I plan on moving to BMO in the next few weeks. You know, before I change my name."

"Ah, there are my two Canadian representatives," Jon said enthusiastically, arms extended, strutting into the room with a grand entrance, as he made a beeline toward their table.

"Mind if I join you? I'm not interrupting anything, am I? I mean, I could fly back to Detroit and come back tomorrow," he said sarcastically.

"Good to see you've maintained that edgy wit of yours. In fact, we were just discussing Canadian citizenship. I told Sapphire she can stay at a flat I own in Toronto while she gets her sea legs under her."

"Why not the U.S.? I thought it would've been your top choice." Jon said as he grabbed a chair at their table.

"I decided against it for a couple of reasons. First, your politics is for shit and for a democracy, your government has been ineffective for decades. Second, it was too much of a hassle to immigrate to the States compared to Canada. Besides, I prefer Toronto, in city where I can use my French and English interchangeably."

"Sounds like you've got everything worked out. Seen any of our Russian friends floating around at the conference? Are there any other Russian scientists here besides you?"

"Actually, I'm not here at all," she winked. "As far as scientists go, I can identify just one. I know her, and she is benign when it comes to Russian politics. She is a pure researcher, and hydrology is what she's known for, specifically the Arctic Circle. The Russian Navy has used her occasionally for special projects."

"Wait? What? That's a bit troubling. Sapphire, what's her name? I want to run a full background check on her with my friend at Langley to make sure she won't cause us any issues, or anyone else seated at this table. After the Diaz fiasco, we can't be too careful."

"Her name is Dr. Yekaterina Volkov, but her friends and colleagues call her 'Kat'. Go ahead and check her out. I'm curious to see if you find anything."

Jon leaned over and took a whiff, almost putting his nose in Elena's cocktail. "Will do. What are we drinking here? It doesn't look like vodka."

"It's an Angry Canadian," she smirked. "Our friend just introduced me to it an hour ago."

"Jon, what's your current thinking about Chirkov?" Elena chided, trying to make idle conversation.

"Look," Jon snorted, trying to order a drink from the waiter. "Chirkov is sixty-two and still going strong. I think he's part cockroach and part octopus. Cockroaches can survive nuclear wars, and octopus can grow back tentacles after they've been severed."

Later that night, Jon received a full-blown report on 'Kat,' from Chip at Langley. It turned out that she wasn't exactly your ordinary scientist working as a hydrologist in Russia.

Jon revealed his finding later that night at dinner. "Her father had a decorated career with the Russian Armed Forces and was responsible for building Russia's three most recent naval bases in the Arctic region," Jon told Elena and Phillippe, who were huddled in his room booked under the alias Jack Walker. They discussed the logistics of 'how and when' Elena would be transported to Toronto.

"It looks like our friend Kat has been integrally involved with the plans to build the most recent two naval bases," Phillippe interjected. "As Trudeau, who at seventy-two and is one of the oldest Canadian prime ministers to hold office, said at a press conference two years ago, 'Russia's been breathing down our neck in our region in the Arctic Circle for more than a decade, and we need to take all necessary precautions to defend our territory and natural resources.'"

Phillippe began to take charge of Elena's real-time defection. "Sapphire, I'll drive you personally. So, everything is settled, eh?"

"I'll keep an eye on Kat and who she associates with during the conference," Jon added.

"Can you bug Kat's phone?" asked Elena.

"I think that might be a stretch. She carries it with her everywhere she goes, so probably not."

"I'm beat," Elena whispered. "Time to hit the sack."

"Me too," echoed Phillippe.

They left Jon's suite and headed back to their respective rooms. Earlier that evening, Jon had taught Elena and Phillippe the cell phone fingerprint ID trick. He had installed his own app that screened fingerprints on the doorknob of their respective hotel rooms. After scanning their own prints first, the phone camera would then scan the door each time they entered to check for inconsistencies. It was a brilliant strategy because the hotel staff wore gloves and left no fingerprints.

Elena arrived at her room first, scanned the doorknob, and immediately noticed the flashing red light on her phone, indicating her room had been violated. She panicked and started sprinting down the hallway toward the elevator just as she heard a door open behind her. She ran with purpose into the stairwell, down two floors, practically jumping a full flight of stairs at a time with the use of the handrails until she reached the second floor.

Elena was breathing heavily as she stumbled towards Jon's room and rapped loudly on his door with her bare knuckles. Jon answered, saw the look of panic on Elena's face, and pulled her in. He noticed beads of sweat running down her temples, merging under her throat, and continuing down her neckline.

"The scan?" he uttered, conserving his words. Elena rapidly shook her head up and down. He quickly grabbed an old Diablo 12-gauge pistol with a full-hand option from under his pillow. It was more of a traditional grip angle instead of a two-fingered one.

"What the fuck is that? You really are a cowboy, aren't you? You could kill a charging Rhino with that thing!" Elena said, still gasping for air.

"I prefer it for close range encounters, especially when there is more than one target. Can't miss." Jon made sure his Diablo was loaded. "Change of plans. We're leaving immediately for Toronto. Fuck the conference. The Russians are on to you. We need to get out of here! Call Phillippe and tell him to meet us in the lobby. No time to pack. Y'all just leave your gear here, and we can have a service deliver it to a hotel lobby in Toronto in case someone's following the van."

By a stroke of luck, Phillippe, a creature of habit, had gone down to the lobby for a nightcap before heading back up to his room. His phone began to vibrate on the table.

"Bonsoir, Sapphire. To what do I owe the pleasure?" he asked calmly.

"Court. We are leaving. Now. Stay right where you are, and we will meet you in three minutes. My doorknob print didn't sync. I imagine yours won't either. Why don't you call a driverless cab to take us all to a rental car facility in another part of town? Whoever is chasing us must've staked out your car. No sense in walking into a trap."

"Will do."

As Jon and Elena quietly entered the stairwell, they noticed a man standing near the door entrance slightly ajar, peaking into the lobby. Jon, with his handheld shotgun in tow, peered around the corner and saw the back of a rather large man in a trench coat screwing a silencer into the barrel of his gun. Before Jon could aim his Diablo at the intended target, Elena leaped over the railing and down a full flight of stairs, landing on top of the Russian with the full force of her body weight. The gun was jarred loose, sliding across the floor, barely out of reach. He groaned loudly upon impact, his head smashing into the cement floor. She quickly wrapped her powerful legs around the dazed Russian's neck and squeezed, cutting off his oxygen. His arms flailing, he pulled a stiletto from his pocket and made a vain attempt to stab Elena in the stomach but missed as she banged his head hard to the floor. The knife slipped out of his grasp as he took his last few breaths. She choked him out in less than thirty seconds while yelling, "Я хочу, чтобы вы это помнили, когда будете умирать."

Jon was watching the entire scene, as if in slow motion, walking purposefully down the stairs, his handheld shotgun aimed at the Russian's chest just in case he was able to free himself from Elena's python-like grip. Elena sprung up and they each carried one arm of the lifeless victim toward a utility closet and left him there for some unsuspecting housekeeper to find the next morning. Jon grabbed the dead man's gun, stuffing it into his coat.

Elena brushed back her hair and rearranged her clothes as if nothing had happened. She strolled into the lobby, making eye contact with Phillippe. They both nodded in unison, with Jon following close behind, searching the room with beady eyes for anyone who looked like an accomplice.

The car pulled up seconds later, and they were out the door and hopped into the driverless vehicle. "Sapphire, why didn't you let me take him out?" asked Jon.

"Two reasons. One, I figured it was better to not fire a gun in the hotel as that would have alarmed others that might be lurking around. And two, I wasn't sure how good your aim was with that portable cannon you were packing and was worried about being collateral damage from the shotgun spray."

"And just for my own edification, what were you screaming at him in Russian?" Phillippe was in the front, listening intently.

"'You were beaten by a woman. Die, motherfucker!' If this thug had tapped out, I might have let him live long enough for you to shoot him at close range." A smile formed around her lips, as she looked at Jon, batting her eyelashes.

Phillippe was in the front swirling his ice cubes in the glass he had inadvertently taken from the hotel bar. "Good thing I was thirsty and didn't head back to my room without a nightcap, eh?"

The driverless cab pulled up to the remote rental car agency on the west side of town. Phillippe rented a car under his alias, Etienne Tremblay, hoping it would cover his tracks. Jon stood outside the door, checking to see if they had been followed. He had given Phillippe his Diablo for protection, although Court wasn't sure what to do with it since he'd never fired one before. Jon was feeling emboldened, and if push came to shove, he would much prefer using his Glock compared to the weapon he carried in his tan trench coat pocket.

Jon dug into the details after they got in the rental car. Since Phillippe was the most familiar with the drive, he quickly got behind the wheel. "Think of it this way, Court. We have the edge because our enemy can't really see what you're holding, and we have the element of surprise. The bonus is one pull of the trigger could take out two people standing in the same vicinity of one another," he grinned.

"What's our Toronto ETA?" Jon asked. "It looks like ninety minutes. We're heading to my house. I'll call June on the way and make sure nothing unusual is going on, and let her know I'm on the way with a couple of passengers, eh?"

Jon felt relieved that he had smoked out Kat and her band of merry men, and managed to help Elena successfully navigate her defection without firing a shot. Jon's gun rested on the seat next to his right hand.

Jon's glasses showed Wolf's number calling. Jon answered promptly.

"How's it going up there north of the border, eh?" Wolf asked cheerily.

"*Comme ci, comme ca.* We just had a little incident at the hotel. Turns out Elena was being followed by some unfriendly Ivans, but we got out without so much as a scratch. They weren't as fortunate. Heading to Toronto now. Phillippe is driving us to his place. Should arrive in a couple of hours."

"Never a dull moment, eh, Buck?"

"Nope. Business as usual. We had to eliminate a Russian agent hanging around our hotel that had been tailing Elena all the way from Moscow. Elena took him out without firing a shot. All quiet at Darwin?"

"So far, so good. Sounds like I keep missing all the action. What was that?"

"I gotta go." *Click.* A black sedan had pulled up next to their car on the passenger side and fired a couple of stray bullets that hit the window. Instinctively, Jon and Elena both ducked as Jon grabbed the shotgun next to him.

"Court, hold her steady," Jon screamed. He opened the window halfway, took aim, and fired two shots, one at the front tire on the driver's side and the other at the driver's head.

"Got 'em." Jon stared out the rearview window, watching the anonymous black sedan veer across the three-lane highway. The driver was slumped over the wheel as the passenger struggled to move the list-less body out of the way. Jon's eyes followed the car as it hit the guard rail that separated the six-lane highway and flipped over three times before coming to an abrupt halt upside down. The car disappeared from Jon's field of vision.

Everyone was silent until Jon spoke. "One thing for sure. These guys don't quit. They're incorrigible."

CHAPTER 13

ACROSS THE POND

End of March 2045

They pulled into a quaint neighborhood, and the smell of lilacs permeated the car. After two left turns and a right, Phillippe pulled into the driveway and then his garage. After a harrowing journey, they had arrived safely, entering Phillippe's home through a narrow door in the garage. The house had an eighties look, decorated with all kinds of antiques, mostly elephants made of ivory and seashells of all shapes and colors. At the end of the hallway was a walnut brown, recently varnished grandfather's clock that was similar in height to Jon, positioned next to a powder blue bathroom.

June, Phillippe's second wife, greeted them in the kitchen. "What can I get you?" June asked. "How about a pot of hot tea?"

"Sure, just what the doctor prescribed," Jon replied.

"Anyone else?" she asked, looking in An's direction.

"How did y'all meet?" Jon asked inquisitively.

Phillippe responded first. "Well, that's a long story but suffice it to say that my first wife went to school with June's brother, and he introduced us six months after my first wife passed."

"I'm so sorry," An said, acknowledging the hardship that Phillippe had endured earlier in his life.

Jon slept restlessly, agitated by the chain of events that had occurred during the past twenty-four hours. The next morning, Jon and An said goodbye to their Canadian cohort, thanked June for her hospitality, and left to catch a flight back to Houghton, where Wolf was waiting to pick them up and transport them to Darwin, the impenetrable fortress where Jon could protect An from all her adversaries, both real and imagined.

The plane sat on the tarmac, hydrogen-powered engines running silently before take-off. Jon sat next to An in an aisle seat across from her, and he was feeling a faint sense of satisfaction that in ten days' time, he managed to blow up a pipeline in the Gobi, escape unharmed, spent three nights in Joshua Tree with An, disposed of a Russian entourage tailing An in Montreal, and get Elena and An out of their hostile countries of origin and safely into North America. He was certain that the job of keeping F.O.R. out of harm's way was far from over. *Not by a long shot.*

The next morning there was a scheduled hologram video call with all F.O.R. Jon and Wolf, and An were physically together at Darwin. They broke down the mission and brainstormed about what they could have done to improve upon execution of the plan. They all talked about how they would communicate going forward.

After the meeting concluded, Yael called Wolf and asked him why Jon was the ideal leader of F.O.R. "The truth is simple. Jon is a supernova and is about leaving the world a better, more secure and sustainable place. Every waking day, he seems to gather more force and momentum toward his quest. His mantra is just because things aren't our fault doesn't mean they aren't our responsibility."

She patiently waited for Wolf to finish, thanked him, and hung up. She decided to have some mint tea, relaxing in her condo looking out over the water of the Mediterranean. After taking the final sip of tea, she decided to make the same call to Jon. Yael thought she would get a more unbiased response if she asked them separately. "Wolf never met a room that he couldn't blow the roof off with his intellect and his almost limitless reservoir of spirituality. He has a tranquility about him, constantly firing on all cylinders, raising the games of others. In the end, he makes F.O.R. stronger and not dependent on any one person.

He is the ultimate leader intellectually, emotionally, and morally, but what he is best at is building ships," Jon told Yael.

"Ships?" Yael replied. "Whatever do you mean by that?"

"You know, relation*ships,* friend*ships,* and partner*ships.*"

After an exhausting three weeks, Jon was ecstatic to be back in his underground bungalow, especially during the winter months before spring, where he would be holed up somewhere anyway. He was sitting at his desk with An fast asleep in the next room. With eyes glazed over he sat staring at his fifty-inch touch screen. He was hell-bent on doing high-level research on Antarctica, a continent located at the epicenter of the next mission. He understood that the White Continent held eighty percent plus of the world's freshwater supply and housed glaciers the size of Rhode Island and Delaware.

Both Jon and Wolf were more concerned about the underground lakes and rivers than the mass of surface ice. He desperately needed help, an ally who had expertise. *But who?* Jon's mind churned during a listless night's sleep.

He awakened the next morning from his cell phone buzzing. It was 5 a.m. He groaned and reached for his phone. He bumped his head on the corner of the nightstand. "Ow, dammit." He suspected it might be Yael and reached again for the phone in the dark, knocking it off the table. He fell out of bed, hit the floor, grabbed the vibrating phone that was flashing a number he did not recognize.

"Hello. Sol?"

A man with a British accent was on the other end of the line. "Ello! I was wondering if you could help. I'm looking for a chap by the name of Jack Walker."

A puzzled look appeared on Jon's sleepy face.

"Who is this?" Jon asked in a brusque manner bordering on rudeness.

"I'm sorry, my good man. This is Dr. Michael Sinclair calling from Cambridge. It is urgent that I reach a Mr. Jack Walker."

"How did you get my number?" Before Sinclair could answer, Jon was bombarding him with more questions. "Who are you and who told you to call Jack Walker?" Jon wondered if it was some type of bait and switch tactic.

"Ah, yes indeed! A Miss Yael Solomon from Israel, who I met at a water conference in Tel Aviv last week. She thought I should speak to a Mr. Jack Walker. You see, I am the foremost expert in the world on Antarctica. I have spent much of my career at Cambridge doing research and traveling to and from the White Continent. If not there, then on Greenland where I purchased a home about twenty years ago. I have developed strong connections with certain higher-ups in the British Navy as well. Is this Mr. Walker by chance?"

Jon's brain clicked in. "Yes. I am Jack Walker. Pleased to meet you Dr. Sinclair. How can I help?"

"Jack, I can introduce you to some particularly important people in the British Navy who are longstanding relationships of mine. It will take me forty-eight hours to gain clearance for you, and then I could set up meetings for us, say Tuesday of next week. I realize this is rather short notice, but Miss Solomon spoke with a sense of urgency about the two of us meeting in London. She thought my background in nuclear and the newer mini-submarines might be of value."

"I see." That's all Jon needed to hear. His mind began to clear, wondering about booking a flight from Detroit to London when Sinclair interrupted his train of thought.

"Well, Jack. Shall we give it a go?"

"Sure, Dr. Sinclair. I will make plans to meet you in London as soon as we hang up. And who are the two people we will be meeting with next week?"

"Jack, you must trust me on this. I cannot share their names with you until you land, but I can assure you that this trip will be worth your while. Top secret business if you catch my drift. Will that be satisfactory for you?"

"I'll be there. Just tell me where and when."

"Send me your flight information, and I will meet you at Heathrow. Here's my private email address. Might I suggest that you may want to arrive the night before or no later than Tuesday morning at ten o'clock? We can knock off both meetings in three to four hours tops. The two meetings are a few kilometers away from each other, and we can take the tube."

"Great. I look forward to meeting you, Dr. Sinclair."

"Please. Call me Michael."

"Michael. There's one more thing?"

"What's that?"

"My actual name is Jon Oliver Buckingham."

He hung up and looked at An, who lay silent and still. Jon knew that this was an offer he couldn't refuse. He got up, tiptoed out of the room, and began looking for Wolf to tell him the good news. Jon found him meditating in the workout room and started jabbering before Wolf opened his eyes.

"Besides, Sol is now two for two with her introductions that yielded great benefits to F.O.R." *Speaking of Yael, I wonder why she didn't give me a heads up that Sinclair would be calling. It wasn't like her to drop the ball like that. At least an email or a text.*

An stirred, and was now half-awake. Rubbing her eyes gingerly, curiosity grabbed her by the throat. She walked out of the room to find Jon and heard him speaking with Wolf down the hall.

"Who was that calling at such an ungodly hour?"

"Some guy from London. Yael met him at a water conference in Israel a couple of weeks ago." Suddenly, Jon felt a surge of anxiety.

An took one look at Jon and sensed something was wrong. "What's the matter? You don't look right."

Why didn't she call to give me a heads up? Jon wondered. "Sol. I think she's in trouble. Can you call her and make sure she's okay?"

"Maybe you're just exhausted from the travel back and forth through multiple time zones. If I phone her up right now, will you promise to go back to sleep and get some rest?"

"Deal."

"I'll be in after I reach her," An said in a motherly tone. She grabbed her cell phone, strode down the hall, and shut the door behind her.

Jon went back to the bedroom and flopped on his pillow. An speed-dialed Yale. No answer. She tried again. Still nothing. An assumed that Yael was out for a jog along the promenade overlooking the Mediterranean. *But she normally takes her phone with her,* she wondered.

It was 1:30 p.m. in Tel Aviv. Yael stared out her bedroom window, watching the bright sun fluorescing the azure-colored water. Her windows were open, and she was listening to the steady waves caressing the shore while thinking about Jon living twenty feet underground in a bunker that held Wolf, An, and him like a cradle in the Upper Peninsula of Michigan. She felt a tinge of envy, wishing she could trade places with An.

Jon was more than six thousand miles away, yet Yael could feel his arms wrapped around her, as if they were connected by a silver, ethereal cord from Jon's soul to hers. She felt Jon's presence.

Every Friday afternoon at 1:30 p.m. her mother's call arrived like clockwork from Jerusalem. On this day, Yael focused the conversation on her new beau. "*Ima*, he's like a thunderbolt. He is intelligent, powerful, focused, funny, warm, and vulnerable all at the same time. When we are together, he puts me at ease.

Sometimes it feels like we met in a past life, and our souls have been connected for centuries. I feel a certain unconditional love from him, nothing like I've ever felt before," she crooned.

"Is he Jewish?"

"Not exactly, although his great-grandmother on his mother's side was Jewish until she converted."

"Oh, I see," she said, her voice trailing off with slight disappointment. Their conversation always ended with 'I love you' and 'Shabbat Shalom' exchanges. *It could be a lot worse*, she thought to herself smiling. She went back to her bedroom for her daily yoga stretches. Minutes later there was a knock at her door. She was alarmed by knuckles wrapping on the entrance to her abode.

Who would be knocking on my door on Friday afternoon? Maybe it's Jon? she asked rhetorically, as she reflexively grabbed her Beretta M1951 pistol from underneath her pillow. *Nope, Jon would have told me he was coming and not taken the risk that I wouldn't be home.* Yael went from calm to high alert in a split second. Her military training had prepared her for anything at any time. She heard footsteps and voices speaking in

Russian outside the front door of her first-floor condo nestled between two others on either side.

A second series of knocks, only louder, almost banging. The other male was trying to look in the window, one that's view was blocked off by thick blue curtains. Yael, adrenaline flowing everywhere through her taut body, got down on all fours and crawled out of her bedroom behind her couch into the kitchen. She could hear her cell phone buzzing against her antique nightstand. *Shit. Left my phone. Oh well.* She slowly rose to her knees, using her hands to pull herself up onto the kitchen sink, peering with her eyes to identify her unwelcomed guests. Her right hand firmly gripped the pistol.

She noticed a black BMW sedan parked on the street, and with her peripheral vision, saw two strange, anonymous men standing by her front door, weapons drawn. She cocked her semi-automatic pistol but quickly decided against a firefight in broad daylight. She was outnumbered, and the intruders had automatic weapons. Blood rushed to her ears. She started crawling toward the garage military style and feebly tried to repress the panic spreading like cancer inside her, trying to nurse some calm from her IDF training.

I knew I should've taken the third-floor condo. Too fuckin' expensive. I wonder if they think I'm home, and that's why they knocked? Damn. She covered her mouth. *It can't be. One of them looks exactly like the guy that Jon and I took down at the restaurant in Tel Aviv a few days before we met in Be'er Sheva.* She heard her phone buzz a second time, clicked her glasses, and saw that it was An.

She heard him speak Russian to his accomplice, but couldn't quite make out what they were saying. *I never forget the face of a thug. Or a voice, for that matter.* Underneath the sink, she reached down and pressed the silent alarm button wired directly to the Lev Ha'ir police station a few blocks north. Yael held her breath, quietly opened the door to her garage, and crawled in. She pulled back the carpet just off the entrance to her door, lifted the ring attached to a large piece of tile, shut the garage door behind her, and climbed backwards down the stairs into a fifteen-meter tunnel that flowed into an empty park across the street. There she would be safe and out of the line of fire.

As she gently closed the hinge to her secret passageway, Yael heard the front door being bashed in by the unwelcome intruders. Before being out of earshot, one of them had entered her home. Her sacred space had been violated. It took her thirty seconds to crawl out to the tunnel's exit. She turned the latch and gradually pushed open the door covered by real grass. As she started to climb out, there were sirens blaring from two police cars screeching around the corner and figured the Russians would be distracted.

Assuming that no one was home, the weapon-toting thugs were caught by surprise. One of them, overflowing with false bravado, raised his SKS/Simonov self-loading carbine and opened fire on the Israeli police car that had pulled up ten feet behind the BMW. Yael mouthed the words *big mistake*, as the second police car opened fire on the BMV, flattening two of its tires facing the street. One of the men panicked and started to run. Yael was watching this unfold as the man hit the concrete sidewalk holding his left leg with both hands, bloodied by a gunshot wound from an exploding bullet.

Good shot, she said under her breath. The thug's accomplice was crouched down behind a stone wall four feet to the left of her front door, a wall that had already deflected several bullets. After seeing his comrade taken down by the Israeli police, he immediately raised his machine gun and his free hand.

"Drop your weapon."

"Don't shoot. Hold your fire. I come out to surrender," he said, as he threw down his semi-automatic on Yael's manicured front lawn in front of her mangled front door. Three Uzis were now pointed in the direction of the defeated Russian agent, and a fourth officer was running with a pistol in hand to handcuff the downed attacker.

Most of the neighborhood were standing outside their doors, watching the scene unfold. Soon an ambulance siren blaring could be heard around the corner, as it pulled up behind the police car. Two people got out, lifted the handcuffed man off the street, and carried him to the back of the ambulance. The ambulance pulled away, headed for the nearest ER.

Yael surveyed the scene, and started walking back towards her house, shouting in Hebrew, "My name is Yael Solomon. This is my home, and I am the one who pressed the silent alarm. Thank you for your help, officers. These are the same Russian thugs that confronted me and my friends in a restaurant last month. They must have been following me, and as you can see, are heavily armed. I am a water researcher and scientist down in Sde Boker. They may have been attempting to steal state secrets."

The lead police officer happened to be fluent in Russian and Hebrew.

"Thank you, officer," said Yael in Russian.

"Yael, I am Officer Lebedev. Are you OK? You must be shaken up, but I do need you to come down to the station and answer a few questions," he responded in a heavy Russian accent. Knowing he was of Russian descent, Yael looked at him, and responded back in Russian.

"Officer. I'm happy to comply. Should I follow you in my car or can I get a lift to the station?"

Upon taking a second look at Yael wearing yoga pants and a tight-fitting peach tank top, Lebedev responded, "I'll drive you. Hop in, and then we'll have someone take you back. I'm assuming that given the condition of your front door that you have little interest in staying here tonight. One of my men will be patrolling the area through tomorrow morning to make sure there are no other stragglers hanging around. It should give you time to get your door replaced."

Yael loved Israeli security and police. They were so thorough and made her feel safe, not like in other countries. It was not a fair comparison given how many Israeli citizens went through the IDF, but that was not Yael's concern.

The questioning lasted forty minutes. Most of it involved the tussle Yael got into at the restaurant bar in Tel Aviv, and why she didn't report it that very night. "I was with some colleagues during my last encounter with these assholes." She desperately wanted to keep F.O.R. anonymous and off the map while speaking to the police because they had used a military base for the taking-off point.

"I turned them over to security at the restaurant and hoped that they'd take care of it. Not sure what happened after we left."

By the time she finished it was 4:30 p.m., and Yael decided to check into a local hotel right near the beach. Her adrenaline was running like a wild stallion. She phoned Jon. His soothing Southern drawl was the exact medicine she needed to quell her anxieties.

"Sol, I'm so sorry that happened, and hope you're safe," Jon said in a concerned tone. "I 'sensed' something was wrong but thought we'd gotten rid of those cowboys."

"For a second, I got excited because I thought it was you at my front door surprising me, but I guess it wasn't meant to be."

"Hey. Sinclair called this morning. He told me that you sent him. Is that correct?" Jon asked hesitantly.

"Yeah. My gut told me he could help the cause."

"Well, most important is that you're safe. Now that I realize what you just went through, I wish I was there. Call later when you get settled. I'd like to find out more details about what happened. I realize you're tough and resilient, but that kind of surprise would scare the tail off a peacock."

Jon walked back into the kitchen where An was helping herself to some oatmeal topped with almonds and walnuts. "I have some news. Remember the two Russians at the bar in Tel Aviv?" Jon asked An.

"How could I forget?"

"Well, they just showed up on Sol's doorstep about two hours ago. They were toting automatic weapons and busted down her door. Fortunately, Sol had a silent alarm in place that went straight to the police, then escaped through an underground tunnel that the former owner had built."

"That's awful. Is she OK?"

"Yup. Sol's tougher than an ornery wolverine." Jon spoke with a false aura of confidence. Inwardly, he was afraid of Yael being so far away, that he was unable to protect her from the random dirtbags roaming about Tel Aviv. Powerlessness was a newfound emotion for Jon. He had never cared enough for someone like Yael, apart from his own mother.

CHAPTER 14

LONDON BRIDGES

March 2045

As promised, Sinclair met Jon at Heathrow in a private car, where they were driven to Cambridge for their first meeting. During their shared car ride, Jon pumped Sinclair for information about the people he was about to meet.

"Jon, I have arranged meetings with Admiral David Brown, head of the British Navy, and Dr. Calvin Foerster, a dear friend who knows more about submarine warfare than anyone in all of Europe." Jon was speechless. *Perhaps I underestimated Sinclair's connections. He under-promised and over-delivered.*

"Dr. Sinclair, is there anything I should know about the Admiral? Like his approach, his pet peeves, anything?"

"Nothing to be concerned about. I have gained the Admiral's trust over the past thirty years, and well before he was an admiral. Let's just say that he is sort of a buttoned-up chap. He doesn't leave anything to chance, assumes nothing, and tries to de-risk a military threat or mission as much as humanly possible."

Focused on the next mission, Jon shifted the conversation and was soon picking Sinclair's brain about the annual average ice melts in Antarctica.

"Before I answer your question, allow me to begin with the Arctic region, including Greenland, and work my way south. Except for the northern half of Greenland, the thin ice shield covering most of the Arctic Ocean to the mile-thick mantle of the polar ice sheets, ice losses had almost doubled from about 760 billion tons per year in the 1990s to more than 1.35 trillion tons annually in the past decade. That is an increase of more than sixty percent, equating to twenty-eight trillion tons of melted ice in total."

"What's your prognosis?"

"Simply put, roughly 1.2 trillion tons of ice have melted a year for the last twenty years. More troubling, methane gas underneath the frozen tundra now exposed due to climate change has been leaking into the atmosphere," Sinclair spouted with perfect recall. "To date, Arctic ice has declined 87% from where it was seventy years ago."

"That is off the charts."

"Agreed. The bad news is that there is good reason to believe that the rate of melting will continue to accelerate until it all turns into seawater. Also, a 2039 NASA-backed study on the Greenland ice sheet found that no less than fifty percent of major glaciers that terminate in deep, warming ocean waters have been severely compromised. These statistics are from a new study that my colleagues and I recently published in the Journal of Polar Science Advances."

"It's like the Ice Age in reverse," Jon belted out.

"Indeed. The United Nations Intergovernmental Panel on Climate Change (IPCC) found that ice sheets could drive as much as ten meters of rising sea levels in the next fifty years. All that ice lost on our fragile planet correlates to a direct decrease in freshwater that currently exists as ice today."

"Can you please explain what that means?"

"I'll give it a go. The single largest total is some 7.6 trillion tons and is a result of the melting of the floating ice cover of the Arctic Ocean. They don't necessarily raise sea levels. Nor do the 6.5 trillion tons subtracted from Antarctic ice shelves. Those were already afloat. What raises sea levels? If all the ice in Greenland melted, it would raise sea levels by twenty feet or more."

"That's 14.3 trillion tons of ice, a number I have a hard time wrapping my head around. It's almost inconceivable."

"It appears that the Good Lord gave us an ample supply of freshwater in the form of ice that we have squandered due to neglect and arrogance. And I would be remiss if I didn't point out that between Greenland and Antarctica, ninety-four percent of all the planet's freshwater still sits in frozen form. The two ice masses combined have lost 6.3 trillion tons since 1994, and estimates are that it could lose another trillion tons in the next five to ten years."

"Not good. And I'm sure you're aware that during the same period, the world's mountainous glaciers collectively have lost over six trillion tons of ice. They've contributed to rising sea levels as well."

"I'm curious. Where did you get that information from?" a dubious Sinclair inquired, given any good scientist would verify first and then trust.

"From someone I know at Columbia University's Lamont-Doherty Earth Observatory who's an expert in glacier ice that's melted and continues to melt."

"Alas, it's not too late to save Greenland, in particular, because the Chinese have been rebuffed by Denmark to commence mining rare earth minerals there. They did let Canada and a select handful of US firms begin the mining process about twenty years ago. Greenland and Denmark finally relented because the annual tax revenue for the government plus a plethora of local jobs is producing over $300 million annual tax revenue. Not too shabby when you consider that Greenland's total population is a mere 200,000."

"At least China's not stealing the minerals like they're doing with the subglacial lake water from Antarctica."

Sinclair sat in stunned silence before he spoke. "What did you say? How could they possibly be stealing water from Antarctica when there's two-hundred meters of solid ice covering the surface? That's preposterous."

"My hunch is that China is going from the bottom up, and not from the top down. Since we are opening our kimonos, I have glaciologist contacts at both UC-Irvine and NASA's Jet Propulsion Laboratory. They utilize hundreds of satellites as well as instruments deployed by aircraft and ships, revealing the shape of the land under the ice. Over three hundred glaciers have terminated in the sea over the past two decades. Currently, estimates are that more than five hundred subglacial lakes exist underneath Antarctica's surface."

The driver tapped the brakes and pulled up to the entrance of their first meeting. "I just hope that the West Antarctic ice sheet doesn't suffer a similar fate in the near future," Jon said with a tenor of worry in his voice. "Or we're in cow manure up to our necks."

"Let's continue this conversation later, and focus on the meetings at hand, shall we?"

Jon gave Sinclair an imperceptible nod as they both exited the car from different sides. For the first time, he got a full view of Sinclair and observed he was tall and lanky with silver hair mixed with light brown patches under his derby. Sinclair had a long, deliberate gait and appeared to be quite formal, except for his dry British humor that occasionally escaped his lips.

As they approached the doors to what appeared on the outside to be an ordinary building, Jon was mesmerized by what Sinclair had managed to pull off with two days' notice. The property possessed an immaculately cured landscape that surrounded the stone structure.

What Jon discovered upon passing through security was nothing short of eye-opening. They were met outside the first-floor entrance by four British naval guards. Every office was constructed with 3/4-inch-thick bulletproof glass. A second layer of security met them on the third floor, stationed outside of Brown's office, the size of a presidential hotel suite. It was museum quality and decorated with all sorts of awards, medals, and military paraphernalia.

"Come in," the admiral said in a stern voice followed by a firm hand-shake. Two armed guards remained in the meeting room with holstered firearms, sitting in the back just out of earshot. Admiral Brown, Sinclair, and Jon were sitting in the corner in old English leather chairs at a small-lacquered coffee table, where they were conversing back and forth. Jon was awestruck about being in the presence with the likes of Brown.

He and Sinclair were getting schooled in submarine robotics and next-gen technology. The British Navy had spent 3.1 billion pounds on a nuclear-powered behemoth machine that could stay underneath the surface for six months at a time, and thus avoid both satellite and intermittent sonar detection.

Admiral David Brown continued spouting confidential information about U.S., German, Chinese, and Russian submarine technologies. "First things first, gentlemen. The number one priority for all nations' naval superiority is the ability to be stealth. Next, in order of importance are range, mobility, endurance, payload, and last, but not least, survivability. Submarines of the future will need to be flexible with the ability to be reconfigured, both internally and regarding off-board vehicles, sensors, weapons including laser functionality, and robotics. All those 'toys' will be able to manage deep-sea construction and demolition.

"Admiral, if I may sir. You obviously know about the project just completed by the US Navy for seabed warfare. After the cost overruns, it came in at $5.3 billion. But did you know this vessel is able to deploy mini-subs and drones at crushing depths? Now that they are working on the second and third ones, it has become a great neutralizer to China's push to control the seven seas."

"I'm well aware of the submarine but didn't know about the mini-sub deployment capabilities. But let's call it what it is. Insurance that the pipes on the ocean floor, responsible for sensitive financial transaction, energy needs, and more than 95% of global internet communications, are well-protected from sabotage. And that a few hundred cables carry all that traffic, making it an unstable and unsustainable system."

"And that doesn't include all the AI used by the NATO navies, especially the nuclear subs," Jon added.

The admiral cleared his throat as a prelude to changing the subject. "There is something else I'd like to discuss, a sort of fly in the ointment, if you will," the Admiral bellowed. Jon and Sinclair leaned forward on the edge of their chairs.

"What's that, David?" Sinclair asked, gingerly.

"Our intelligence has gotten wind that a Chilean or Brazilian double agent who'd been supplying information to the Russians and ultimately the Chinese about the whereabouts of some rogue independent team that was operating as an unaffiliated international unit. In exchange for those services, the Kremlin was handsomely paying him. I believe he'd been given asylum, and his wife and children are already living in Russia. A palatial estate was provided by Chirkov himself somewhere in the Ural Mountain region."

Brown paused to allow for questions. He eyed Sinclair first and then Jon, whose head looked like it had just spun around. "What's wrong, Jon? You look like you've just seen a ghost!" said the Admiral.

Jon was stuck, reliving his own nightmare, as if he'd just taken a large dose of psilocybin. His mind immediately went directly to the Gobi jump.

Diaz again? That fuckin', no good son-of-a-bitch is like a bad penny. He'd been two-timing the U.S., and he was ratting us out to the Russians and the Chinese. I hope to God that he didn't hand over any information about Angie. I guess it doesn't matter much now. She's safely tucked away at Darwin with Wolf.

Or is she? If I tell her what I've learned, but then I'd be violating the confidentiality of the British Navy. Shit! What in hell's name am I supposed to do? Maybe I should listen to Wolf and just let it all go. Once again, the idea of protecting someone he cared about was drifting in like a Frisco Bay fog. Jon's conscience was being torn to shreds.

Brown's commanding voice snapped him back to reality. "Jon, you look a bit pasty. Shall we take a break or are you ready to continue?" Brown remarked.

Sinclair jumped in to rescue his new friend. "How about some water or tea? Might be jet lag." Sinclair needed to make a good first impression on Brown.

"Green tea would be excellent. Admiral, may I speak freely here?"

"Of course. The only way we're going to help each other succeed is by being transparent. We are in a safe space here." The admiral was a persistent note-taker who had a pen in hand and began scribbling on an iPad scrubbed by the British intelligence daily.

"Admiral, I can shed some light on the spy of whom you speak, someone with whom I've had personal contact. It's my belief that he was working for the Russians, who were handing off information to the Chinese. Apparently, he became an academic pariah and had been pulled into political opprobrium due to a personal financial crisis caused by reckless gambling. It's not like the Russians stuffed cash into a bazooka and just blasted it at him. He walked into the abyss of chaos in exchange for nothing more than a measly twenty-five million Rubles. Apparently, it crowded out whatever amount of integrity he had left."

"All that risk for less than 300,000 British pounds? How could you possibly know that much detail?" the Admiral queried with a stunned look on his face.

"It's a long story, but I do have the inside track. Let's just say that he lost his mind to paranoia and his ability to differentiate between right and wrong to greed. Just a walking tragedy, an accident waiting to happen. Either way, he is permanently incapacitated due to a series of mini-strokes and will not be trouble for anyone in the future. Admiral Brown, I'd like to ask you one last question, if I may sir?"

"Fire away. Ask me anything you want. I will try to answer to the best of my abilities."

"What would you say if I told you there might be escalating submarine activity as we speak in the Antarctic region of the Southern Ocean that might capitulate into a WWIII scenario in the next eighteen months, and possibly sooner? If this scenario grows beyond a skirmish, it's going to result in a naval battle between Russia, the U.S., and China, the likes of which have never been seen. It may draw the British Navy into the fray. And ultimately it will be a face-off between democracy and totalitarianism."

Brown suddenly lost his poker face. "My good man, let me begin by saying that would be a disaster of epic proportions. It would not only require the redirection of enormous military resources. It would be a damning blow for the delicate ecosphere of Antarctica as well as the entire balance of the planet. Overnight, it would set the Paris Climate Accord pact back three decades."

"How bad do you think it could get, David?" Sinclair jumped in.

Brown responded with measured words. "I'd say we could be looking at a prelude to a longer-term Armageddon scenario, like all hell breaking loose. The reason is that NATO is not equipped to defend anyone from the sea, particularly as remote as the Southern Ocean and Antarctica. A region that holds over eighty-five percent of the world's freshwater supply coupled with a potential for a dramatic rise in the sea levels across the globe could not only destroy coastlines and envelop entire islands but threaten the last bastion of freshwater on earth."

Brown looked at the antique clock on the wall to his left. "It would be human nature at its worst, a devastating free-for-all in a region that up until now has been pristine, preserved for millions of years. He peered at his visitors with grave concern. Is there something you're not telling me?" the Admiral demanded.

Jon and Sinclair looked at each other, and then at Brown. Jon spoke first. "There's nothing definitive to say at the present time," Jon confided. "It's between a hunch and a conspiracy theory of mine that I'm struggling with to either confirm or deny. The sooner I get to the bottom of things, the better. The big problem is the lack of intel on the Russian and Chinese submarine fleets south of New Zealand in proximity to 90 degrees south."

Jon paused, took a couple of sips of lukewarm green tea, and continued. "And it has everything to do with the world's waning freshwater supplies. As we all know, a gallon of bottled tap water surpassed the cost of a gallon of petrol over a quarter of a century ago, and there are no refining costs involved in water like there are with oil. The Russians and Chinese are in pursuit of something far greater than monetary value. Based on recent history, they will stop at nothing to secure water. China's very survival as a dominant superpower depends upon it."

"Go on," Brown said, unlit pipe in hand, adjusting himself in his brown leather chair.

"Admiral, all things point to China meddling in the subglacial lakes of Antarctica with Russia aiding and abetting. Especially with the consistent saber-rattling Russia had been doing in Greenland, Iceland, and the Arctic region of Canada. The only saving grace for Greenland has been Thule Air Force Base in the north. I know that the U.S. Air Force and Navy have bolstered their manpower and radar surveillance up there."

"Interesting data points, my friend."

"We all know that there are military and shipping advantages to exploitation of new sea lanes within the Arctic Circle, including the potential for increased sourcing of seafood. Part of my theory is that the military activity in the Arctic is nothing more than a distraction, a decoy giving China the maneuverability and the proxy to exploit the planet's last untouched resource of real significance and ameliorate their ongoing water deficit. Russia would be a direct beneficiary from the water. You know, by protecting and running interference for the Chinese submarine fleet, acting as a smokescreen against Western navies in the Arctic."

With an audible groan, Brown leaned back in his chair, and grabbed his lighter lying on the mahogany table. Immediately, he lit up, taking a few puffs. He swallowed hard, trying hard to maintain a neutral expression. Jon and Sinclair noticed the Admiral's flabbergasted face turning a bright shade of red as if his blood pressure was rising in real-time.

"I've heard quite enough. Here's God's honest truth. The British Navy is perhaps the fourth most powerful unit of its kind on earth, and at this moment we are not prepared for a battle that is over fourteen thousand kilometers from our shores. We are focused on the Arctic region, including Greenland. I'm going to check with my commanders in the Royal Navy Submarine Service later tonight to see if they know of any Russian or PRC submarine activity off the eastern and southern coasts of New Zealand and Antarctica."

Brown paused, took a deliberate drag from his pipe, and continued. "The head commander is Commodore James Parks, who I've known since our time together at the Submarine School at HMS Raleigh at Torpoint in Cornwall. I happen to know that one of our more advanced subs has been deployed to southeastern Australia and has been roaming around the southern coast of New Zealand for over a month now. This is highly classified information, I may add."

"What class sub is it?" Sinclair asked of his friend and trusted confidante.

"It is an Astute-Class S123 Attack Submarine, launched in 2033. It became fully operational six years later, all five billion British pounds of it, and that was only for construction materials, and labor. That number doesn't include fuel, manpower, and annual maintenance. We should make good use of it and start getting a return on our investment, don't you agree, Michael?" Brown chided.

"Sir, I couldn't agree more."

The Admiral looked in Jon's direction, as he took one final puff from his hand-carved ivory pipe. "Gentlemen, as you both know, this conversation is of the utmost confidentiality, and if the contents of this meeting were to get out of this room it could cause a global panic beginning in Western Europe and ending God knows where. Do you follow?"

Brown took for granted that Jon's relationship with Sinclair was airtight but like all good highly-trained and experienced military he had to prepare for a worst-case scenario. Jon appeared to be credible and trustworthy, but the Admiral knew better than to rely on his gut. He sensed that Jon held back some important details earlier in the meeting.

"Of course, Admiral," Jon responded without hesitation, nodding away.

"Jon, if you have any close contacts in the U.S. Navy, I suggest you start there and do some digging."

"I already have, sir!" Jon said with the utmost respect, looking at Brown.

The Admiral hesitated, relit his pipe for a third time, and went on. Even with the ceiling air filters drawing the smoke skyward, Jon had the onset of a headache.

"Splendid. I also know that Chirkov and company have put a stake in the ground and have diverted a significant amount of capital and resources toward improving his submarine fleet, particularly in the category of theater antisubmarine warfare. We are monitoring him quite closely, I may add."

"One final question, Admiral, if I may. What do you know of the mini subs being developed for military use in the last decade? Any thoughts you could share would be much appreciated." Jon wanted to seize the opportunity to gather as much data as he could to finalize the construction of F.O.R. 's mini-sub in an anonymous industrial warehouse in Denver, a submarine that was due for a test launch within three months.

"The last time I checked, our navy was using mini-subs for research and exploration only, but I will be happy to investigate it further, both with respect to the British Navy and other foreign navies."

"That would be greatly appreciated," Jon responded enthusiastically.

Brown pulled out a sterling silver antique timepiece from his vest pocket, and then proclaimed, "You'll have to excuse me, gentlemen. I have a conference call with the Prime Minister and our joint chiefs of staff in forty-five minutes. Need to do some final preparation and apologize for cutting our meeting short. Hopefully, I've given you enough to stew on for the time being."

He stood up, extending his wrinkled hand. Jon, thank you for coming all this way, and if I can answer any questions in the foreseeable future, please don't hesitate to contact me. Here's my direct number."

Brown handed Jon a business card he took out of his drawer, a card that was the same color as his namesake with a private number on the back. Jon, in his tailored navy-blue suit and paisley tie, took the card and placed it in his pocket

"Thank you, Admiral. I'm eternally grateful for all your help and wisdom. As you can appreciate, our cause is of the utmost importance for the Western world and for the future of our planet. Once I find out more about the Russian fleet capabilities and their current technology as it pertains to Antarctica, I will revert back to you. My inclination is that China will take a bit longer to research. It goes without saying that this needs to be a collaborative effort for all of us to succeed," Jon said, as he shook hands with Admiral Brown.

———

Jon turned and walked out the door just a few steps in front of Sinclair, waiting outside by the elevator banks. As Jon looked back over his shoulder, he saw Sinclair say something to Brown, who was nodding his head in approval.

"This Buckingham seems like a bright lad and a level-headed bloke. I also checked on his Seal background and verified the sale of his drone company," the Admiral whispered to Sinclair, who then saluted the Admiral and joined Jon at the elevator bank. The door dinged, they stepped in, and Jon hit 'L'. A few seconds later, the door slid open to the main floor, a lobby so dull it reminded Jon of a bank lobby with no customers in it. After they departed, Jon seized his opportunity to discuss F.O.R. with Sinclair.

"I've got an 11 p.m. flight out of Heathrow to Detroit later tonight. How about dinner? It will give us an opportunity to download our meeting with the Admiral. I can't thank you enough for making it happen, especially on such short notice. Also, I'd like to continue the conversation about what my intentions are in the next six to nine-month time frame." Jon was hoping for a 'yes' answer so that he would have the opportunity in person to invite Sinclair to join the F.O.R. team.

"Certainly. Let's discuss your ideas over dinner and see where the conversation takes us. Why don't we meet at Simpson's in the Strand at around 6:30 p.m. sharp? Figure we'll have ninety minutes to eat dinner and chat, and then it's thirty minutes to Heathrow, leaving you about ninety minutes before the flight. You're in my town and I'm buying! Let's not discuss any sensitive topics on the tube to Calvert's office. It's only a couple of stops away. You never know who may be within earshot if you know what I mean."

As they left the lobby, they took a left turn and walked a kilometer towards a park that led to the tube station. Sinclair turned to Jon and spoke to him in earnest.

"Cal spent the better part of three decades in the British Navy and was a renowned world 'expert' on submarine fleets, including the Russian and Chinese fleets. Jon nodded, listening intently. *How can I begin to repay Sinclair for introductions to people that I would never be able to access on my own?* he wondered as they strolled casually through the peaceful park setting.

"You know the chap whom you mentioned to Brown identified as the double agent? If I may, I'd like to share something with you that I learned the hard way in my earlier days. Vengeance can have a long shelf life, but not anger. Anger lingers, then dissipates inside you. Vengeance not only clouds your thinking, but it can also destroy your physical health if it festers too long. You need to shed it, like a snake molting its skin. Does that make sense? I hope I'm not butting into places where my advice is not welcome."

If I didn't know any better, I might think I'm getting one of Wolf's lectures, Jon thought to himself.

"Not at all. I appreciate the advice, especially coming from someone like yourself. I want to surround myself with people who aren't afraid to call me out on something. So, all good and..."

Suddenly, gunshots rang out as bullets hit the trees they were walking between, causing chips of wood and bark to spray randomly through the air. Instinctively, Jon hit the ground, holding his left shoulder, writhing in pain.

"Michael, get down!" he screamed as he drew his Glock with his right hand.

"You're hit!" Jon's thick brown, sweat-filled hair bounced in the breeze.

"It's just a graze. Call the Admiral immediately and tell him where we are. Ask him to send help. And hurry. Whoever these guys are, they're serious, and don't think they are planning on taking any prisoners."

People were running through the park screaming, scattering like ants as if their mound of sand and dirt had just been kicked over. About two-hundred meters south, there were two Asian men in black coats. One was holding a QBB-95 5.8mm machine gun, the other waiving a QSZ-92, a semi-automatic pistol, barking commands in Mandarin. He signaled his man to move forward with a wave of his weapon. Although Jon couldn't lay eyes on his newfound enemy, he could hear them, and knew instantly they were Chinese. He fired a few shots in their general vicinity to keep them at bay.

Crouched behind an interspersed patch of thick sycamores, Jon and Sinclair knew they were severely compromised, wondering how they were going to fend off their intruders.

"Michael, if we try to make a run for it, we're as good as dead." Sinclair was breathing heavily, having become frail and out of shape from all his hours doing research behind a desk and sitting on airplanes. Mostly to and from Antarctica, and to a lesser extent, Greenland. But his hearing and eyesight were still exceptional.

Through Jon's audible panting, Sinclair heard helicopter rotors approaching from the north. Before he could say a word, bullets from a sniper leaning slightly out of the chopper came raining down out of the gray London sky. The two Chinese were cut down instantly, never realizing what hit them. They died a quick, efficient death.

The helicopter landed in an open area about fifty meters from Jon and Michael. They scurried to the chopper as two naval pilots and one gunner exited. Jon was still holding his left shoulder, bleeding ever so slightly through his shirt and onto the interior of his suit jacket.

"Thank you for your service," Sinclair said, extending his right hand to one of the pilots.

"You're quite welcome, sir. Is your companion hurt? Looks like he's been hit. We can airlift you both to a nearby hospital if need be."

Jon waved them off and looked at the marksman. "Just a flesh wound is all. Appreciate your concern. I'm still standing because you are an excellent shot. Man, you nailed those guys like splitting a log."

Jon turned, walking hurriedly towards the two slain Asians, who were lying face down. He searched them but found no identification. He kneeled, holding his hand on their necks, trying to find a pulse, but they had taken their last breath minutes earlier. As he turned them over on their stomachs, he happened to notice they both had the same distinguishable marks on the right side of their necks just behind the ear lobe. One of them had blood trickling from the corner of his mouth onto his chin. *Clean shot. Went clear through the back of his skull out of his mouth. The last thing he tasted was his own blood. The man was erased like a sandcastle on the beach at high tide.*

He rose slowly, confiscated the two weapons, and headed back toward the Admiral's helicopter, blades still churning in the cold, misty air. Jon addressed the sniper, still holding his rifle.

"I thought you might like the weapons they used. Maybe y'all can identify the source." He handed both weapons to the sharpshooter. As Jon's adrenaline wore off, pain followed quickly. Agonizing, knife-twisting, deep. Jon was in agony but hid his wounds convincingly.

A chic black, bullet-proof armored SUV screeched around the corner, a stone's throw from the whirring blades of the temporarily grounded helicopter. A man in a black suit and white shirt emerged, engine still running. Sinclair recognized the man as the Admiral's personal driver. A smile of relief appeared on Sinclair's face.

"Dr. Sinclair. Good to see you again. How can I help?" The driver addressed the two men now standing in front of him.

"Alan, this is Jack Walker." They shook hands. "Could you be so kind as to give us a lift to London? We were heading for the tube on the way to our second meeting, but since we were rudely interrupted, that's not going to happen," Sinclair said in a loud voice, unaware of adrenaline coursing through his veins.

"It would be my pleasure, sir. Hop in and I'll take you wherever you need to go. There are a couple of bottles of Hildon in the fridge, and a bottle of the Admiral's favorite Scotch inside the leather-paneled door. Help yourself." The driver, sitting in the right front seat, put the fifteen-year-old, bullet-proof Rolls Royce SUV in first gear. The engine hummed as the driver pulled forward with his left hand on the stick shift, his right hand on the wheel.

Jon turned to Sinclair, wincing, sweat dripping from his brow.

"Now the Chinese are on to us too? Dammit! This is not good! I think I'll take that scotch and a bottle of water now. You best call Calvin and alert him to what happened."

"Capital idea," Sinclair responded. He examined the bottle of Glenmorangie 18 Single Malt Signet, and opened the cap. He took a whiff, smiled, tipped the bottle, and proceeded to pour a scotch for Jon.

For Sinclair, the gunfire was a shot of reality that pervaded his psyche. What Sinclair kept hidden from view was his deep-seated fear of death, privately tormented by the guttural fear that affected everyone else. He was always surprised by how effortlessly everybody else suppressed their fear of death. The loud crossfire of guns blazing in the park was as close as he wanted to get, but the surprise attack had brought mortality closer like a deafening roar. The Scotch would help settle his nerves, but not his mind. He poured himself a shot and tossed it down his throat.

Sometimes I wish that I could outthink death, he thought. *My emotional insulation stripped away like ripped up old carpeting. I always understood death as a reality but instances like this bring it uncomfortably closer. It's the finality of it all. And this is how it happens. Death makes its entrance, risks camouflaged. Some are temporarily spared while others are cut down, never to see the dawn of the next morning's sunrise. It's the pure randomness of it all that befuddles me.*

Jon knew instinctively that you can't manipulate death for any length of time. Reality eventually replaces delusion, a passage he'd gone through many times before.

"What's Hildon anyway? Never heard of it," Jon inquired, a welcomed relief that broke Sinclair's mortal train of thought.

"Hildon is Britain's finest natural mineral water and is typically reserved for places like the House of Commons, Buckingham Palace, and the Royal Opera House. It begins as rainwater in the chalk hills of Hampshire countryside. It takes almost fifty years for the water to seep through to an underground aquifer underneath the Hildon Estate built in the 1800s."

"I get it. The chalk acts like a natural filter, giving the water higher than normal levels of calcium and shielding it from pollution."

"It is also bottled without any chemical treatment process, and in case you're interested, contains low levels of sodium. Cheers, Jon!" Their glasses clinked. "You still up for a good meal?"

"I sure as shit am. I'm hungrier than a grizzly comin' out of hibernation!"

"Let's get you back to the hotel and get you cleaned up and packed. Then, Christopher will drive us to the restaurant and you to the airport when we've finished. I'm not letting you take any public transportation for what's left of your stay in London. Call it British hospitality." Jon grinned and nodded in approval.

They arrived at the restaurant on time and were seated immediately at a table in the corner reserved for Dr. Sinclair. Dinner was both remarkable and satisfying. Hand-carved meat was served from a silver-domed cart with built-in heating underneath. The waiter donned a white jacket, in a black tie with black pants, and served them glazed carrots, potatoes, and green beans almondine. The fine dining experience at a posh London restaurant was a reward of sorts for what they endured in the past several hours.

"Would you mind telling me more about your theories of Russia's military presence in the Arctic as a decoy for ulterior motives in Antarctica?"

"Certainly. In my estimation, Russia is doing an end-around in the Arctic to get to Antarctica, and it has nothing to do with establishing military superiority. It is about helping China capture as much of the existing freshwater as they can to use as leverage in the long run, and as a long-term source for bargaining and food production. Of course, Russia will have access to all the water that China pipes back to the mainland in exchange for watching over the PRC."

Sinclair motioned Jon to continue.

"I can only imagine that once they have satisfied their countries' demands, Chirkov and Xi will hold other countries hostage for an absurd profit, bringing governments to their knees like choirboys in church. Take Africa for example. You know as well as I do that unlike oil, water is mostly about life, death, and power as opposed to commerce, transportation, and manufacturing, especially since the world has progressed with hydrogen, and the by-product is water."

Toward the end of dinner, Jon became cognizant of why he was there, and even with his flesh wound, possessed the presence of mind to pitch the F.O.R. idea to Sinclair. He cleared his throat and took a sip of water.

"I was wondering if I could share with you in confidence what I've been doing for the last twelve months, and then jointly determine whether you would want to be part of our team on a go-forward basis." Jon had finally exposed the elephant in the room, but the elephant was more like a blue whale.

"Exactly what team are you referring to?"

"We call ourselves F.O.R., or Forces of Rationality."

"Interesting name. I'm all ears. You've got me as a captive audience during the next hour, so be careful what you wish FOR," Sinclair bellowed with laughter following his play on words. By the time they finished dessert, and the check came, Sinclair had agreed to become an official member of F.O.R.

Minutes before boarding his plane back to Detroit, Jon phoned the Admiral's personal cell number to thank him for saving his life. "Glad to be of service. It's damn good fortune that we met before the incident, so I was able to get you out of a pinch. Kind of fortuitous, don't you agree?"

"I couldn't agree more, Admiral, but I still owe you one."

CHAPTER 15

FOLLOW THE RUBLE

April 2045

Back at Darwin Jon slept on and off for a couple of days, and then tirelessly went back to work on planning F.O.R.'s next mission. It was Tuesday night, and he knew the upcoming journey was going to take longer so he planned accordingly. More complex, more expensive, and more dangerous. A mini-submarine armed with next-generation laser technology and weaponry.

Jon would need it completed and tested in another three months, a tall order. He and his crack engineering team had been working on it for over two years in an anonymous warehouse somewhere in east Denver. They had started planning and construction eighteen months before the Mongolian mission ever took place. Only Jon and Wolf knew of its location and its status.

In high school, Jon used to read about da Vinci in his free time and study his sketches and drawings of prototypes for the future. He loved to pontificate about da Vinci. *This guy created the invention of a submerged warship, or what was a precursor to today's submarine. He called his invention 'a ship to sink another ship.' Amazing stuff. When he wasn't painting the Mona Lisa, he drew sketches of helicopters, parachutes, gliders, automobiles, machine guns, tanks, and more. He was clairvoyant, and a true Renaissance man. He even locked his drawings in a safe, hidden from view because he thought that war was already too violent. He took precautions to prevent his inventions from falling into the wrong hands.*

"What did you and your engineers model your mini-sub after? I'm assuming you didn't reinvent the wheel here?" asked Sinclair, who phoned in from his Cambridge office and research facility.

"We took the NR-2, the US Navy's mini nuclear-powered sub developed in the early 30s. The NR-1 built in the late 1960s was first but very obsolete. The main difference between the NR-1 and the NR-2 was that the 2 could hover at 7500 feet below sea level, while the NR-1 could not go deeper than 4500 feet. Ours is equipped with two lightweight high-speed torpedoes and countermeasures with an outer shell so strong that it could withstand attacks from other subs and UUVs. And here's the kicker. It can descend comfortably to 9,000 feet."

An strolled around the corner to engage in the conversation she'd overheard. "What have you discovered about the balance of power in submarine warfare between Russia and the U.S. Navy?" she asked.

"It looks like this. The U.S. now has the USS South Dakota, the latest Virginia class sub, commissioned in February of 2034. The navy now has thirty-one, with a goal of forty-six total commissioned by 2049. It sounds like overkill and way too redundant. It's like throwing money down the torpedo tube. Besides, the greater the nuclear sub-arms race between Russia, China, and the U.S., the more likely things will end badly."

This piqued An's curiosity. "Any idea how much each of those babies cost to build from bow to stern?"

"They're not cheap, that's for sure. The last cost estimates were $3.25 billion in 2033 for the latest class of U.S. submarine. And that doesn't include the cost of operating and maintaining them. Here's what's disturbing. I've been reading the minutes from the U.S. House of Representatives, Committee on Armed Services, Seapower, and Strategic and Critical Materials Subcommittee Research & Development, and it ain't pretty."

"How's that?"

Jon clicked on his glasses twice and printed out a couple of pages of minutes from the wireless printer twenty feet away. "Check this out, and I quote: 'Collectively, not only do the Russians have more stealth subs, they also have the fastest ones. This is due to their vessels possessing the highest power density because of liquid-cooled metal reactors. They also have the deepest diving subs as well as the hardest to sink. And non-magnetic subs are constructed from titanium, and they are loaded with the largest SSBN and SSGNs.'"

"What about the U.S. capabilities?" Jon held up his index finger and continued reading. "'The U.S. has the safest, quietest subs, and the best overall.'"

This was written by one of the admirals in the U.S. Navy: "'Our navy still maintains certain advantages and has been pursuing a strategy using composite materials that yield a six to one improvement in strength to weight capacity. They also managed to develop an eight-fold payload increase for a submarine of that size. Combined with our stealth superiority, we're still the global leader. If my son were in the Navy based on a submarine, I would want him on a U.S. submarine. They are still the safest and most capable with the best technology that exists in the seven seas.'"

An crossed her arms, shifting her weight from one foot to the other. "Either way, I don't know about China, but it sounds like the Russians are more of a legitimate threat."

"I suggested to Admiral Brown that they are in cahoots with the Chinese protecting their subs from attacks by the Western world, namely the U.S., England, and Germany," Jon stated. "I know they have first-strike capabilities."

Wolf quietly pondered the subject. "What about China's takeover of North Korea, making them the dominant player in the submarine race? Must have been a helluva sales job by Chirkov to convince China that the whole Mongolia incident was just vicious rumors, don't you think?"

"I'd say so."

"If I could sum it up in one sentence, it's this. Russia now has fourteen naval bases in the Arctic Circle. I told Sinclair and Admiral Brown that this seemed like a gigantic head fake in that NATO and the U.S.

consistently spend time and resources preparing to defend against Russian submarines, particularly the Arctic Circle and mid-Atlantic Regions."

Jon pressed An. "Say, I was wondering if you have 'friends' back in your lab who could provide us with some intel on Chinese submarine technology, especially underwater drones. I'd like to understand how developed they are with the ability to suck water out of subglacial lakes and reservoirs in Antarctica, and how far along they are in building a pipeline that eventually reaches China."

Earlier that evening, Wolf left to visit his mother, who had come down with the virus of the month. Jon was in a deep REM cycle when An walked into the room and shook him violently.

"Jon. Wake up. What's that beeping noise?"

"What?" Jon snapped with irritation in his voice. He looked at his watch. "It's three in the frickin' morning. Shit, that's the alarm going off. Must be intruders. These systems don't lie! Get dressed. Now."

"Couldn't it have been a moose that set it off?" Angie asked innocently, pulling on her wool socks.

"Not a chance. Follow me to the control room," Jon said, putting on his hiking boots, untied.

As Jon sat down in front of four giant screens, he flipped on one of the camera switches facing north. Nothing. A similar result occurred as he activated the south and east-facing cameras. Still shaking his head in disbelief, Jon switched on the west-facing camera.

"What the...? It can't be." Jon exclaimed. The approaching five thermal figures glowing on screen from the heat sensors were within five hundred meters of the entrance and closing fast. Visible beads of sweat had formed on Jon's forehead. An was perfectly still, standing behind Jon, peering at the screens.

"It looks like they're carrying the same plastic explosives that we used in Mongolia," she suggested. Her heart pounded.

"We could wait this one out, and try the gas, but it looks like they learned their lesson and have gas masks on," Jon said calmly, until he noticed two more commandos standing right near his trustworthy, bullet-proof Tesla Cyber Stealth, resting ninety meters west of Darwin.

"What about drones?" An whispered in quiet desperation. Jon was totally focused and seemingly ignored her, thinking about the worst case.

"Damn. How'd they find the bunker and my jeep at the same time?" he asked rhetorically with a slight panic in his voice. "The odds are infinitesimal unless someone tipped them off to our whereabouts. We can wait it out or ..." Jon stopped in mid-sentence.

"Or what?" An pleaded, waiting for Jon to complete his thought.

"You know what? Everyone has a plan until they get punched in the mouth." He tapped his glasses and dictated a text to Wolf over their secure intranet. Jon wanted to see if Wolf was close enough to help them. Jon was prepared to initiate Plan B until he got a text back from Wolf within seconds of sending his. Help was on the way. Both he and Wolf had remote warning systems on their smartphones that would alert them of intruders, even if they were miles from Darwin.

I'll meet you at the east escape hatch in exactly eleven minutes. Get moving!' Jon read the text out loud so An could hear it.

"There are two armed guerillas standing within meters of my truck, and another five are almost right on top of us," Jon texted feverishly.

In times of stress, Wolf was the man of few words.

"Trust me." Based on experience, whenever Wolf used that phrase, it was a lock. Jon knew he could count on Wolf to be there at the exact time he indicated.

'See you in ten. Angie is with me.'

Jon grabbed two camouflage, bullet-proof vests from the closet, and tossed one in An's direction. He grabbed his fake passport and disguise, and a couple of infrared flashlights that could blind the enemy at short range. Seconds later, they were both waddling like ducks on land through the tunnel, heading toward the escape hatch.

Based on his precise calculations, they would be at the exit about forty-five seconds before Wolf's ETA and would wait for his signal. It was brisk in the unheated tunnel, but in the excitement, they were feeling the heat from their own bodies, fueled by adrenaline.

Jon sent one last text to Wolf that said *'launch'* indicating that they were directly under the main exit. Wolf knew that meant Jon and An were on the ladder, waiting on the top steps, crouched down with their heads slightly bent. Jon's hand was on the latch button, waiting for a signal from Wolf. He could hear An's labored breathing right underneath him. Seconds later, they heard gunfire and what sounded like a heavy vehicle vibrating a few feet above them.

Wolf texted back, *All clear. Let's get it on.* Jon pressed the button firmly, and the submarine-like hatch opened. They climbed out, and the hatch closed behind them within seconds. Jon looked around for Wolf's vehicle. He knew it had to be within a few meters of where they were standing. Even though the lights were off, Jon could feel the vibrations of the electric engine running. He wheeled around, putting on his prescription NVGs.

"What the fuck is this?" Jon uttered with a smirk on his face.

Wolf had his window slightly cracked open, and yelled, "That look on your face is the pain in my ass. Stop messing around and get in unless you're tired of living," Wolf grinned.

Jon couldn't believe his own eyes. Wolf was driving an old Mansory fashioned after the Mercedes G63. It was pitch black with smoked windows and came with international standard VPAM 7-protection. In 2035 it was the top-of-the-line penetrator-resistant vehicle able to withstand roadside explosives. The wheels were protected by an armored plating that Jon hadn't seen since his days of Seal training.

An followed Jon as they dove into the back seat through the rear right door. Jon was laughing, rubbing the last remnants of sleep from his eyes, as he stared at Wolf in disbelief. An was sitting stoically, unsure how to process it all. Wolf punched the accelerator. She stared out the window observing the landscape of Copper Harbor streaking by. There was a full moon, the first green blush of spring.

"I've seen you do some crazy, wild ass things, but this is truly fucked up. Where on earth did you get this tank, and how did you manage to pay for it?"

They heard gunfire crackling against the rear windshield, housed in one-inch bullet proof glass. Wolf pulled a lever, instantly transforming the vehicle into an 875-horsepower destroyer. The car lurched forward in overdrive.

Although the vehicle he controlled with his hands weighed in at just under three tons, it seemed to float along the forest road as if he were canoeing on a placid Lake Cloud. Wolf was driving like he hadn't a care in the universe, gliding along at a speed that belied his calm demeanor.

"It was a series of coincidences. Couple of years ago, I did a side job for an ex-military contractor, and he hit some hard times due to an unexpected divorce. He couldn't pay me in cash and offered me this thing in exchange for construction services. This one-man-army vehicle cost $1.40 million new ten years ago. He owed me about $135,000 and I took the car in lieu of cash and didn't even have to pay taxes. Not bad, eh?"

"How come you never told me about it? This piece of metal has more in common with a tank than it does any road vehicle with four tires. Nice goin'."

"Whoever was shooting at us is now out of range and we're out of sight," Wolf laughed. "I bet they didn't see this thing coming. No time to deploy the anti-tank missile decoy when I hit the overdrive button. Too many trees."

An giggled in response to Wolf's sense of humor, knowing that they were safe for the moment. Wolf was heading due north in the direction of the lake where Jon's seaplane rested comfortably in a hangar. Jon started to wonder if the plane was in one piece, or if the terrorists had found it and there was a surprise ambush waiting for them. The fact that he had only flown once in the dead of winter and never at night, weighed heavily on his mind.

"Wolf! Do you think our friends who we just left in a pile of dust came by boat, plane, or car?" Jon asked.

"How should I know, and what difference does it make? The immediate issue is what we do now. Take the plane or keep on driving?" asked Wolf, his eyes on the rearview mirror, looking at the silhouettes of Jon and An glued to the back seat. Wolf tapped the brake pedal, slowing down enough that his two passengers could feel the car decelerate. Wolf's Arctic-colored blue eye was now gazing at what lied ahead, but Jon already had a plan B and C in his mind.

"Let's drive up toward the ridge that overlooks the harbor where the float plane is docked to make sure everything is copacetic."

"Can you please stop using those big, fancy words? I know you have two PhDs from prestigious universities, but you don't need to impress anyone," Wolf said laughing so hard he almost drove off the side of the road.

"Keep your eyes straight ahead for chrissakes. I don't wanna die in this contraption with you behind the wheel." They drove another ten minutes to the top of a ridge as Jon broke the quiet.

"You never answered my question. How come you never told me about this thing?" Jon bared his teeth with the shimmering moon spreading its light among the pine trees.

Wolf, his handsome chiseled face, shrugged his shoulders. "I don't know. Just never felt like it was that important at the time and figured one day it might come in handy. Looks like I was right." Wolf deliberately pulled over to the side of the road, as its deep tire treads dug into the loose gravel. He turned off the headlights, and they exited the beast on four wheels, a mutant compared to other SUVs. The road was lined with pine trees on either side. Wolf had adeptly parallel-parked in between two trees, six feet off the winding road, and far enough back where a stray car's headlights couldn't see Wolf's Masonry.

Wolf pressed Jon's NVG Zeiss 20x60 T*S to his forehead as if he was looking through the beady eyes of an owl in the dead of night. He took a breath and exhaled, expelling a visible mist. A sudden gust of bitter wind from Lake Superior, whipping up pine needles resting on the forest floor. Like nettles, they stung the hands and faces of three vigilantes standing like mirages in the night. The Zeiss binoculars were powerful enough that anyone using them could read the date of a quarter on a picnic bench two hundred yards away. Wolf was a startled like a horse by a copperhead from what he saw. Jon promptly snatched them from Wolf. "I don't like it. Not one bit."

"What's the matter?" Wolf said, pointing to the float plane with words painted *Last Chance* on the side facing them. It was outside the hangar, floating listlessly on Lake Superior.

"Check out the little gift fastened to the underbelly of the plane. These jokers obviously found our ride, assumed it might be our escape route, and that I'd be in a hurry and overlook the bomb they fastened underneath my plane."

"Sorry to disappoint, guys, but your plan is not happening. That's strike two," Jon delivered sarcastically.

Wolf stared into the sharpened lenses. After no more than five seconds, he located the vehicle-borne improvised explosive device. "Can you tell where the explosives originated from?"

"Looks like the kind they would use in the Middle East. Probably Russian."

"Let me see," An said, as she caustically yanked the binoculars from Jon's neck. She whispered loud enough for all to hear.

"That's trouble with a capital T. I know that incendiary device, and I can see some Chinese characters inscribed on the side!"

"So much for my theory it's the Russians," Jon responded, shaking his head. "Who knows? Maybe it was Russians using the latest and greatest in Chinese explosive devices. The silver lining is that they may outnumber us, but we have superior technology on our side."

Seconds later, Jon pulled out another phone that doubled as a portable drone device and activated it. Loathe to kill anyone, he preferred to take them as prisoners and interrogate them. He was unsure how many of them were floating around Superior's shores and figured his uninvited guests would be able to escape the same way they got in. Jon acted decisively, and half a minute later, his self-constructed drone zeroed in on the enemy and was spraying 22-caliber bullets. Jon watched as two of the intruders raised their machine guns to fire at the approaching drones, but the darkness put them at an extreme disadvantage. "Got two of 'em!" he shouted as if he was dominating a video game.

He activated a second drone that soon eliminated another set of soldiers. It almost felt too easy, perhaps a bit unfair, like using a high-powered rifle with a scope to kill a deer a half mile away. But Jon was in no mood for fair play.

"Four down, two to go. Wait! It looks like the other two are in a pickup truck heading northwest toward Copper Harbor. Wolf, what should we do?"

"Well, the last thing you want is some huge explosion if you decide to incinerate their car, so I'd let them be."

"No," An jumped in, imposing her will on her two male companions.

"Take them out. They need to be eliminated. I'll explain later."

Not ten seconds had passed when Jon activated a third drone loaded with AI and heavy-duty weapons. It could fire small, lightweight missiles that could penetrate two inches of armored steel.

"More than enough to stop those bastards in their tracks," Jon said under his breath. Seconds later, they heard an explosion that could be seen along the perimeter of the lake, bursting flames lighting up the dreary night sky.

"Got 'em all!" The three exhaled in relief, hoping the excitement was over.

"Bravo! Good to see that our drones stood the test of time," said Wolf.

Jon had a gut feeling there were more out there than the six he'd just taken out. "Call your men and ask them to take care of the bodies and the car. And let 'em know that there may be others lurking around the premises."

"Nevertheless, the bombed-out vehicle is going to be a tall order," said Wolf, as he punched in an automated private number on his cell phone.

They got back in Wolf's armored truck, and Jon was in command behind the wheel. There was a tug of war going on between the left and right sides of Jon's brain whether they were going to head back to the bunker or leave the area entirely. His internal debate ended abruptly. Returning to the bunker was not an option.

"Probably came through Canada into Michigan if I had to guess," Jon mumbled loud enough for his companions to hear him.

"Does it really matter? What's the plan?" Wolf asked calmly.

"Have you called in your cleanup crew to dispose of the trash?"

"One step ahead of you. I already gave them a head's up. Just called to have them clean up our backyard. My guys should be on the scene shortly."

By the time Wolf's men arrived, the four bullet-ridden, blood-soaked men motionless, scattered in various positions. It was just a matter of time before their bodies would be laid to rest in the bowels of icy Lake Superior, weights attached to them so they would not float to the surface. His men disposed of the six-seater and its charred remains at a local junkyard owned by one of Wolf's cousins.

"Do you think there's any others?"

"Anything's possible. My sense is there were more of them stationed around the perimeter so they could activate the bomb under the plane wirelessly with a regular smartphone. Either way, I'm not taking any chances. If the plane is still in one piece when we get back, all the better. I just paid my insurance premium for the year, and not concerned about it."

"May need to find another location or maybe build a shed in a different place to hide the plane from the bad guys just in case there's a next time. Can't be too careful these days." Wolf's voice trailed off, and the car was enveloped in silence for the next few minutes, as Jon streaked around one winding curve after another. It continually tore at his pride and trusting nature that someone had leaked information of the whereabouts of the bunker, the one safe place where Jon and Wolf had been conducting their proprietary, high-level research.

Am I blinded by inherent trust? What if Wolf misread one of his own men? Jon thought, recoiling at the idea percolating in his mind.

"An. Let's have it. Why the decision to kill those guys rather than capture and interrogate them? You must have your reasons."

"I did speak to my friend in China, and he confirmed that there is a rogue group of Russians and Chinese operating out of Lisbon. I think it's gotta be them. They have an alternative to cyanide they'd ingest before being captured alive."

An deferred to Wolf. "I'm sure Wolf knows more than me because he's the local, in-house nature boy," she snickered. "It's a combination of the seeds of two plants. First, the seeds from castor plants. One seed has enough ricin to take a life within minutes. The other is referred to as the suicide tree, *Cerbera Odollam* in Latin. Its seeds contain a strong toxin named cerberin, a compound that disrupts the rhythm of the heart. The reason for its wide use is its taste can be masked by spicy food. Either way, the two in combination have a deadly 100% kill rate."

"Thanks for the tutorial. All you did was raise my paranoid meter."

Jon had already decided that he was going to have his friend Chip at Langley contact the Canadian border patrol to identify Russian and Chinese infiltrators. He was heading southeast toward his friend Denny's pad on a remote lake three miles up the road. Jon called him and was about to test his new relationship in a big way.

CHAPTER 16

FRIENDS WITH BENEFITS

March 2045

"Hello?" Jon spoke, staring at his glasses driving Wolf's getaway tank.

"Denny here. Is that you, Buck? To what do I owe the distinct displeasure of a call in the middle of the goddamn night?" Denny chuckled. Jon knew that Denny was awake at all hours.

"Yeah, it's me. I was wondering if you could do me a big-time favor. I need you to fly me and two of my colleagues to MSP International. I mean the closest lake to the airport and drop us off. I know it's a big request, and I'll explain later, but there is a big sense of urgency here."

"Is that it?" Denny was now bellowing with laughter. "Talk about dropping a bomb. But, for you, no problem. I've been looking for an excuse to fly my new plane at night anyway," he howled.

"Great. We'll be there in thirteen minutes. Thanks, Denny. I almost forgot. One more thing. I was wondering if I could leave the vehicle I'm driving in your garage while we're away. Shouldn't be more than three or four days."

"You got it, my friend. See you when you get here. Don't be late. Otherwise, I'll have to start worrying about you." Denny hung up and shook his head of graying hair for agreeing to such a crazy stunt on short notice. He went directly to his refrigerator, where he always kept a spare cup of iced coffee for situations like this. Then he went around back to top off the tank of his new Viking Twin Otter Series 900 hydrogen-powered seaplane that would take him there and back. Denny had painted the name *Sweet Ride* on the tail of his plane.

Wolf was in the back seat of his military-grade vehicle booking three one-way tickets to Denver. "We're all set. Mr. and Mrs. Jack Walker have seats together," he exclaimed. "At least on the one-way to Colorado."

Jon made a sharp left turn into Denny's driveway, throwing Wolf against the back door on the passenger side. The garage was already open with an empty spot on the right side. Jon pulled in and tapped the brakes. Denny was outside on his front porch watching and couldn't believe the size of the hunk of machinery that had just turned into his driveway. Wolf's SUV fit neatly into his oversized garage with about three inches to spare.

The team got out as Denny stared at the truck. "That's the largest goddamn thing on two axles I've ever laid my sorry eyes on. Where in hell's name did you get it?"

"It's Wolf's, and it's a long story. He'll tell you on the way to MSP."

"Deal. Follow me, guys. My plane is in the back. I just bought it a couple of months ago, and she's a real beauty," Denny stated proudly. "This flying machine holds 8-10 comfortably and tops out at just over two hundred mph. She was manufactured in Victoria, British Columbia, and has a range of 800 kilometers. Its price tag is not for the faint of heart, coming in at $2.2 million Canadian. I can justify the cost 'cause I run that damn pain-in-the-ass passenger business during the summer months to and from Isle Royale. I can depreciate it for tax purposes."

The three tired evangelists followed him around his two-story A-frame, composed of cedar with brick covering the front and back patios. The height and the width of the house conveniently blocked the view of his flying gem. As they turned the corner, Jon took one look at Denny's toy as his jaw hit the ground. "You weren't kidding, were you? This is magnificent."

"Stop your drooling and get in. I thought you were in a hurry. It's about two hours and thirty-five minutes of airtime to Flying Cloud Airport. I'll land on the adjacent lake, and from there you can catch ground transportation to MSP."

"I prefer a human driver, and I believe there's a few still floating around the Twin Cities."

"That's accurate. Let me see. This time at night it shouldn't take longer than twenty-five minutes by car. What time's your flight, Buck?"

"Departs at 6:30 a.m." The last thing Jon heard before nodding off was Denny's command. "Ladies and gentlemen, fasten your seatbelts. We're ready for take-off," as Denny pulled the choke a couple of times and fired up the hydrogen-fueled engine. It purred as he came around and took off from the lake nestled between his house and the woods of Porcupine Mountain. Everyone was asleep except Wolf. He was always on high alert, even when flying above the clouds. It was ingrained in his DNA.

Aside from a few wind pockets, the flight was artfully smooth. Denny landed gently on Flying Cloud Lake exactly two hours and thirty-one minutes after take-off. *Four minutes ahead of schedule, thanks to the slight tailwind. Not bad. Maybe I should charge 'em extra.* He pulled the plane around, idled it, and docked at a local diner to refill his coffee mug, the one that read *Denny's Air.*

"Denny, I can't thank you enough. What do I owe you?"

"You don't owe me nothin' except a tip for getting you here ahead of schedule. How about some help refurbishing and enlarging the dock in my backyard? I'll need you and your friend for three to four hours one afternoon, and then we're square. Sound good?"

"Done. Best deal I've gotten in a long time. Happy to help. I'll let you know when we're headed back into town. Should be early next week. Fly safe!"

"You, too." Denny waved to them as they walked off the dimly lit dock fifty paces from the parking lot where an UberLyft driver in an electric black Toyota was waiting patiently for them, engine barely audible.

"Are you Jon?" inquired the brown-skinned female with an African dialect rolling off her tongue.

"Yes, I am. And you must be Aaliyah?" Jon asked politely as he got into the front seat. "I'm surprised there are still UberLyft drivers around with all of the self-driving cars up here."

"I am indeed. Yes, I am one of the fortunate few who has survived the job carnage created by self-driving vehicles. Let's get you folks to the airport. ETA is twenty-three minutes. If you're thirsty, I have some glass water bottles in the cooler. Minnesota's finest, filtered from Lake Superior. Help yourselves!"

Jon took a sip of the cold, clear water. "Aah, that's damn good." He remembered something that Yael and he had talked about back in Sde Boker. *Aliyah* was the Hebrew word used to describe Jews who emigrated to Israel from other countries to obtain citizenship. The literal translation in English was *'the act of going up, and elevating oneself spiritually.'*

His lips curved into a smile, daydreaming about the time with Yael on the beach overlooking the Mediterranean in Tel Aviv. Minutes later they arrived at MSP Airport. The car came to a gradual halt.

"Thank you, Aliyah. Great name by the way."

"I think so too. Safe travels." He felt good vibes from Aliyah and give her a generous tip. Wolf was feeling something much deeper. *She feels strangely familiar, as if I knew her in a past life,* he thought.

As they got out of the car, Jon felt a tinge of remorse about killing the men back at Darwin, the same men that were trying to kill or kidnap them. As they walked into the terminal, Jon's conscience started down a negative spiral, but remembered a quote from George Eliot that Sinclair had told him at dinner in London. *"The important work of moving the world forward does not wait to be done by perfect men."*

Jon sighed and found his way to An and Wolf, who were already seated in the lounge where their plane would board. It was 4:50 a.m., and there was nobody in the airport, save a few TSA folks, and some robots that were multitasking between security and cleaning duties.

An gazed at Jon's tired face. "So, what were you going to do if Denny wasn't around and unable to fly us here?"

"That's a reasonable question without a good answer. At least I don't have to be concerned with some Russian or Chinese deadbeats stalking us in Colorado," he said to An. He curled up on three empty seats and used his green, crumpled-up camouflage ski jacket as a pillow.

Wolf, sitting upright on an uncomfortable faded green plastic airport chair, was in deep thought, striking a statuesque pose akin to Rodin's *Le Penseur*. He was a choreography of inner reflection. Jon was about to share the story and the details surrounding the incident at the park in Cambridge, starting with his wound that had healed but decided not to interrupt him and save it for the plane ride.

Jon, eyes open, daydreamed again that Yael was in some sort of trouble, but managed to come out unscathed. Jon had forgotten about her close encounter with the Russians. He felt connected to Yael in ways he had yet to understand, like a future reality was about to collide with his spiritual side that she had awakened. Their connection was like the Maasai warriors Wolf had told him about who communicate telepathically when on hunting expectations so as not to alert the hunted animals they were approaching.

While walking around Porcupine Mountain a few months ago, Wolf tried an experiment with Jon to communicate telepathically. It turned out that Wolf could hear Jon's thoughts, but Jon was unable to receive Wolf's. As they began to board, Jon felt a certain calmness. The plane took off and soared quietly into the atmosphere. Twenty minutes later, An lifted the window covering only to get a glimpse of the sun that shone its magnanimous, piercing yellow rays. Ninety minutes later, the wheels hit the runway with a screech, jolting his nervous system. The three were groggy and ravenous, but feeling rejuvenated, knowing that their former predators were left in the dust near Darwin.

They were among the first passengers to exit the plane. Their vitals continued in overdrive from their harrowing experience in Porcupine National. Jon headed to his car with An. Wolf stayed behind to make sure they weren't being followed.

"Pick you up right here," he shouted to Wolf as he and An walked away.

"Why do you think that Wolf and you make such a strong partnership?" An probed, curious to see how Jon would answer her question?

"Why do you think so?" Jon responded, still yawning.

"OK. For starters, you are the perfect yin to Wolf's yang."

"Can you be more specific?"

"Sure. Yang is often depicted by creativity and associated with heaven, heat, and light. Yin, on the other hand, is typically tied to the words, 'eagle' or 'victorious' in the English language. The way I see it is you are a depository of enormous earthly knowledge, and Wolf is a vessel filled with eternal spirit and limitless wisdom."

"You definitely got the gist of it. Can I ask you a question?" An nodded in the affirmative.

"What was the real reason you wanted all those guys dead last night?"

"I was concerned because the explosives had Chinese characters on them, that they might recognize my origin and identify me. I'm unwilling to take even a slight risk since the government knows where I used to live. I fear for mama and lao lao."

Once outside the airport, Jon logged onto his glasses via his high-speed intranet. He checked remotely using the cameras inside his plane to see if it was in one piece. A feeling of relief came over him.

Jon called Denny, still in the air. "Hey, Denny. Thought I'd give you a heads up that there are explosives under the plane that can be detonated remotely, so it's best to stay clear of it for now."

"Thanks for the warning," Denny said with a sarcastic tone. "What are friends for? Later Buck."

CHAPTER 17

SUNNY SIDE UP

April 2045

J on picked up Wolf as promised. "I'm starving," Wolf groaned.

"Me, too, and I've got this darn kink in my neck," An said looking wide awake after resting her head on Jon's shoulder for most of the flight.

"Guys, I know a great place in Dillon. We can stop on the way to my home away from home," Jon smiled as he drove off in his 'mountain' car.

An wore the biggest smile as she climbed into the back seat, ready to ride the Rockies. "Nice wheels," she laughed. "I bet it's an awesome ride."

"Y'all are about to find out. What can I say? My ol' man drove one just like it as a teenager, and he always wanted me to have one. The only difference is you can't hear me coming. When he used to turn his ignition, the neighbors could hear the engine rumbling four blocks away. This one tops out at about 210 mph. The sight of this car in the winter really turns heads, especially the ski crowd and the townies who work at the resorts. They check it out like they are eyeing a beautiful woman, especially the truck drivers that do long-hauling. It's like eye candy for them."

"I bet," An commented, a huge smile on her face. She had never seen anything quite like it in all her years living in China.

"Y'all, those guys were playing for keeps. They were going to blow up the plane right before we arrived so they could move in and capture us once they turned our escape plan into ashes. One thing is for sure. They don't know squat about the interior of the bunker or the defenses we put in place. Those guys were after Wolf and his breakthrough microplastic innovations. No question."

Jon had cameras running 24/7 outside and inside his home overlooking Lake Dillon. It was an insurance policy against inconvenient people who knew where he lived and decided to plant a bomb somewhere where Jon might not be looking. "You know guys, you can't be too careful these days. My definition of caution is part *practical realism steeped in skepticism and mixed with a healthy dose of cynicism.*

In the mountains, Jon drove his sixty-seven-year-old, fire-breathing dark green muscle car, a 1970 Chevelle SS with a hydrogen-powered engine installed by a San Diego outfit, a company who had moved a mile inland because the rising tides from Arctic ice melting had eroded the beaches and invaded the shores. For an immodest sum, they converted Jon's classic car turbo-charged engines to hydrogen fuel. His badass piece of technology on wheels was lighter than an electric car without the lithium batteries adding extra weight. Jon was proud of his Chevelle. It brought him right back to his teenage years.

Wolf had already checked in with his men twice to see if any terrorists were lingering around Darwin. "Nothing, Buck," he said, as let out a gigantic sigh of relief from deep within his lungs.

"Guys, the bunker is clear, and the car and bodies have been disposed of. It's like nothing ever happened back there." Jon headed on I-70 west to the Dillon exit, about seventy-five miles from the airport. "The Sunburst Café serves breakfast all day long, and I'm gonna treat you to the special. Trout, eggs, and home-baked muffins. Sometimes they throw in a Burgerhop for good measure."

"What's a Burgerhop?" An asked inquisitively. "Never heard of it."

"It's a new chain, and it makes burgers from any kind of bug that hops. You know, like grasshoppers, crickets, and termites. And if you're lucky, you'll get a termite queen. They are a delicacy in certain countries, along with dragonflies. Big businesses in Uganda and other African countries with limited supplies of traditional protein due to lack of freshwater. High in protein, but no chemical or hormone injections like chicken or beef. Plus, it takes virtually no water to produce them in mass quantities."

Wolf couldn't help himself. "Fried spiders are a delicacy in Cambodia. One of the edible spiders is the Thai zebra spider, but it is venomous and aggressive. And the labels on cooked tarantulas come with a warning: remove as much hair as you can and don't eat the fangs." Wolf roared as he glanced over at An's twisted facial expression.

"Ecch, count me out. I assume there's no maggots, woodlice, or scorpions in the recipe, right?"

"I've checked it out. None of those ingredients are in Burgerhops. You might find some crushed ants in there, but otherwise all good. The ants are also high in protein."

An wanted to dig deeper and was yearning for Wolf's purpose. "I've been meaning to ask you. What was the turning point in your life? You know, the catalyst to devote such a big part of your life chasing around the world dictatorships who are messing with the world's freshwater supplies."

"I couldn't sit back any longer and watch the bad actors get away with highway robbery and squander precious resources. The problem with us is I'm not sure whether we're hunting or being hunted. What was it for you, Angie?"

"It would have to be when a polluted river in the Zhejiang burst into flames after some person randomly tossed a lit cigarette in the waterway. Somebody took a video and posted it on the internet, but the Chinese government took it down. The flames on the water rose over five meters high, and it made me physically ill when I watched i. It occurred in 2014 during my PhD. What about you?"

"I reckon it was way back in the sixth grade. I had Mrs. Potter for my teacher in science class. She was the best teacher in all Wartrace. We had one class about water pollution and how the Dow Chemical plant up the road was poisoning all the fish within a ten-square-mile radius.

And when she said it was killin' all the frogs too, I got really upset and my brain went into overdrive. She ticked off all the other chemical plants that were around destroying all the wildlife, and I still remember every last one of them. They're all white-collar criminals and should be doing time in a Tennessee state prison."

"Best of luck rounding them up," said An.

"Yeah. Half of them could be dead by now. I discovered later that the real villains were utilities, the largest polluters of streams, lakes, and rivers."

After wolfing down breakfast and chugging glasses of freshly squeezed orange juice, the three spent an hour shopping in Silverthorne. Wolf and An walked away with three days' worth of winter clothes. Given the time of year and the climate back at Darwin, they purchased flannel shirts, wool socks, winter hats and gloves, corduroys, and sweaters to offset the frigid climate. An never needed warm clothing until she set foot in the States. The shopping experience was a struggle for her, having never been exposed to this kind of material abundance. The selection of choices was overwhelming.

"C'mon guys, let's get moving." Jon couldn't wait to take a hot shower. Only a ten-minute drive to Frisco separated Jon from the two large solar water heaters he had installed, and there would be plenty of hot water for everyone.

We need to focus F.O.R.'s energies on the next mission. A continent that has no cities or full-time citizens, not even a paved road or a restaurant. Code word will be Southland, and it's important from here on out Antarctica is not referred to by its name. Even the White Continent is too revealing.

Jon downshifted as he turned onto his street. There were three inches of fluffy, light snow on the ground. His driveway was completely clear because of heaters underneath powered by wind. Jon wanted to give his neighbors the impression this was his permanent residence and he lived there all year round.

"Wolf, we need to set up a video call Thursday of next week on our secure intranet with everyone, and let's make sure we include Sinclair. I want to introduce him as the newest official member of F.O.R."

"Who the hell is Sinclair, may I ask?" An asked, slightly perturbed that she hadn't heard about him sooner.

"Sorry. Thought I told you about him. He's the gentleman I met after the early morning phone call, remember? I then flew to London for a couple of meetings he arranged with the upper echelon of the British Navy. Yael turned me on to Sinclair, who she met at a water conference in Tel Aviv."

"We've been downloading our laser hologram plans based on the latest submarine data after the meeting with the highest-ranking Admiral of the British Navy. I'm hoping we have access to a couple of cutting-edge 'secret weapons.' The ones that will give us a sustainable advantage, given our smaller stature."

———

In 2044, Jon spent most of his time shuttling back and forth to Denver from Frisco, supervising the construction and engineering of his prized minisub. It was being constructed eighty miles away in a plain, forty-thousand square foot warehouse with thirty-foot ceilings in an industrial park five miles west of the airport.

The group had three relaxing days consisting of home-cooked meals, hiking, hot tub time, reading, and watching a few movies. On the way to the airport, Jon stopped in front of an inconspicuous-looking rectangular shaped building in the middle of nowhere. The name on the building was Acme Technologies, and the security was airtight. It required biometric fingerprints and retinal scanning to enter the premises and only one person was allowed in at a time. Jon was the only one who knew how to override the system to allow Wolf and An to see it. Jon also had eleven minicams hooked up in the warehouse that allowed live viewing back at Darwin as well as his home in Frisco. It had enough firewalls to stop hackers from getting a gander at his latest and greatest engineering feats.

Upon entering the second door, An gasped. "Holy fuck!" She just stood there, her mouth agape, taking it in. "I don't mean to ask what's up with the mini-sub, but what's up with the mini-sub? I'd no idea you were this far along."

"Why does An look like she just drank from the wrong Grail cup?" Wolf whispered to Jon, with his hand covering his mouth. Wolf and Jon had a bird's eye view of the mini sub from almost every angle over the last fourteen months. To see it in real-time living color was mind-boggling.

Part of Jon was always torn leaving Frisco because it had everything that he wanted, except one thing-- Yael. There were so many activities that they could do together. Fly fishing, biking, hiking, sailing, and skiing, along with clean air and complete solitude at nine thousand feet altitude. With no real industrial activity within sixty miles and a room with a view that was second to none, it was Jon's happy place.

He wanted desperately to bring Yael into his mountainous world, but he would have to be patient. Heading to the airport, Jon's noiseless car was gliding along at 85 mph. An was munching on some chocolate-covered ants in the back seat. 6,000 miles away, in Sde Boker, Yael was sleeping in her bungalow, and having a horrible, restless sleep with twisted nightmares about something awful happening to Wolf. To make matters worse, Jon was unable to protect his best friend in her dream.

As if they were connected telepathically, Jon called Yael on the drive to check-in, and woke her out of a fitful sleep right before her dream ended.

"Hey, Sol! Que pasa?"

"Do you know what time it is here?"

"Oops. Sorry about that. Got my time zones crossed. I thought it was 7:30 a.m. your time, but now I realize it's 5:30 a.m. Well, either way, Boker Tov!" Before she could tell Jon about her nightmare, he barreled ahead with his agenda.

"I want you to meet me in Hobart at the beginning of next month. Can you get five or six days off work? It's mission-critical."

Yael struggled to sweep away the lingering cobwebs in her brain. "Hobart? The only Hobart I know is in the Midwest near you, I mean Darwin."

"Think again, my dear. Hint: It's on the other side of the world about ten thousand miles from Indiana." Yael found herself quickly checking her phone and faked her way through a conversation to avoid the embarrassment of not knowing.

"Oh, you mean Hobart in Tasmania? Of course." She adeptly back peddled her way out of it.

"Yeah, that small island about an hour south of Melbourne by plane."

"I'll need to check my schedule and see if I can get the time off. What's in Hobart that's so earth shattering?"

"That's for me to know and for you to find out. I'll tell you when you get there. Besides, you are wicked smart and can probably figure it out. Let me know as soon as you can."

Wolf was astounded. "When it comes to travel, you're 100% OCD."

They said goodbye seconds before An washed down her last chocolate ant with a bottle of Vilca Bamba water she'd grabbed from Jon's fridge. He was busy daydreaming about a romantic getaway with Yael on neutral territory, the ideal blend of business and pleasure.

Wolf recently connected Jon to a famous researcher in Tasmania. Not just any researcher. One that was working at the University of Tasmania studying glaciology using satellite images embedded with AI; namely, the ice sheets of Greenland and the subglacial lakes underneath Antarctica. Adrienne Bernays was valedictorian with a double major in biology and physics at Heidelberg University in Germany. Five years later, she received her doctorate in Glaciology from the Institute of Antarctic and Southern Ocean at the University of Tasmania.

CHAPTER 18

WHERE WATER TASTES LIKE WINE

April 2045

It was a six-hour flight, and they were cruising at 35,000 feet. Their Destination, surrounded by the relentless, unforgiving Southern Ocean on all sides with its own zip code, was the epicenter of the harshest environment on the planet. The private flight cost $40,000 per person. Jon thought it was worth the outlay to explore Antarctica with his newfound ally.

The Gulfstream, with green jet fuel packed into the wings between the forward and rear spars, was unusually quiet. Soaring high above the clouds into the multi-colored horizon, six miles above where the Atlantic and Indian Oceans joined hands, the aircraft was eerily quiet. They were sitting four feet away from each other, conversing in a normal voice.

Jon looked at Sinclair. "Any guesses which countries are in the GAC? I'll bet you can get most of them."

"Hmmm. Let me see. Russia, Canada, the U.S., and Denmark because of Greenland, Norway, Sweden, and Iceland. That should do it."

"You forgot one?"

"Ah, yes. I'm such a Wally. It's Finland."

Sitting beside Sinclair on the way to the White Continent, he couldn't help but notice that this world-class researcher from Cambridge was a dichotomy, someone who smiled and laughed often but had a serious side as well. He also leaned toward a more formal presentation of self in everyday life. Jon had been a witness to his more formal demeanor when they spoke to Admiral Brown in London.

The excursion they were embarking on was unique in many ways. Instead of taking a scheduled flight from Punta Arenas in southern Chile to King George Island, he had met Sinclair in Cape Town. He had flown from London and had been conducting research in Cape Town about repeated freshwater shortages.

Jon broke the temporary silence. "It looks as if the Russians got to the Arctic too late, at least in terms of capturing any freshwater from glacier melts. Perhaps that's why they are in Antarctica with the Chinese?"

"At least the Russians intervened twice to prevent the weaponization of water," Sinclair pondered.

"I know they brokered a deal between China and India to stop the PRC from building dams, diverting the water from the Himalayas, and averting a major skirmish, if not a prolonged war between two countries that contain more than twenty percent of the world's population. What's the other one?" Jon asked.

Sinclair's eyes stared at Jon, with his glasses resting on his nose. "You remember what Turkey started over twenty-five years ago when they violated the 1987 agreement with Syria and Iraq? Geography had given Turkey control of more than 90% of the water that flows into the Euphrates and 44% of the Tigris.

"That started when I was still a student. Wasn't 60% of water supposed to flow to Iraq, but they ended up diverting about 40% to Syria? And then they tried to blame the Kurds, and Russia had to intervene on Syria's behalf in 2025 to prevent a major war between Syria, Turkey, and Iraq."

"Well done. I'm duly impressed." Sinclair congratulated Jon for his recall of events as they unfolded in the Middle East.

"Let's get back to the Arctic Sea ice," Sinclair suggested. "By 2032, sea ice had shrunk to historic low levels. The last time I checked with NASA and the U.S. National Snow and Ice Data Center the Arctic summer sea-ice cover had declined by over 210,000 square miles, slightly less than twice the size of the UK. It's below the lowest levels since the data was first analyzed in 1972."

"What's your prognosis for the future?" Jon asked, thinking he knew the answer before Sinclair responded.

"Here's the crux of it, and something that has yet to occur in Antarctica. The water is absorbing the heat. This happens mostly when there isn't enough ice in the Arctic Ocean to reflect the sun's rays back into space. So, it becomes a vicious cycle. As the ocean temperature rises, it accelerates the ice melt. The heat absorbed by the ocean further impacts ocean currents and can weaken the jet stream. By contrast, the ice on Antarctica fell as low as 723,000 square miles almost twenty years ago but has been holding steady ever since."

Jon had an epiphany. "So, that explains what happened in parts of Australia, the Western U.S., Africa, China, Russia, and India from 2025-2039. And the multiple deep freezes that hit Texas, Los Angeles, and the Southeastern U.S. where pipes became frozen and there was no water available for weeks.

"That's correct. But there is something significant that you left out, resulting in a dramatic effect in rising sea levels since 2029."

"What's that? Why do I have a funny feeling this conversation is going south? Get the pun? *South.*"

Sinclair smiled and continued his pontification. "Here's something to consider. The Geological Survey of Greenland identified in 2039 that Greenland's largest remaining ice shelf broke off a massive ice chunk that was three times the size of Yosemite. If my math is correct, that's the equivalent of about 10,000 kilometers, a record loss for Greenland's ice sheets. It's beyond frightening because that mass of ice alone could cause sea levels to rise a good two meters or more over time."

"Times have changed, I'll give you that much," said Jon. "The U.S. managed to tip the balance of power ever so slightly when they delivered five Virginia-class nuclear subs to Australia back in 2031. Since the Chinese built a landing strip on the northeast side of Antarctica near Ziong Shen, things have metastasized into something sinister."

"Due to the ownership claims that countries have with a presence in Antarctica, and Australia's share of the continent is 42%, the best launching point may be from Melbourne, perhaps even Tasmania."

Suddenly, a fighter jet appeared on the horizon, and then buzzed the plane. Jon was nervous the Russians knew he was on the plane and started to turn pale. "It's a cheeky move, and nothing to be concerned about. It would be unusual if a Russian or Chinese jet didn't check us out as we approached our designated landing strip. Those blokes are just doing their jobs."

"What about the 1959 Antarctic treaty that your grandfather signed? No settlements, no population, no government in Antarctica? The PRC and Russia have violated most of it because there's no governing body to enforce any of it."

"As far as research stations and proximity to Antarctica are concerned, I'm afraid not. Several countries have research stations that are not part of their claimed territories, starting with the U.S. and Russia. There are over eighty-five research stations scattered across the continent. China alone has established six stations in the last decade alone, including one equipped with an airstrip constructed of ice and stone."

Jon grabbed some salted cashews from the bowl in front of him, and stuffed them in his mouth. It was his favorite nut because he used to eat them on the bus riding home in grade school. "An told me that the PRC has been abusing the privilege by flying military planes and landing them on that airstrip. Who's going to stand up to China and tell them what to do?" Jon asked rhetorically.

Jon noticed a thirty-something blond flight attendant out of the corner of his right eye strolling up the aisle with a robotic cart trailing behind her. She asked the two journeymen if they wanted anything to eat or drink. Upon getting a closer look, her stoic face turned into a slight smile as she gazed into Jon's blue eyes.

"Do you have any green tea by chance?" Jon inquired.

"I'll have a Guinness, thank you," Sinclair added. She nodded and then went back to the small kitchen at the back of the plane.

"I've got last one question I've been dying to ask. In your professional opinion, what would the world look like if all the ice melted?"

Sinclair hesitated before answering. He knew what he was about to say would be tough to swallow. "Brace yourself. Based on the modeling we've done at Cambridge if Antarctica's total of 25.4 million cubic kilometers melted, the oceans would rise seventy meters across the globe."

Jon slumped back in his seat, his imagination running wild with disaster scenarios. "Florida disappears along with most of the eastern seaboard starting with Maine. The west coast is an unmitigated disaster and so is Europe, Asia."

"I'm afraid that's just the start. The Hawaiian Islands, Fiji, the Solomon, and Cook Islands would cease to be, along with countries like the Netherlands, Denmark, Bangladesh, most of the Philippines, and Japan. The UK and Uruguay would lose most of their land mass to seawater, along with the eastern fronts of China and Russia. And let's not forget about Taiwan either."

"It would be a frickin' disaster," Jon responded meekly.

Sinclair nodded. "I've gotten some intel that India, with their Maitri location, is contemplating putting a second stake in the ground on the northeastern part of Antarctica. Somewhere between Novolazarevskaya, a Russian territory, and Syowa, Tokyo's sole location."

"How did you come by that information?" Jon's curiosity was piqued as he leaned over to better hear Sinclair's response.

"Simple. They hired me as a consultant to help them figure it out," Sinclair said with a smirk that turned into gut-wrenching laughter.

Jon spotted a large military drone out his window. "What the hell's this?"

"Probably Russian if I had to guess." Sinclair responded matter of fact.

"But I thought there was no military allowed on the continent?"

Sinclair sighed heavily. "In theory, that's correct. The Chinese and Russians are deceptive in their claims of using research drones exclusively. Everyone knows the truth, but again, who's going to police these things? Certainly not NATO."

"There's still one thing on my bucket list. I'd like to ski Mt. Vinson in Antarctica," Jon shared.

"So, what are you waiting for?" Sinclair teased.

"Well for one, I've been a bit busy traveling the last nine months.

And the dates are somewhat limited. Restricted travel from December 5-21, 2044, and then again December 31-January 15, 2045. The windows are too narrow, especially with our upcoming mission. Also, I'm not crazy about the carbon footprint it would leave, both to and from the continent as well as on the climb. It just seems fundamentally wrong to me. So, what is Antarctica like?" Jon inquired with a boyish curiosity.

"Well, let's see how I can best describe it." Sinclair remained silent for a good thirty seconds. "Antarctica is like a giant Garden of Eden ice cave, except its beauty comes at you like a fist out of nowhere. This wondrous continent is the final frontier for freshwater, and we can't afford to mess it up like the Russians did in the Arctic. It's our last stand. Mars is at least half a century away from being habitable. Not to mention that Venus is completely off the table. Its average surface temperature is nine hundred degrees, and its clouds are mainly composed of sulfuric acid," Sinclair said like a Sunday morning preacher from his pulpit.

The robotic cart arrived with their beverages. Sinclair took a few gulps of his Guinness, allowing it to glide down his throat. The intercom went live. "Gentlemen, we just got buzzed by a Chinese fighter jet checking us out. We are now in descent mode and should be landing in thirty-five minutes. It can get turbulent with the high winds as we get closer to the surface, so fasten your belts and hang on to your beers," the pilot said with a thick South African accent.

Jon was looking out of his window, sipping his green tea, stunned by the beauty and undisturbed ice resting peacefully at the tip of the Southern Ocean. It was craggy, white, and unblemished. No signs of any pollution from the air.

"Do you know the history of the island we are about to land on?"

"Not really," he responded.

"A little more than 500 million years ago, Antarctica was part of the supercontinent Gondwana. Over time Gondwana broke apart, and Antarctica as we know it today was formed thirty-five million years ago. By comparison, Iceland is approximately sixty million years old with some help from an underwater volcano." Jon's versatile mind was struggling to wrap his head around a continent of ice that was originally part of a tropical paradise.

"I can top that. Isle Royale, a stone's throw from the shores of Lake Superior, is believed to be 1.1 billion years old," Jon added. "It's a forty-five-minute flight by seaplane from where Wolf lives."

"Did you know that up until twenty years ago, the only runway in Antarctica was McCurdo Station, large enough for the Lockheed C-130 Hercules to land on?"

"Yeah, I read something about that. They call it White Ice. Asphalt was impossible and so they packed groomed snow on top of a layer of sea ice. It's the darndest thing. Every summer they rebuild it, and it remains in operation until December. At that point, the ice is too damn unstable."

"Within the past ten years, the Russians have constructed several of their own runways close to their research stations. Australia built one near their Davis Research Station in 2031. Antarctica now has over fifty landing strips, and China has been trying to build its own airport in northeast Antarctica. Ludicrous!"

Ten minutes later, Jon spotted the massive white land mass. The Gulfstream descended, and gently hit the ice runway as the tires thumped on landing. The sleek jet took about thirty seconds to come to a complete halt. Ice landings were always tricky, and the experienced pilots didn't want their expensive piece of equipment to spin out and slide into the hardened snowbanks.

As the plane came to a halt, Sinclair put on his winter hat, gloves, and a pair of prescription sunglasses before exiting first. Sinclair had almost forgotten how fierce the gusting wind could be down under. The frigid winds proved to be a rude awakening, stinging his clean-shaven face.

As Jon emerged onto the steps, he was awestruck by the bright, glaring summer sun. It hit his eyes like lightning bolts, and his pupils instantaneously shrunk to the size of pinheads. Jon reflexively grabbed his sunglasses and wrapped them around his temples.

This place is like a destination between two worlds. A mountainous continent of solid ice, an endless, white ice desert unmarked as far as the eye could see. The howling silence that engulfs it is deafening to the soul, as if frozen in time and space, like experiencing the edge of civilization. If I stayed here too long, it would be like a slow suicide into nothingness.

Sinclair was thinking something altogether different. *The visibility is good, the sun is shining, and the sky is clear, but why do I feel as if I'm in a fog?*

"Michael," Jon shouted. "I need to make a quick call."

As soon as he got clear of the tarmac, Jon phoned Wolf to see if he could get a solid connection all the way to Darwin's bunker. He tapped his glasses with his gloved index finger. "Wolf?"

"Hey! Where are you?" The high, gusting winds battered Jon's phone, making it hard for him to hear anything.

"I'm a few miles south of New Zealand. I think it's our lucky day. We just hit the jackpot with Sinclair," Jon said in between crackles of static.

"How so?"

"You gotta talk louder. For starters, Sinclair is the former chairman of SCAR, better known as the Scientific Committee on Antarctica Research. You know, the organization that devotes all its resources toward Antarctica and preservation of the continent." A sudden gust of wind was hurling hard snow crystals that felt like sewing needles stinging his face.

"I've heard of it. Fill me in on the details later."

Jon was now shouting into his headset. "I'm going to traverse the northeastern part of Antarctica over the next thirty-six hours with Sinclair to see if we can find out what the Russians and the Chinese are up to above sea level. Call you in a couple of days from Cape Town. Is all quiet on the northern front? How's An?"

"Yeah, all good." The tension in Wolf's voice was palpable and gave away some of his deepest fears, nine thousand miles away through demonstrable static.

"You're not convincing, my friend," Jon shouted into his phone to overcome the combative wind.

Jon looked up and noticed that Sinclair was waving for him to come inside the shelter. "Court just phoned, and there's something else you should know. In the last twelve hours, Russian subs sank two large fishing boats, one Icelandic and the other off the southwest coast of Greenland. Clearly no accident."

Jon was speechless. "Are you there?"

"Roger that. Gotta go."

"Michael," Jon shouted as he approached the hut. "We need to talk. Pronto!"

————

Jon and Sinclair boarded the plane back to Cape Town, and Jon continued the preamble of his theory, hoping that Sinclair would jump into the fray of F.O.R. to take on two formidable militaries in the coldest region on earth, and where submarines and drones would be lurking.

"Jon, I hear what you're saying and respect your intentions, but is it not a fool's errand? Why would anyone want to get involved with their respective militaries on a continent that is thousands of miles away from civilization? It doesn't make sense. Unless..."

"Go ahead and say it. It's the freshwater supply, isn't it? All eighty-four percent of the clean water that is left on our fragile planet. And some of the most powerful and hostile governments are in the hunt, transcending any sane approach to the sanctity of Antarctica's pristine reserves. We both know what's been going on in the Arctic Circle, Iceland, Greenland, the Canadian Arctic, and even Scandinavia. It's not a land grab. It's a water grab." Jon was listening intently, waiting for Sinclair to finish. The plane took off, and the conversation continued.

"As members of F.O.R., we view ourselves as self-appointed stewards to look after the earth's limited resources, trying to maintain an equilibrium between water, power, and equality."

Sinclair's eyes grew wider with each spoken word uttered by his newly minted friend. "Thanks. I've been studying the satellites in orbit to see if any of them might be observing their targets and noticed something strange going on during the last eighteen months or so."

"What's that?"

"Remember way back in 2027 when NASA launched the Ice, Cloud, and Land Elevation Satellite-2, or ICESat-2? It used a laser altimeter, firing pulses of photons split into six beams toward the Earth's surface three miles below. Each pulse contains trillions of photons, but only a handful of photons are reflected back toward the satellite. It provides data that is accurate to within a few inches. Does that ring a bell?"

Jon noticed a red flashing warning sign light up. "This is your captain speaking. Due to high winds at this altitude, the flight is going to be choppy for another ten minutes. Please keep your seatbelts fastened."

"I was sitting for my second PhD, so the answer is no."

"Fair enough. Essentially, there are two issues, and one is rather obvious. Seven countries have launched similar satellites into orbit, including Russia and China. Why would Russia and China suddenly become so interested in what's going on in Antarctica, especially given there is no real strategic military advantage? And it's not exactly close to either country."

Sinclair looked directly at Jon to make his next point. "The second issue is potentially destabilizing. After consulting with a glaciologist at NASA's Jet Propulsion lab in Pasadena, I discovered that the resolution on the NASA satellite is so high that it can detect tiny rifts and other small features on the surface."

"Not catching your *drift*?" Jon said.

"Remember when it was discovered that the floating ice shelves were thinning, allowing more ice to flow from the interior to the ocean, along with the theories about how that will contribute to rising sea levels? Well, guess what? For some reason, the sea levels adjacent to the shore-line for the past three years have stopped rising and I think I know why. It goes well with your conspiracy theory. We both know there are close to five hundred massive freshwater lakes underneath Antarctica, correct?" Sinclair espoused.

"I think either the Russians or the Chinese- and I'm leaning towards the latter- have figured out how to suck out the water from subglacial lakes and underground rivers beneath the ice caps," Jon stated with authority. "For all we know, they may have already begun running a pipeline or pipelines from eastern Antarctica all the way up to God knows where. I believe their scheme is to pump the water through to mainland China."

Jon paused, content that Sinclair had come around to his way of thinking. "They may be using a special kind of ductile iron for their pipes, including a small graphite coating on the inside of the pipeline. It's superior transporting water versus traditional PVC piping."

"Ironic," Sinclair said, staring out into space. "Not only is it viable, but China has been the largest graphite-producing nation in the world for thirty years, more than seventy percent of world production. That is, up until six years ago."

Sinclair had planted a seed of his own in Jon's mind.

"What do you mean?"

Sinclair grinned, as if he were Sherlock Holmes himself that had just solved a murder mystery. "In the past several years, I have watched as China's exports of graphite have plummeted sixty-five percent."

Jon looked perplexed. Sinclair was about to shed some light on Jon's conspiracy theory. "I think they're using the material for their pipelines to extract water from the subglacial lakes and pipe it under the Southern Ocean all the way to New Zealand's southwest coast. I'm not lost on the idea that graphite has replaced traditional leads, the ones that have led to unconscionable lead poisoning. You recall the incidents in Pittsburgh, Detroit, Cleveland, and Chicago, don't you?"

"Sure do. The hundreds of cities in the U.S., China, Europe, and Russia that have experienced high levels of lead and C8 compounds in drinking water simply because the powers that be consciously allowed the infrastructure to rot. The difference is that China deliberately chose to reduce its graphite exports and has kept it a secret from most of the world because they can. The Chinese tried in vain to hide this from the outside world."

"No disrespect here. But how on earth could they accomplish all that? We're talking about the harshest environment on the planet, where temperatures can approach minus fifty degrees Fahrenheit without factoring in the windchill. It's inconceivable that..."

"Maybe. Maybe not. This is all taking place underwater and not on the surface. In 2035, the PRC began developing long-range, robotic submarines using advanced deep-water technology to lay pipeline," Jon said in a serious manner.

"Is that it? There must be something more." Sinclair was probing to extract everything from Jon's mind.

"There's one more thing," Jon said hesitantly.

"Let's have it. We've only got thirty minutes of airtime remaining until we land in Cape Town," Sinclair fired back, staring at his satellite watch.

Jon inhaled, his chest expanding slightly. "The Arctic region has already been eviscerated, and the sea ice there has decreased in surface area by about 80% over the last fifty years. The ice in the Antarctic region did a one-eighty. My sources tell me it's increased slightly during the past two decades for reasons that are still being debated among scientists." He spoke to Sinclair as if he were a doyen, and his conspiracy theories were irrevocable, irrefutable truths.

"Hmm, it is true that the Climate Change Committee for Antarctica is made up of the European Union and twenty-five other countries," Sinclair stated, stroking his chin. "If memory serves me correctly, ideas proposed by the E.U., Australia, Chile, and Argentina were blocked repeatedly by Russia and China."

The plane hit an air pocket, and everything on the refreshment cart ended up in the aisle. "Maybe it was just a smokescreen," Jon chimed in. "And Greenland, where natural resources were in abundance, exceeded the grasp of the megalomaniacs in China and Russia because of its natural barriers and Thule Air Force base sitting like a watchdog atop Greenland north of the Arctic Circle."

"Aah. What those cheeky bastards really had in mind was a future territorial lunge to exploit freshwater from subglacial lakes."

"Now do you know why you're needed on our team? In ten minutes, you figured out what the U.S and British Navies are just starting to grasp." There was an irritating tension hanging in the air.

"Precisely. You're on to something. How can I help?"

"We need your guidance on the subglacial lakes underneath those massive ice sheets to lead us to the most likely places where underwater pipelines are being used, and then we dissect them on the Southern Ocean floor. Look, the credits didn't roll after the nuisance we caused in the Gobi. They ain't gonna roll if we're successful in the Southern Ocean either."

"I understand," Sinclair responded in a deadpanned voice.

"It's like Winston Churchill once proclaimed a century ago. *'This is not the end, nor is it the beginning of the end. It's the end of the beginning.'* The mission in front of us can act as a countermeasure to China's unspoken mantra of ignoring restrictions so they could hijack global resources wherever and whenever they see fit. For obvious reasons, they were looking south, as in ninety degrees. I'll need your guidance with logistics and planning, including a little help from our British Navy friends."

"Fair enough. There is one other detail that could work in our favor," Sinclair offered as a sly grin formed on his face. We need to meet with Calvin, my good friend and colleague who is among the leading experts on global submarine technology. He continues to have his finger on the pulse. Calvin's been retained as a high-level consultant by the British Navy for the last decade, and he's viewed as indispensable. When would you like me to start digging in?"

Jon's eyes opened. "If not now, when?" he said with fire in his eyes.

Sinclair cleared his throat, leaning on his tray table. "I'll give him a call when we land in Cape Town. Let's see if you and I can meet with him over the weekend in Tuscany. He's there for the entire month holding a private summit."

The robotic cart glided up the aisle to clean up the spilled mess and collect waste. "Why don't you give him a call now?" Jon uttered with enthusiasm, tossing his secure satellite watch across the aisle.

Jon beamed. The generosity of spirit that Sinclair displayed by was consistent with F.O.R.'s net-giver philosophy. Sinclair attached Jon's wireless headphones and voice-dialed Calvin's number. Sinclair looked up at Jon, shook his head from side to side, and proceeded to leave a message. "Cal, I'm about to land in Cape Town and thought it would be a capital idea if I divert to Tuscany on my way back to London. I've got a pressing issue that I'd like to discuss with you." Anything else keeping you up at night these days?"

"Yeah, one. I just got wind that China has installed a fifth generation MIRV warhead called the Dongfeng-51 on its subs. Not only can they travel at Mach 25, or about twelve-thousand kilometers per hour, but they have a range of fifteen thousand kilometers. There's no missile defense system, including satellite lasers that can stop them, at least for now."

"I see. How accurate would you say they are?" Sinclair asked sternly.

"Crap. If one were launched from this side of the Southern Ocean, it could probably hit a large barn in Tullahoma, Tennessee on a foggy night."

"Ok. Go on."

"The U.S. has an offensive deterrent of their own," Jon offered.

"And that is..."

"The Navy has Zumwalt Stealth destroyers, and each battleship is equipped with twelve hypersonic missiles. They now have nine Zumwalts wandering around the Atlantic and Pacific with a total of 108 hypersonics, all with nuclear warheads attached. Didn't come cheap either. They spent over $8 billion on R&D, and each one cost an average of $4 billion. Cost overruns galore." Jon took a sip of water.

"The Chinese started developing special long-range, robotic submarines in 2035 using advanced deep-water technology to lay the pipeline. The majority have gone undetected by satellites because of the operating depth of the submarines combined with hundreds of meters of ice that function as cover."

"I see," Sinclair replied despondently. He was leaning back in his chair with hands wrapped tightly around his neck gathering himself for a thoughtful response.

"And that is why you keep referring to Antarctica as the final frontier. It is the last untarnished freshwater supply on the planet besides Greenland."

"Isn't it true? Antarctica and its freshwater supply are the end of the line. There's just nowhere else to go. Even landing on Mars is a bad joke."

"Why do you say that?" Sinclair asked.

"According to my friends at NASA, the best case is when the earth and Mars are 35 million miles apart every couple of years, and it still requires over six months of space travel. Besides, the surface of Mars is too cold to support life, and there's too much radiation. The atmosphere is 95% carbon dioxide."

The plane hit the runway in Cape Town, barely making a sound. Jon scanned his phone for messages. There was one from Admiral Brown. "Please call at your earliest convenience."

Chapter 19

Anarchy on Ice

May 2045

Wolf wasn't working exclusively on a solution in the depths of Darwin for dissolving microplastics from fresh and seawater. He was also trying to configure a device that could remove microplastics from the air. Wolf was concerned about the more than three thousand tons of tiny plastic fragments reigning down from the skies on the Western U.S. every year, where regions had turned into dust bowls.

Jon came out of the bedroom rubbing his eyes, yawned audibly, ready to start the day. "It's the equivalent of between four to six hundred million plastic bottles raining down from the sky," Wolf preached. "You do realize that the world still produces about 300 million metric tons of plastic a year. Half of it is single use, non-recyclable plastic and is tossed out. This stuff is in the air we breathe," Wolf said, as he raised his voice in a rare moment of disdain.

"That's madness," Jon exclaimed with an irritated tone. "I thought you always preach that you can't go against that which is."

"I don't mind being wrong on the way to being right. I'm even more incensed about corporations like NESCO that produced 1.7 billion plastic bottles a day. The killer is that it takes two liters of water to produce a one-liter bottle of water," Wolf suggested. He closed his eyes, sending prayers to the universe.

"One thing's for sure. It's the plastic that we can't see that's the problem." Jon knew that others were also working on the micro-plastic dilemma. They're still decades away from any viable, cost-effective solution," Jon added. He promptly voice-dialed Sinclair at Cambridge and then Sinclair did a three-way holographic video call.

"Calvin, I'd like to introduce you to Jon Buckingham.

"Ello, Jon. Pleased to meet you."

"And you as well, Calvin. Sorry things didn't work out for us to meet in person. You must know that it took all my willpower to skip two days in Tuscany, but duty called."

"I understand. No apologies necessary. How can I help you in your upcoming mission's chances? It sounded from Michael that you have big plans cooking." Calvin spoke deliberately, carefully choosing his words, as if he were trying to parallel park his mind into a small space with no rear-view mirror.

Jon and Sinclair looked at each other, shrugged, and Jon motioned to Sinclair to go first. The three spoke for almost a full hour.

"So Calvin, do you really have concrete evidence that the Chinese have been snooping around Antarctica for the better part of a decade, particularly the northeastern peninsula?"

"Unequivocally, my dear friend. And with the Russians involved, anything is possible. Your theory that the Chinese could be attempting to steal billions of gallons of water from subglacial lakes and rivers clearly *holds water*," Calvin laughed uncontrollably at his own play on words.

"Thanks for your time, Calvin. Much appreciated."

"It was my pleasure. And Michael, thanks for introducing us."

"Cheers, gentlemen. Michael, I'll call you tomorrow."

Jon turned to Wolf and asked his friend a penetrating question.

"I thought of a new mission statement for the team. Ready? 'We are a momentary flame in history with the purpose of saving all the water. We're prepared to go anywhere and do anything as long as its forward.' Whaddya think?"

Wolf grinned. "I think it's a tad ambitious, but overall, the power is in its simplicity. Suddenly, the alarm signaled intruders were approaching, and put the two F.O.R. founders on edge. "Wolf, check that out please," Jon said calmly.

Thirty seconds later, Wolf called Jon into the control room. "Looks like a herd of elk mimicked the real thing. False positive," he said with relief.

"What's the latest on the West Coast company you've been speaking to for the past three months?" Jon asked Wolf.

"Bottom line is that I need some negotiating advice." Wolf had worked in earnest with a company called Green Resolve Plastics. He passionately believed GRP was a 'paradigm shift' in the world while using green hydrogen as its primary energy source. GRP's mission was to prevent additional water damage caused by plastic pollution. The company had developed a breakthrough ocean-degradable biopolymer called PHB using air and greenhouse gasses.

Wolf also held certain patents that prevented GRP from getting to the production stage, serving as a gentle coercion for them to work together. The company was now commercially viable, ready to deliver a unique level of material with proven certified sustainability.

"Then what's the issue?"

"The vulture capitalists have their talons deep into these guys. They are holding the company hostage from getting additional capital, sorely needed to get to commercial sales. You've had experience in this area. What should I do?"

"Let me talk to them. I'll get to the truth and make sure they are flying straight with no bullshit."

After one thorough phone conversation representing Jon as Wolf's anonymous agent, he was able to work his magic. "Gentlemen, may I put you on hold for one minute? Thank you. We'll be right back."

He turned to Wolf. "Are you 100% convinced that there are no competitors breathing down their necks?"

"If I license three of my patents, they will be impenetrable from a competitive standpoint and will own the market, at least until the patents expire twelve years from now," Wolf said triumphantly.

"A word to the wise. When you are negotiating a business deal, 'NO' is a complete sentence. Otherwise, you run the risk of negotiating against yourself." Jon pressed the mute button firmly, putting them back on.

"Gentlemen, we'd like to make y'all a proposal, but before we do, can I ask how much money are you looking for? Also, what are the investment terms the vultures are proposing?" Jon's casual bedside manner was disarming.

"Sure thing, Mr. Walker. We are looking for $35 million to achieve positive cash flow. If we can get reasonable terms, there will be no further dilution." Wolf was nervously shaking his leg up and down.

"The lead investor is proposing a convertible note with an eight percent coupon that pays in stock, with a strike price that puts the valuation right around $70 million."

The CEO spoke next. "Look, guys, I'm just a fellow PhD trying to do the world some good and slow down the single-use plastic pollution that has been decimating our planet for better part of a half century. The real issue is they want a third of the company, and then they're entitled to tell us what to do, and when."

"I understand. Been there before when I sold my company several years back," Jon replied empathetically. "Tell you what. How about giving us three percent of all gross sales in exchange for licensing our patents until we get one hundred percent of our money back? And once we reach that point, how about a percent on all gross sales from that point forward, until such time when either the company is sold or goes public?"

"We're in agreement with you so far."

Jon was now in his element, rolling up his business sleeves. Wolf stood by like someone sitting in the passenger's seat of a NASCAR going two hundred miles an hour. He could barely keep up. Everything seemed like a blur.

"If we give you the $35 million at a $80 million valuation, do we have a deal? That will give us 30% ownership, excluding any future dividends. And if you decide to raise capital in the future, we get the right of first refusal?"

"Excuse us for one minute." Wolf was now in full panic mode. He was in unfamiliar territory dealing with such big numbers and was much more methodical when it came to business. The language of investments was foreign to him, and he typically moved deliberately. He was clearly outside his comfort zone.

Jon probed Wolf one last time. "You're absolutely sure about this, right?"

Wolf looked at Jon with intent before answering. "Buck, it's right down the middle of F.O.R. 's lane. To be able to help a company succeed that can rapidly scale the supply of a natural, cost-effective, biodegradable replacement for plastic."

"Guess I'm sold," Jon laughed, breaking the tension. But even in the aftermath of the negotiations, Wolf remained steadfastly uneasy.

"It's just an enormous sum of money, and I don't want you risking a chunk of your net worth. What if the company craters for some reason?"

"Stop your frettin', will ya? I'm a big boy. Like the sayin' goes... It's better to be half right on time than 100% right too late. The worst case is if the company tanks you will own the rights to your patents again. I did a back of the envelope calculation, and figure the patents alone are worth $40 million. I can live with that kind of downside."

Jon tapped the mute button on his watch. "I believe we have a deal."

"Great news," the CEO responded. "I don't mean to be pushy but is it feasible for you to close next week and wire by a week from Friday?"

"Sure. The money will be coming from a numbered account in Panama. One last request. Can we be an observer and sit in on the board meetings?"

Silence ensued. The two officers of the company couldn't believe their ears, especially after all the back-and-forth negotiations with the venture firm in Austin. All their interests were aligned, a dream-like scenario for GRP.

"Gentlemen, we agree."

"Great," Jon replied. "Y'all will be hearing from our legal counsel by email. Appreciate it if you can get them the paperwork and send wiring instructions, too."

"Thank you. I say with all sincerity that it's been a pleasure and we at GRP look forward to a long-term, mutually beneficial relationship." Jon hit the off button. He noticed Wolf staring at the ceiling in a trance-like state.

"Wolf! Snap out of it. Do you have a will by chance?"

"I don't. Why do you ask?"

"You need to create a will that gives me half the stock. If something were to happen to you or me for that matter, we need to have an agreement between us."

"Why only half? You're putting up all the money, and I don't think it's fair that I should get fifty percent of this deal."

"We're partners, aren't we?" So long as I recoup my investment from gross sales, I'm good."

Jon reflected upon how his mom's theory proved out. *Nothing of long-lasting significance and substance can be accomplished alone.* They held each other in selfless admiration and high esteem.

"All this damn negotiating makes me hungry. Want anything?"

"No, thanks. I'm fasting today. Just lemon water for me."

CHAPTER 20

DRACO SPIRITUS

June 2045

Thanks to a little help from her friends, An had been living in Denver for over two months as a full-time researcher and part-time professor in the hydrology department at Denver University. It was her dream job to be living and working in the U.S. Breathing fresh air in Colorado without a mask was a privilege she never took for granted. Denver's worst days of inversion layers and smog were infinitely better than breathing China's air under their best conditions. In 2045, the PRC required specialized masks in China's five largest industrial cities to protect its citizens from lung cancer and other health concerns.

She was also tasked with keeping an eye on the progress of F.O.R.'s mini-submarine project in a 40,000-square-foot warehouse in an industrial park located west of the old Denver airport. Jon and others were working diligently toward bringing An's mother from Shenzhou to Denver.

Yael decided to make the journey from Tel Aviv to see Jon and Darwin, in that order. Originally, she was going to pay a surprise visit to Jon by coordinating with Wolf but decided against it. She knew Jon's habit of traveling at a moment's notice and wasn't chancing it.

"How long has it been since we've been together? Over three months?"

"Don't remind me. The night I left Mongolia, I was sweatin' like a pig over a Fourth of July barbeque pit," said Jon. "Besides, we are only four months away from the Southland mission, and let's just say it's good timing on your part."

Jon met Yael at the airport in his refurbished Tesla Cyber Stealth, wowing her. Not only did the truck have bullet-proof glass it also had two ¾ inch steel doors with a chassis supporting the truck that could withstand a roadside bomb detonation. But the two features that Jon valued most were the truck's ability to change its outside 'skin' to camouflage and blend in with the surrounding environment within seconds, as well as the pickup's float capabilities and maneuverability on water for hours while traveling at a speed of eight knots.

Yael exited the small plane, and Jon was waiting on the side of the runway, standing next to his Tesla. "Nice truck, or whatever you call it," Yael said right before she gave him a huge hug and a long, sensuous kiss. They had electric pickups in Israel, but nothing like the Cyber Stealth.

"I'll take that kind of greeting any day of the week, but only comin' from you, Sol." Yael took a Shakespearean bow, as she exuded a smile that projected dozens of positive emotions, including joy, love, friendship, and connection.

"Glad to see you're traveling light."

"I learned in my university days how to travel minimally," she grinned.

On the drive toward Darwin, Yael was torn between staring at Jon and the spectacular nature she was witnessing, visible through the front windshield.

"There's nothing close to this in Israel. It's exquisite, and the only U.S. cities I've ever visited were New York City, Los Angeles, Miami, and of course Denver."

Jon nodded. He was single-mindedly focused on making sure that no one was following them as he approached the camouflaged parking space in the middle of Porcupine National Forest, constantly checking his side and rear-view mirrors. As they parked, Jon switched the outside of the car to a forest-like camouflage from its previous all-black exterior.

They exited the car and walked ninety paces toward the entrance to Darwin. Jon pressed a small knob on his watch, and the hatch opened. Like a chameleon, the hatch's top was perfectly disguised with dirt, wild grass, twigs, and moss about four inches thick.

Yael was startled and took a half step backward. "Didn't see that coming. Impressive." They quickly descended into Darwin as Jon hit the button a second time and the hatch closed above them with a soft thud.

"Wolf, where are you? Sol's here."

He walked out of his research lab wearing shorts, sandals, and a hoodie.

"Shalom, Wolf! Good to see you again," she said, extending her hand.

"The pleasure is mine." They sat down at the counter in the kitchen.

"You must be hungrier than a shark in shallow water. What can I get you?" Jon asked, trying to be the consummate host.

"I'll have whatever you're serving. Don't mind me. When it comes to food, I'm easy. But I would love something hot to drink, and just happen to have some *nana* tea in my bag. Would either of you like to try some?"

"What's *nana*?" Wolf asked with a perplexed look on his face.

"Oh sorry. Nana means 'mint' in Hebrew."

Jon poured everyone hot water, and Yael handed tea bags to Jon and Wolf. They caught up for a few minutes before Yael turned the conversation on its head.

"I'm curious. Do you have a name for the minisub yet? I know you've got fancy names for everything, right?"

"As a matter of fact, we do, Miss Smarty Pants. Wolf thought of the name. I'll give him the honors of explaining how he came up with it."

"I call it the *Spiritus Draconis*. Or Draco Spiritus for short. "

"Hmmm. Latin, I assume?" Yael inquired.

"Sure. Why not? Any guesses as to what it means?" Wolf shot back.

"Not a clue. My Latin is somewhere between sub-par and non-existent."

It was like opening a bottle of nitroglycerine to see Wolf's brain in overdrive. Like a tapestry, he fused the name together from various parts of his life. "The loose translation is Dragon's Breath. It is the name of the largest underground non-subglacial lake on the planet, located in Namibia."

"That's a strong start," Yael said in a complimentary tone.

"It covers over five acres. In Africa, with its inherent droughts and arid climate, this is rather unique. The name also has another meaning. Our mini sub will have the first effective underwater laser embedded into it. Hence, the dragon breathing fire analogy. What do you think?"

"Is that all you've got?" Yael teased Wolf playfully.

"There is one more thing. My theory is that the Chinese are going after the largest underground glacial lake in the world, Vostok Lake. It is conveniently located under Russia's Vostok station located on the surface of the central East Antarctic Ice Sheet. What's crazy is that the lake is over 13,000 feet below the surface of the ice, and almost sixteen hundred feet below sea level."

"The lake is massive," Jon added. "It covers almost five-thousand square miles with an average depth of fourteen hundred feet. It's about 1300 cubic miles, making it the sixth largest lake on the planet measured by volume."

Yael placed her hand on her chin. "So, let's recap here, shall we? You used geology, chemistry, biology, geography, physics, and language arts to explain this scenario. Kind of surprised you didn't use astronomy, but I'll let it slide."

"Well, that's not exactly true," Wolf said unabashedly. Scientists have hypothesized that the sub-glacial lake water itself may have been isolated for between fifteen and twenty-five million years. Because Lake Vostok may contain an environment sealed off below the ice for millions of years, astronomers and astrophysicists have hypothesized that the conditions of Vostok Lake may resemble the ice-covered oceans that exist on Jupiter's moon Europa, and Saturn's moon Enceladus."

Yael waved her arms above her head. "OK, Wolf. No mas. I surrender. You win. Now all you need to do is to explain to me and the rest of F.O.R. how under water lasers are going to work since no one has ever used them successfully."

"There's a bunch of physics involved, and it must work in deep water where the pressure is extreme. We are going to take Draco, sever the pipeline that China is running from the subglacial lakes, and then notify the UN and NATO that China and Russia are attempting to steal the planet's last bastion of fresh water." Wolf shrugged his shoulders in his own self-effacing way.

"Wait. Russia?"

"Yes. We assume that Russia is in cahoots aiding and abetting the Chinese with part of their submarine fleet."

"Somebody's gotta do it, and it might as well be us, right?" Jon said. "I'll tell you something that's been gnawing at me for years. Why would Chinese researchers at the best universities be so interested in subglacial lakes emptying into the ocean?"

Wolf, as if right on cue, walked over to a file that Jon kept in a cabinet under his workstation that required biometrics to open it. He pulled out an abstract written by two research facilities in China. One in Wuhan, and the other in Beijing.

"There's no logic as to why the PRC would be funding these kinds of research projects unless they had long-range plans to steal the water." Wolf's words were hanging listlessly in the air, as he slapped a white paper on the counter.

Scientists Track the Sudden Disappearance of an Antarctic Ice-Shelf Lake:
Massive Water Drainage into the Southern Ocean
Chinese Journal of Geophysical Antarctica Research July 2039

A global team of scientists from China has observed the sudden drainage of a massive, ice-covered lake within an Antarctic ice shelf. Scientists estimate that 650 million to 750 million cubic meters of water were drained from the bottom of the lake underneath a 5,000 feet thick shelf of floating ice. After the unnamed lake drained, a crater-like depression known as an ice doline in the ice surface appeared, covering eleven square kilometers.

"Well, I'll be a damned catfish on dry land. That's about the same volume of water as in Lake Cumberland. We used to weekend there on my grandpa's houseboat," Jon exclaimed. "What took place is known as hydrofracturing. The flow into the ocean beneath would have been so intense it would have simulated the velocity of water flowing over Niagara for three days!"

Jon was pacing back and forth, thinking about how he was going to deliver the message to his fellow F.O.R. compatriots. He would have to include in great detail why the mission would succeed against all odds.

———

"I believe everyone's on the video call," Wolf stated.

Jon started right in. "Greetings, everyone. I believe it's the proper time to make a full confession to my 'family.' I have an ace up my sleeve. My father advised me that if you're going to sit at a high-stakes poker table, you need to have an edge. My ace in the hole is an underwater laser expert who's on the 'cutting' edge in her field." Jon heard murmuring from Sinclair and Phillippe.

"Her name is Dr. Shanaya Praani. Shanaya graduated from the Indian Institute of Technology and received her doctorate in Quantum Physics from Stanford, where she is currently doing post-doc work."

"Let me guess. I suppose her name has some hidden meaning?" Yael asked.

"Why would you think differently?" Jon replied. "Shanaya means 'first ray of the sun' and Praani is a Hindi word for water. How's that for destiny? Her research achievements have provided a blueprint for operating quantum tech in space and underwater. And like all of us, she came from humble beginnings."

"Can you clarify a few things? Have you checked her out?" An asked from her Denver three-bedroom condo.

"Just to clarify, I'm not talking about Praani joining the mission or F.O.R. It's more about working with her on finalizing the mini-sub's underwater laser capabilities for two reasons. One, the ability of an underwater laser to disable certain submarine software and electronics. And two, I want a laser that can cut through at least two inches of pipe underwater. Any questions?"

"Sounds too good to be true," Elena piped in from Toronto. "How did you meet her and how long have you known her?"

240

"Got introduced by a colleague I've known at Stanford for a decade, and who I did my PhD with at Cal Berkeley."

An was digging in. "How does your colleague know Praani?"

"Simple," replied Wolf." My colleague is part of her research team."

Sinclair pressed the issue from his London flat. "I'm aware that fifteen years ago the U.S. Navy started mounting lasers on its Virginia-class subs to counter air and surface attacks, especially drones. We also know there are five U.S. nuclear submarines in existence that could destroy the world in less time than it takes to order a pizza, and have it delivered. I know the Russians and Chinese have their fair share as well."

"That's reassuring," Yael added. "Please enlighten us." Yael caused a smile to emerge on Sinclair's face, even when discussing a most somber topic.

"I'll be brief. Your Navy's Ohio-class ballistic submarine can hold up to twenty-four UGM-133 Trident II D5. If each missile can carry twelve W88 475 kiloton thermonuclear warheads, it equals two-hundred and eighty-eight targets."

"What's the circular error of probability"? Yael asked after a moment.

"Ah. Good question, Sol. It's accurate within a 90-meter circumference."

"That's depressing," Wolf sighed.

"I'll second that," said Elena. "And you better believe that the Russian and Chinese Navies have the same military threat technology."

"Yes, but the true shitstorm scenario is that each Ohio can carry twenty missiles," Jon added. "Due to the Chinese Navy's continuous saber-rattling in the Pacific, the U.S. Navy has deployed seven of these subs in the Pacific. They all have first-strike capabilities and could hit over 4600 targets in thirty minutes, assuming they were all fired simultaneously. The bottom line is that there's no way to defend against a launch of this magnitude. It's that simple."

"That's extremely comforting," Phillippe bemoaned with sarcastic flare.

"I think Sapphire is correct. You've got to figure that the Russians and the Chinese have developed similar nuclear redundancy. Isn't that right, Dr. Sinclair?" Jon stammered, enveloped in a haze of fear at the thought that civilization could be destroyed in less time than he could fly his plane to Isle Royale.

"That's correct, but for the sake of time I'll spare you the details."

"Angie, where is China getting all the money to fund their growing submarine and naval fleets? I know its economy and population have been stagnating for the last decade," asked Yael.

Sinclair jumped in to clarify. "What our intelligence gleaned is that at the time of the annexation of North Korea by China, the North Korean Navy had over one hundred submarines operating in its fleet. At the time, the U.S. Navy had a slight lead, say seventy-one versus sixty-eight for China."

"Does anyone know what the rarest precious metal is with the highest density?" Jon queried the team.

"I'll bite. It's osmium, isn't it?" Wolf suggested.

"Give the man a prize."

A light bulb went off in Sinclair's head. "Everyone believed that its primary use was for jewelry. I learned several years ago from a British physicist that when this rare material is heated up to 400 degrees Celsius, it becomes crystallized and is harder than diamonds. Calvin told me that the Chinese were starting to use it in the construction of nuclear submarines because as osmium cools down, it becomes a super-conductor enabling the transport of electricity without loss. Raw osmium comes out of a mine as a rather unspectacular gray powder and is extremely poisonous. Once it is heated, its crystalline structure changes, and when cooled it becomes harmless."

"Damn the PRC!" exclaimed An incredulously. "Never saw the osmium thing coming, even as they went on a rampage purchasing African mines."

"Not to worry. Remember when I mentioned a while back that I had a connection to a huge mining operation in Perth?" asked Jon. "Just before I began construction of our mini sub, I got a call from down under that they had discovered an area with abnormal amounts of rhodium and osmium. After telling the mine owner I was working on a project that could disrupt the Chinese and the Russian arm's lead, I 'persuaded' the mine owners to sell me whatever I needed at cost."

"And how does that help us again?" Phillippe asked in a dubious manner.

"My crack team of former naval engineers figured out how to incorporate it into the outer shell of our mini-sub to increase durability as well as for conducting electricity. Because of it, we may have a leg up on the Chinese and Russian submarine fleets. Remember, the goal is to disrupt the pipeline and protect ourselves from Chinese and Russian subs in the process."

"Hallelujah," said Elena. That same night, Yael and Jon were alone for the first time since Israel. Wolf was visiting his uncle at the local hospital. For dinner, Jon made Yael his special trout recipe with a spinach salad, complete with mandarin oranges, baked potato, and green beans almandine. He surprised her with her favorite dessert. A chocolate sundae with chocolate chip avocado ice cream, and a generous heap of coconut whipped cream.

She looked at him with her playful Cupid eyes and walked over to hug Jon from behind. "I didn't know you could cook a meal like this. You're so multi-faceted. There is one other thing that whipped coconut is good for!"

Jon blushed a pale shade of red as Yael gave him the look of a wanton lover, grabbed his hand, and escorted him to the bedroom. She gazed at him, her aqua eyes intense and fascinated by the prospects of what would happen next.

"I figured the Israelis were direct and aggressive, but you're somethin' else," Jon said with a thick nervous Southern drawl.

"You're not complaining, are you?" Within seconds, Yael was on top of him, writhing in full-blown, unbridled ecstasy. Her back was arched, head tilted to the side, hair flowing as her fingertips braced her upper body on Jon's stomach lightly for support. Her rhythm was mystical, as if from another time and place, like nothing Jon had experienced before. Yael felt like she was outside of her body looking in, as she surpassed her imagined limits of what she thought sex could be. She came into his arms, breathing heavily.

The next day, Jon was on the phone with Elena trying to determine if she had the experience and the capability of helping him run the minisub if the situation called for it. They were stuck on the topic of Russian politics, and the contamination of Lake Baikal.

"Chirkov is a maniacal, one-man psychodrama. Someone with an outsized inferiority complex that drives his predatory instincts, stalking the world with a chip the size of a basketball on his shoulder. He did nothing other than put up signs to protect Baikal. And let's not forget what happened in 1961 when Khrushchev was in power."

Jon's mind went hurtling back through history. "Wait. You mean the Cuban missile crisis?"

"Before that. Does Tsar Bomba ring a bell?"

"Not really," Jon said disappointedly because he didn't know the answer.

Elena's voice dropped an octave to convey the horror she was about to describe. "The former Soviet Union exploded a nuclear bomb in the Arctic region, and it just happened to be the largest bomb ever tested. It is believed that people felt the heat some 275 kilometers away. So powerful that certain people saw the flash from over a thousand kilometers away. Who knows what the long-term damage is and how many centuries the side effects will linger, causing carnage among wildlife and water in the region?"

"How big was the bomb?"

"Thank God they only built a fifty-megaton bomb. It weighed over twenty-seven tons and was twenty-six feet long. Khrushchev had originally ordered a hundred-megaton bomb, but the Soviets didn't have a plane large enough to make the drop."

"That's downright ugly."

"Can you believe that a two-thousand-pound parachute was used to release the bomb? When it finally exploded, the murderous mushroom cloud reached an altitude of two hundred thousand feet, the equivalent of thirty-eight miles. Thankfully, no one was killed, at least not directly from the blast itself." Jon gulped hard with a sinking feeling.

"I guess this is as good a time as any to bring up my past," she suggested, trying to be as transparent as possible.

"What's on your mind?"

"I experienced a couple of anxiety attacks while I was in the navy when we were submerged underwater for more than seven to ten days at a time. I don't suppose we will be down there anywhere near that length of time?"

"Doubt if we will be underwater for more than five days consecutively."

"I'll bring my meds along just in case."

"Great. Thanks for your honesty. Good thing F.O.R. takes the Latin phrase *Si vis pacem, para bellum* to heart." "I'm impressed with your command of Latin but have no idea what the hell you just said."

"It means *If you want peace, prepare for war.*"

CHAPTER 21

THE TASMANIAN ANGEL

July 2045

With a three-hour layover at LAX before his flight to Sydney, Jon had the forethought to bring running gear in his backpack. Weather permitting, he would go for a run in LA before boarding the nine-hour marathon flight over the Pacific.

His five-mile run was a welcomed relief, and he managed to grab a shower in the Qantas executive lounge. He always slept better after a good run.

Yael arrived in Melbourne a half hour before Jon's flight, and spontaneously decided to meet him at the gate. She noticed two Russian-speaking men sitting in front of the bistro where she was working on her laptop. Yael took a deep breath and thought, *just my mazel if it's the same two guys who broke into my condo.* She made a conscious decision to confront her potential nightmare head-on, rose from her seat, and walked right past the two men speaking Russian.

Yael caught a slight 'whiff' of their conversation and breathed a sigh of relief knowing it was not the two men from Tel Aviv. As she strolled into and out of the bathroom, she noticed upon her return that the two men were gone. Strange. *They were sitting there a minute ago with beer and appetizers, and now they're nowhere to be found.*

Yael looked up at the monitor and noticed that Jon's flight had landed, and caught the tail end of the plane pulling into the gate. Even though she'd been with Jon less than a month ago at Darwin, she was excited to see her love and the genesis behind F.O.R. She didn't have to wait long because Jon was the second one off the plane, backpack in tow. He saw her standing there, slid his backpack off his left shoulder and caught her as she jumped into his arms.

"Wow. I feel like I'm home," Jon emoted. They kissed and then gazed into each other's eyes. After a minute of holding her, Jon picked up his backpack, grabbed Yael's hand, and started walking toward the rental car pickup. Yael spoke about the Russians at the bistro, and how they had abruptly vanished.

Jon shrugged. "Do you think it's something we should be concerned about?"

"No idea, really, other than we should be aware of our surroundings."

Jon had arranged to rent an all-electric Canoo pickup truck. The bed of their rental was designed to retrofit a variety of camper shells. When she laid her cyan-colored eyes on the tan vehicle, she let out a squeal that turned some heads.

"I thought you'd like it. We can drive right up to a beach of our choice and camp out close enough to hear the waves caressing the shore. I canned the hotel on the beach idea. I hope that's alright with you. Besides, no one will be able to find us where we are going because we don't even know ourselves yet."

"Fabulous. I have to say you're a hopeful romantic, and I like it."

"But not a naïve romantic." Jon explained some of the Canoo's safety features. "The windshield and all the windows are bullet-proof, and I brought my portable honing device to detect intruders. I'm a realistic romantic."

"Where are we headed? Or are you going to keep me in suspense? I've only been to Australia once before and spent most of my time in Sydney, so this is all new to me."

"I've got the perfect plan. We're gonna find a spot near Bondi

Beach. This afternoon we're going to wander around on Coogee Walk, and if we make it far enough to Tamarama, Bronte, and Clovelly, we'll eat an early dinner at the restaurant of your choice. Sound good?"

"It sounds better than good!" Yael said with a sparkle in her eye.

Around dusk, Yael and Jon made love on a secluded sandy cove about thirty feet from the waves sliding up the beach. They went back to their pickup camper and slept soundly the rest of the night, only to be awakened by the sound of ocean water caressing the shore. The sun's rays were dancing on the water, creating a mystical reflection that led all the way to the horizon and back.

Jon was mesmerized, admiring Yael's inner and outer beauty.

"What?" she said blushing.

"Why do I feel like I woke up next to an angel? You level me with your voice, your laughter, your scent. I never take you for granted. And for the record, I've never said that to anyone before."

"I don't know what to say, except that I'm honored, and I love you too?"

Jon and Yael took a quick skinny dip, dried off, dressed, and headed for Sydney airport, where they caught a 10 a.m. flight to Hobart. Jon had one last surprise for Yael. They were going to meet the renowned researcher Dr. Praani, who had arranged for Bernays to be there as well. It was serendipitous that Praani was in India visiting family.

Jon was able to convince her to stop into the Tasmania University lab on her way to Stanford where she was teaching a PhD class for the semester. The meeting was scheduled for 1 p.m. at Praani's office.

Jon and Yael arrived a half hour early to spend time alone with Bernays. The walls and desk were decorated with assorted pictures of Praani's family, all the way back to her great-grandparents. The largest wall had a mural of a sunrise in Dong in the state of Arunachal Pradesh over the Bay of Bengal, a yellow haze that streaked orange with an azure background. The big, bullet-proof window overlooked a rose garden dotted with pink, red, and yellow flowers that bloom all year round, a miniature version of the Chandigarh Rose Garden. It was an idyllic and peaceful setting for someone who spent half of her life entrenched in far flung, mundane research labs and crammed into airplane seats.

Jon led the discussion. "Dr. Bernays, this is Dr. Yael Solomon from

Sde Boker in Israel. I hope you understand that everything that we discuss today will be kept confidential among us all."

"Jon, please call me Adrienne. This is the second time I've made the request." She winked at Yael. "And Yael needs no introduction. I'm aware of her work in desalination. And her work on retention of groundwater and the reduction of evaporation."

"Of course, Adrienne. Incidentally, have you been approached or been working with any Russians or Chinese scientists lately?" Jon asked tactfully.

Bernays was startled by his direct questioning. "Interesting way to start a conversation. In fact, I have been approached by two scientists from the PRC about a collaborative effort. However, I respectfully declined their overtures. I couldn't bring myself to do it. I knew they had an agenda diametrically opposed to my own."

"May I ask why?" Yael chimed in.

"Certainly. It is more about their track record concerning human rights violations, and oppression than anything else. The Chinese have been conducting naval maneuvers in this area for more than a decade now, and they've practically overrun New Zealand and other islands nearby."

"We all know that they've had a freshwater deficit for the last two decades," Jon added. "They're trying to branch out to other areas in proximity to figure out how to deal with their acute supply/demand imbalance. The Russians? They're a different story with their own agenda."

Jon and Yael looked at each other, and then at Bernays. They were nodding their heads as if to say that they agreed wholeheartedly with both Bernays's philosophical and moral points of view. Just then, Praani strolled through the door.

"G'day everyone. Dr. Solomon, I'm Dr. Praani. Pleased to meet you."

"Likewise," said Yael.

"As they say in the South, *damn glad to meet you,*" Jon echoed. That was all she needed to break the ice. *Just think. Three of the most high-powered intellects on the planet and it's a privilege to be in the same room with them.*

Jon relished the idea of hanging around intelligent people regardless of gender or race. He wasn't intimidated by their brilliance either. In fact, he welcomed the opportunity and relished the three hours they had together.

"Adrienne, can you tell me about the silicone robot? Can it really dive as deep as the Mariana Trench while navigating the pressures of the ocean floor?"

"A few of my colleagues and I developed a newly improved, self-powered soft robot using underwater wave technology. It moves around like a manta ray with two fins that can glide and can take pictures as well as videos, with the composition of squid or jellyfish that roam near the ocean floor."

Jon was feeling empowered as he switched on his engineering mind. "And how do you design electronic components to withstand the crushing pressure?"

"We were able to spread out the electronic circuitry with a silicone matrix that is more flexible. When you apply battery current, the softer material of the robot's body can convert electrical into mechanical energy."

"Fascinating," Yael replied. "And this works at depths of 9,000 meters?"

"Yes. We continue to have reliable results in the Mariana Trench 10,900 meters below the surface. And our robot was able to reach speeds of ten centimeters per second. We are working on a non-traditional deep-sea explorer, not unlike mini-submarines used for research, comprised of a combination of this malleable silicone material, and traditional composites capable of withstanding intense hull pressure."

Praani was sensing some strange energy from Jon. His head was about to explode with excitement. "Dr. Praani? Are you thinking what I'm thinking? The implications are mind-boggling and..."

Praani walked toward the window facing the rose garden. She was feeling calm yet confident about her invention. "Do you mean, could my underwater laser attach to a device like this? And could it operate effectively near the ocean floor?"

Like all good scientists, Praani measured her words carefully before elaborating. "I don't see why not. And I suppose your next question is how long it would take to evaluate it and find out?" she asked, smiling.

Jon admired pragmatism and ability to cut right to the core. "Dr. Praani, how did you know…?"

"Great minds think alike?" They all laughed.

"I'm not sure I would put myself anywhere near the same category as y'all, but I'll take the compliment."

Drs. Praani and Bernays were highly curious about Jon's mini sub back in Denver. "Jon, can you give us the dimensions such as weight, height, the volume of water dispersed, and the materials it's made from? That would help us answer your questions," inquired Praani.

Jon pulled out his laptop, placed it on the table, and started to log into the Denver facility's cameras. "I'll do one better. In seconds, we'll be able to have a full 360-degree view of our home-made mini-sub."

Fortunately for Jon, some of the engineers were already there working, even though it only was 7:30 a.m. mountain time. "There she is!" Jon said with enthusiasm. "Ain't she a beauty?"

For about thirty seconds, Praani and Bernays were both speechless, as they eyed the sea-going vessel, manipulating various camera angles.

"That is a real piece of art and science," said Praani. "Where is it being constructed and housed currently?"

"Afraid that's top-secret. I can't really divulge that kind of information with the mission so close. Let's just say it's somewhere west of the Mississippi River."

"Impressive, but I would still need the dimensions and the material it is made from to determine where and how the underwater laser would be fastened for maximum results. What are your plans for the laser?"

Jon hedged. "That depends on the kind of power it can generate. I would like to state off the record that the purpose is to cut through some piping laying on the ocean floor that is bare minimum two inches thick."

"Can you be more specific, Jon?"

"'Fraid not. With all due respect, I cannot disclose anything else."

Praani walked around her mahogany desk and opened her laptop, as she went into her analytical mode before asking her next set of questions.

"Do you have evidence, either satellite or underwater photos, that this alleged pipeline truly exists? And how deep the spot is on the ocean floor?"

"Good questions. Let's just say I have very reliable secondhand information from a non-U.S. naval officer that the pipeline does indeed exist. As for the depth of the ocean floor that varies between 8,000-9000 meters."

"I'm stunned," Praani replied, lowering her glasses and giving him a dubious look. Bernays agreed. There was enough silence filling the room they could hear planes taking off while Praani was developing her own theories.

"I'm ready to give you all the support I can with respect to your vision. This seems too big for scientists with a conscience, a heart, and a soul to ignore." Praani concurred. "I'm right behind you, Adrienne."

"Great. I'd like us to put together a sixty-day plan of how we are all going to work together to make sure our mission is a success, of course with y'all's input. Confidentiality, including phone conversations, P-mails, and P-texts need to happen on F.O.R.'s private intranet. You'll have P-mail addresses later today."

Bernays glanced at Praani before speaking. "Your mission is of the utmost importance. Thank you for including us."

Praani turned to face both Jon and Yael. "Ditto. Let's go to work, shall we?"

CHAPTER 22

READY. FIRE. AIM.

June 2045

"Welcome to the fifth official call for Southland. I received confirmation last night from Michael's intro to the British Navy," said Jon with Wolf sitting next to him in Darwin munching on some raw veggies. "Apparently, one of their subs wandering around the Southern Ocean originated from underneath Antarctica. Both the Chinese and the Russians have created landing strips of their own and have not only moved military equipment onto the northeastern part of the continent, but we believe that one or both navies are operating robotic nuclear-powered submarines and undersea drones in the Antarctic region." Elena's holograph looked concerned.

"On another note, wanted to give credit to Wolf for the contributions he made to Draco. He was at the forefront of a project that could succeed against all odds." Wolf was a bit embarrassed at the praise being heaped on him.

"Excuse me, but who exactly are you referring to? It's certainly not anyone I know. Why don't you give your vocal cords a chance to catch up with your brain?" Wolf said grinning. The team roared with laughter.

"I get the hint. Let's talk about what is going to give us the edge for Southland. Draco can hold a maximum of three people and is fifty percent faster than its bulkier nuclear sub counterparts, notwithstanding their ability to outmaneuver and dodge torpedoes fired at its smaller hull. And it can reach depths beyond traditional nuclear subs equipped with complete robotic tech."

Elena piped in from a secure line from Toronto. "You alluded to sharing big news on the call, correct?"

"The big news is that Sol and I met with two world-class scientists, one of them courtesy of Wolf. Dr. Praani is on the cutting edge of underwater lasers, something that can 'cut' through two-inch thick metal lying on the ocean floor. And should we become the hunted as opposed to the hunter, these lasers possess state-of-the-art stealth capabilities and can fire underwater, traveling distances of up to four-hundred meters. They can also disable software and electrical systems of unmanned underwater drones."

Yael added her own expertise. "Like Israel's Iron Lasers, version 3.0 of the Iron Dome. These new lasers are equally effective both as offensive and defensive weapons. They can short-circuit a torpedo's software before it reaches its intended target. Think underwater taser."

"What's the net effect?" asked Sinclair.

"The recipients of these laser shocks are unable to fire a torpedo for five to seven minutes. And under the right circumstances, it will render these naval weapons useless, like pieces of floating metal, and allow Draco to fly the coop."

"Excuse me. Do you have hard evidence that these underwater lasers can disable a large underwater drone or torpedoes fired, or is it merely anecdotal?" Phillippe asked respectfully, sitting at a desk in his stark Toronto office.

"Good question. The short answer is yes. Let me come back to that later if I may. In addition, their stealth capabilities enable mini- subs to become submerged ghosts. They can literally drop off the screens of the most sophisticated sonar equipment housed within today's most advanced submarines, destroyers gliding along the water's surface, and reconnaissance planes flying overhead with state-of-the-art sonar detection."

"Is the Draco's driverless feature operational?" asked Elena.

"The short answer is no. The main issue is that we need to be within ten kilometers to operate it, and in Antarctica, that's going to be a helluva challenge, even for us."

"Do we have approximate coordinates for this pipeline matrix?" Yael asked.

"It is my belief they have a pipeline in place that is intended to flow towards the coast of southern New Zealand. I have reason to believe this is where their newly constructed naval base is stationed. I'm going to let Angie answer the rest."

There was a palpable tension building on the holographic video stream.

An cleared her throat. "I'll tell you what I recently told Buck. These are only hypotheses but keep in mind that the PRC is still smarting and quite displeased that they spent $12 billion on a pipeline from Lake Baikal to Lanzhou. It's money in Chirkov's pocket that China will never recoup."

An paused, pulling some notes from her phone based on a previous discussion with Jon. "Again, please keep in mind that what I say next is based on conjecture. The PRC could run the main line from New Zealand all the way to Jakarta, through Malaysia, and then under the South China Sea between the coasts of Vietnam and the Philippines. Given that rising ocean tides have left parts of those coastlines submerged, it serves as an excellent smokescreen for the PRC's plans. Where it ends up in mainland China is anybody's guess."

"Where would you run the pipeline?" Phillippe asked.

"If I were running this project, the primary cities that I would target are Qinshan to the south, adjacent to the nuclear power plant, Zhanjiang to the southeast, or possibly Beihai on the southwest coast. I am trying to get more information, but it is too much of a risk to ask my friends to dig deeper."

Elena pulled up a map of the southern coastline of China projected from her smart pen onto a wall. "Interesting theories, Angie. What about Guangzhou?"

"Doesn't hold water. You would have to thread the needle between Hong Kong and Macau. Too many eyes in that region."

"Why not go all the way to Fuzhou? It's much closer to Shanghai," Elena suggested to An.

"True. But the pipeline would have to go right past Taiwan. The military conflict potential would negate that as a possibility. It would never fly."

"Guess I'm satisfied that Angie has narrowed it down to three cities."

"What's a realistic timetable to launch?" Yael asked Jon.

"Five months from now during Antarctica's summer, we're going in by sea with Draco that'll be transported by a private freighter sailing from Hobart. The barge that will carry her is also equipped with two choppers on board that are equipped to land on ice or snow, even another sea-going vessel. Draco will be accompanied by a nuclear-powered yacht. The barge is loaded with special hydrogen-powered cranes that can lower our sub into the water."

"Wait. Did you say a nuclear-powered yacht?" Elena asked.

"Yes. And I'm gonna defer details on that for the time being."

"Why not leave from New Zealand? Isn't it twenty-five hundred miles south of Australia?" An inquired.

"The short answer is that you and I both know they're too many Chinese hanging around and the PRC has a naval noose around New Zealand. It's way too risky to launch from there. Besides, Australia is still our ally, and I trust them implicitly, especially given my relationships in Hobart."

"Who is going to navigate the sub?" probed Phillippe.

"Draco will be navigated by Elena and myself. We plan to attach the laser in Hobart and test it underwater before Draco gets on a slow boat to Antarctica." Everyone looked at Elena as if she was some kind of guinea pig being sacrificed for the greater good.

"That's great, but where are you going to get the money to pay for all this? Even you can't bankroll a project of this magnitude by yourself, yes?" Elena's voice echoed off the walls of Darwin. She looked past Jon and noticed a framed quote in the kitchen. *If the world was perfect, it wouldn't be. Yogi Berra*

The quote may be apropos given our circumstances, but who the hell is Yogi Berra? Elena thought.

"And how long have you been working on the construction of Draco that started at ground zero?" Phillippe asked with an edgy tone as F.O.R continued to grill Jon.

"One at a time, please. A group of former high-level retired engineers from the Navy and I have been working on this sub for over fifteen months before y'all went on the joy ride with me to Mongolia. To answer your question, Elena, I could bank the project myself, but decided to diversify the expense with a successful tech friend of mine. They have no idea what purpose the mini-sub is going to serve except they believe in preserving Antarctica. Call me the 24/7 optimist."

"How long will the mission take?" Phillippe asked with a firm curiosity.

"I can give you a range but can't or won't say definitively. My best guess is minimum of a month, and a maximum of two. I'm prayin' it will be on the shorter end of that range. It's the best I can do but can say with certainty that it won't be a quick jaunt like Mongolia."

"Can you subsidize us for time missed at work to cover the two-month gap?"

"That was already in my plan, but I never communicated it to y'all. I think we've covered it, except that we have the wind at our backs with some senior command of the British Navy aiding and abetting us," Jon grinned.

Yael suddenly emerged like a butterfly from a cocoon. "It's a relief that you're not asking me to be on Draco. Israelis can't take that kind of cold." She lit up the holographic call with her reassuring smile.

Wolf spontaneously decided to go for the close.

"OK. Let's do roll call as a formality. Who's in? Or perhaps a better question. Is anybody out? I would prefer your answer now, but if you need another day, I understand. Also, want to acknowledge that this is a much higher level of risk, and the commitment may be for a month and not days like the last jaunt," Wolf said empathetically. "Keep in mind that the potential reward is significantly higher as well."

Wolf proceeded to go around the holographic video, asking the F.O.R. members, one by one on his 85-inch OLED screen.

"Angie?"

"Yes. Of course, I'm in. You got me out of China, didn't you? I'll support you any way I can."

"Thanks, Angie. Sapphire?" Wolf continued.

"In. You know what I think of Chirkov and his band of thieves. Fuck those fuckin' thugs!" Elena bellowed with insane laughter.

"Court? What say you?"

"I had so much fun the first time around, how could I say no?" Phillippe responded without hesitation. "Definitely in, and besides, I'm used to the cold."

"Michael Sinclair? As someone who did not participate in the Mongolian mission, how do you vote?"

"Wolf, it's a must for me. I really don't feel as if I have a choice in the matter. We just cannot afford to allow Antarctica to become a statistical artifact, and another wasteland like the Arctic has become over the last fifty years."

"Sol? We assume you're in but always like to ask the question."

"Wolf, I'm beyond flattered by your invitation, but I really need a day to reflect on my decision. I live by a saying, 'Just because we can, doesn't imply we should.'"

The room had the air of a funeral as if someone near and dear to them died.

"Sol, there is no 'should' in this case," replied Jon with confused eyes.

"Look, everyone. I'm 99% certain, just need a little time to process things. You know, being away from Israel for up to two months is something I've never done before." Yael's hesitation caused a ripple of anxiety throughout the team.

Jon's jaw clenched ever so slightly. He assumed that Yael was a slam dunk because she not once, even for a moment, had ever led him to believe otherwise. Yael had taught him so much about himself by being true to herself. In fact, she was irreplaceable from Jon's perspective. And in more ways than one.

"Sol? Just so you know, and I'm certain that I speak for the entire group, we are not taking 'no' for an answer. Take as much time as you like. I don't want to put any pressure on you, but besides me and Sapphire, you are the only one in the group that has experience with submarines and can be trained quickly to operate Draco in case we need a backup plan at the last minute."

Wolf called out Jon's name.

"Buck? For the official record, are you in?"

Jon gave Wolf the 'look' of shock before he responded. "What?" Elena and Yael said in unison. "You've got to be kidding, right?"

Jon hesitated for effect. "Guess so. I'm fully vested. Besides, the pay is great." Jon managed to cut the tension in the air.

Wolf ignored his friend's sarcasm. "Looks like we've got a quorum."

Jon closed the discussion. "To reiterate, the mission will be a surgical operation. We must remove the far-reaching tentacles of the Kremlin and the PRC and prevent them from stealing the contents of the subglacial lakes. I'm cautiously optimistic now that the leaks of our former Chilean friend have been cauterized. Details to follow in a couple of weeks. Stay safe everyone." They all disconnected as holographs disappeared one by one.

Jon was left wondering about Yael. He would be bearing more than his share of the burden if she declined to participate. He knew with every cell in his body that it was mission-critical to have her on board. He longed to be with her again. More like ached.

Jon turned toward Wolf. "If Sol refuses the mission, they might as well dip my balls in Tennessee honey, tie me naked to a tree in the middle of a bee farm, and then throw rocks at the hives. That might be less painful."

Wolf looked at his friend, who was completely vulnerable, hanging by a thread. "Whatever you say. You're the boss. I'm just an hourly worker." They both cracked up.

With the addition of Sinclair, the improved F.O.R. team wasn't naïve. Not by a longshot. They knew exactly what they were getting themselves into. The phrase 'this time is different' was top of mind. While the first mission took five days out of their lives from beginning to end, this one had the potential to take months, and had the feel of indefinite. They all had a healthy dose of fear, heading into a future that was at best risky and opaque. And they had this in common. All were idealists grounded in realism. F.O.R. was fighting on behalf of something that transcended all else, including their lives as well as their own countries.

It was now apparent to Jon that they all could carry more than their own weight. It was their passion and native intelligence that ruled the day, binding them together into a collective fate.

An silently raged, sitting in her home in Denver. *Now that the PRC is desperate, money is no object. Especially with the country's farming industry and drinking water supply hanging in the balance. They're about to use a show of force to provide enough clean water for their own farmers and citizens. I'm completely freaked out. They will stop at nothing.*

Phillipe was pondering the question driving from his Toronto office to his three-flat. *Canada's sitting pretty, at least for the moment. We've got fifteen percent of the renewable global supply of fresh water. Combined with the fact that Canada only has approximately one-half of one percent of the world's population, we're in a unique position except for one minor detail. We're vulnerable from the North and our army and navy suck. Hope the country we border protects us.*

Yael was sitting in her condo with a view of the Mediterranean in the background. She felt alone, not lonely. *Just because I love the man who founded F.O.R. doesn't mean I have to go on his crazy, convoluted mission. I'm torn between my country and the team. They're like family to me. I just don't know.*

What Wolf didn't say out loud was that he thought the damage was done, not only with Antarctica but also the extraction of water from subglacial lakes. *It appears irreversible. The hands of time could be slowed by hydrogen. The implementation of green hydrogen on a mass scale could be helpful, but I'm not convinced damage caused by climate change has any chance of being reversed.*

CHAPTER 23

RACE TO THE BOTTOM

August 2045

J on wasn't taking any chances with his recently created multi-million-dollar piece of highly sophisticated, technologically superior submergent war machine. Jon and Wolf were standing on a remote dock in Long Beach, waiting for Draco to be loaded on from an oversized railcar that originated from Denver to a cargo ship. Before the cargo vessel containing *Draco Spiritus* set sail, Jon had arranged a preemptive move with Admiral Brown in case the Russians or Chinese had gotten wind of F.O.R.'s plans. A British nuclear submarine was scheduled to meet the cargo ship carrying Draco near the Hawaiian Islands and would serve as an escort for the journey to Tasmania.

Jon peered at the cargo ship with his binoculars, let them fall around his neck, and with an astonished look on his face, turned toward his partner in crime. "Really, Wolf? *Tethys*?" Wolf had the cargo ship repainted in large black letters.

"Tethys is the Greek goddess of freshwater. Surprised you didn't know."

"Whatever. You are the only person on the planet who would do this."

Except for Jon, Wolf, and Sinclair, the remainder of F.O.R and the crew would be unaware of the British Navy's presence. "You do realize that Admiral Brown has assured me that their sub would remain submerged the entire journey, always within 3500 meters of Tethys. Brown is our guardian angel and our insurance that we get in and out of the cold, pristine hell of Antarctica."

––––––––

Everyone arrived in Hobart within hours of each other. Yael from Tel Aviv, Phillippe and Elena from Toronto, Jon and Wolf from Darwin, An from Denver, and Sinclair from London. It was the only chance for Bernays and Praani to meet the entire team in person.

Praani and her engineers were working furiously on the final details of attaching the laser to Draco. Time was not on their side. Their one advantage was that Hobart was the home port for both the Australian and French Antarctic operations, and an ideal location for the launch.

Jon showed up at an obscure, secluded dock the morning after they all arrived at 7:30 a.m. It was away from the Macquarie docks on the Derwent River where most of the cruise ships were resting. This incognito location was chosen to prevent Draco from being spotted by tourists, satellites, or Chinese intelligence drones that may have been lurking overhead. When Jon felt it was safe, he contacted Wolf and Elena to meet him at the secure dock.

Besides Sinclair, the rest of the F.O.R. team was a bit surprised that Hobart was the chosen location, mostly because they assumed it would be on the mainland of Australia, where they would have military protection.

"You know what I like about this place?" Jon announced.

"No. What?" Wolf asked.

"Despite Tasmania being the smallest state in Australia, over forty percent of its territory is reserved for national parks and world heritage wilderness. It's practically timeless. Kind of like the UP in Michigan."

"How long do you think we will be at sea once we set sail from Hobart?" Elena asked trying to prepare herself for the first leg of the journey.

Jon looked around the dock to see if there were any stragglers or uninvited guests. He noticed a few tourists, nothing out of the ordinary. "Well, normally it's about 5300 kilometers, so I would have originally answered your question with eleven to twelve days. I do have good news."

"What's that?"

"You know the atomic yacht I rented? It's a floating five-star hotel that will get us there in less than half the normal time. It has some tantalizing weaponry like the USS Zumwalt (DDG 3000), the newest, most lethal battleship in the U.S. Navy roaming the Pacific. It can use decoys against torpedoes and its rockets can hit a target up to one hundred miles away. Plus, its sonar and radar capabilities are beyond reproach."

"What?" Elena responded, practically picking her jaw up off the floor. Jon, with a smile plastered all over his boyish face pulled out a picture of the magnificent floating vessel. It looked like a spacecraft on water, impenetrable from the harshest environment on the planet.

"The maiden voyage left Tokyo on December 7, 2041. Although it was never publicized, the highly secretive excursion went around Antarctica and back to Tokyo. The passengers were mostly scientists and a couple of rich, eccentric billionaires who were sworn to secrecy."

"I imagine your rental is expensive," Yael added.

"Yeah, this baby costs $1.2 million a month, or $2 million for two months, but it's worth every penny. It was recommended by Admiral Brown, and he told me that if I used his name, we would get a discount." Jon shrugged his shoulders. "It was constructed in Seoul."

"What about the crew?" Yael asked.

"Most of the crew are ex-navy that defected from Russia."

"How many people will we be?"

"There are ten of us, including two engineers from Praani's lab in case something goes wrong with the underwater laser. And fifteen crew, including the captain and the cook. The only hassle is those batshit crazy Tasmanians. They won't permit nuclear-powered vessels to port in their pristine country. Go figure."

"Ingenious," Elena responded. "I've read about this. The company that owns the atomic yachts gives about ten percent of their profits toward climate change."

"I'm aware of the donations, and the PRC's new underwater research lab like the one that was built off the coast of Curacao in 2026. It's like a frickin' Four Seasons underwater hotel. It has pods that contain laboratories, personal quarters, medical bays, and even a 'moon pool,' where divers can explore the ocean floor. And it's powered by a combo of wind, and ocean thermal energy. It was the first of its kind to have underwater greenhouses for growing food."

"Not surprising," An stated. "That may all be true, but the PRC has a more calculated agenda. Former colleagues of mine tell me that their lab has been masquerading as a research facility, and it's probably serving as a substation checkpoint for their freshwater pipeline project."

"Just another reason why we don't want to launch near New Zealand."

"By the way. There's a town called Darwin in northern Australia," Yael said playfully. "How come we aren't making a stop there before setting sail? It could be like a good luck charm or something? C'mon, it's only 2300 miles from Sydney, and I read it takes sixty-four hours to drive."

"Maybe, if we all come back in one piece after Southland," Jon sighed. "We're going to meet up with the others for lunch, and hatch our final strategy to take out a few pipes without PRC or the Russians knowing we're in their pool."

Elena's impulsive temper got the best of her. "Yes, but we all know those fucking bastards have already broken the Antarctica treaty multiple times. No military submarines are allowed on, around, or under Antarctica. It's so lame that they are claiming only research submarines are there. Anyone with a brain and a little common sense knows it's a pack of lies."

The following day, Jon and Elena prepared for their test dive with the new laser attached, courtesy of Praani and her team. He allowed everyone onboard the docked submarine. "Y'all, only three at a time, including Praani and Bernays."

As they climbed aboard Draco rocking gently side to side, they were stunned by the interior control panel, the furnishings inside, and all the amenities you would expect in a studio apartment in Manhattan. They took turns in two shifts of three for a couple of minutes.

"Draco's dimensions are stunning. What's the length" Praani inquired.

"It's twenty-four feet. That's still only a quarter of the length of an adult Blue Whale. I'm hopin' that we blend in and will be mistaken for whales on some of the Chinese and Russian sonars."

"We can hope, can't we?" Sinclair added. "And the height and width?"

"Eleven feet, six inches in height with a width of slightly under ten feet."

"If it holds three people comfortably, then why are only two going on the dive?" asked Bernays in a calculating, analytical manner.

"It's a question of risk tolerance. It's the same reason that the engineers who worked on Draco certified her for dives down to depths of 9500 meters, and we're only taking it to a maximum depth of 7600 meters on its mission. She has a 100-millimeter titanium pressure hull, the equivalent of 3.94 inches thick for y'all non-metric system folks. And has been machined 99.937 percent of a true spherical form. Our practice target area is about halfway across the Ditch."

"The Ditch?" Sinclair inquired.

"Yeah. The people here refer to 'crossing the ditch' as the water between Australia and New Zealand. It's like calling the water between Great Britain and North America the pond."

"What's different about this sub compared to what the U.S. Navy might build?" Phillippe asked.

"My former naval engineers in Denver stumbled upon a relatively new substance called Graphene."

"You've got my attention," Yael added.

"It's got the thickness of a single molecule and can conduct heat like no other material. And get these eye-popping stats. It's lighter than paper yet 200 times stronger than steel. And it's almost invisible. If you were to cover a football field with a single sheet of it, the darn thing would weigh slightly over one gram."

F.O.R. let out a simultaneous gasp. "Tell us the catch," An probed.

"The catch? Graphene is extremely expensive to produce."

"How expensive is extremely?" asked Sinclair.

A quirky smile formed on Jon's face. "It's irrelevant because Wolf has connections in Vancouver who figured out a way to mass-produce it for pennies on the dollar. I guess my grandpa was right when he told me it's a who you know world."

"Anything else we should know?" Philippe inquired.

"Yeah, all you need is electricity to power batteries. And we can power them with hydrogen and never run out of energy. These new babies have up to five times the life span of current charge/discharge cycles. And they will charge up to fifty times as fast. So, if we get hit, we won't all be blown to kingdom come."

"Comforting," Elena quipped. "That does wonders for my anxiety."

"Why didn't you tell us sooner?" Sinclair inquired.

"I couldn't chance it, especially after what happened with Diaz."

They arrived at a quaint café The Catch which was known for its fresh fish. The special was Barramundi and everyone ordered it except Sinclair.

"I'll have the prawns if I may. And go easy on the butter sauce."

While dining in the private room, the group continued to pepper Jon.

"What's Draco's endurance? How long can it last underwater on one dive?"

"Good question, Court. It has an endurance of ninety-six hours, not including emergency life support. So basically, the actual number is seven days."

"Basically?" Elena asked.

"Any other questions before Sapphire and I submerge?" The waiter appeared to clear plates and asked if anyone wanted dessert. Jon jumped in and ordered.

"Let's have one Pavlova and one Lamington. And seven forks! We can share them. Trying to watch my figure y'all." Jon smiled big, covering his entire face.

"I have a question," Yael stated. "Do you know the diameter and thickness of the pipe you are going to test the laser on? And how do those dimensions compare to what you believe to be the pipe running from the subglacial lakes?"

"The short answer is the longest offshore oil pipeline on the planet is about forty-eight inches in diameter. The actual thickness is only three inches. Pipelines carrying water are vastly different 'cause you only have to puncture one part of the pipe to create the desired amount of chaos."

"Allow me to interject for a moment?" Sinclair suggested. "There are underwater pipes laid by oil companies on the ocean floor and in trenches where transportation of water is important in the process. All the Chinese had to do, with the Kremlin's help, is to create or even convert pipelines for water use only."

"Not to get too granular here, but these pipelines are protected from external corrosion through the process of high-efficiency coating and cathodic protection," Wolf added.

"The oil companies spent billions to figure it out," Jon added. "Those babies can range in diameter from five inches for gas lines all the way up to six feet, though the thickness of the pipe walls is typically three inches. We are going to use our laser to cut through the outer pipe wall, under the assumption that these pipes are two and a half inches thick."

"Why not go the maximum three inches?" asked An.

"Because we are assuming that the thickness of the pipe wall is much less when movin' water through it as opposed to oil. Once the pipe is punctured with Praani's laser, the water flow will be interrupted indefinitely. Why? Cause the saltwater will move through the hole in the pipe quickly, rendering the freshwater undrinkable and worthless for agriculture."

"What happens next?" Elena asked.

"After they repair the pipeline, whenever that should take place, the PRC shitbags are gonna need to flush the entire pipeline from beginning to end for them to eliminate the saltwater that got into the pipe. Even if they manage to repair or plug the hole in short order, it will take them weeks if not months to flush it a hundred percent clean. By then, the entire world will know about it."

"I just can't fathom how many millions of gallons of the most pristine water on the planet will go to waste," Wolf pondered aloud.

"God help us. We could use that for our water shortages!" Praani shrieked.

———

The following morning, Elena and Jon arose, grabbed some coffee and a couple of muffins at the hotel cafe and headed toward the dock at 7 a.m. They needed to run through the system checks. The others arrived around 7:45 a.m. to see them off. As they all stood on the dock holding Draco, Jon extended his hand toward Elena's.

"Shall we, m'lady? Our chariot awaits us!" They strolled to the entrance hatch of Draco, disappearing out of sight as the rest of F.O.R. waved goodbye.

An and Yael turned and jogged back while Phillippe and Sinclair took a leisurely stroll. They were all heading to the office of an Australian Navy friend of Bernays to track the path of Draco with an advanced sonar system. The estimate for the practice voyage was between three and a half to four hours. The office was small, but well ventilated.

"It's a good thing Sapphire's in the sub and not in this tiny room. It wouldn't have done wonders for her claustrophobia," An laughed.

Elena entered Draco first. She took one look at the chairs in front of the control panels and gasped with delight. "Are you fucking kidding me? Brown padded seats? Are they real leather? Surprised you didn't put a small bed in here with satin sheets and pillowcases. This is more like a limo than a sub."

"Oh. The bed is in the back." Elena did a doubletake. "Just kidding."

"Only the best for the best. And it's fake leather, by the way." Like a pilot of a plane sitting at the control panels, Jon proceeded to go through all the checks one last time to make sure Draco was prepared for the dive.

"Nice touch with the da Vinci quote." Hanging from the inside read the following. *I have been impressed with the urgency of doing. Knowing is not enough. That we be willing to apply knowledge is not enough. We must do." — Leonardo Da Vinci*

"I still can't believe the White Continent is 5.5 million square miles."

"Yeah, but consider that Denali Park contains Wonder Lake and Mt. McKinley, and is more than double at 12.7 million square miles," Jon added.

Elena examined the control panels, for the moment ignoring the weapons part and focusing on the laser technology since this was a practice run. Jon watched from a screen located on top of Draco as the outside crew unhinged the floating vessel from the dock. Within seconds, the sub was on its maiden voyage and disappeared from the surface like a whale that had gathered enough oxygen to go for a deep dive. Elena let out a gasp as Draco submerged, heading for its intended target.

Once underway, Draco penetrated the sea with ease at a thirty-degree angle. The darkness crept up to Jon's eyeballs, save the dull blue lights on the control panels in front of him. It was quiet. The sub moved like a large, flowing manta ray. Designed using aerodynamic engineering, it did not use a ballast like traditional research subs that were more akin to a blimp. Draco had the ultimate mobility, enabled by propeller screws and special pump jets.

"I need to make a small confession here. I'm a little nervous about the Draco's hull being able to withstand the pressure four or five miles down. Hope I can keep my claustrophobia in check," Elena shared.

Jon gave her a reassuring smile. "Allow me to put your mind at ease. It's constructed with materials superior to what James Cameron used for the Challenger Deep dive in 2012. His personal submersible record reached a depth of over 35,700 feet. That's just shy of seven miles deep."

Jon was well prepared because he and his Denver engineers had built a simulation program using advanced artificial intelligence for operating Draco underwater, duplicating volatile undersea conditions.

He had been on the simulator no less than seventy-five hours until he felt satisfied that he could operate Draco under duress. He even knew that controlling the two hydroplanes mounted near the aft in the vertical plane were utilized to change the lateral direction of Draco when she was in motion.

Jon examined the control panel. He eyed the button for the main ballast tank. Draco was built with many features in mind that might be found on a larger submarine, including a periscope, communications, radar, and a weapon sensor mast. The control panel included a pair of hydroplane fins at the forward and aft used to manipulate the heave and pitch independently from one another.

"How do you know how to operate this thing having never been in it before? I hope you're going to teach me the ins and outs during the practice run. You always have a Plan B, and guess I'm it.

"Yeah, I'm going to teach you how to fly straight, and you are the Plan B," he winked assuredly.

There was no accommodation room in a small submersible. There were only small compartments for underwater gear if they had to abandon Draco in case of an emergency. The weapons panel used to control the underwater laser and fire torpedoes were in the same vicinity, within reach of both of Jon and Elena.

"In case you're wondering, this thing is loaded with two small high impact torpedoes along with countermeasures that have the latest acoustic decoys. If we're fired upon, Draco also has a sonar decoy that presents a false target."

"I know you mean well, but Jesus, Buck. Your little speech just ratcheted up my anxiety level a few notches," Elena said with a tentative smile in her eyes.

"There's a small toilet and a fridge in the back. I stocked up with bottled water and soft drinks. There's no vodka back there. It's an alcohol-free vessel."

"Well, let's look at the bright side. We're only going to be down here for five hours max," Elena kidded Jon.

"Looks like we are seventy minutes away from the pipeline. I'm setting her on auto pilot for the time being. I wanna see how effective her AI software is. Why don't you test our communication system with F.O.R. to see if they are tracking us real time and whether there are any issues on their end."

Elena firmly pressed down on the intercom and spoke into her mic. "Aye, Aye, captain! This is your first mate speaking. Can *y'all* hear me?" Elena asked.

CHAPTER 24

TESTING THE WATERS

September 2045

Although they found themselves in calm, non-threatening waters, the world had accelerated in the past fifteen years when it came to the advent of new and improved submarine technologies. None of this was good for humanity and only increased the possibility of another world war.

"Admiral Buck? How're we doing?"

"I'm now an admiral? Well, in that case, things are under control."

To Jon and Sinclair, it was only fitting that a war of this magnitude would take place on the seas. The five major oceans represented ninety-six percent of the water that blanketed the globe. After it annexed North Korea, China was firmly in command of the Pacific, particularly in proximity to its coastline. With the largest fleet of submarines in the world, the PRC continued to make overtures toward Taiwan and Guam to the east and Vietnam and India to the south.

Jon was trying to make small talk with Elena to distract her, but it backfired.

"Certainly, there are only two countries in the world that can intervene and slow down the aggressive saber-rattling behavior of the PRC. One is the U.S. and the other is Russia, a distant second."

"Yeah, but Russia's fate may be like that of the female spider that kills and eats its male companion after they mate. Chirkov had all the incentive to look the other way when it came to his partner in crime. Russia was busy with its own movement westward, still trying to conquer countries supported by NATO."

"Interesting analogy," Jon said to Elena.

"All this talk about my former country is seriously stressing me out. Let's just chill."

"Roger that, but one more thing. Do you know what excites me most about our upcoming mission?" Jon asked, checking the monitors for depth and distance to the target.

"I couldn't begin to guess." Elena got up to grab a water bottle.

"That seven people are going to fuck with two major superpowers who are infinitely more powerful than we are. It's a modern-day David and Goliath story."

Having submersed itself more than two thousand meters below the surface, Draco was surrounded by absolute darkness. "For the sake of my claustrophobic tendencies, can you please concentrate on driving this damn contraption?"

Jon looked at her. "We're still on autopilot for chrissakes." Slow and effortlessly, the oblong-shaped vessel drifted lower. It felt to both Jon and Elena as if they were in outer space except for one minor detail.

"There is light in space from the stars with the sun reflecting off the moon. And other planets, but there's nothing down here."

There was only a single, shadowy light refracting the water from the nose of the submarine. Down below 5,000 feet, there was not even a glimmer, save for another submarine lurking beneath the deep silent sea. Completely devoid of any noise except a random whale call.

Elena's raspy voice broke inner Draco's serenity.

"How long until we reach our destination?" Before he could answer, something strange but familiar was sounding off in the crevices of Jon's mind.

He heard Wolf's voice. "At the current speed and trajectory, your target is thirty-nine minutes away."

Jon spun to his right, facing Elena. "Did you hear that?"

"Hear what? Dear Lord, don't tell me you are hearing things," Elena said rolling her eyes.

"Sorry, must have been my imagination." At that precise moment, Jon knew that Wolf was communicating with him telepathically. They had tried it once before, but it resulted in a one-way communication from Jon to Wolf.

Jon glanced at the dashboard. "Thirty-nine minutes until we reach the pipeline we're going to torch. My estimates from Praani are that it should take no longer than five minutes to burn through it. Hopefully less."

Elena was consuming all her energy trying to control her predisposed claustrophobic tendencies, an exercise in futility. For her, being trapped thousands of meters below sea level for hours at a time was a minute-by-minute struggle. She tried everything. Breath control, positive thoughts, body relaxation techniques, and meditation. Nothing seemed to work. The only things that calmed her nerves were sex, smoking, a shot of vodka, or a combination of all three.

"I'm starting to lose it."

"What does that mean? Is it the claustrophobia?" Jon couldn't help but notice her uneven labored breathing, as if she was nine centimeters dilated and about to deliver her first child. Elena nodded without answering. She had placed a paper bag over her nose and mouth, desperate to quell her anxiety. Jon grabbed her left hand and spoke in a delicate tone to his co-pilot. "It's alright. Don't fight it. If it's gonna happen, then let it be."

Just then she looked up and saw a giant squid propelling through the deep. The ancient creature was frolicking forty meters in front of Draco's headlights.

"Look. Over there!" she pointed. Within seconds, Elena forgot all about the wrestling match with her nerves, distracted by the best that the sea underworld had to offer.

"That is freakin' magnificent," Jon exclaimed. "To think these creatures have been around for over five hundred million years. I read somewhere that the largest squid ever recorded was forty-three feet long and weighed over a ton. That's over three times as long as the sub we are sitting in."

They stared in solitude until the squid moved out of Draco's path. Both were in awe, having witnessed something together for the first time. *It seems that the unplanned experiences are always the best surprises,* Jon surmised.

From that point forward, the practice mission seemed anticlimactic. They arrived at the target, and as Elena initiated the laser with the press of a button, Jon put his hand on hers as he guided the laser with an AI-loaded joystick.

In less than four and a half minutes, the pipe lay cut in half. Jon took a picture for posterity using the underwater camera near the light at Draco's bow, as if he were taking a picture with a flash. They rode back to the surface in silence.

"My fantasy is seeing a whale underwater," Jon confessed. "And you know how partial I am to blue whales. It's one of my greatest obsessions, for reasons I can't comprehend."

Two hours passed. As they glided toward the surface, still maneuvering in absolute darkness, lurking seventeen hundred meters beneath the lukewarm surface water, Jon heard the familiar otherworldly voice again.

"*Veer left twelve degrees,*" he listened to Wolf telepathically.

He did as he was instructed. "What the...?" There, sixty meters in front of him was a majestic blue whale mother swimming with her calf. Their grey eyes seem to hold ancient knowledge, wisdom that spanned ten million years.

"Sapphire, wake up. You gotta see this," as he thumped the back of his hand against her chest. "It's frickin' unbelievable!" he screamed, pointing in the direction of his newfound family. "The largest creatures to ever roam the planet. What a gift! Thank you, Wolf."

Startled, a confused look appeared on Elena's face. "Why are you thanking Wolf?" she asked, still dazed from fighting off her creeping claustrophobia.

"It's a long story. Some other time." Again, they experienced something joyful and awe-inspiring in a few hours. They knew it would be difficult to put into words. It felt like a time warp, and they were excited to share it with the team. That night while they enjoyed a celebratory dinner together at The Devil's Work, Praani's favorite restaurant in all of Tasmania, she received an alarm warning from her redundant, underground office. Praani was methodical and had developed a backup plan years ago, creating a fully equipped, duplicate lab ten feet underground a half-mile away.

While in a self-driving UberLyft, Wolf asked Praani a one-word question. "Why?" he gently probed.

"I had seen one of my mentors do it, and it made all the sense in the world. Besides, there was no downside, and it was a suitable place to hide if there was a Class 5 hurricane, a nuclear attack, or just in case our high-speed connections went down in the office you were in yesterday. No one knew of its whereabouts except me and my close-knit team. And now F.O.R."

They were dropped off at the entrance, a mundane, four-inch-thick door, painted gray. *This looks like the entrance to a power plant or utility.* Jon checked his advanced GPS system, and it hadn't shown up anywhere. He and Praani both noticed that the outside alarm had been disabled. As they walked downstairs two flights of stairs in pitch-black, Praani noticed that the second entrance to the office was damaged as well. The intruders were not prepared for a third alarm, connected to the laptops in her basement lab that strongly resembled a dungeon. No windows, no pictures on the walls, nothing but concrete and used furniture.

Files were in disarray, turned upside down and dumped on the floor. The tech thieves, who had disappeared into the night, had tried to download the contents of the computers onto their phones, but to no avail. Praani and Jon checked out the tiny cameras that were the size of a quarter, and they had been sprayed with black paint, so there was no evidence of who the attackers were.

An was convinced the PRC was behind it. They wanted desperately to have what Praani wasn't selling. "Dr. Praani. I'm so sorry this happened. It looks like the work of the PRC," An surmised. "Looks like they were in a hurry too."

"Whoever it was, they were probably after your next-generation underwater laser system, if for no other reason than to weaponize it," Jon stated.

Praani was visibly shaken. "Well, nothing we can do now. We certainly can't call the police because they don't even know this place exists. I'll get my team in here tomorrow at sunrise."

————

Twelve hours later at 8 a.m. sharp, Draco Spiritus was loaded onto the barge. Its destination was a drop-off ninety kilometers off the northeastern shores of Antarctica, where some of the roughest, unforgiving waters and fiercest of winds on the planet presented themselves to the unprepared seafarer. The captain of the cargo ship was a veteran of the Southern Ocean.

The crew of the barge and the nuclear-powered yacht, Erebus, were handpicked by Jon, Wolf, Elena, and Sinclair to ensure safe passage and a successful mission. Draco was draped with a thick, gray tarp, and strapped onto the deck with chains composed of tungsten, titanium, and carbon steel.

Sinclair had arranged for a nuclear sub courtesy of Admiral Brown to accompany the cargo ship. There was also a container below deck that housed an identical laser to the one that Jon and Elena had tested off the coast of Tasmania. Part of Jon's redundancy and Plan B.

Given the speed of the superyacht that Jon had chartered, the F.O.R. team hung around Hobart and gave the cargo ship a three-day head start. The barge could take up to ten days to travel the 5400 kilometers. Erebus, housing all F.O.R., would take a mere five days for its journey.

Jon was betting that the superyacht would pass as a tourist expedition while it traveled down the northeastern coast of Antarctica for a couple of days to see if they could find out what the Chinese were up to. They would be launching drones from the yacht and checking satellite reports to obtain as much information as they could before meeting up with the cargo ship, where Draco would be lowered into the frosty, grey waters of the Southern Ocean.

They were two days away from launch, and the superyacht was

scheduled to arrive from Seoul in less than forty-eight hours. Before Erebus set sail, Phillippe took Yael and An shopping to pick out some cold-weather gear. "Ladies, I know that this is foreign to you, but if you are not properly prepared for what you are about to expose yourself to, then it may be quite uncomfortable."

"I'm used to temperatures that are over 100 degrees warmer than where we are headed," Yael bemoaned, perusing the waterproofed parkas with fleeced hoods.

"Why can't we just stay in Hobart, where it's a balmy 32 degrees? Celsius, that is," An asked, as she tried on bright red waterproof overalls designed to withstand wind chills of -20 degrees. Both Yael and An were squirming about what they might have to endure and bonded over their aversion to cold and ice.

"I like the fuchsia jumpsuit. It's waterproof and lined with material that will keep me warm in sub-zero temperatures. The thing looks like it glows in the dark, and if I get tossed overboard at night, you guys will be able to see me," An teased.

Phillipe cracked up. Yael picked out a bright yellow outfit for the same reasons as An, yet didn't feel the need to verbalize it.

The next day Jon called F.O.R. for one last strategy session to unpack the risks of the mission. Praani had arranged for the team to use a conference room in her office with a view.

"Y'all realize that this ain't no dress rehearsal. If we fail, the world will continue to spiral. This isn't a problem that Silicon Valley or Austin, Texas with its trillions of dollars can solve," Jon said, starting the meeting.

"Based on what Angie uncovered, it appears the Chinese have been laying the groundwork for a decade, setting the stage to perpetrate the biggest heist in our planet's history, stealing our most precious resource. At least people have finally woken up to the idea that the supply of earth's clean water supply is not forever. It appears that infinity is shrinking at a rapid pace," Sinclair added.

"Angie, do you have anything to add?" Philippe asked.

"I do. The PRC is in deep shit. Beijing has been importing water from other areas of China and Russia since 2039, and that's why China will never again be the host country for the Winter Olympics.

No water to make snow, no bottled water to provide for their citizens."

Elena decided to inject some humor into a conversation that was headed south. "I guess the *Buck* stops with us."

Yael laughed. "Nice one, Sapphire."

Jon rose from a black faux leather chair made of recycled materials, drew the automatic shades with the flip of a switch, and projected a 3D map of the Southern Ocean and Antarctica on the wall from his laptop. A laser device emanating from his smartphone guided the room to the underwater pipeline targets as well as Russian and Chinese bases.

"This is where the Chinese are stealing the subglacial lake water, and here is where Sinclair and the British Navy calculate the location of Russian subs stationed to protect the Chinese drilling operation. And over here in the northeast corridor is where the Russians have above-ground stations located."

"Do you think the cargo ship or Erebus are vulnerable to military attacks from the air?" Yael questioned.

"I don't think so. Long-range missiles could be a different story. Our radar and drones will spot them as soon as they become airborne. I'm banking on the fact that neither the Chinese nor the Russians have hypersonic missile launchers in Antarctica. Why would they bother?"

Jon scanned the room. "Any more questions?"

"Yeah, I have one for you," Wolf asked. "How old do you think you'd be if you didn't know how old you were?" Everyone sat stunned. "I'm kidding. Do we have the Boar or any of the anti-drone technology aboard the yacht or Erebus like we used in Mongolia?"

"Good question. And the answer is yes." The team breathed a collective sigh of relief knowing that at the very minimum, they had the capacity to defend themselves against certain types of air attacks. Only two F.O.R. members knew that surface to air missiles or submarine attacks with high-speed torpedoes were a different story, and extremely difficult to defend against.

Jon pre-empted the next round of questions. "On the torpedo and missile defense side of the equation, here's what we've got. Due to its speed and maneuverability, Draco is the least vulnerable to attack, particularly under water. She's equipped with torpedo decoys and coupled with her size and mobility should be able to sidestep torpedoes, and could easily be mistaken for a small whale. Plus, her acceleration from a dead stop is an added defense mechanism."

One of Praani's co-workers knocked on the conference room door, peeked her head in, and asked if anyone wanted something cold to drink.

Wolf responded. "How about some iced green tea for this guy, and a pitcher of iced coffee and water? Thank you for asking."

"What about Erebus?" Yael asked with an unemotional curiosity. "Does it have any serious firepower?"

"Yep. Erebus is a warship disguised as a yacht. It's equipped with an anti-defense missile system for smaller projectiles. So long as she remains close to the cargo ship, the system can protect both ships. Erebus also has its own torpedo defense system, but the cargo ship does not. And the *piece de resistance*? Erebus is equipped with a powerful laser that can repel other ships, drones, and military aircraft, so long as they are above water. This gives us the element of surprise and a leg up."

Praani's co-worker returned with the beverages, and they decided to take a ten-minute Vitamin D break outside in the warm air heated by the Australian sun. They continued the conversation in a courtyard gazebo overlooking the luscious rose garden. The more questions the team asked, the better they were feeling about their own safety.

"What about the cargo ship?" Phillippe asked.

"Given its inherent lack of defense systems, the plan is for the cargo ship to stay eighty miles north of Antarctica after it has lowered Draco into the water. This will reduce the risk of attack. Having said that, it does have a small defense system, comprised of an upgraded version of the SeaRAM, an anti-ship missile defense system that protects itself and other ships from missiles and subsonic threats. You know, drones, enemy aircraft, and even small boats, but not cruise missiles."

"It's designed after our Iron Dome laser system," Yael interjected. "I'm highly confident that this system can be an early warning sign and defend against an attack from the sea or air."

"Jon, you should probably add that the cargo ship also has two SH-60K helicopters," Phillippe reminded the group. "They're designed to comb the sea for hostiles. They'll also serve as an escape route if the cargo ship is attacked. The ship even has an elevator that can lower the choppers to an internal hangar below deck where no one can see them. They are undetectable from radar. Again, I didn't skimp. Courtesy of the Danish and U.S. Navies that patrol Greenland's borders."

"Yeah, and the only things missing are that it's not armed with anti-submarine missiles or torpedoes. The point is we don't want to engage in any skirmishes with Russian and Chinese submarines in the middle of the Southern Ocean. According to the calculations fed into our A.I.-driven quantum computer, we would come out on the losing end 99.9% of the time. This mission will make Mongolia seem like a milk run. We'll always be under threat. Meeting adjourned."

———

They all boarded the superyacht ready to set sail. The officer at the top of the gangway checked documents for all passengers as a routine security precaution. He checked the proprietary guest list, and the F.O.R. entourage boarded. The officer hailed the steward to escort them to separate rooms adjacent to one another. Jon stretched out on his premium bunk bed, hands behind his head clasped together. *It isn't exactly the presidential suite, but it'll do. Least I have my own bathroom.* As Jon's eyes glazed with fatigue, he decided to test out the gym. The winds were so fierce at night that a wave could come over the side of vessel, and the superyacht was well-equipped with shatterproof glass along with sixteen bedrooms and thirteen baths, a makeshift surgical center, a state-of-the-art sick bay, and a full-time surgeon on staff.

Each passing day, the ocean water turned darker, the brisk air got windier, and the sky grayer, as the temperatures plummeted precipitously. Nothing but views of the water intersecting with a distant horizon, absent land.

On the third day of the journey, Yael was up on deck chatting with An and Elena. "It feels primal," declared Yael, the whipping wind slung icy sleet, stinging her tan cheeks. "Like Genesis and creation. Nothing but water and sky."

"It's crazy to think that our only connection to civilization is the ship's high-speed satellite. Otherwise, it's hard to gauge what century we are in," An said. The hard waves of an ominous sea rocked the superyacht side to side.

"This part of the Southern Ocean is as empty as the bank account of a gambler who lost his last hundred dollars," declared Jon, who had entered the door to the top deck. "I would know."

Erebus was also equipped with both surface and underwater radar. The hull was constructed with titanium-reinforced steel. Small torpedoes could not penetrate the massive yacht's exterior. The only stipulation that Jon put on F.O.R. was to have three meals a day together at 7:30 a.m., noon, and 6:00 p.m. Given the intensity of the situation, Wolf insisted that everyone sleep separately. He did not want to tempt fate. There was no room for distraction or drama.

The superyacht also came with a handpicked chef, Dmitri. Jon took the team's suggestions and sent their wish list to the head chef three weeks before launch. He had secured a month's supply of eggs, fresh frozen fish, and bug burgers, plant-based proteins, fresh and frozen fruits, and vegetables, and an assortment of non-dairy desserts.

Other than dim lights encircling the upper deck, the nights on deck were a blueish black hue, with the moon hidden behind the clouds and a dense fog, enough light to see a few feet in front of them where they were able to identify each other by the silhouettes of their bodies.

Amazing. Bundled up in bright yellow and fuchsia cold-weather gear and still invisible in the dark, colorless night, Jon thought to himself. The engines purred, eerily quiet, and made for easy conversation save the occasional gusts of wind lashing out from the southeast. Since no one in F.O.R. was permitted to smoke on the yacht, certain members of the crew could be identified by the orange ash at the end of their cigarettes.

During the day, one F.O.R. member was assigned an hour at a time to sit in front of the two radar screens in a small room on the lower deck to look for suspicious activity, both in the air and underwater. Yael realized that this was not a kid-friendly cruise ship, but the issue that unnerved Sinclair was that the captain carried sidearms. It was a mutiny prevention strategy.

Elena, An and Yael were in Elena's room. An noticed a stuffed animal that was an octopus on her bed.

"What's the story with this?" she asked Elena lightly.

Elena shook her head and then answered. My maternal grandmother knitted it for me when I was a child. Fake diamonds for the eyes, and eight tentacles, just like the real thing. She even put a smiley face on it. I named it Inus, after the middle sibling between my mother and her sister who had died. She had an incurable disease and this all happened when my mother was ten years old."

"That's precious," Yael said, looking at Elena differently after her story.

They proceeded to don their cold-weather gear, and headed up to the top deck, where they continued the conversation. The air was dense with humidity.

"All I know is the last place I'd want to be right now is Moscow. Too easy to be killed or poisoned by the Federal Security Bureau. And if you leave that shithole excuse of a country, the dirtbags in power will order the Foreign Intelligence Services to track you down. And if they want you eliminated, one of those agencies will get to you and there's nothing much you can do about it."

An started to laugh. "Except if you manage to change your name, your identity, and your country of origin, and then rewrite your entire life story in the process. I imagine it is no better or worse than the PRC's MSS Ministry of State Security," she said. "The last time I checked their annual budget was an outrageous $14 billion."

Jon appeared out of the darkness, standing within feet of his team. "And there's not a goddamn thing we can do about them pursuing any of us either. Except to expect nothing and be prepared for anything." Jon's breath lingered in rigid polar air.

CHAPTER 25

TRUTHS COME IN BLOWS

October 2045

At 6 p.m. sharp the F.O.R team sat at a table in the Erebus dining room. They were given a choice of omelets, fresh fish that was tested for forever chemicals, or a vegan meal. After dinner, things started to loosen up. Everyone was sitting around laughing and telling stories, revealing parts of themselves from lifetimes ago. *It feels like I'm sitting around a campfire on a crisp fall night in the Smokey Mountains with a fire crackling in the background*, Jon imagined.

"I remember when my friends and I would go frog gigging," said Jon.

"Excuse me. What did you just say? Frog what?" Yael asked. Jon couldn't stop laughing and told Yael to hang on. It took him a minute to find equilibrium.

"I said frog gigging. We used to go out on small lakes or ponds on a warm humid night with a canoe, spear, and flashlights. When you shine a light in a frog's eyes at night, the frog freezes and can't move. Then one of us would get close enough spear it in the gut and bring it back into the canoe."

"Ugh, that sounds so barbaric," said An.

"That's not the barbaric part. Not by a longshot. After we took the spear out of the frog's stomach, we held it by the legs and bang its head against the side of the canoe to make sure it was dead, and couldn't hop back into the water."

"I'm starting to get nauseous just thinking about it," Elena said, her hand over her mouth. "What's the point of your story?"

"That you can't take the country out of someone, no matter where they find themselves later in life. You're not going to change people unless they want to change themselves, that's all."

"What about you, Sol?"

"There were a lot of scorpions in Israel, especially in the desert. We learned two things at a young age. One was that the smaller ones were deadlier and more venomous than the larger variety."

"I get it," said Jon, as he looked at An. "Kind of like Angie here being the most lethal in hand-to-hand combat. "What was the second thing?"

"The most effective way to kill a scorpion without 'touching' it? Light a ring of fire around it. The scorpion tries to put out a fire with its thrashing tail. Eventually its stinger will thrash its own body and kill itself. I've actually seen it with my own eyes!"

"Any one of y'all like to share? C'mon, Wolf. I'm sure you've got some good ones."

"If you insist," Wolf said with an outsized grin on his face. "When I turned fifteen, it was time for my rite of passage into manhood. My father sent me out into the wilderness in the dead of winter to live off the land for a week with nothing but a hunting knife, a bow and six arrows, a few matches, an insulated, camouflage-colored winter jacket, one pair of pants, a sleeping bag, a pair of gloves, a couple of winter hats, and snowshoes attached to my waterproof, ankle-high boots. And no cell phone or a way to communicate with the outside world."

Court's face told all, and his mouth went agape. All he could muster was, "Really? That must've been rough."

"It was the middle of winter, and the day temperature hovered around fifteen-twenty degrees. When the sun went down, and the wind came cascading down the mountains and through the valley, it could get down to minus ten or twenty below with the wind chill."

"That's the kind of temperature where my piss could freeze in mid-air!" Jon grimaced. "How could you sleep outdoors in that kind of weather?"

"I had to dig a hole in a bank of snow to insulate and protect myself from the wind. Learned that technique from my old man."

Wolf had three things going for him that were absent from Jon's life. First, his father was an incredible teacher and mentor and had helped hone his life skills. Second, Wolf was blessed with incredible night vision. Third, he was a natural at bow hunting and had military-like accuracy. Jon had been exposed to bow hunting a couple of times before, yet never came close to mastering it. He felt admiration as Wolf continued.

"Truth is, I often hunted best at night by the light of the moon. That way I had nothing to worry about the next day and could eat and sleep during the daytime when it was warmer. I managed to cover about forty miles over six days and came back with two dead rabbits attached to my belt. They were gifts to my family. It was trial by fire, or should I say *ice*, but I managed to survive."

Jon broke the awed silence of the group. "I just wanted y'all to know that your welfare is of the utmost importance to me."

"Fuck my welfare," Elena said laughing. "I'm here to stop the evil axis. Namely, my former country and Angie's, who continue committing heinous crimes against humanity and nature."

"No worries, Sapphire. This will be over sooner rather than later and we're all going to come out the other side in one piece," Sinclair interjected.

"I'd like you to put that in writing," Elena said sharply.

"Let's call it a night. We all need to get some rest."

Out of nowhere, the hair on Yael's arms raised up. She couldn't quite figure out what was going on until she noticed the waiter's gait walking back to the kitchen. She was frozen like an ice sculpture. Even though he spoke almost perfect English, she was sure he was one of the Russians who had broken into her house and that she knocked to the ground in the Tel Aviv restaurant.

Yael calmly turned to Jon, who was sitting to her left, and whispered in his ear. He nodded. As the waiter approached bringing her a chaga mushroom and dandelion root tea boiled with desalinated sea water, she asked in Russian, "Can I have some ice, too?"

His reflexive response was 'Da' followed by "Yas koro vernus." Jon jumped up, pulled his Glock tucked into the back of his pants, and waved it in the unsuspecting waiter's face yelling, "Get the fuck down. On your knees. Now! You're like a bad penny coming back where you ain't wanted."

Jon pointed his cocked gun at the Russian's forehead. The waiter hesitated. "Move asshole." Jon motioned with his gun. "Or I will shoot and ask questions after I've iced you."

The newly minted hostage did as instructed. Elena cuffed him, and the two of them tied him to a pole on the ship's deck. After discovering his cabin number, Jon instructed Elena to search his room for any weapons and check his cell for the last few calls, listening to any voice-mails still on his phone. Ten minutes later Elena returned, holding plastic explosives and a semi-automatic pistol constructed from stainless steel.

"Who sent you?" Jon howled at the top of his lungs. He didn't answer.

"Who sent you? Sapphire, tell this lowlife in his own language that we are going to throw him overboard if he doesn't talk."

Elena did as she was instructed, repeating her message twice. The Russian smirked and spit at her. Jon spun out of control with rage, a familiar response when he was being deceived and felt threatened. "You have no idea what kind of hurt you just walked into," his wild blue eyes scanning the deck.

Jon untied and picked up the handcuffed Russian like he was a lightweight duffle bag, put him over his right shoulder, and walked briskly across the deck toward the side of Erebus.

"No, Buck. Wait. We'd rather have him alive for questioning. He might prove useful," pleaded Sinclair, who was convinced Jon was dead serious until he saw him wink at Elena as he walked by with his victim pleading for mercy.

"OK, OK. I talk. Please don't throw me overboard," the waiter pleaded, hoping to buy more time. Jon could smell his lies. Jon dumped him onto the deck, and asked, "Are you working for the Russians or with some rogue agency?" He said nothing. Jon was growing less tolerant by the second. "Last chance. Who's paying you to chase us all over the globe?" The waiter gave him a blank stare so Jon asked Elena to repeat the questions in Russian. Still no response. Not a word.

"Have it your way," Jon said in a calm yet maniacal tone, as he emptied his gun chamber of all but one bullet. Only Jon knew what order the live bullet was in, as the Russian watched helplessly, trying to figure out when the next time Jon pulled the trigger it could go right through his head and come out the other side with part of his brains attached to the bullet.

"Let's play, shall we?" The Russian's eyes were trembling, as Jon pulled the trigger. The click caused the defenseless Russian to shudder uncontrollably.

"OK. Достаточно."

"What'd he just say?" Jon asked, turning to Elena.

"He said *enough*!" The phony waiter proceeded to confess everything, and each time he hesitated, Jon put the gun up to his forehead and mercilessly cocked the gun back, his right index finger on the trigger.

Elena continued her relentless grilling. As she grew frustrated with his lack of response, Yael yelled in Russian, "Let's throw him overboard, mafia style. You know, with weights attached to his ankles!"

After that statement, the waiter glared at Elena and started to confess his background. He was part of the secretive Sino-Russian organization that was working in tandem as one unit from two separate countries. The same organization that had attacked Jon and Sinclair in Cambridge, and Darwin twice.

As Jon and Elena conferred on whether he was telling the truth, the Russian grabbed a gun with handcuffs still on both hands and took aim at Yael. As he tried to cock the gun, An, who was behind him, delivered a roundhouse kick to his temple as the fired bullet went well over the bow and missed its intended target.

"That kick was groanworthy!" Wolf said aloud.

With eyes on fire, Jon grabbed the Russian, who had just committed an act of suicide by firing at his beloved soulmate, and chucked the limp body overboard. Everyone on deck heard Jon's last words as they echoed into the night.

"Fuck you, you mother fuckin' scumbag. You're gonna freeze in hell." There was a feint scream and a muted splash as his body hit the water. F.O.R. stared at Jon as if he was an alien from another galaxy.

Everyone except Elena. She merely shrugged. She held the gun that the former waiter had used in vain against Yael. "He earned himself a one-way ticket to the Southern Ocean. I have no regrets whatsoever."

"Let me take a look at the weapon," Jon said as he extended his hand to Elena. "Hmmm. It's stainless steel. Odd that stainless steel weapons can sometimes give metal detectors the slip."

Yael got busy interrogating every worker, chef, and crew member to make certain the Russian that hounded her was working solo. She worked off a list that the captain gave her, including the sanitation and housekeeping staff, the engineers, and the deckhands. Before Yael could get to the galley crew, Elena discovered from her own investigation that the waiter had an accomplice, a Russian female sous chef.

Elena immediately told Jon. "The goddamn sous chef? You've got to be kidding me!" Elena and Yael handcuffed her to a secure copper pole, and duck-taped her feet for good measure. "That should hold her," Yael said to Elena.

"Let's take turns standing guard. I'll take the first shift." They told Jon, and he immediately rejected the idea. "Let's have Angie or Court do the night watch Sapphire. We've got some monster days ahead of us, and I need you to rest up."

Later that night, Jon asked Yael to meet him on the bridge. It was only the captain and the two of them in the room that controlled the yacht's coordinates and speed. It resembled an older 747 control panel with a few differences.

After the helter-skelter incident with the waiter, Jon made an executive decision that was simple and straightforward. He decided to take Yael and Elena with him on the Draco voyage. In his mind's eye, it was the ultimate Plan C.

"Sol, if Sapphire freaked out from claustrophobia during the practice mission, who knows if she will fold under pressure or not."

"I understand. Can't see any downside, except that I don't have a frickin clue how to operate Draco."

"You're the only insurance we've got. I'll break the news to Sapphire tomorrow. Besides, the two of you have been getting along famously, and I'm sure Sapphire will be elated and relieved that all the pressure is not on her anymore."

The following morning, Jon made the announcement in front of the entire team. "First, we need to surrender all hope of a better past. We are where we are, and there's no rewinding the clock. Sometimes you are in the middle of a fast moving river headed over a waterfall and there's nothin' you can do about it except relax, go with the flow, and then kiss your ass goodbye. To increase the odds of a successful mission, I decided to include Sol aboard Draco as a backup."

Jon looked at Yael with confidence. "And because of your experience in the IDF Navy, you're the logical choice. As we saw back in Hobart, Draco can fit three comfortably, and I will make sure we have all the necessary equipment in case of an emergency."

"God forbid if we need to abort the mission midstream," Yael murmured.

"You know I'm a team player, but only on two conditions. First, if the mission is successful, I get a bonus payable in shekels, and two, just promise me I won't have to swim in that unbearable, not fit for humans, freezing water. Israel hasn't invented a wetsuit yet that will protect me from water that is sixty to seventy degrees colder than the Mediterranean. Are we clear?" Everyone laughed,

"Maybe you'll get lucky and swim into a hydrothermal vent."

"What the hell is a hydrothermal vent?" Yael asked Wolf.

"Hydrothermal vents are the result of seawater percolating down through fissures in the ocean crust. Cold seawater is heated by hot magma and reemerges to form vents. Beware if you find one because temperatures could run as high as 700° Fahrenheit. Don't worry, Sol. Hot seawater from a hydrothermal vent does not boil because of the extreme pressure at the depths where the vents are formed."

"Hmm. I suppose that's comforting and one way to stay warm."

The next morning came early and without a sunrise. The day had finally arrived for Jon, Elena, and Yael to board Draco. The remaining F.O.R. team would stay aboard the superyacht and monitor Draco.

Wolf and Sinclair would man the underwater radar keeping tabs on the mini sub while An and Phillippe would coordinate with the crew of the yacht and communicate with the cargo ship about any approaching enemy ships or drones. The three warriors were waiting on the deck of Erebus to be airlifted to the cargo ship, where a humongous crane was ready to place them in the water. It was a dull gray backdrop with intermittent gusts of wind up to thirty-five miles per hour and waves that swelled ten to twelve feet high.

"How long until we are in the water? " Jon asked the captain of the barge, a slender, thick-skinned man in his mid-fifties. "Mr. Walker, the entire process should take no more than eight minutes under normal conditions. This is anything but normal, so figure twice the amount of time. Just trying to manage your expectations," said the captain, who doubled as the crane operator and would lower Draco into the turgid waters below.

Fifteen minutes passed, and the barge captain called Jon's cell. "I wish the weather was clear. It's just schizophrenic out here, changing by the minute. Were gonna need to wait this one out, and then I'll have a chopper transport the three of you," he screamed, a whirlwind gale spraying seawater on the deck.

Thirty minutes passed, and Jon's phone showed the captain's number flashing. "With this weather, we don't have much margin for error," the captain shouted into his phone. "Looks like we got ourselves about a twenty-minute window here. I'm sending the chopper. Be ready to go, mate."

Jon knew the helicopters were designed for travel in windy, polar conditions. He showed little concern for what was about to happen as if he embraced it, but Yael and Elena were quite the contrast. Jon could see the trepidation on their faces, as they quickly donned their extreme winter gear.

Jon approached Wolf before boarding the chopper. "I heard your voice telepathically, when Sapphire and I were on the practice dive off the coast in the ditch. Thanks for the tip on the whales, too. It was spectacular and wish you could have seen what I saw."

"How do you know I didn't see it?" Wolf asked. Jon shook his head in bewilderment. A part of Wolf remained an enigma to Jon.

The chopper arrived in six minutes flat. Hauling them up in a harness one at a time from the yacht's desk was no easy task, as they were swaying back and forth from the intermittent gusts. "Everybody good?" one of the chopper's pilots yelled. Wasting no time, the pilot hightailed it back to the cargo ship.

Exiting the helicopter, the three Draco submariners were getting blown about like tumbleweeds. They quickly entered the sub, sat down, strapped in, and prepared for a rough submersion. Jon waved to the captain, who was sitting in the crane operator's seat. Jon gave him a thumb's up, the signal that they were ready.

Thirty seconds passed, and everyone felt the crane hoisting Draco up, and then overboard, as they were placed as gently as possible in the raging ocean. Once the crane detached from Draco, Jon put in the coordinates 77.500 latitude, 106.000 longitude, heading directly toward the eastern tip of Lake Vostok's subglacial lake. The only way to approach was from underneath the gigantic ice mass to prevent troops that heavily guarded the surface from spotting them. Up until this point, the plan to catch the Russians by surprise was merely a theory.

For her maiden voyage, Yael was given a quick tour around the interior of Draco. It took Elena less than a minute to complete the task. "And finally, here's the entrance to the bathroom and this is where the drinks are stored."

"How's everyone feeling?" Jon asked.

"I feel like I have — how do you say in English? — butterflies in my stomach," Yael answered.

"My stomach feels more like bats flying around inside me," Elena laughed.

"We're on our way. How many of us have seen a giant squid and a Blue whale with her calf in the same two-hour period? Raise your hands." Jon chuckled trying to lighten the mood as Draco submerged in dark waters.

"What are you smoking?" Elena smirked.

"Just tryin' to entertain y'all." Underneath Jon's bold façade lurked a basic motive of distraction to keep everyone calm, including himself.

"How about some music?" Elena requested. Jon was not amused. "Let's not give enemy sonar any more advantages than they have. We are the underdog here."

"Not even smooth jazz?" Elena smirked. Jon ignored her request.

"One more question. This is for Sol. Which lake in Antarctica is so salty, even more than Israel's Dead Sea, and stays liquid even at extreme temperatures?"

"That one's easy. I haven't a clue."

"It's called Deep Lake. It's considered one of the planet's least productive ecosystems, as the cold and hypersalinity prevent almost all life from thriving. The lake is sixty meters below sea level and only gets saltier the deeper it gets."

Draco drifted lower, and other than their own voices, the three were surrounded by a dark silence. They were thirty miles from the north-eastern shore of Antarctica, cruising at a casual twelve knots at a depth of forty-four hundred feet below the surface. The nothingness frayed Elena's nerves, and Yael was meditating to offset the sensory deprivation.

As Draco approached the icy shores, Jon was satisfied with his margin of error, at least for the moment. Jon noticed Yael's eyes opening and had a burning question for her. "I'd love to hear why you believe Israel succeeded in desalination when everyone else failed. Just curious."

Yael wrapped her sun-streaked hair in a ponytail as she began to answer Jon's query. "I thought that the nanomembrane manufacturers of seawater and brackish water using reverse osmosis membranes and polymer technologies would do the job and lower the cost of desalination."

Elena joined in. "So, what happened? Why didn't it take hold like your projections indicated?"

"These membranes deliver best-in-class flux and rejection yet were unable to yield clear drinking water."

"Why not?" Elena persisted.

"Well, it's a very fluid situation," Yael winked at Jon. "Two reasons. One, the proliferation of drugs flushed into the sewer systems contain molecules, a subset that is too small to be blocked by the membranes. The second reason pinpoints why Wolf's breakthrough research is invaluable. Compounding the issue is the abundance of microplastics in the air and the water that couldn't be screened on a large scale, even though over a thousand commercial sites in sixty countries have embedded these membranes in their desalination systems."

Jon subtly pressed a button, and the remainder of F.O.R. huddled on the yacht became part of the conversation. Yael and Elena looked at each other with expressions of surprise. "How's everybody doing down there?" asked Sinclair.

"So far all is going according to plan. How's the weather up there?" Jon's insides were in knots. He would never let on how the safety of his two companions was his only priority. Elena started to experience a sort of claustrophobic creep. Yael had been in so many military combat situations before but never in a mini sub where there was limited room to maneuver. She felt calm but even the simple task of stretching her legs had to be finessed. Jon clicked off.

He went back to his strategic thinking. Part of his plan banked on two assumptions. *I hope I've got this right. The part of the pipeline that's been completed and constructed within thirty miles of where Draco began its surgical mission, was under the icecap. And I'll be finer than a frog hair split four ways if our advanced sonar picks up the pipeline on the ocean floor. I'm still bettin' this baby could eat corn through a picket fence.*

What Jon and Wolf couldn't de-risk was that Lake Vostok lay two miles underneath the surface of Antarctica, and worst case, the origin of the pipeline was over six hundred miles from the eastern Antarctica shoreline. Even at a max speed of fourteen knots, it would take Draco over two and a half days to get to the source of the pipeline.

Jon made a calculated bet that the giant underwater compressor, being used by Chinese engineers and hydrologists, extended at least two hundred miles from its source. He could hide both his most positive and negative emotions from the others. It was none other than fear.

Even with the extended pipeline to our advantage, there's a small chance I'd need to engage emergency power. Shouldn't be a problem but I'd rather not go there. The goal is nothin' short of making it back to the cargo ship with Draco in one piece. Just crazy that I'm bettin' the Chinese have made significant progress and that the pipeline has been built out at least two hundred miles.

Once Jon saw that Yael and Elena were fast asleep, he began whispering words laced with an inner vulnerability, as if his alter ego were sitting right next to him. *What if somethin' happens to the cargo ship or Erebus is captured by the Russians? Or worse, the PRC? Then we're all fucked. It's a damn good thing that I had my own state-of-the-art underwater drone technology. Better to be safe than sorry. It's a beautiful thing that I never filed patents. That way no one could reverse engineer this baby. It may be the biggest bet I've ever made because it has nothing to do with money and everything to do with saving my team's lives. C'mon, Jon. Keep your shit together. Focus.*

Hours passed. Jon was fighting off the sensory deprivation and was daydreaming about the future that he and Yael could have together if they both came out of this alive. Tel Aviv, Colorado, Darwin, even Nuuk were possibilities. *I want at least two kids. Of course, I'd prefer twins, one of each, but I'll take them any way I could get them. I wonder if we'll give them Hebrew or American names.*

Suddenly, the alarm on the radar went off like the thunder he often heard at ten thousand feet up in the Rockies. The three of them were jolted back to the present, dazed, but Wolf's voice coming through his headset was unmistakable.

"There's trouble ahead. Looks like a Russian nuclear attack sub with all the bells and whistles standing guard about three thousand meters off your starboard. And it's not a drone either. Not sure if they've seen you yet. They might just think that Draco is part of a school of whales careening around Antarctica. The good news is that you must be close to the pipeline. The bad news is obvious."

"I see it," Jon spouted.

"There's a high probability it's Russian and heavily armed," crowed Elena.

"Wolf, I've been saying for a year that we've been knocking on the door."

"Now we're banging on it, ready to bust it down," Wolf replied.

"We might be able to sidestep her and continue in stealth mode. What do you think, Sapphire?"

"You know as well as I do that whales travel in schools, rarely alone. Usually the mother, the father, the calf, and another adult whale. That's one way to view an escort service, *da?*" Elena laughed until she had tears in her eyes.

"Not sure what to tell you other than let's start scanning for the pipeline on the floor. If we don't find it right away, we might have to go to Plan B. By the way, what is our Plan B?" Elena whispered.

"I haven't a clue, except to cut bait and run. Do you have any bright ideas?" Jon smirked, staring at Elena straight-faced until he couldn't manage it.

Yael was sitting beside Elena shaking her head. "C'mon. Of course, I have a Plan B! Don't you know me by now?" Just as Jon finished his sentence, a second alarm and a smaller submarine came up on the radar. It was behind them and rapidly approaching from the northeast.

"I'm taking the scan off auto." Elena stared at two screens in her line of sight, her face bathed in green haze. The light from the screen cast shadows of curls on her forehead. She was aware of even the slightest nuance. Her eyes widened, and her voice trembled. The phallic-shaped, spherical object seemed like a cluster of cancer cells moving through the bloodstream toward its intended target.

"Check this out," said Elena, pointing to the screen closest to Jon. "This one's coming up our ass and hard. It's moving at thirteen knots, and it could be getting ready to fire."

"Maybe it's a school of mermaids," Jon cajoled with a drawl. The uninvited intruder slithered undetected through the frigid waters of the Southern Ocean, like a Copperhead rearing its fangs, ready to strike Draco's portside.

"No torpedo tubes open," Yael cringed, looking over Elena's shoulder. "It could be a drone, and if it is, can't be a friendly one either."

"What the... It looks like it's gonna ram us," Elena cried out. Jon stood up from his chair and knocked his head on the ceiling light encased in a metal covering. "That's not possible. Russian drones were used strictly for reconnaissance and surveillance. Not for ramming."

"Still closing fast," Elena screamed with panic in her voice.

Jon plunged into the chaos. "I'm firing the laser to slow this underwater UFO, and to throw it off our trail," were the last words anyone heard before impact. A loud bang followed, forcing Draco to roll 360 degrees, stabilizing on its side. Elena wailed at the top of her lungs as her leg was partially crushed by the indentation made by the drone. Yael, fastened in securely, hung on with desperation, watched Jon crash into the padded ceiling and then drop six feet like a hundred-pound kettle bell. Draco spun in the water and righted herself.

CHAPTER 26

UNDERWATER TRIAGE

Early October 2045

J on felt like he was flying and falling at the same time. Yael was drowning in empathy for Elena, who was writhing in pain. She felt a helpless emotion rising from her soul. Jon got up, steadying himself. "All systems are still a go. I'm going to zigzag and then make a beeline to the surface. I want them to think I'm some kind of sea creature and it's feeding time. That should throw them off our trail."

"You're gonna do what? Are you crazy?" Yael howled in a voice an octave higher than normal. She glanced in Elena's direction and noticed Elena grimacing, slumped over, as she passed out. Yael took a closer look and noticed a dent in Draco where Elena's right leg used to be. The IDF naval veteran was unable to differentiate between the inside where the mini- sub started and where Elena's leg ended, pinned against the titanium interior.

"Jon, hurry. We've got to do something. Sapphire's in a world of hurt. Got to get help. Now." *This mission has become a free-for-all hellscape*, Yael shuddered. *A place of darkness where no one's accountable for anything that happened in the Southern Ocean underneath the white continent.*

Jon was wobbly from what he assumed was a concussion. "Sol, take the controls. Must've banged my head real hard. Feels like someone just smacked the back of my skull with a two-by-four. You need to get us to the surface," he said, "and quickly," before laying his head back down on the floor, barely conscious.

Yael was in full multi-tasking mode, trying to balance her role as emotional support to Elena while navigating Draco out of range. Her stint in the IDF Navy did little to prepare her for the utter chaos she found herself in. She swallowed hard, a futile attempt to keep her emotions neutral, trying to move herself into a Zen state. An undercurrent of anxiety refused to stop rippling through her body.

She began to relax slightly, thinking about how Jon had once sung her the song, *"Momma said there'd be days like this, there'd be days like this my Momma said..."* It calmed her fraying nerves, especially after hearing her friend howling in agony like a wolf caught in a steel trap. *Sometimes it's more painful to be a helpless bystander than to experience the pain.*

Seconds later, as if on autopilot, Draco made a beeline for the surface like a dolphin gasping for oxygen to restore its depleted mammalian lungs. Draco cracked the surface like a breaching whale, violently displacing the greywaters, as gravity abruptly yanked it back down to the surface.

A long, pronounced moan that transformed into a piercing scream emerged from Elena's throat through pursed lips. Jon lifted his head off the floor far enough to notice her leg was wedged in. Without warning, three mini bots appeared from a vent on the floor, scurrying about repairing any damage caused by the ramming drone. The delay was caused by the drone that rammed Draco until the AI could reboot itself. The bots were moving randomly in all directions, like mice who had just discovered cheddar crumbles on the floor. The bots quickly repaired the interior damage and patched two miniscule leaks. The damage was done. Jon knew it, even in his half-conscious state.

"Sol, call the choppers and give them our coordinates," Jon groaned trying to beat back a massive headache and remain conscious. "We've got to get Sapphire to the ER on Erebus. and fast."

Yael had one eye on the radar and the other on Elena, her facial expression a mixture of pained compassion and severe stress. Elena knew instinctively that the chances of saving her leg were slim and had already accepted her worst-case fate.

"The pain in my leg feels like a bonfire," pleaded Elena.

"They'll be here in eight and a half," Yael barked. She had managed to dislodge Elena's badly damaged leg and wrapped it in bandages to stop the bleeding, keeping her hanging flesh attached to her right femur and calf. "Stay with me," she pleaded.

She had given Elena a shot of morphine to ease the excruciating pain and was doing her best to comfort Elena, whose head was in her lap. Eight minutes later, the crew of Draco could hear the chopper buzzing overhead, lowering the makeshift hospital bed. Yael and Jon quickly loaded Elena onto the bed and fastened the restraints. The wind and waves were so remarkably calm that it felt to Yael as if the Red Sea had parted, making the effort to get a prone body out of Draco's hatch easier and more efficiently than imagined.

"Я хочу, чтобы вы завершили миссию," Yael mumbled in Russian loud enough so that Elena could hear, *Fortune favors the bold.* Elena had a sudden burst of energy. "I understand that I am no longer vital to the mission."

She nodded off, resting her eyes. Jon looked at Yael as she pulled on the metal cable for the pilot to hoist up Elena.

The chopper hydraulics promptly reeled Elena up as two men lifted her inside. The helicopter pilot immediately headed due northeast toward Erebus, where the doctor was waiting to repair what damage he could. Yael closed the hatch and noticed blood all over her hands, spotting her left shirt sleeve all the way up to her elbow. The blood didn't faze her. She was only concerned about the well-being of her comrade and friend.

Jon stood up and gingerly sat down next to Yael. "Hey. Looks like I'm getting a second wind," he cajoled and winked at her. Yael was relieved to see her soulmate fully conscious, and back in the driver's seat. *Let's hope that robotic, voice-activated surgical device can save Sapphire,* he prayed.

"Sol, what's the status? Heard anything from the chopper pilots or Wolf?" he asked. Jon felt tinges of guilt pulsating through his brain.

Guilt borne from the idea that one of his magnificent team members could lose a limb, or worse, her life. It was his nightmare scenario, and he was experiencing it all in real-time. He tried valiantly to keep his emotions in check, stoic-like, refusing to emote to Yael.

The wounded drone drifted like a disabled *kamikaze that had been shot down before completing its mission.* By trying to take out Draco, whose outer frame had been reinforced with an extra layer of titanium and graphene, it had destroyed its own software and any ability to communicate back to the mothership, the Russian nuclear attack sub.

Like a dead fish, the drone lay listlessly on its side, with no ability to navigate in the silent undersea world. Jon and Yael had no clue that they'd bought a small window of opportunity to complete the mission. Jon reflected with certainty that none of the drones could be armed with torpedoes due to weight limitations. Although he had underestimated the speed and accuracy of the drone to disable other drones, they were effective only as early warning intelligence against enemy subs and other underwater drones.

Above the surface, Wolf, An, Phillippe, and Sinclair were safely tucked away below deck on the atomic yacht. They had been viewing in real-time everything that had just gone down on their 3D, artificial intelligence-laden radar system. An let out a sigh as the Russian sub seemed to have lost track of Draco, and was heading in the opposite direction. Wolf was left wondering why he didn't see the drone sooner before it blindsided Draco at ramming speed. *Perhaps the PRC had developed stealth mode capabilities for their drones,* he thought.

"Buck, maybe they think you have friends and are now looking for ghosts," Wolf suggested telepathically. "Either way, good job, and we will see that Sapphire gets the best medical care possible. I see it's clear where you are, so why don't you head southwest and continue to hunt for the pipeline below."

"Will do."

"Jon, who are you talking to?" Yael asked innocently.

He ignored her question. "How're you feelin', Sol? Ready for Round 2?"

"At the moment? I feel lightheaded, clueless with a feeling of doom, like a kite dancing in the eye of a hurricane. But I'm ready for one more dive to finish what we came halfway around the world to do."

Jon nodded and manually set the controls to head toward where Wolf indicated the pipeline would be. Just as quickly as Draco had broken the surface, it dove back to the depths below, almost as if it had done a delayed U-turn. The collision had all but destroyed Draco's capabilities to be operated via voice control. To Jon, it was a victory of sorts and a small price to pay, except for the life-threatening injury to Elena. He also had a secret weapon, something he had revealed to Wolf only.

Behind his screen was a green button. He tapped it three times, a protocol that he had developed back at Praani's lab with a little help from her engineers. Impervious mirrors appeared from Draco's six corners, generating infrared rays that enabled Draco to disappear from the radar screens of all predators with one caveat. If anyone was communicating by radio for more than ten seconds at a time, the enemy would discover its whereabouts.

And it was not a moment too soon. Yael had picked up a blistering, green blip on her radar screen. She was sure it was a torpedo, but there was no enemy sub anywhere to be found.

"Jon," she shouted. "Looks like a projectile headed our way, but I don't see anything on the screen that could have fired it."

"Releasing countermeasures. I sure hope these babies work as advertised." Sweat was streaming down Jon's forehead and he wiped it away with his sleeve. A Russian sub four nautical miles in the distance had picked up the skirmish between its drone and Draco right before the drone's communication system went dark.

Fifty-two hundred meters to the west, the captain of the Russian nuclear sub sat calmly in his designated chair, with a hot coffee mug in his hand that said in Russian, *Please don't launch any ICBMs until I've had my morning coffee.*

"Load torpedoes," the admiral voiced firmly from the bowels of the Typhoon-class submarine. "Prepare to fire tube 1." The senior lieutenant sitting directly right of the captain opened the firing key and hit the bright red button.

"Torpedo launched!"

"Time to target?" the captain unshakably asked the chief engineer.

"Captain. Estimated time to target two minutes, twenty-three seconds," not looking up from the timer in his hand. Two minutes passed. "Twenty seconds to target, captain. Ten, nine, eight..."

What the Russian captain failed to anticipate was that the drone lay directionless as a shield between the torpedo and its ultimate target. The drone was four hundred meters away from Draco, closest to the torpedo. As the Russian torpedo detonated its unintended target, the explosion of the Chinese drone sent shock waves so powerful that it slammed Jon and Yael against either side of Draco.

"That was way too close for comfort," Jon said in his Southern drawl. "They must've picked up our signal when I was talking to Wolf before the drone rammed us. We should be completely invisible. Surreal how the two realities of F.O.R. and the Russians were separated between the thin veil of life and death."

"Admiral. Looks like a direct hit. I don't see any signs of movement on the screen," the first lieutenant yelped proudly. Cheers could be heard on the bridge.

Jon refocused his short-lived daydream to the objective at hand. He decided to head southwest, gliding lower at a sixty-degree angle doing nine knots. Yael was sitting to his right, in the same seat that Elena was in when she received the unexpected, crushing blow. Her eyes were like cyan lasers intensely focused on the green radar screen, scanning relentlessly to identify something, anything resembling a long cylinder shape. The radar screen she eyed had been using AI-embedded software that could identify anything with a graphite component.

A voice jarred Jon out of his celebratory dreamworld. "Buck, come in please. I have an update on Sapphire. Do you copy?" Wolf asked.

"I copy. Make it quick. We're using the invisible shield to confuse Russian radar. What's the news?"

"The docs couldn't save her leg below the knee, but all her vital signs are healthy and strong. They gave her morphine and blood pressure medicine to bring it back to a normal range. You can imagine how sky high her vitals were after what she went through."

"Appreciate the update. Will keep you posted on any pipeline sightings. Gotta go. Out." Again, Jon felt a familiar twinge of guilt. This time it was more like a power surge than the smaller pulses he'd experienced earlier. There were things he desperately wanted to say but could not. The emotions he was feeling and trying to process took a back seat to the mission's ninth inning as he stepped into the batter's box. *This is the best way to honor Sapphire and the loss of her leg,* Jon rationalized in the heat of battle.

Yael gazed at Jon as the water surrounding Draco became the color of dusk before it reverted to a pitch-black ocean. Yael noticed a slight spiritual conflict on Jon's face, reflecting the contours of his brownish-blond eyebrows. His eyeglasses framed the hardest-working, altruistic pair of blue eyes she had ever seen. She let out a romantic sigh infused with admiration.

"I'm feelin' something heavy in the air. What's with the sigh?" Jon asked.

"Not important, would take too long to explain. Some other time, yes?"

"As you wish." Diving headlong into another confrontation with his mortality, Jon had compartmentalized any fears or worst-case outcomes and had refocused his intentions on the objective at hand. Gliding lower, Jon leveled out at a fifteen-degree angle, with Yael sitting to his right. He looked at her with soft eyes. "Maybe we should switch seats?"

"Not necessary," she replied. "You know I don't have a superstitious bone in my body."

Twenty minutes went by. Nothing. No sign of the pipeline. Jon was sitting in his chair, fidgety, resting his blood-shot eyes. His mind drifted back to his childhood, fishing with his Grandpa Al from a houseboat on the Tennessee River catching rockfish by the buckets. He could hear the frogs croaking on the riverbanks and the crickets chirping that served as treats for the amphibs. He could smell the water and feel the humidity on his skin.

Seen plenty of people willing to die for their country. Never seen people willing to die for freshwater. Normal people just don't act that way, but whoever accused Chirkov or Xi of being normal?

Yael slapped him on the right shoulder. "Wake up!" Jon was startled out of his few precious moments of childhood serenity.

"Whaddya got?"

Yael pointed with her unpolished index fingernail. "Look. Right there." She pressed her finger on the screen. "Do you see that?"

"I think you're onto something. It's only five hundred meters below us, and at our cruising speed, should take no more than three and a half, maybe four minutes tops." Jon was experiencing maximum anxiety, even though Yael felt drenched by a wave of optimism pouring over her.

Jon redirected Draco from the instrument panel in front of him and was heading toward what was a possible false target. It didn't matter. They had to take calculated risks, and this was just one in a string of many. Draco was no more than 600 feet away and closing rapidly. Jon throttled back the engine as they glided to a gradual, floating stop, hovering a few feet over the pipeline. Yael was waiting for her beau to execute a plan with insurmountable odds. The pipeline looked infinitesimally small on his screen.

"Come in, Wolf. Do you read me?"

"You're coming in a bit muffled. Go ahead."

"Do you see any enemy drifters around us?"

"Nothing. Do you copy? Nothing at all."

"Yeah, I copy. We're going in. If we have time, we'll cut the pipeline twice. Half a mile apart. Out." Immediately, Jon went to work as he activated the underwater laser, praying that this laser device would succeed as planned, just as it did at the bottom of the Tasmanian Sea. *OK, Draco, Let's see what you've got...*

The difference between the bottom of the Southern Ocean and the Tasmania Sea was the laser in Tasmania was voice-controlled, and it hadn't been disabled by enemy drones that short-circuited the voice activation system. Jon steadied his nerves, took a couple of deep breaths with long exhales, and began to visualize the laser cutting through the pipeline.

"I got this. Here we go." He activated the laser, carefully manipulating the joystick to focus in on one specific area. He could feel but not see through the mirky water. The joystick responded to Jon's every subtle movement. What seemed like an eternity later, he slumped back in his chair, mentally spent.

"Voila," and proceeded to bring the laser's arm back toward Draco.

"Not bad," Yael said in a celebratory mood. "It took three minutes and fifty-seconds, a minute and two seconds faster than your practice run." What neither of them had anticipated was the entire pipeline was wired with a Chinese-engineered alarm system that pinpointed the exact location of any damage or punctures and then sent a message to surrounding subs and drones.

"I'm setting our coordinates fifteen-hundred meters east of here. I'm going to create a little mischief here by cutting the pipeline in two places. I figure two bites of the apple is better than one. That'll hold 'em for a while." Yael watched beads of sweat drip from Jon's nose. She observed fear on his face. Not the fear of dying, but the fear of failure. *It's risky to overstay our welcome down here. I got a bad feeling about this...*

Wolf's voice was coming in loud and clear. *You got company. It looks like a drone coming up your tailpipe, and another sub coming at you from a westerly direction above and closing fast.*

He turned his chair toward Yael. "Whaddya think?"

"About what? I don't know if you're hallucinating after you banged your head, but I have no idea what you're talking about." It took Jon the blink of an eye to realize that Wolf was communicating telepathically again. He did a quick calculation in his head and made a unilateral decision to 'park' Draco near the bottom, activating the mirrors again. Draco was lying still like a hunted fish in a coral reef, waiting for a hungry eel to pass by.

"It's a good forty minutes to the barge and about fifty-five minutes to Erebus if we're moving at thirteen knots."

Yael was staring intently at the radar. "I just spotted a drone coming from one direction and what appears to be a Chinese sub coming from the other. It looks like the drone is heading to the broken pipeline for probable damage assessment. The sub to the same spot there from the other direction, so we have a clear shot."

As if on autopilot, Jon floated down to the pipeline and hit the button, activating the laser's arm. Knowing that he successfully executed severing the pipeline twenty minutes earlier gave him a confident edge for the second time around. With a steady hand and a clear mind, Jon accomplished the task in a little under three and a half minutes.

"Done. That'll keep 'em busy and give us time to hightail it to the barge." Yael felt triumphant. Jon refused the complacency trying to penetrate his mind, and would not rest easy until they were safely hauled out of the Southern Ocean and Draco was placed on the cargo ship's deck. He waited five minutes to get clear of the pipeline he'd just severed and then spoke into his headset. "Wolf, we got a two-fer and heading full speed ahead back to Tethys. How's Sapphire?" he asked tentatively. "Can she talk?

A raspy voice was speaking. "Did you get the pipeline?"

"Sapphire, good to hear your voice. How about twice?"

"The first cut we severed completely, but we were in a hurry on the second one, so I just severed it halfway through. They could take weeks to repair both, especially at that depth. Should give us plenty of time to alert the international community and expose them as the common thieves that they are."

"How're you doing? I want the truth. No sugar coating." *Sapphire is a warrior. She took a blow for the team and was able to come out the other side.*

"Well, I'm adjusting to my new reality. The doc told me after a few procedures and rehab I'll be able to run harder and faster than ever, now that I'm part bionic," a feint laugh emerged from her lips. "And the best part? I pity the poor bastard who gets hit by one of my kicks with my bionic leg. It's going to be a one and done knockout kick. Maybe I have a second career in MMA. I look at the bright side, don't need to paint my toenails anymore," she said in a hoarse voice.

Yael noticed something coming from the corner of Jon's eyes. Upon closer examination she realized that his sweat was masquerading as tears. *I wonder. Are those tears of joy or tears of guilt? Or both?* She didn't want to interrupt the moment and realized that his tears were a combination of feelings across the emotional gamete, something she had not seen before.

CHAPTER 27

ROCK ME BY THE WATER

November 2045

J on and Yael had made it back to the cargo ship safely, hoisted from the murky waters, and then helicoptered back to Erebus. Their journey northeast across the Southern Ocean was augmented by a royal escort from a British nuclear sub, courtesy of Admiral Brown.

At a favorite watering hole in Tasmania, they gathered around a large, walnut table in the corner. Jon raised his glass high.

"Here's to Admiral Brown, Bernays, Praani, Cal, the British Navy, and finally, each of you." Everyone was standing but Elena, who was sitting on a high top chair, still in the initial stage of a recovery that would take months. As the team of everyday heroes that few knew about indulged themselves and roasted each other, roars of laughter echoed off the walls, heard by the locals who frequented the pub. At 4 am, the bartender announced last call. They strolled arm in arm back toward the hotel, and noticed the emergence of the sun's rays piercing the cirrus clouds on the horizon, presenting a new day. They slept it off for twelve hours, and met in the lobby the next afternoon at 6 pm sharp. With many hugs and tearful good-byes, F.O.R. went their separate ways.

———

Two months later at a low-key restaurant near Jaffa, there was a bachelor party in progress for Jon. In attendance were the entire team plus Yael's brother, the base commander in the Negev where their journey began. "Does anyone have any concluding thoughts or anything they'd like to share about the last nine months?" Wolf asked humbly, scanning the eyes of everyone in the room. He looked at Jon, waiting for him to initiate the informal debrief.

"Guess I never stopped believing that our missions and the triumphant outcomes were as inevitable as the tide rolling in and out. F.O.R. can never stop. The only way out is in. The only way in is through. And our adversaries can't run forever, and we can't hide from them either."

Jon looked back at Wolf from across the table. "And you, my friend. What did you learn from all this?"

Wolf let out an audible sigh. "It's not just what you do in the end that matters. It's how and when you do it. I no longer take at face value that seeing is believing. Seeing is understanding, and right actions are the outcome of believing." Wolf had once again eloquently surpassed the expectations of the team.

"Anybody else?"

Yael spoke up. "I do in that it's more about human nature. It seems that nothing much of human nature has changed in the last thirty-five hundred years. The only thing I see differently today is that water is to survival like lust to a teenage boy." Everyone stared at Yael and then erupted in laughter.

Jon looked at Elena tenderly. "And you, Sapphire, would you like to say anything? Jon asked, holding his breath.

"Sure. I've learned through experience to never sit near the side of a mini-sub." They all roared, with feelings of relief and admiration for their comrade.

"Court. What about you?"

"To quote one of your favorite philosophers, *Society never advances. It recedes as fast on one side as it gains on the other.*"

"I see you've been studying up on Emerson. Well said, Court." Jon raised his glass toward Phillippe.

"An, and then Michael. Care to share your native intelligence with us?"

"It seems as though evil people and most of the shallow, weak-minded lemmings that roam this planet appear to measure their self-esteem by what they have, and not by who and what they are becoming."

There was silence followed by applause.

Sinclair looked around the room distracted by the mundane.

Noise from conversations in the restaurant, the constant coming and going of servers bringing them food, and the occasional dropped glass or silverware.

"I'm usually quite adept at public speaking, but I seem to be at a loss for words. I'll say this. No person should ever stand in awe of others. To travel across the oceans and stand on different continents is not only a privilege but a miracle of sorts. I hope the shared experience we've had continues. This last adventure will be etched in my mind forever. Nothing brings me more joy and satisfaction than when we achieve the triumph of principles. Thank you all."

———

With a serene look of solitude on his face, Jon gazed to the west at the fiery red Mediterranean ball of fire staring back at him, disappearing gradually as if it transcended time itself. Jon sat placidly in a blue and white striped seersucker suit. The water on the horizon matched the color of his Yael's eyes. Their journey was on a continuum of time, never to be a distant memory.

Elena, without crutches appeared in his field of vision. Jon gave her one of his signature bear hugs, lifting her off the ground. His spirit soared by how adroitly she strolled onto the beach. It helped lighten his guilt load, yet embers lingered. Jon would need more time to wipe away the memories of when Draco got rammed and what transpired after.

"Wow. You look great and are walking without a limp. I'm so

grateful you're able to be here, and that you've healed, emotionally and physically."

She blushed. "The rehab was hell on crutches. But you know me. I was not to be denied." She looked deep into Jon's eyes. "Please don't feel any burden for what happened. It wasn't your fault. Are you hearing me?"

He nodded tearfully, as salty drops began trickling down his cheek. Elena reached out and wiped it with the back of her hand.

"That's the Sapphire I know. 100% no bullshit."

Before Jon could complete his thought, An approached them, arms extended as if she wanted to hug them both at the same time. "Thank you again for getting me out of the Godforsaken country, and for your help with Mama and Lao Lao, too. I will be forever grateful to you and F.O.R." She kissed Jon on the cheek and then hugged Elena.

Jon eyed Wolf, dressed in a white suit with tan sandals on his feet. He grinned at the dichotomy of what his friend was and how he would always be. "Welcome to my wedding. I'm glad that my best man is standing in one piece, and that you've sailed through both missions."

Wolf embraced Jon and said, "It's binary. Either you become a diamond or get crushed by the pressure."

Phillippe and Sinclair approached from the hotel parking lot across the street. Sinclair had neatly trimmed his auburn gray facial hair. Sinclair looked at An. "I knew the PRC was in desperate need when they started converting petrol stations to water stations."

"Look at you. You're all business, even on my wedding day."

Wolf put his arm around his adopted brother. "We should be going. Are you ready to change the rest of your life in the best of ways?" he asked.

Jon nodded, steadied himself to walk tall along the beach toward the tent. He stepped onto a red carpet that rolled up to the entrance of a giant tent covered with white orchids, where he would wed his soul mate on her own turf, and where he first bonded with Yael twelve months ago to the day. *Feels like I've known her for years.*

He noticed navy patrol boats vigilantly scouring the sea, and an electric helicopter hovering above, engine noise muted. *The Israelis can never let their guard down completely, even for one day,* he thought.

Jon entered the tent, and spotted his mother who was sitting in the front row beaming with pride and love. Her first time in Israel, Sally was savoring every moment of her son's wedding. He walked up to the rabbi who was to marry them, shook his hand, and bent down to kiss his mother. Jon stood on the opposite side of where Yael's brother, in full military uniform, was standing under the white-laced chuppah smothered with a multitude of violet, orange, and yellow orchids.

Violins were playing the song "Here Comes the Sun" by the Beatles, as Yael strolled down the aisle, arm in arm with her mother and father on either side. Her braided hair was so blond it had to be real. Jon teared up, his eyes moistened by the humidity and the overwhelming, intense joy he felt.

Jon said his vows in Hebrew, Yael hers in English. Their eyes locked. He whispered to his bride, "With all we have been through together, never once did I doubt that one day we would be standing together."

Yael said, "I do." The rabbi responded, "You may kiss your Kallah." In a twist of tradition, Yael stomped on the glass instead of Jon. They walked back down the aisle, and outside the tent, just in time to take in the reddish-pink sunset beaming through some interspersed cirrus cloud cover hanging lazily in the sky.

Jon noticed an unknown number appear on his glasses. *Who could it possibly be? Everyone important in my life is right here,* he wondered. *Whoever this is, their timing sucks.* He hesitated. Filled with dissonance, and against his better judgment, curiosity got the best of him. He tapped his sunglasses and took the call.

He instantly recognized Admiral Brown's voice. "Jon? I hope that this is not an inconvenient time and that I'm not intruding on your personal life."

"No problem, Admiral. To what do I owe the distinct pleasure of this call?"

"In the spirit of full disclosure, I have a friend of yours on the line as well."

"Hello, Jon."

"Chip, is that you? How in the world did you get connected with the Admiral? Either way, it's good to hear your voice. Just got married in Tel Aviv," Jon gushed.

Chip smiled through the phone, and the Admiral said, "Mazel Tov."

"Sorry to interrupt your joyous occasion. I need to tell you what this call's about."

"Any chance this can wait 'til tomorrow?" Jon heard the Admiral groaning in the background.

"'Fraid not. Listen carefully," Chip responded with a seriousness that overshadowed Jon's celebration that was about to occur. "There was a device stolen from Cambridge that has the capacity to produce hydrogen from tap water and moisture from the air. It had four failsafe mechanisms built in, including one that would shut it down if it were moved from its location. I'm talking about twenty meters or less."

"I'm listening, Chip, but I don't have much time. Please get to the point," Jon said with a slight irritation in his voice, starting to question the timing and importance of a call on his wedding day.

"Here it is. An international organization stole it, and Admiral Brown believes it is the same group of thugs and bandits that tried to take you and your F.O.R. friends out of the picture more than once. I'm talkin' about the Chinese and Russian rogue cohort."

"Chip, I'm still not trackin' you. What's so damn important about a stolen hydrogen-producing device? They're everywhere."

The Admiral intercepted his question. "Jon, this is not your ordinary device. You see, it can be weaponized and tilt the balance of power in favor of whoever has it. We never filed patents on it because we didn't want anyone to know about it. I fear that someone might be able to reverse engineer our hydrogen-producing technology, and I'm extremely concerned about it falling into the hands of Russian or Chinese scientists collaborating to use it as a weapon of mass destruction."

"I'm with you, Admiral. But why call me?"

"The weapon had a tracking device that was disabled yesterday. Its last known whereabouts were on the northwest coast of Greenland near the town of Sisimiut, the second largest city in Greenland, and a couple of hundred miles north of Nuuk. My understanding from our colleagues at Cambridge is that the colder and purer the water that the device intakes to produce hydrogen, the more concentrated the hydrogen output will be. In short, the weapon is most potent and potentially dangerous where the built-in tracking device last emitted a signal."

Jon's voice trailed off. "I see. How can I help?" He knew exactly where his friend and the Admiral were going with this ill-timed conversation but decided to let it play.

"Do you still have Draco? And is it in good working condition? Specifically, its underwater laser?" Brown asked in a stern, serious tone.

"Wait. What the hell is Draco?" Chip inquired, quite alarmed, given that he was unaware of Draco's existence. He was taken aback by the idea that one of his best friends had kept this type of secret from him, and felt as if he had failed in part of his role with CIA in not knowing about something of this magnitude.

"Admiral, the truth is I donated it to the Smithsonian." Jon laughed at his own joke, but no one else on the line thought it was funny. "It's actually sitting in an undisclosed warehouse in Liverpool, courtesy of your good friend Sinclair. For the record, I planned a honeymoon starting the day after tomorrow in a small town called Darwin, Australia."

"Jon, how would you feel about taking your honeymoon in Greenland? We have contacted Thule Air Force base and they told us there's nothing they can do. The only way the terrorists wouldn't see you coming is by submarine, and only a small one like Draco could move in undetected."

"Buck, let me tell you how serious the situation is," Chip added. "If we can't figure out a way to neutralize, destroy or recapture this device, a WWIII scenario would be *fait accompli*. Of course, you'll have the full support and backing of the U.S. and Royal Navies, including a new battleship we designed to handle extreme polar conditions." Silence ensued. Chip and Admiral Brown could hear the wind blowing through Jon's device

"Every minute counts. Take an hour to think about it and call us back with your answer. I assume that all F.O.R., including Sinclair, are at the wedding, and if we've got any chance of succeeding, you'd all need to be involved."

The phone clicked off. Yael took one look at her new husband and knew something was off. She could practically hear him thinking. *It's not shocking that this happens, but shocking that it's happening on my wedding day. We're all so vulnerable to governments that have a warped sense of entitlement.*

"Jon, who was that? Did somebody die? You look like you just lost your best friend." Jon smiled, took his new bride by the hand, and walked back toward the tent and the party inside. "Let's go celebrate our new life together. Is there any chance I can convince you to postpone our honeymoon and take a diversion?"

Yael responded appropriately. "Is there something you're not telling me? I suppose if it's somewhere warm."

"Just be mindful that we live in a world of not yet," his voice trailing off, as he put his arm around her and opened the entrance to the tent. As the tent closed behind them, they began their new journey together.

AUTHOR'S NOTE

I vividly recall sitting in an environmental studies class at the impressionable age of twenty. It was the only undergraduate level environmental studies class offered at the university I attended in the mid-70's.

No question that I was daydreaming when I was startled back to reality after the professor's indelible prediction: "Lake Michigan could run out of water by the year 2000." That statement certainly got my attention, especially have grown up in Chicago until I left for college. I was frightened for the remainder of the class, and then I let go of the fear-mongering statement.

For some reason, that prediction was stuck deep inside me all the way until the late 1990's when I knew without a doubt that the premonition would not occur, and Lake Michigan was going to survive longer than my children and possibly grandchildren. As I sit here forty-five years later, the "when" of this novel was a seed planted that has been germinating ever since.

The "why" question is complex, as I have been tracking global freshwater supplies ever since May of 1975. When it comes to the world's freshwater supply, it appears that mankind is in a squandering phase of folly, spinning hopelessly out of control without a long-range solution.

Tempting fate at its very core, this novel is meant to be a wake-up call for humanity, and the possibility of what the state of our watery world may evolve into in the next quarter of a century, as the supply of fresh water decreases at an increasing rate. It is going to be a geopolitical mess at the minimum, and something that could morph into mass emigration to high per capital sources of drinking water, military skirmishes, riots, and dare I say an Armageddon scenario, like the story of Noah's ark in reverse due to extreme droughts. Or to paraphrase a saying, "It's the rising tide that destroys our planet's coastlines and islands." Again, For All the Water is not meant to be a scare tactic novel, but a wake-up call for every one of us.

Consider certain facts and recent events-

The cleanest drinking water by country in the worlds are:

- Denmark (purported to have better tap than bottled water)
- Iceland (95% of water comes from springs in the ground)
- Greenland (owned by Denmark)
- Finland
- Columbia
- New Zealand
- Sweden
- Canada

The ten worst countries for access to clean water (Source: World Health Organization)

- Niger, the least developed country in the world, according to the UN
- Papua New Guinea, 100x the population of Greenland
- Republic of Congo
- Chad, 3x the population of Finland
- Ethiopia, 3.5x the population of Canada
- Eritrea
- Somalia
- Uganda, 5x the population of Sweden
- Angola, 6x the population of Denmark

- Mozambique, 10x the population of New Zealand

Notice the pattern that most of these countries have sparse populations and no country with over 55 million people made the list.

Almost half of the population worldwide depends on access to the water flowing from the Tibetan Plateau. There is tension already brewing between China and India as China becomes stressed for water, a thirst that may only be quenched with Tibet's Yalong Tsangpo River, known in India as the Brahmaputra. According to the *Asia Times*, Chinese Prime Minister Wen Jiabao admits the "survival of the Chinese nation" depends on whether it can secure enough water. International interests have been escalating because of China's big plans to divert the Yalong Tsangpo river to use for hydro-electric power as well as a water source for its dry regions in the north and northwest.

Uruguay, a stable democracy with a tradition of farming and livestock prowess, is experiencing a crushing shortage of freshwater due to an extended drought- its worst in 74 years. The state has resorted to mixing its dwindling freshwater with salt water to extend its life, a health risk for many of its citizens. Montevideo, its capital and largest city, is down to a few days' supply. Consider the economic devastation given that greater than 80% of the land can be used for agriculture and the economy is dependent on the export of meat, grains, and dairy, all of which thrive on the abundance of freshwater.

Arizona, particularly the large-populated Phoenix area, has deliberately slowed down the construction of residential properties, partially due to rationing and diverting its main source, the Colorado River. Recently, a spokesperson stated that the decision was based on a 100-year analysis of the water tables, and that there is no imminent danger of running out of water. What makes anyone think that politicians or bureaucrats in Arizona would admit to their constituencies when water supplies will dry up to the point of rationing?

Predictions in the next 20-25 years are a rather stark reality, and the following are based on a diminishing supply and an increasing demand of fresh water. At the current consumption rate, cities such as Beijing, Sao Paulo, and Cape Town — a city that has already run out of water several times and where you can shower for ninety seconds, drink a half liter per day, cook one meal, and wash hands twice a day, leaving enough left over to brush your teeth and doing laundry.

A glaring example is Bangladesh, a delta region of some 170 million people. Although fresh water has been plentiful for centuries, the increase in droughts, deluge, cyclones, and saltwater have wreaked havoc on its citizens. As land washes away, people are forced to move to other villages and towns. The have learned the art of drinking rainwater, every drop of it. The region has a total of 64 districts, and half are vulnerable to water insecurity caused by climate change. The inherent danger of excess salinity contaminating the soil and freshwater is a constant threat due to rising sea levels.

The catastrophic element is the scarcity of water, evident in every continent simultaneously, except for Antarctica, which researchers tell us holds over 80% of the world's fresh water supply, albeit in the form of ice. The situation is so acute that more than half of the drinking water in Bangalore is lost to wastewater, and 85% of the water in city lakes is not drinkable. In Chennai, India ten million liters of drinking water are trucked in per day. Mexico City, Cairo, Istanbul, Jakarta and even Melbourne are looming cities for water instability and scarcity.

Throw in the Hail Mary of water desalination for drinking water on a mass scale along with the plethora of microplastics invading our water, fish, vegetation, and even our lungs, and we have a problem of complexity that will involve multiple, simultaneous solutions. I pray that we never get to a point of where *For All the Water* takes the reader, which would ultimately involve naval warfare. The kind of U.S. and Russian submarines that could unleash 192 nuclear warheads with a range of 3,000 nautical miles and wipe125 major cities off the map.

The 'how' quandary refers to the platform, or the ability to reach and influence as many people as I possible. I thought long and hard about writing a non-fiction version of *For All the Water,* but quickly concluded that a mass scale audience could not be reached with this format. I have tried in vain to read non-fiction books about this topic and others, and after reading no more than 30-40 pages, laid them to rest in an empty bookshelf that has turned into my personal graveyard for unread books. The ultimate platform in terms of 'reach' would be to create a movie based on the book, a process that has already begun.

For further information or to contact the author: https://stewartrflink.com/

If you enjoyed For All the Water, be sure to pick up a copy of *For All the Power* coming soon.

For Twitter @waterwars

Made in the USA
Monee, IL
03 December 2023

48112208R00194